First Born

Also by Lindsay McKenna
in Large Print:

Destiny's Woman
Heart Lost (Corazon Perdido)
An Honorable Woman
Hunter's Pride
Hunter's Woman
Man of Passion
The Untamed Hunter

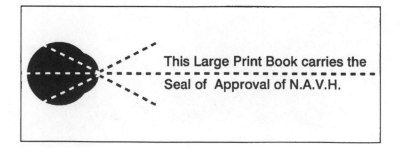

This Large Print Book carries the
Seal of Approval of N.A.V.H.

FIRST
BORN

Lindsay McKenna

Published in 2004 by arrangement with Harlequin Books S.A.

Wheeler Large Print Compass.

The text of this Large Print edition is unabridged.
Other aspects of the book may vary from the original edition.

Set in 16 pt. Plantin by Liana M. Walker.

Printed in the United States on permanent paper.

ISBN 1-58724-800-X (lg. print : hc : alk. paper)

First Born

National Association for Visually Handicapped
-------------------------- *serving the partially seeing*

As the Founder/CEO of NAVH, the only national health agency solely devoted to those who, although not totally blind, have an eye disease which could lead to serious visual impairment, I am pleased to recognize Thorndike Press★ as one of the leading publishers in the large print field.

Founded in 1954 in San Francisco to prepare large print textbooks for partially seeing children, NAVH became the pioneer and standard setting agency in the preparation of large type.

Today, those publishers who meet our standards carry the prestigious "Seal of Approval" indicating high quality large print. We are delighted that Thorndike Press is one of the publishers whose titles meet these standards. We are also pleased to recognize the significant contribution Thorndike Press is making in this important and growing field.

Lorraine H. Marchi, L.H.D.
Founder/CEO
NAVH

★ Thorndike Press encompasses the following imprints: Thorndike, Wheeler, Walker and Large Print Press.

Chapter 1

Trouble hunted him. And Chief Warrant Officer Jason Trayhern knew it had found him today. As he climbed the concrete steps of the Ops building at Fort Collins, Colorado, he began to sweat beneath his flight suit. Taking off his cap, he entered the swinging doors. As he did, he could hear the whapping sound of the Longknife Squadron Apache combat helicopters taking off and landing on the other side of the massive operations facility. How he wished he were up in the air now!

Mouth tightening, he nodded perfunctorily to the meteorology and air-control-desk personnel who stood on the other side of the tiled lobby. He knew both of them well. One didn't fly without getting a meteorology report from the weather desk, or a flight plan from the air desk.

Locating Major Butler's office, Jason girded himself internally for his meeting with his commanding officer. The passageway was clear of personnel for a moment, so he took a quick swipe at the perspiration on his brow before he entered the office. He didn't want

7

Major Butler to see him sweat. He wouldn't give the bastard the satisfaction.

Jason knew the routine. This was the second time he'd been called in by his C.O. for the same damn reason. Mentally trying to barricade himself from his writhing feelings of fear, rage and frustration, Jason took a deep breath. Then he squared his shoulders, put his chin up and moved through the open door, displaying the cocky attitude he was known for.

Butler's secretary, Mona Evans, a civilian in her fifties, looked up from her desk, her small, gold wire glasses halfway down her prominent Roman nose. "Ah, Chief Trayhern. Thank you for coming."

Jason stood at attention in front of her desk. "Yes, ma'am. I'm here to see Major Butler, as ordered." Of course this was an order. One didn't just waltz into the C.O.'s office without a prior appointment.

"Right," she murmured, putting her appointment book on the desk. "One moment . . ."

As he watched her get up, walk to Butler's door, open it and disappear inside, his gut tightened. He'd rather be facing El Quaida, with a Stinger missile aimed at his Apache helicopter, than be here right now. What would his father think? Morgan Trayhern, USMC, was a living legend in the military. Everyone, no matter what their service affiliation, admired and respected him. Jason fought a surge of anger. He didn't give a damn what his father thought. All his famous father cared about was his reputation — not his firstborn son. But his mother, Laura? Groaning inwardly, Jason momentarily closed his eyes and fought a wave of sadness at the thought of the disappointment she might feel to learn her oldest son had screwed up — again.

Jason loved his mother with his life. It hurt him every time he knew he'd disappointed her. What would she think now?

The door to Butler's inner office opened.

Mona smiled gently and pushed her glasses back up her nose. "Major Butler will see you now, Chief Trayhern." She stepped aside. "Go right in. He's expecting you."

I'll bet he is. . . . "Yes, ma'am." He kept his voice deep and unruffled, though he was anything but. He felt as if he had a hundred angry rattlesnakes writhing inside his gut.

Major Yancey Butler raised his head and pinned his narrowed gaze on Jason as he entered and snapped to attention.

"Shut the door," Butler ordered, brusqueness in his tone.

"Yes, sir!" Jason turned and shut it, did an about-face and then snapped back to attention. Butler was lean as a hungry wolf, with short black hair and gray sideburns. His green eyes glittered, sending a frisson of terror through Jason. Butler wasn't taking any prisoners today, judging from the thunder-cloud look on his face.

Sitting back in his burgundy leather chair, the man said, "At ease, Chief Trayhern."

Jason swallowed, spreading his feet apart and placing his hands behind his back. His commanding officer's pale face was speckled with copper freckles reminding Jason of a spotted Appaloosa horse. The thought made him want to laugh, though now was not the moment for humor. Today was not the day to flaunt cocky grins or shoot off smart re-marks.

"Son, you're like a cat," Butler began silkily as he opened Jason's service record in front of him.

"Sir?" Jason's brow furrowed with confu-sion. Where was Butler going with this? Heart pounding in his chest, Jason felt his adrenaline surge as a bad feeling pervaded his system. He wanted out of here. Out of Butler's office and out of the Longknife Apache squadron he'd been assigned to. It had been hell on him ever since he'd arrived at this base.

"You know a cat has nine lives, right?" Butler said finally.

"Yes, sir."

"Well, Chief Trayhern, you've used up, by my count, eight of your nine lives thus far." Grimly, the major folded his hands on the desk. "You got tossed out of the Naval Academy in your third year after a drug scandal. Though the charges didn't stick, your reputation was tainted. Then you came begging the Army aviation people to give you one more chance. We decided, since your record was clear, to take that chance on you."

Jason stood very still. He'd heard this litany before.

"After your officer training, you went to Fort Rucker, Alabama, and learned to fly the Apache Longbow combat helicopter. But there was a problem with you there. You were arrogant, Trayhern. Hard to get along with. You never saw yourself as a team member. The colonel of the flight school kicked you out of his squadron and put you in mine. You've been here six months, and I can't say it's been a positive experience for any of us. Two times now I've had seasoned combat pilots ask to transfer you out of their cockpit because you couldn't get along with them. With you, it's your way or no way, and that's not what Army aviation is all about, son. The Army is about teamwork. But you don't want to be part of a team. You want to lead, and listen to no one but yourself. This is *not* an Army of *one*, Mr. Trayhern. It's an Army where everyone works together."

Tapping his finger on the maple desk, Butler said slowly, "When Chief Doughtery requested another pilot to fly with, and he

11

told me why, I saw the handwriting on the wall. I have given you more chances than you deserve, Trayhern. I've asked you to fit in, to be a part of our team. And for some reason, you fight it. You rebel against the status quo for no good reason." Shaking his head, he muttered, "I gave you all these chances because I know your father, Morgan Trayhern. He's a hero to all of us. He's a man who did the right thing, fought back, made things better for everyone around him. He's a helluva role model in my opinion."

Unlike his son. Jason filled in the rest of Butler's sentence. Bile curdled in his throat. "Sir, with all due respect —"

"Just stand there and listen," the major growled.

"Yes, sir!"

Grabbing a set of orders, Butler scribbled his name across the authorization line with barely contained ferocity. "Mr. Trayhern, you're down to your ninth life. I've been in touch with Colonel Red Dugan, who commands the 2-101 Aviation Regiment of Apaches at Fort Campbell, Kentucky. Presently, all squadrons there are undergoing qualification trials before they're shipped overseas for duty in Afghanistan. He has agreed to put you into the Eagle Warrior Squadron under his command. If I didn't have so much respect for your father's name, I would be sending you to personnel to be processed out with a bad conduct discharge. Instead, you're going to Screamin' Eagle country, the 101st Airborne Division, air assault."

Jason's eyes widened slightly as shock slammed into him. His mouth dropped open. Quickly, he snapped it shut. *Butler wanted to give him a BCD? Oh, God, no!*

"That's right, son. You heard me." The major lifted his hand and held his thumb and index finger an inch apart. "You are this close to getting canned. Is that what you want?"

"No, sir!" Gulping, Jason wondered if his C.O. could hear his heart hammering against his ribs. It had been humiliating enough to be kicked out of Annapolis. Now he was in danger of a BCD. His head spun with questions. What had he done so wrong?

"I want you to know one thing," Butler growled as he handed Jason his new orders. "Colonel Dugan is a friend of your father's. I called him and talked over the fact that you're a real problem for the Army. I asked if he thought he could straighten you out and avoid a BCD." The officer nailed Jason with his gaze. "Son, you'd better hear this loud and clear. Colonel Dugan is your *last chance.* You screw up there, like you have with me and my squadrons, and you're out, famous father or not. We don't want to make headlines for Morgan. He doesn't deserve this.

And the press would have a field day with it. Your attitude could give the Army a black eye if you don't shape up. You understand? You have one last chance to vindicate yourself, get your head screwed on straight and learn to work as a team member, not a rebellious loner."

"Yes, sir. I understand, sir."

Butler nodded. "One more thing, Chief Trayhern. Colonel Dugan is a warrior of the first order. He won't take any shit from you. You got that? You had better head to the Eagle Warrior Squadron with a new attitude, because this time your father's name is *not* going to save you. . . ."

At 0530 the sun was starting to rise above the trees at Fort Campbell, Kentucky. The 2nd Battalion, 101st Aviation Regiment of AH-64D Longbow combat helicopters were surrounded by tall, stately maples, oaks, elms and ash trees, and Annie Dazen loved the sight. The deciduous trees reminded her of her home in the mountains at the White River Apache Reservation in Arizona, where scrub oak and slender ash trees mingled with thick stands of mighty Douglas firs. The military base stood at five hundred feet above sea level in the rolling countryside near the Tennessee state line. There were over ninety-three thousand acres of softly undulating Appalachian Mountains and valleys to fly over

14

while she sharpened her skills as a combat pilot. The landscape was the only thing she liked about the base's environment, though. Kentucky was a hot, sultry place during the summer and she preferred the dry desert climate of her home over the humid atmosphere of the base. No, she'd take the mountainous terrain of the reservation over the high humidity and tropical temperatures of Kentucky any day.

Every morning Annie went out in back of the hangar where her Apache helicopter was kept, her medicine necklace in her hands, to send a prayer to the rising sun. She was Apache, and in her tradition prayers were said at sunrise and sunset, the most powerful times of the day.

She stood alone in the morning quiet, an unusual state for the sprawling base of fifteen thousand people. At 0600, when helos from the various squadrons wound up for takeoff on another day of training, the place became a beehive of activity. Annie missed the great yawning silence of the reservation. There, one could hear the winds singing and sighing in the pines — the voices of the Tree Nation.

As she stepped away from the huge hangar and stood on the red clay, facing east, Annie gazed down fondly at the necklace in her hands. It had been in her family for hundreds of years, passed down to the eldest daughter of each successive generation. It was a medicine necklace, one with mysterious power, beauty and healing qualities.

Stringing the necklace between her hands, she lifted it breast high and closed her eyes. Annie grounded herself by imagining dark tree roots encircling her ankles and going down through her black leather flight boots deep into Mother Earth. Taking a deep breath, she whispered, "Father Sun, I honor you on this new day. Please guide me, help me to follow my heart and bless Mother Earth. Aho."

The necklace in her hands grew very warm. Annie was used to feeling her fingers tingle as she recited the ancient prayer. The heat soon increased and she felt the energy flow gently up her arms. A familiar calming sensation moved into her chest and remained there, like a warm, fuzzy blanket from child-hood, one her mother had tucked around her at night.

High above, Annie heard the shriek of a red-tailed hawk. Opening her eyes, she gazed into the pale blue sky, which was misted over by the high humidity of the July morning, and saw a mature red-tail circling. Its wings were outstretched and its rust-red tail fanned as it floated on an updraft of warm air. Lips lifting into a smile, Annie called, "Ho, little brother, what message do you bring me?"

She knew that when an animal showed up after her morning prayer, it was a message from the Great Spirit. What exactly it meant, she didn't know, but she always paid attention and tried to figure it out. Closing her eyes, she pictured the hawk in her third eye, located in the middle of her brow. An unsettling sensation blanketed her. Frowning, Annie opened her eyes. When she looked up again, the hawk was gone.

Odd. Annie didn't like the feeling cloaking her. Was that the message the hawk had come to tell her? That she should be unsettled? Unsure? She felt as if lightning had struck nearby and shaken her up. Birds were always considered messengers, bringing a warning, good or bad, of things to come. Usually within hours of their appearance Annie knew she would receive word, either in person or through a phone call, a letter or e-mail, of something or someone coming into her life.

Unzipping the right thigh pocket to her dark green flight uniform, Annie pulled out a soft brown deerskin pouch. Lifting the necklace, she gently tucked it back into the pouch and returned it to her pocket. The first rays of Father Sun were streaking across the tips of the elms and maples. It was now 0600 and the day had begun in earnest. All flying was done early in the morning when the air was still cool, and therefore more stable, making for easier flight training.

Turning, Annie walked back to the hangar.

Opening the aluminum door, she stepped inside onto the meticulously clean concrete floor. Her desert camouflage Apache Longbow was in for software upgrades and sat near the far opening of the hangar. Her crew, two men and a woman, were busy working on it. Usually they worked early and left in midafternoon, to avoid the blistering summer heat.

The welcoming smell of coffee wafted toward her. Flaring her nostrils and inhaling deeply, Annie made her way around two other helos in the hangar. The coffee dispenser was on the wall to the right of the open bay, and Annie headed straight to it. A day didn't begin without coffee!

As she stirred in cream and sugar, she heard booted feet coming in her direction, mingling with the clink of tools and the hushed voices of crew members. She looked up as she took a sip of the brew. Sergeant Kat Lakey, her crew chief, was hurrying her way, dressed in a green T-shirt, cammos and black boots. At twenty-five, Kat was a year older than her. Annie was happy this woman took care of her bird, for Lakey was the best crew chief on the base, in her opinion.

" 'Morning, Kat. You look like you're on a mission. What's up?" Annie grinned, looking pointedly at the watch on her right wrist.

Kat smiled and halted. "Yes, ma'am, I believe I am." Hooking her thumb toward the operations building in the distance, she said, "While you were out just now, I received a call from Ops. From our squadron commander, Colonel Dugan. He wants to see you immediately. I saw you step back into the hangar and thought I'd tell you. He called about two minutes ago."

Sipping more of the coffee to hide her surprise, Annie nodded. "Okay . . . Geez, it's early for him to be up and moving around, isn't it?"

"Yes, ma'am, I think so." Kat raised a brow. "But Colonel Dugan is famous for saying the early bird gets the worm."

"Yeah, you're right about that one."

"You know what it's about, ma'am?"

"Hmm? Me? No. Why? Do you? You're good at knowin' all the base gossip, Kat. What dirt have you heard lately?" Annie grinned at the sergeant. Kat had a mop of brown hair and a long, narrow face blanketed with freckles across her cheeks and nose. Her gray eyes twinkled with silent laughter.

"No, nothing new, ma'am. I know we're going to start combat training flights tomorrow, though. With live ammo." Kat rubbed her hands, grinning wolfishly. Live ammo wasn't used often. It cost money for shells, so usually electronic laser shots were used in training. Everyone looked forward to having the Apaches' considerable arsenal be "hot and live" — real rockets, missiles or bullets instead of a namby-pamby red beam of light to equate a kill.

Chuckling, Annie nodded. "Yeah, I can hardly wait. Okay, I'll grab a ride over to Ops. You doin' okay on the software checks? I want my bird in top shape for tomorrow's live-fire exercises."

"Goin' fine, ma'am. She's not a hangar queen." Kat chuckled.

Annie smiled and said, "Thank goodness she's not that! Okay, I'll get back over here ASAP."

"Ma'am . . ."

Annie hesitated. "Yes?"

"Do you think this might be about Chief Dailey's leaving? You do need a new pilot to fly with you. Could the colonel be callin' you over to let you know a new team member has been assigned to us?"

"That would be my thinking, Kat." She lifted her hand. "I see the base bus that'll give me a lift to Ops. You'll be the first to know when I get back."

"Yes, ma'am."

"At ease, Chief Dazen," Colonel Dugan said. He pointed toward a brown leather chair set off to one side of his dark green metal desk. "Sit down, please."

Annie smiled quickly and nodded. "Yes, sir." She perched on the edge of the chair, hands on her thighs, and gazed at him expectantly. The look on Dugan's oval, pock-marked face puzzled her. He was frowning, his short blond hair gleaming with reddish highlights beneath the fluorescent light above his desk. She knew he was in his mid-fifties, but he appeared far more youthful.

There were what appeared to be several personnel jackets scattered across his desk, and he was thumbing through them. Annie smiled slightly as she watched him. She liked her commanding officer. Red Dugan was a legend in his own time. He'd been one of the first to fly the lethal Boeing Apache combat helicopters, had helped create the curriculum to teach pilots how to fly it at Fort Rucker, and had a long, impressive combat record to boot. Annie had flown with him from time to time and had learned a lot from the highly decorated pilot.

"Annie, there's no nice way to say this," Red muttered as he lifted his head after moving the files around on his desk. "I have a problem, and I hope you can help me solve it."

Ordinarily, her C.O. never addressed her by her first name. In fact, Annie could count on one hand the times he had done so in the year that she'd been with the Eagle Warrior Squadron. Something was definitely up. "Okay . . . sir. Sure, what can I do to help?"

He smiled a little. "That's one of the reasons I've chosen you for this, uh, assignment." Lifting out a file, he set it on top of the others. "Two days ago, I got a call from the C.O. of another Apache squadron who told me he had a problem pilot on his hands. This pilot, CWO3 Jason Trayhern, is now being reassigned to us."

Frowning, Annie said, "Okay, sir." She bit back any questions she might have. Although her curiosity was burning her alive at this point, one didn't throw questions at a commanding officer. One waited for the C.O. to lay out the plan of action instead.

Opening the file, Dugan growled unhappily, "CWO3 Trayhern is a problem, Annie. But his father, Morgan Trayhern, is highly respected by all branches of the military. We try to take care of our own. Have you heard of Morgan Trayhern?"

"Yes, sir, I have. He was a Marine Corps officer in the closing days of the Vietnam War. His company got overrun and only two people survived, him and another guy."

"Yes, and there was a cover-up by our government on this particular operation when the company was lost. They painted Captain Trayhern as a traitor to whitewash the debacle, which was really the fault of the commanders above him. He, in the meantime, had suffered a severe concussion and was taken to Japan to recuperate. It was then that the CIA got involved. Morgan had amnesia and didn't remember who he was, so, with the approval of the French government, they invented a new name and history for him and sent him off to the French Foreign Legion after his recovery. Out of sight, out of mind, or so the government officials thought. Trayhern remained there many years until one day his memory came back, and when it did, he returned to the United States to clear his name."

"His family has a long history of serving in the U.S. military," Annie said.

"That's right. Their service record stretches back two hundred years, a real role model for the military way of life in this country. Despite that, Morgan Trayhern had to go through a lot to clear his name and restore his family's honor after he was branded a traitor." Dugan smiled faintly. "The man did it. He investigated on his own and finally was able to identify the men who had colluded against him." Waving his hand, the colonel said, "That's history now. But since then Morgan started a supersecret agency known as Perseus, which works closely with the CIA. His expertise has been focused on helping people around the world when the country in question can't or won't handle the problem. Suffice it to say, Mr. Trayhern has worked with every U.S. military service, and continues to do so to this day. I've met the man myself, and he is a true hero. He's someone the military does

23

not want to let down if we can at all help it."

Hearing the awe in Dugan's voice, Annie was impressed. "And his son is coming here? He's being assigned to us?"

Nodding, Dugan set his lips in a frown. "Yes."

"Then, sir, if you don't mind me asking, why are you looking so unhappy about all of this?" If the son was anything like the father, Annie thought, he'd be a real asset. A hero in the making.

"Because, Annie," Dugan replied, looking at her across the desk, "the two Trayherns are nothing alike. Have you heard of Jason Trayhern?"

"Uh, no, sir."

"When he was a third-year cadet in the Naval Academy at Annapolis, he got enmeshed in a drug ring scandal. He was never found with drugs, but names of cadets who had purchased them were found on his laptop computer. The people who conducted the investigation at Annapolis think his roommate set up Trayhern to take the fall. Jason and his lawyer had said from the get-go that Trayhern was framed. But the cadets have this skewed honor code and they don't rat on their brother or sister cadets. No one came forward in his defense, so they booted him out."

"Ouch. What must his family have felt

like?" Annie murmured. "Or him, if he was innocent? I'd be really angry about it."

"Precisely. It was a black mark against the Trayhern military dynasty, a blemish of the worst sort."

"And he talked to the investigation officials?"

"Yes, he did, but the 'blue wall' closed ranks — the cadets refused to give up the real culprits to clear Trayhern's good name. If someone had come forward to vouch for him, more than likely Annapolis officials would have allowed him to stay, all things being equal." Dugan opened his hands. "I know from talking with one of the admirals at the school that they really wanted to save the senior Trayhern from this kind of embarrassment. But his son was caught with the evidence on his laptop and couldn't explain how it got there."

Shaking her head, Annie said, "Well, sir, we don't know all the details."

"Yeah, that's right." Running his hand through his short blond hair, he added, "And that's why I've chosen you, Annie, to deal with Trayhern. I need the most astute, intelligent pilot I have in my squadron to handle this mess coming our way."

Annie sat up straight. "The mess being Jason Trayhern?"

"That's a roger. We're getting him dropped on us because he's a loner, Annie. He's not a

25

team player. He's said to be rebellious, angry and arrogant, from what Major Butler has told me. Two pilots in his regiment petitioned Butler to have Trayhern replaced, because the man simply refuses to get along with anyone else in the cockpit."

"Oh, sir . . ."

"Sorry, Annie. You don't deserve this kind of partner, either. I'm sorry we had to give Chief Mike Dailey a medical discharge. No one wished more than me that his high blood pressure problem could be resolved. You two were my ace team in the squadron, and I really hated to see him go. But we can't have a pilot at risk in the cockpit, either. And now you're the only one in the squadron without a copilot."

Annie thought back to earlier that morning, when the red-tailed hawk had screamed out for her attention. When she'd asked what message it brought, the exact feeling she had right now had blanketed her. She felt upset. In chaos.

"So you're assigning Chief Trayhern to me?"

"Yes, I am, Annie." Dugan shrugged. "Ordinarily, we wouldn't be having this conversation, but the situation is unique. I know Morgan Trayhern personally. I'm sure that, as a father, he's going through hell right now because his son has gotten booted out of two Apache squadrons in a year's time. This boy of his is a real burr under the saddle — his and ours. I had a choice in whether or not to take Trayhern. I'm doing this as a favor to his father. We're going to give Jason Trayhern one last chance."

Chewing on her lower lip, Annie sat there digesting the problem. "Sir, we're slated to go over to Afghanistan in a month."

"I know that. And Annie, I know what you're up against. If there's anyone in my squadron who can turn this man around, it's you. You're the only woman pilot on base, and I know this sounds like gender prejudice, but maybe, just maybe, Trayhern won't take the same arrogant tack he's taken with other pilots he had to work with if he partners with a woman."

"And if I can't get him to be a team player, sir?"

"All you have to do is come to me and tell me." Dugan shook his head. "I hope it doesn't come to that. I don't want to be the one to boot Morgan Trayhern's son out of the military, and if that happens, no service will *ever* allow Jason to reenlist. He'd be out. Castigated. But if you come and tell me he's not fitting in, then I will give him a bad conduct discharge without any qualms."

Annie found she had a hundred questions racing through her mind. Time was so short — only one month before combat duty. She knew it took at least three months for two pilots to get used to each other. They sat in the Apache together, flew together, worked together, and their relationship was like a marriage of sorts.

"Sir? Has Chief Trayhern ever worked with a female pilot before?"

Dugan smiled grimly. "No. As you know, there are only three women in the U.S. military who have qualified for Apache training thus far. That's not counting the Black Ops squadron in South America, of course, which is nearly all female. He's flown only with men."

"What makes you think he's going to respond positively to me, then? If he's never flown with a woman, how do we know *how* he'll respond to me?"

"That's a good question," Dugan murmured. "And I don't have an answer, Annie. But I'll tell you one thing — your marks listed in your personnel jacket, in flying and training, are 4.0. You're the best I've got. Your crew has won every trophy in and out of the squadron, and I know it's because of you, your ability to lead, as well as your ability to be a team player. You don't leave people out or behind, Annie, and that's the mark not only of a good leader, but of a real people manager."

She saw his hazel eyes brighten with hope. The praise was wonderful, but the assignment sucked. "I do try hard to make everyone feel a part of my tribe." She grinned wryly.

"There's a lot to say for you being Native American, Annie. I've learned a thing or two from you myself. I'm convinced that what you've learned from being brought up in your community can help us here in the Army, too. Teamwork is everything. I've seen you take people who felt disenfranchised and make them a valuable part of your squadron 'family.' " He smiled again. "And if Jason Trayhern is to have a prayer of learning how to fit in, I can't think of anyone better than you to be his teacher."

The responsibility was nearly overwhelming. Annie felt the weight settle on her shoulders. It was bad enough that she had to train hard and rigorously herself for the next month, to get ready for Afghanistan, where her life would be on the line every single day. Her copilot had to be someone she trusted with her life. How was she going to manage to do all of this?

Looking up, she murmured, "Sir, this is an incredible challenge for me."

"I know it is, Annie. And I'm sorry to lay it on you. But no one is better qualified to save this young man from himself. He's a fine pilot, but he's a loner. Do your best, okay? I don't expect miracles, and if it doesn't pan out, it's not going to reflect poorly on your personnel record, believe me."

"Okay, sir, I'll give it a go." She managed a lopsided grin. "But I don't know who I feel worse for, him or me."

Dugan chuckled. "I understand. Listen, stay in close touch with me on this. I want to know what's going down with him." Glancing at his watch, he continued, "Chief Trayhern will be arriving here at 1000 hours. He's to come directly to me, and I'll give him a talking to and a warning. Then he'll go through personnel, and finally, he'll be taken over to your hangar. At that point, he's all yours. Because the regiment is going over to Afghanistan in a month, I'm assigning him temporary billeting at the B.O.Q., Bachelor Officers Quarters, here on base."

"Yes, sir. It wouldn't make any sense to try and find an apartment for only thirty days. By 1300, he should be through personnel paperwork?"

"Yes."

Annie stood up and came to attention. "I'll do what I can, Colonel Dugan."

"Good enough, Chief Dazen. Thank you in advance. Dismissed."

"Yes, sir!" Annie did a snappy about-face and left his office.

Once outside the three-story redbrick building, she decided to walk the mile back to the hangar area. She needed time to get over the shock of her new assignment and try to adjust to this bad news.

The sun was hazy, the humidity stifling, and she was already sweating heavily. The street was busy with traffic, both desert-brown Humvees and many civilian cars. People in uniform and flight suits walked here and there with crisp efficiency. The home of the Screamin' Eagles was a workaholic's paradise, Annie thought. People were proud of the 101st Airborne's historical tradition and strived to make it the top aviation division in the Army as a result. Everyone who wore the screaming eagle patch on their uniform did so with pride.

The tall, spindly pines planted between large-leafed maples stood at attention along the concrete sidewalk as she walked across the bustling Army base. The main headquarters, painted white, lay in the center of a diamond-shaped expanse of lawn bracketed by asphalt highways. Green shrubs along the walls of the diamond were trimmed to military perfection. But Annie was unable to appreciate the manicured beauty that surrounded her. Her mind and heart were elsewhere.

One month. One month to tame a lone wolf who didn't want to be part of anyone's team. And this wasn't just any lone wolf. No, this was a famous one with a jaded past. Annie's brow knitted as she walked. Settling her cap more securely on her head, the bill drawn low to shade her eyes from the sun, she kept to the inside of the sidewalk. When she passed an officer, she saluted. Enlisted personnel who passed saluted her. Warrant officers were not quite officers, but they were treated with deference nonetheless.

Automatically, Annie unzipped her right thigh pocket and pulled out the deerskin pouch that held her medicine necklace. After she'd shifted the necklace to her left hand to leave her right one free to salute with, she instantly felt the object's warmth, finding it comforting and soothing to her anxiety and concern. Annie didn't understand exactly why the necklace reacted when she was upset, but it did, and she absorbed the calming energy from it.

A pair of raucous blue jays screamed as they flew from one elm tree to the next ahead of her. That wasn't a good sign — birds fighting and squabbling with one another. In Annie's world of mystery and miracles, she knew nature talked to her, about herself and what was to come, whenever she would listen. Well, those birds had her full attention now. Would she and Trayhern be just like the blue jays — squabbling, bickering and screaming at one another? In four hours, she'd find out.

Chapter 2

Four hours later, Annie was flat on her back beneath the carriage of the Apache along with Specialist 3 Lance DeLong, one of her mechanics. They were lying side by side, looking up into the area where the chain gun was situated. The cannon, which looked like a long-barrel machine gun suspended beneath the fuselage of the Apache, could spit out 30mm rounds, instantly destroying whatever it hit.

Annie was so intent on what Lance was saying about a piece of hardware within the mounting that she failed to hear the solid, confident stride of someone coming her way. Only when the highly polished black shoes came to a halt less than two feet from where she lay did she realize they didn't belong to one of her crew.

Hands freezing momentarily on the gun mount, Annie turned to Lance. "The new pilot is here. Can you handle this repair alone?" She searched the twenty-year-old's round face.

"Aw, shucks, sure I can, Ms. Dazen. Not a problem." Lance grinned, showing his uneven teeth.

Annie nodded and grinned back. "Okeydokey." She rolled out from beneath the fuselage, her heart skittering with dread at meeting this infamous pilot. The polished shoes backed up to give her plenty of room to roll to her hands and knees and then get to her feet.

Raising her head as she brushed herself off, Annie saw the man was dressed in his class A Army uniform and standing with his feet apart, like a boxer ready to be struck. As her gaze ranged quickly upward, she realized that Jason Trayhern was tall, at least six foot two inches. When she looked into his square face and met his frosty blue eyes, her heart contracted in fear. The narrowed look he was giving her was one she might give an enemy.

Dusting off her hands, she thrust one forward. "Mr. Trayhern? I'm Annie Dazen, pilot in charge of this girl here." She hooked her thumb over her shoulder at the huge Apache helicopter behind her.

Jason scowled. Annie Dazen wasn't anything like he'd expected. Standing at five foot nine inches tall, dressed in an olive-green T-shirt and cammo fatigues, she was curvy but clearly in top physical form. Her skin was a deep copper color and her thick black hair lay in one long braid down the middle of her back. But it was her eyes that drew him, melting the glacial reserve that usually protected him. They were a warm golden-brown,

34

and they sparkled with life. The careless smile on her full lips told him she either didn't know who he was or could put on a helluva good facade. As he gripped her hand, he found her long fingers strong and resilient. He tried to ignore the warmth radiating from her, and gave her hand a perfunctory shake.

"Yeah, I'm Jason Trayhern," he said abruptly. He released her hand because it felt like fire itself, and saw her smile widen.

"Welcome to the Eagle Warrior Squadron. You're now part of the 101st Screamin' Eagle family, and that's a proud heritage to carry." Annie gestured around the huge hangar, which held four Apaches in for routine maintenance. "This is our home away from home. You'll be spending a lot of time down here with us."

Her voice was like smooth sipping whiskey, and it ruffled his icy armor. "I would expect to," he said, biting off his words with official coolness. Her hair was coming loose from her braid, and her T-shirt was soaked with sweat. And no wonder. It was eighty-five degrees in here, and the humidity was just as high. He was sweating in his class A uniform, and envied her in the everyday clothing most people wore on the base. He desperately wanted to get out of his uniform.

"Well," Annie said, "I assume you've already talked to Colonel Dugan? Been

35

through the personnel game?" She tried to sound upbeat and glad to see him. Truth be told, Annie wanted to step away from this warrant officer, who was a grade below her in rank. That made her the commanding officer, and he had to follow her orders, not vice versa. Oh, it was true, he was ruggedly handsome, with that square, aggressive chin. She was sure most women would swivel their heads to look at this dude. He was definitely easy on the eyes. Yet Annie could feel his tension, and saw it reflected in his narrowed, darting gaze. A part of her felt sorry for Trayhern, because being new was always a pain in the butt. His mouth was thinned, too, telling her he wasn't at ease in the situation. Seeing a film of sweat covering his brow just beneath the edge of his beret, she realized he must be very hot in the wool uniform.

"Yeah, I went through those volleys."

Annie heard the repressed anger in his taut tone of voice. Though he held a black cowhide briefcase in his left hand, there was no question he was in a fighter's stance. Why? There was no one here to make him feel that guarded or intimidated. Maybe that was the problem, Annie thought. He didn't trust anyone.

Giving him her best official smile, Annie said, "Well, come with me. I'll take you to the squadron locker room. We'll get you squared away with a locker, and in the meantime enjoy the wonderful air-conditioning inside."

"Sounds good to me." Jason glanced around. He noticed that nearby crews, three to a helo, were all circumspectly looking at them. He was sure everyone knew that Dazen was getting a new pilot who'd just been transferred in. But did they know about him? The truth, that is? Had his black cloud of bad luck followed him here, too?

As he swung in behind Dazen and followed her across the spotlessly clean concrete floor toward the west flank of the hangar, he realized that this was a spit-and-polish operation. Not that the squadron he'd left hadn't been, but Jason could spot little things that told the tale. He'd heard that the 101st was a top-notch unit, and now he believed it. The Screamin' Eagles were the best. He was surprised that he'd been sent here, because normally only the cream of the aviation crop landed here. He hadn't expected such a plum. When Butler had called him in for new orders, Jason had thought he was going to be relegated to some Army outpost — out of sight, out of mind.

Now he tried to ignore the gentle sway of Dazen's hips as she walked in front of him. He didn't want to be drawn to her as a woman. Colonel Dugan had read him the riot act, making it clear that if Jason screwed up here, he was out. Period. A BCD.

Wouldn't that be wonderful? More than anything, Jason wanted to avoid a bad conduct discharge. That black mark would haunt him the rest of his life, he knew. It was wretched enough that he'd been kicked out of Annapolis in his third year. He'd never live that down in a million years, given the military dynasty that was his family heritage.

Grimly, he forced himself to quit thinking about the sordid past. All it did was bring up pain, and that was something he was trying to avoid at all costs. He'd had enough of that to last for ten lifetimes.

Dazen opened a door, and when they stepped inside a narrow passageway, a delicious coolness hit him.

"Whew!" Annie said, wiping her forehead with the back of her hand, "what I'd give to have air-conditioning out in that hangar. Southern weather sucks!" And she laughed.

He walked at her shoulder. "You aren't from the South?"

"Me?" She looked up at him and grinned. "No. I'm a full-blooded Apache from the White River Reservation near Show Low, Arizona. Land of desert, high mountains, low humidity, lakes and thousands of pine trees." She saw his eyes thaw ever so slightly. "Where do you come from?"

"Hell," he answered abruptly.

Annie slowed her pace for a second. The passage was empty of people at this time of

38

day. For a moment, she wondered if he was serious. "Is that a polite way of telling me to mind my own business?" She kept her tone light and slightly teasing as she watched him take off his beret and wipe his brow.

"No." Jason settled the beret back on his head. He refused to be drawn into friendly banter with her. She was his boss. There was an invisible line of demarcation between a junior and senior officer. No matter how much he wanted to respond to her sunny personality, he couldn't allow it.

"In there is the men's locker room," she said, leading him through. "Off-limits to women, but there're plenty of open lockers available, from what the guys have told me. Just pick one and get the combination lock that's hanging on it. The combo to open it is written on a piece of paper tied to the lock."

"Okay." He looked down at her expectantly. "After getting a locker, what's next?"

Shrugging, Annie said, "They said they're putting you up at the B.O.Q. until we ship to Afghanistan. Have you stopped over there to get a room assigned to you yet?"

"Yeah, I've got it. Room 202, in case you need to ring me for anything in the future."

Annie nodded and mentally tucked the number into the back of her mind. "You got wheels?" Nashville, Tennessee, was only sixty miles away and he might have taken the bus down here. Unless he'd driven his car from his last base, in Colorado.

"Yeah, I've got wheels."

"Okay, why don't you get your locker and head back to the B.O.Q.? Once you change into your work uniform, come on back to the hangar. There's plenty of indoctrination you need to get up to speed here. I'll be out there with my crew, so just hunt me up when you return."

"Yeah, fine. By the way, is there a phone around here I can use? I need to make a call. Maybe in your office?"

"Sure, let me show you where. We'll be sharing the same office." She gave him a measured look. "You'll be spending a lot of time in it, for the next week anyway, familiarizing yourself with our manuals of operation."

Jason followed her down the passageway. Reaching an intersection, she turned left toward a cluster of ten small offices, five on each side of the corridor. There was a hall window in each, with venetian blinds to keep out prying eyes if the warrants wanted privacy from passersby.

The first office on the left was hers. Annie unlocked it and entered, and when Jason followed, the heavenly coolness enveloped him even more strongly. Automatically, he gave a little sigh of relief as he shut the door behind him.

Annie walked around the metal desk, which was covered with neat piles of papers. She touched the black phone. "If you're making a long-distance, nonmilitary call, just dial the operator and use a credit card."

"Got it," he said, setting his briefcase on the floor next to the desk. "Thanks."

"Sure." Annie opened a drawer and drew out a key. "Here, you might as well have this. It's a key to the office. Just lock it up when you're done?"

She saw him wrestle with his icy reserve, as if considering whether he could let down his guard. The iciness won out. She saw his eyes harden as he pulled out her chair, took off his garrison cap and sat down. "Yeah, no problem. Thanks, Ms. Dazen."

She lifted her hand. "I'll see you later, Mr. Trayhern. Welcome to the Screamin' Eagles."

He watched her push open the door and then disappear. Well, that hadn't gone as badly as he'd thought it might. Maybe Dazen didn't know of his jaded history. At least he hoped not. Frowning, Jason pulled a credit card from his wallet. It had been a week since his transfer, and he hadn't called home for a week before that. He was sure his mother would be worried about him by this time. Normally, he called his mom once a week. And every time he did, he hoped his father wasn't around so he wouldn't have to speak to him. Jason tried to time his calls for just before lunch hour, knowing his mother would likely be there alone in his family home in Phillipsburg, Montana. His dad always drove home from the office in order to have lunch with her, so Jason tried to call before he arrived. Avoiding his father suited him just fine.

Picking up the phone, he punched in the numbers. Heart beating a little faster in expectation, he gripped the phone in hopes that his mother was there — and alone.

Laura Trayhern had just finished getting her two-year-old into her special kiddie seat at the kitchen table. Kamaria looked up at her now with wide blue-gray eyes and smiled. "Spoon, Mama?"

"Oh, you are such a cute little tyke," Laura whispered, pressing a kiss to her adopted daughter's soft black hair, which Laura had just brushed and braided. Reaching toward the counter, Laura retrieved one of the wooden utensils that sat in a yellow ceramic cup next to the range.

"Mama . . ." Kamaria held up her arms as she approached.

"You are irresistible!" Laura chuckled and gave the child the spoon before she tied a pink terry-cloth bib over her daughter's purple Barney T-shirt. "There! Okay, wail away and do your musical renditions." Kamaria liked to beat the spoon against the table in time to whatever music was playing on the small radio perched on top of the refrigerator.

Laura was heading for the fridge when the phone rang. Detouring, she looked back to make sure Kamaria was okay. Strapped in her chair, her fifth child sat quietly, looking around the cedar-paneled kitchen and waving the spoon like a flag. Sunlight poured through the windows, highlighting the gauzy white cotton curtains on either side of the sink.

"Hello? Laura here. . . ."

"Mom?"

"Jason! Oh, I'm so glad you called! Is everything all right? We didn't hear from you last week."

"Yeah, I'm fine, Mom. I'm sorry I didn't phone."

"Are you all right?" She hastily wiped her hands on a kitchen towel, frowning at the note of trepidation she heard in her son's voice. Leaning against the counter, she watched Kamaria, who was now beating the spoon against the table in time with a jaunty ragtime song.

"Uh, yeah . . . fine. Is . . . Father around?"

Sighing, Laura said, "No. He's still at Perseus."

"Oh . . . good."

Pain flitted through Laura's heart. "He loves to hear from you, too, Jason. I wish you'd stop avoiding him. I don't like having to give him secondhand information from you all the time."

"Yeah, I know, Mom. Sorry. Maybe someday . . ."

She knew better than to push her son. He took after her husband, Morgan, in so many ways. Both of them had a stubborn pride that made them unapproachable on certain issues, especially old, oozing wounds that had never healed. She moved to the sink, cradling the phone between her head and shoulder. Picking up a knife, she began to slice an apple for the Waldorf salad she was going to make for lunch. "Well, how goes it? Are you getting a lot of flying hours in? Last I heard, you were unhappy because you weren't getting them."

"Yeah . . . well, Mom, some things have changed. That's why I didn't call earlier."

She held the knife suspended above the apple. "What do you mean, Jason? What's changed?" The last time he'd used those words, he'd been abruptly transferred out of Fort Rucker to an Apache squadron in Fort Collins, Colorado. Heart sinking, Laura wondered what had happened now. Somehow, Jason's life was dogged by bad luck. Not that he didn't bring some of it on himself, she knew. Her son wasn't perfect, no matter how Morgan wished he were.

"Well, Mom, I'm in a new squadron. The 101st Airborne. How about that? The

Screamin' Eagles. The cradle of Army aviation. I've been assigned to the Eagle Warrior Squadron here at Fort Campbell, Kentucky."

"That's unexpected, Jason. What happened?" Her voice was low and hesitant. In the back of her mind, Laura knew Morgan would be upset. Unless his military cronies had already called him about this transfer and Morgan hadn't told her yet. He'd do that, too, because he knew she'd be worried about Jason. Ever since he'd been kicked out of Annapolis, his life had gone from bad to worse.

"I, uh . . . well, I demanded a transfer and got it."

"But . . . you seemed happy with your old squadron."

"I know. . . ."

"Why, Jason? What happened?" Laura set the knife and apple aside. She turned to keep an eye on Kamaria, who was sucking contentedly on the spoon now that the song had ended.

"I just couldn't get along with the pilot I was assigned to fly with."

She heard the frustration in his voice. "But you didn't get along with the first one, either. That's two pilots, isn't it? Jason, what is happening?" She tried to keep the worry out of her voice, but Laura knew it wasn't working. Gnawing on her lower lip, she felt her heart breaking once more for her son. She was no

45

newbie to the military system. In fact, Laura had been a military writer for decades, and continued to publish articles within high-command military circles. She knew the dope on transfers as well as anyone. And Jason hadn't been at Fort Collins long enough to ask for — and receive — a transfer unless something had gone terribly wrong.

"I just didn't get along with them, Mom. That's all."

Laura heard the steely defensiveness in her son's deep voice. Once more he was putting up walls to keep her out. "And they let you transfer? Again?" Laura knew the service would not tolerate something like this for long. She was surprised he'd gotten a transfer at all. And she knew he wasn't telling her the whole truth. Jason was hedging. He always did when the news wasn't good.

"Yeah, they did. Things look good, though. You'll never guess who I've been assigned to."

Hearing the hope in his voice, Laura smiled softly. "Tell me."

"I'll be flying with a female pilot, Mom. CWO2 Annie Dazen is her name. She's a full-blood Apache from Arizona. How about that? She's one of a handful of women who have ever made it through Apache school, and she was at the top of her class, from what Colonel Dugan told me. He's my C.O. now, by the way."

"A woman. Well, maybe you can get along with her?" Laura chuckled, and she heard Jason give a strained laugh. Her heart lifted. Oh, how she wanted him to have good things happen!

"I'm going to try," Jason said, becoming serious once more. "I'm assigned to the B.O.Q. right now. That's temporary. I want to give you Dazen's phone number, because her office is my office, in case you need to reach me. You got a paper and pen?"

Laura turned and pulled out a small plastic box that sat next to the wall phone. "Yeah, go ahead, honey." Taking out an index card, she wrote down the number he gave her.

"I'll be in touch, Mom. I'll call you next week, okay?"

"Okay. You sound good, Jason. Better than I've heard you sound in the last year."

"Maybe this new pilot will be good for me."

"Do you like her?"

"I don't dislike her. She was real friendly and warm toward me when we met."

"Do you think she knows about your past?"

"I don't know. If she does, she isn't showing it. At least, not yet. But we just made intros, so I really don't know."

"What does she look like? Is she married? Have kids?" Nowadays, the Army was family. Back in the sixties, most people in the service had been single. Now it was made up of married couples and families — a huge change for the military to adjust to.

Jason laughed. "I haven't a clue. She wasn't wearing a wedding ring, but in our business, we don't wear jewelry when we fly."

"Well, find out, okay?"

"Mom, you are so nosy sometimes!"

She laughed a little. Kamaria waved the spoon and Laura lifted her hand and waved back. "I'm a woman, dear, and those things are important to us. What does Ms. Dazen look like? You said she was Indian?"

"Yeah, she's tall and well proportioned, from what I can see. She probably lifts weights. There's no fat on her. But she isn't a twig, either. There's some meat to her bones."

"Black hair? Copper skin?"

"Yeah, that, too. Nice eyes."

Laura heard his tone of voice thaw a little. Her heart thumped with hope. *Oh, please, God, let Jason get along with this woman. Let there be peace, not war between them.*

"What color? Brown?"

"Golden color, really. I can see her pupils in them. She has large, alert eyes, Mom. In some ways, she reminds me of an owl. Not because of the shape of her eyes, but that gold-yellow color. Remember that great horned owl that used to nest in the pine trees on the east side of our home?"

"Oh, Miss Lucy. Sure." Laura had named the huge brown-and-white owl that used to roost high above their two-story cedar home in the woods.

"Eyes like that. Pretty."

"Sounds as if you like her already."

"Well . . . I wouldn't go that far, Mom. She's okay. She's friendly and seems to want to make me feel at home."

"That's a good sign."

"Yeah, maybe. It will probably all change when she finds out about my infamous past."

Laura hurt for her son. She knew that gossip followed everyone in the military like a curse. Sooner or later, Dazen would find out about Jason's shameful history. Gripping the phone a little more tightly, she whispered, "Well, maybe Ms. Dazen isn't going to hold it against you."

Sighing, Jason said, "I'll find out, that's for sure."

"Do you need anything, honey?"

"No, just to hear your voice. It reminds me of home."

Laura closed her eyes. Jason loved being home. He loved living in Montana. He loved working with plants and animals. In high school, he'd excelled in biology. But Morgan had wanted him to go to a military academy to carry on the proud, two-hundred-year-plus tradition of the Trayhern family. Since Jason was the oldest male he was expected to go into the military. Laura knew he really hadn't wanted to. Instead, he had wanted to become an ecologist and work outdoors, somewhere in nature. But that wasn't to be.

"Well, you can come home on leave, son. Your bedroom is unchanged from the day you left it." Laura knew Jason would never come home, not until he healed the rift with Morgan. Jason always spent his thirty days of leave overseas, instead. It had been nearly three years since Laura had even seen her son — not since the Five Days of Christmas party right after his first year in Annapolis.

"Yeah, I know, Mom. I should come home . . . but, well, you know how it is."

"I know . . ."

"Listen, I gotta run. I'll be in touch next week. Love you. Say hi to Pete and Kelly, and give little Kamaria a hug from me?"

Tears burned in Laura's eyes. She cleared her throat and whispered, "I always do, honey."

"And how's Katy? What have you heard from her?"

Laura knew it hurt Jason that his younger sister, two years behind him in age, had taken up the family honor and volunteered to go to the Academy to represent them. Before Jason left, he'd been very close to Katy.

"She's doing fine, honey. She's flying Seahawk down in Columbia for the Black Ops stuff."

"Just like Dad. . . ."

Laura heard the grimness in Jason's tone. Morgan had been a Marine. Jason was supposed to have taken the same route, but hadn't, due to the scandal. "Yes, she's following him into the Corps."

"I see. . . . Well, I gotta go, Mom. . . ."

"Take care of yourself? We love you. . . ."

Just as Laura hung up, the front door opened and then quietly closed. That would be her husband, Morgan, coming home for lunch. She tucked the notecard with Jason's office number on it into her apron pocket. Morgan came through the entryway, wearing a white, short-sleeved shirt and tan chinos, and still looking every inch a Marine with his military-short black hair, which had gone gray at the temples. Her husband was one of the most powerful men in the world when it came to espionage. His company worked beneath the auspices of the CIA, and Laura was proud of Morgan's ability to help people around the world get out of trouble.

Today, though, she saw he was worried. His square face and gray eyes looked tight with tension. She walked up to him and placed a kiss on his cheek. "You look awful, darling. What's wrong? Is a mission going bad?"

Morgan bussed his wife's velvet cheek, inhaling the faint jasmine fragrance she wore. Placing his hand on her waist, he pressed her against him for a moment.

"No, not a mercenary mission," he answered. Releasing her, he made his way to the table where Kamaria sat. The little girl twisted toward him, a smile of unabashed welcome on her face. Leaning over, Morgan placed a kiss on his daughter's pink cheek.

"How's our little musician doing?" he asked, turning to Laura as he rested his hand upon Kamaria's tiny shoulders.

Laura pulled a turkey-and-cheese casserole out of the oven and placed it on a pot holder in the middle of the maple table. Immediately a delicious smell filled the air. "Beating along in rhythm with whatever comes on the radio. Her hair is long enough to braid now. With the temperature so warm today, I thought she might like to have it up off her neck. Do you like it? Come and sit down. Everything's ready to eat."

Morgan sat at the end of the table next to Kamaria. "Yeah, she looks cute in braids. Umm, that smells good. Turkey casserole?" He enjoyed being with his wife and daughter for lunch every day. Eyeing Laura, who was wearing jeans and a pink tank top, he admired her figure. His wife had carried four of their children. She was in her forties, and looked more beautiful to him than ever. Her waist was not as small as it used to be, but then, she was a mother. To him, she was still the special woman he'd met so many years earlier at an airport near Washington, D.C.

Kamaria thumped his arm with the spoon. He grinned and wiped her mouth and chin with his napkin, mopping up the drool that was soaking her T-shirt at the collar.

Laura placed the Waldorf salad in front of him, then put a portion of casserole on a plastic plate in front of their daughter.

When Laura sat down, Morgan gently placed the fork in the toddler's small hand to show her how to hold it properly. The daily lessons were slowly having an impact. Kamaria waved the fork around before plunging it like an airplane into the casserole in front of her.

Laura finished serving and said, "Why are you looking so upset? I can see it in your eyes."

Grimacing, Morgan said, "I can't hide a thing from you anymore, can I?"

"Not after all these years of marriage, darling."

"I'll tell you after lunch. Let's enjoy the time we have now."

Nodding, Laura acquiesced, filling him with relief. Since the terror his family had suffered during a kidnapping by drug lords years ago, Morgan knew he couldn't protect them from everything, and that ate at him. The kidnapping had been the druggies' way

53

of paying back Morgan for disrupting their cocaine trafficking out of the Caribbean and South America. He shuddered as he remembered how he, Laura and Jason had been taken to different parts of the world and held without ransom.

Morgan had felt so powerless. Once they'd been rescued and brought back together, Morgan had moved his family out of Washington, D.C., to the protective mountains of Montana.

Since then, he'd done everything in his power to keep his family safe. He had taken Perseus deep underground. To this day, no one except high-echelon members of the CIA and top-ranking military personnel knew the whereabouts of his supersecret organization. And since that time, Morgan valued and cherished moments with his family as never before. But whenever he was faced with a new trial, he couldn't help but think of the emotional impact of the kidnapping on his family. Especially Jason, who had been six years old at the time. Jason didn't trust anyone anymore, least of all his father, who had been unable to keep him safe in a world gone bad. And Morgan, no matter how he tried, could not repair that terrible rift that lay like the Grand Canyon between them. Over the years, it had driven them further and further apart, until Jason refused to talk to his father, even though Morgan tried often to reestablish connection with him.

As she ate her salad, Laura watched Morgan guide a spoonful of casserole into Kamaria's bow-shaped mouth. Laura's heart swelled with joy. Little Kamaria had been found in the rubble of a Southern California earthquake she herself had been caught in. While Laura was recovering in the hospital at Camp Reed, she had helped take care of Kamaria. When she'd discovered that the little girl had been orphaned by the quake, Morgan had agreed with her request to adopt her. Morgan liked the name of his sister and mother for the baby. Laura liked Kamaria. She ended up with a huge name of Rachel Alyssa Kamaria Trayhern.

Laura knew having a baby in the house again had been very healing, especially to Morgan, who had never had this kind of relationship with his two eldest children, Jason and Katy. Now he was devoting quality time to Pete and Kelly, their fraternal twins, and Kamaria. Laura knew he took parenting very seriously and was trying to make up for all the mistakes he believed he had made with their first two children.

Even now, as Morgan smiled at Kamaria, he turned to his wife and said, "I wish I knew then what I know now." His voice was low with pain, and Laura felt for him. "What if I'd spent this kind of time with Jason? Would things be different now?"

Laura reached over, taking his hand to comfort him, all the while wondering if he already knew about Jason's transfer, and if he didn't, how he would react when he found out. . . .

Chapter 3

After lunch, Morgan stood with Laura in the backyard, watching as Kamaria happily played in her sandbox with a red plastic pail and scoop. The dappled sunlight felt good, and he slid his arm around his wife's shoulders. "I didn't want to spoil our lunch," he began. His mouth flexed and in a lower tone he added, "I have some bad news about Jason."

Knowing what was to come, Laura leaned against his tall, strong frame, studying the darkness in his gray eyes.

Sighing, Morgan closed his hand around her right shoulder. "You know Red Dugan? The C.O. of the Eagle Warrior Apache Squadron with the 101st Airborne? I think you met him at that military convention in D.C. last year. Anyway, I got a call from him today. He told me that Jason had been transferred to his squadron at Fort Campbell. Dugan told me on the q.t. that Jason literally got kicked out of his old squadron. He has a personality problem, Laura. Pilots on two different Apaches asked for him to be transferred to another team. That kid is causing nothing but trouble no matter where he goes."

Trying to wrestle with his anger, frustration and shame over his son's actions, Morgan continued, "I'm sorry to have to tell you this."

Laura looked up at her husband. Although little Kamaria was only two years old and wouldn't understand adult problems, Laura kept her voice low to protect her from the discussion that was to come.

"Synchronicity strikes again, Morgan. I was going to tell you once lunch was over that I just got a call from Jason." She saw surprise flicker in his eyes before they narrowed with pain. Her heart ached for him. "I didn't want to tell you earlier and ruin your lunch. I know how upsetting this is for you. Jason never wants to talk to you, and tries to time his calls to when you aren't around." She shrugged helplessly. "I was going to tell you now, but you beat me to it."

Raking the fingers of his free hand through his hair, Morgan gave a jerky nod. He walked on across the wide green yard, with Laura at his side. "I swear that kid is hell-bent on self-destruction. I don't know what to do to stop him." He turned to his wife, who seemed so small next to him. She was petite, yet strong in ways he never would be. "Red told me in no uncertain terms that this is Jason's last chance. If he can't get along with the new pilot assigned to him now, then he's out — with a bad conduct discharge."

"Oh, God," Laura whispered, pressing her fingers against her lips. "When he called earlier he never mentioned anything about that."

"Of course he wouldn't. He evades, Laura. He never tells either of us the whole story. We only get it piecemeal from my friends at the Pentagon. If not for them, we wouldn't have a clue."

"Well . . . he sounded good, Morgan. He really did. Even hopeful. And he was more open than usual. He's been assigned to a female helo pilot — one of the few women currently flying the combat birds in the U.S. military. Jason said he likes her. Well, he didn't go that far, but he sounded more hopeful than I've heard him sound since he joined the Army two years ago." She reached out and slid her fingers down Morgan's arm.

Feeling anguished, Morgan groped for Laura's slender, warm fingers and gently wrapped his around them. Looking over her head, he saw Kamaria toddling around in the sand, waving the red scoop in her right hand, the pail in her left. One of their cats, a calico by the name of Tortie Girl, was walking in front of her, tail held high, as if to tease his daughter. The look of joy on Kamaria's face as she gently reached out to touch Tortie Girl's tail with the red shovel made him feel a little better. Kamaria smiled more than any of his other children. But then, Morgan reminded himself, she hadn't suffered the strain of his parenting during the difficult times in his past. With a sigh, he hoped he was a changed man and that his youngest daughter would grow up without that stress affecting her.

"What else did he say?" Morgan murmured, looking at Laura once more. It hurt to know that Jason never wanted to talk with him. But why should he? They were icy cold with one another and the conversation always ended up with Morgan berating Jason. He knew he shouldn't, but he didn't know how else to handle his troubled son.

Laura slid her arm around her husband's waist and leaned her head against his shoulder. The warm summer breeze was wonderful, the scent of the pines a balm for how she felt right now. She shared the rest of her conversation with Jason with Morgan, as she always did. Her heart ached when she saw the worry and frustration in his eyes as she stood with him at the far corner of the fenced yard.

"Did Red say anything about Chief Annie Dazen?" she asked when she was done. "That's who Jason's assigned to."

Shaking his head, Morgan muttered, "No. He did say that he was giving Jason the very best chance he could by putting him with the top pilot in their squadron. And I owe Dugan for that."

"He's doing this because of you, Morgan. Everyone in the U.S. military respects you, no matter what service they're in."

"I guess so," he mumbled, "Red told me that. And I thanked him."

"A BCD? Oh, God, Morgan, I hope Jason turns around. He's been in a downward spiral ever since being kicked out of Annapolis."

"He's angry." Morgan's mouth flattened as he looked sightlessly at the mountain that rose in front of them, hundreds of fragrant pine trees blanketed the slope, standing at attention like green guardians. "He's angry at me. Probably doesn't trust me after what happened when he was six. He's carried that anger ever since the kidnapping. I know where it's coming from." Shaking his head, Morgan rasped unsteadily, "I screwed up so badly when he was young. . . ."

"Shh," Laura whispered. She turned and placed her hands on his upper arms, giving him a slight shake. "Listen to me, darling. You did the best you could. I was concerned about our high visibility in the Washington, D.C. community back then. And yes, we did talk about moving, or at least keeping our address secret. We just didn't do it soon enough."

Miserably, Morgan looked down at her. "I

should have listened when you first suggested the move. So much bad came out of the kidnapping . . . for everyone. . . ." He lifted a strand of her shoulder-length blond hair and gently placed it behind her ear. Laura had also been kidnapped, and raped repeatedly by the drug lord, who was trying to get even with Morgan for his efforts to disrupt his billion-dollar drug trade. His wife had spent years in therapy, climbing out of the hell that experience had left her in, and it had forever affected her — and him — as a result. Morgan now realized that when a woman was raped, a part of her was murdered, never to return. In an alarming way, the drug lords continued to get even with him to this day for his arrogant belief that no one would dare to harm his family. He had been so terribly wrong in his assessment of their safety back then.

"Jason is still paying a price for my bad judgment. My arrogance. I don't blame him for being angry with me, Laura. I just wish like hell he'd quit rebelling against the world because of it. It's *me* he wants to get at."

Tears stung Laura's eyes as she searched her husband's gaze, which was filled with pain. She could see he wanted to cry, but Morgan never cried. He was a warrior from a dynasty of warriors who had served their country faithfully and fully. Tears were not an option for him, no matter what. If only

Morgan could cry and release some of that pain that never left him. Laura always found release from crying. It was like a storm moving through her, cleansing her of ugly feelings. Afterward, she always felt lighter, cleaner, and relieved of the burdens that had made her weep.

"Listen to me, Morgan. Jason got the best psychiatric counseling we could give him. We did all we could to undo the damage done to him by that drug lord over in Hawaii." Sliding her hand against his face, she whispered, "All we can do is love him and be there for him, darling. This is painful for everyone. We're all hurting, and it hasn't gotten any easier as he's grown older."

A groan broke from Morgan's tight lips when he saw tears brimming in Laura's eyes. Threading his fingers through her hair and taming the strands tossed by the breeze, he said, "Let's hope that Annie Dazen is a guardian angel for him, because it's Jason's last stop on this downward spiral. If he gets a BCD . . . well, I don't know what will happen to him. No corporation will want him. No one will hire him. It's a black mark on him for life."

Nodding, Laura said, "Yes, let's hope Annie can pull a rabbit out of the hat for all of us." Morgan himself had been marked as a traitor to his country, she reflected. And yet, in time, he had managed to clear his name.

A BCD, however, was different. She hoped it didn't happen — hoped her son's life wouldn't be marked forever.

"Let's get to work, Mr. Trayhern," Annie said when she saw her new copilot come through the door at the side of the hangar. Dressed in his flight uniform, he walked proudly, with his broad shoulders squared and his chin lifted almost arrogantly. At 1500, the temperature was nearing ninety and the humidity made the air feel like a soaked sponge. She had changed into her one-piece flight suit, and had her helmet sitting on the fuselage skirt.

"You look like you're ready to go up." Jason saw her slightly tilted eyes sparkle with mischief above her high cheekbones, her full mouth slightly curved in one corner.

"Yes, we are. You got your helmet with you?"

He halted before her in the busy hangar. "It's in my locker. I, uh, didn't think —"

"Go get it and meet me out on the apron." Annie turned and called over to her crew chief to get the helo pushed out of the hangar so they could fly it. As she twisted to glance across her shoulder, she saw Trayhern stand uncertainly for a moment, a confused scowl on his features.

"Problems?" she demanded.

"No." Jason studied her face, which was

now dead serious. As nice as Ms. Dazen had been upon first meeting, she was all business now. Turning, he hurried back across the hangar toward the locker room.

A short while later, Annie stood beside the bird as her crew prepared it for takeoff. She looked up at the light blue sky, which was filling with cumulus clouds, and surmised that a storm could result around 1600. Sweat trickled down her rib cage and she turned to see Trayhern trotting out of the hangar.

She was pleased to see that he took her request that they fly now seriously. There was a guarded look on his face and that was fine with her. Colonel Dugan had said to test him immediately on his flight capabilities. The colonel wanted to know just how good — or bad — Jason Trayhern was behind the stick of a helo. And so did she.

As he came up, Annie introduced him to her three-person flight crew. To her relief, he shook hands and murmured words of greeting to each. At least he had some sense of civility.

When he moved to where she stood near the step on the side of the Apache fuselage, Annie pulled on her fire-retardant flight gloves. "You get the lower cockpit." Since she was pilot in charge, she could choose to sit in either spot. She preferred the upper cockpit because it gave her more visibility.

"I need the upper one," he replied. "I fly

better in that position."

Hearing the steel in his tone, she smiled crookedly. "Do you always get what you want, Mr. Trayhern?" He was trying to intimidate her. On purpose? Or was it just his warrior attitude?

"Usually." He saw the challenging glint in her eyes as they narrowed speculatively upon him. Annie was three inches shorter, but with her proud carriage and bearing, he could swear she was his height. Maybe it was her cocky Apache pilot stance. No one flew this combat bird who wasn't an aggressive type A personality, someone who lived for confrontation.

"Not today, Mr. Trayhern. Now, climb up." As she motioned to the dark green metal shield that covered one of the wheels of the helo, she saw him frown. This was the first test: would he take orders from a woman? Standing relaxed, she watched what looked like anger move across his face. Did Trayhern know how easy he was to read? He put the helmet on his head and fastened the strap beneath his square chin. She saw a couple of small scars on his smoothly shaved jaw. Had someone picked a fight with this guy? More than likely.

She watched as he put one black flight boot onto the first rung and hoisted himself upward. The cockpit Plexiglas opened on one side only. Just above it, less than a foot away, were the four blades of the bird. She watched as he expertly slid in and squeezed himself into the narrow confines of the front, lower cockpit. Spec 2 Bobby Warner, one of the mechanics on her crew, climbed up and knelt beside him, quickly helping Trayhern with the array of harnesses that had to be put on and locked securely into place. Once Warner was done, he turned and grinned down at her.

"Ready for you, ma'am." Then he stood up and moved to the end of the skirt so she could ascend.

"Excellent, Warner. Thanks." Annie threw her helmet to him and then quickly climbed into the upper cockpit. This was home to her. She slid down onto the seat, the two HUDs — heads-up displays — in front of her. Each cockpit had the exact same equipment, so if one pilot was incapacitated the other could take over flying and get them home safely.

Warner handed her the helmet.

"Thanks," Annie murmured. Within moments, she was strapped in and ready to go. Plugging the cord from her helmet into the radio receptacle, she switched to intercabin intercom.

"You read me, Mr. Trayhern? Over."

"Read you loud and clear, Ms. Dazen."

"Good." Annie looked over and gave Warner a thumbs-up. Below, standing near the nose of the helo, where Annie could see her, was her crew chief. Kat stood with a pair of earphones on, the phone jack plugged into a side panel of the Apache. She would be responsible for starting of the bird.

"Okay, Kat, let's get this show on the road," Annie murmured. She nodded to Warner and gave him the signal to shut and lock each of the cockpits. Excitement thrummed through her. Flying was like breathing to Annie. Her adrenaline surged as soon as she felt the whine of the twin engines. Below, she saw her crew scurrying about efficiently. Kat gave a thumbs-up and Annie pressed the mike close to her lips.

"Okay, Mr. Trayhern, this flight is all yours. Power up."

Annie pulled a clipboard from a side pocket of the cockpit and placed it across her knees. Before she had been assigned with the 101st, she'd been a flight trainer. The clipboard held a list of all the maneuvers she was going to put him through and grade him on. He didn't know, of course, that she'd been an inspector pilot. Annie wanted him to be as relaxed as possible on this flight. There wasn't a pilot alive that didn't tense up and screw up when an IP was in the cockpit, grading him or her. Annie wanted to give Trayhern a chance.

"Yes, ma'am."

She smiled to herself. Trayhern had clearly

dropped the anger she had seen in him on the tarmac, and was all business now. That was good. She heard him communicate with Kat Lakey on the ground. The blessed flow of air-conditioning began just then and Annie sighed in relief, because the cockpit was like a sauna until the cool air got turned on. Sweat dribbled down her left temple and she swiped it away.

When the Apache's first engine started, the familiar high, shrieking whine began. The second engine came on next, and Annie saw Kat pull out the intercom cord and lock the panel down. Then the crew chief backed off and lifted her arm straight up, twirling her fingers, which was a signal for Trayhern to engage the blades.

The shuddering started. Annie absorbed it like a lover. The Apache was the most feared combat helicopter in the world. To her, it was like a dinosaur, ugly as sin, but lethal. When the blades started slowly turning around and around, she felt lulled, like a child cradled by its mother. There was something comforting and soothing about the shaking that went on as the blades whirled faster and faster.

She heard Jason call into the tower at Ops for takeoff permission. Once it was granted, she saw Lakey duck beneath the carriage to remove the chocks from behind and in front of the wheels. Once the crew chief was clear,

Annie heard Trayhern's deep, unruffled voice in her headset. "Ready for liftoff, Ms. Dazen?"

"Yes, I am, Mr. Trayhern. Let's fly. . . ."

Annie held the pen in her right hand, the clipboard across her thighs as the Apache lifted smoothly from the ground. She talked him through the air corridors flight pattern that every helo had to follow when taking off from the base. Once they were out over the countryside, the flat plains of Kentucky changed to gentle, rolling hills, a landscape of green, as they flew across the state boundary into Tennessee. The massive Army base sprawled across the state line, part in Tennessee, but the bulk of it in Kentucky, where ninety-three thousand acres had been set aside for flight training and firing ranges.

At this time of day, flying was often rough, and Annie was jostled continuously as the helo hit air pocket after air pocket. As the summer sun beat down on the earth, thermals rising off the hills created unstable conditions that made flying a challenge.

"I remember this," Jason said, feeling the collective and cyclic in his hands. It felt good to be flying again. They were at five thousand feet and heading to a restricted air space where they could fly maneuvers without hitting a civilian plane.

"What? The thermals?"

"Yeah," Jason said. He'd been nervous, but

the comforting shudder of the helo had taken his anxiety away. "We all went through Apache training school in Alabama. I remember I always got afternoon flights, when the humidity was at its highest. It wasn't fun at first. My lunch was always comin' up. Flying out of this base reminds me of afternoon flights at Fort Rucker." Southern states in the U.S. always got high humidity coming in off the Gulf. At Fort Collins, Colorado, the air was much drier, making it easier to fly.

Chuckling, Annie looked around the sunny cockpit, then drew down the dark visor on her helmet. "Oh, yeah, bag time. How long ago did you last eat?"

He laughed shortly. "Bag time" meant throwing up during flight, into a red plastic bag that was stored in the right pocket of every cockpit. "Not to worry this time around. I learned a long time ago to eat lightly at lunch."

"Fill a few, did you?"

"A couple. You?"

"Nah. Indians don't get airsick."

Smiling slightly, Jason found himself curious about her Native American background. "I see. . . ."

"In all honesty," Annie told him, "I had two hundred flight hours in helicopters before I came into the Army. And I was kidding about Indians not getting airsick. We're

71

human just like everyone else."

"I've never flown with an Indian before. I guess it's something I'll have to get used to." Well, that didn't come out right, did it? He cringed over his spontaneous choice of words. It was one of his problems: foot-in-mouth disease.

"Now, should I take that comment as an insult or a compliment?"

Jason frowned, his gaze flying across the cockpit dials. "No, it's me not thinking," he said abruptly.

"Oh?"

"Yeah, sometimes my mouth gets ahead of my brain."

"Does it happen often?"

"Pretty much. And I apologize."

She heard him almost choking on his words. Was it because he didn't say he was sorry very often? Or was he genuinely trying to get along with her but fumbling it? Annie chose to believe the latter, not wanting to think that he was prejudiced on top of every-thing else. After all, this was his first day in a new squadron with a new air commander. He had to be nervous.

"You don't know much about Native American culture, do you?"

"No . . . hardly anything. You're the first person I've even run into that was Indian."

"I see. . . ." The helo jostled and dropped a good ten feet when it hit a huge air pocket.

Annie smiled as she felt Trayhern adjust and stabilize the bird.

"We moved around a lot when I was a kid. I didn't get to know anyone too well," he told her.

"Typical military brat?"

"Yeah, kinda . . ."

"Not me. I was born on the White River Apache Reservation in Arizona and never left until I joined the Army after high school."

"I've never been to Arizona."

"It's dry and hot. Not like this place. Fort Campbell reminds me of a sponge. I can hardly wait to get to Afghanistan. It's hot and dry there like it is on my res. I'll feel right at home in that desert environment."

"Weather is the least of my problems."

Annie thought it was an odd statement, but said nothing. "Okay, Cowboy, take this bird to ten thousand feet. Now." She smiled at the nickname she'd spontaneously given him. He reminded her of an Old West cowboy — stoic, rough, a little rusty on social protocols, but heroic just the same. If he took umbrage with the new handle she'd given him, he didn't say anything. All pilots had a nickname they were usually called by instead of their real name.

Jason powered up both engines, and the thumping of the Apache's blades deepened. In seconds, the helo was clawing upward, the pressure of the climb pressing Annie against her seat. From ten thousand feet, the carpet of trees looked like lumpy green cottage cheese below them. They were safely within the restricted airspace, and she looked at her HUD to make sure no other aircraft was in the vicinity. Usually, at this time of day, few were flying because of the nasty up- and downdrafts created by the sun's heating of the earth.

"Okay, nice going, Mr. Trayhern." Annie leaned forward and shut off both engines. "You are now without power. Get this bird down in one piece." She heard him gasp once, but that was all. Instantly, the Apache fell, nose first. Without his quick intercession, the bird would have continued to plummet. Trayhern clearly knew what to do. He stabilized the helicopter, using the flailing blades that still whirled above them despite the lack of engine power. An experienced pilot could use the air as a cushion, and the blades as helping hands, to get a chopper down in one piece. As they plummeted closer and closer to the earth, Annie was pleased to see Trayhern moving the wallowing helo toward a small meadow off to the right. That would be where he'd try an emergency landing.

Jason wrestled with the Apache. The last thing he'd ever thought he'd be doing was attempting a dead-stick landing. She'd cut the engines! Just like that! What the hell was she thinking? His anger surged, then receded as he jockeyed the sluggish bird toward the meadow, which was coming up very quickly.

Annie braced herself. At one thousand feet, Trayhern pointed the nose downward. The earth came rushing up fast. At five hundred feet he suddenly eased back on the stick, raising the nose abruptly. The whirling blades caught the cushion of air once more. At the last moment, he steadied the Apache. They hit the knoll with a thud and then rolled forward through the grass, finally coming to a stop.

Annie's teeth unclenched. They were down, the blades spinning slowly around and around. As she relaxed her jaw, she heard Trayhern breathing hard in her earphones. Placing a checkmark in the emergency landing box, she said, "We're in one piece. That's good, Mr. Trayhern. Now take her up again."

Jason suddenly realized she was testing him, and the fact made him angry and frightened. What if he had screwed up? Well, he hadn't on the emergency landing. He flipped on the engine switches, the familiar hum and whine filling the cockpit once more. He busied himself with getting the bird airborne again. Once he had climbed to five thousand feet, he wiped the sweat off his brow. Pulling the dark visor down across his upper face, he pressed the microphone near his lips.

"Why didn't you tell me this was a damn flight test?"

"Why should I?"

"Because I have a right to know."

"No, you don't. You're my copilot, Mr. Trayhern. In thirty days, our collective ass will be on the line over in Afghanistan. I want to make very sure that I'm flying with someone I can trust. Now, get this bird up to ten thousand again. Please."

Grinding his teeth, Jason did as she ordered. None of the other pilots he'd been assigned to had done this to him. It was automatically assumed he was good or he wouldn't be in an Apache squadron.

"What's this all about, Ms. Dazen? Why am I being tested like a rookie?"

"I test any pilot I fly with like this, so you're not being singled out, Mr. Trayhern."

"I don't believe you. There's more to it." He looked around at the hazy afternoon sky, his mind clicking on possibilities. Then he tightened his hands around the collective and cyclic, his nostrils flaring. "I know why."

Annie said nothing. She wanted to see how he handled himself when he was upset. Good pilots disconnected from their emotions when flying. Otherwise, when in combat, the spurt of adrenaline could kill them, caught up as they were in the life-and-death drama of war. And Annie wanted to know now whether he had the necessary detachment to think

76

through the adrenaline rush and haze of fear. So far, so good.

Jason waited. She remained silent. *Damn her.* All of a sudden he wasn't feeling very kindly at all toward Ms. Dazen. She might have a killer smile that made a man feel all warm and good inside, but that was only frosting.

"You know who I am," he said through gritted teeth. "You know I got kicked out of Annapolis on drug charges. You also know that I've been booted out of my previous squadron into this one. And this is my last chance to make it or break it. You know everything about me. That's why you're testing me like this."

"If you were in my seat, wouldn't you do the same thing?"

Her voice was cool and without emotion.

Jason sat there, his gaze flicking across the dials. The Apache soothed some of his rage, some of his fear. But not all of it. "Yeah, maybe I would. If I got handed a black cloud of a pilot who could never say or do the right thing, or do whatever the hell else was expected, I'd be gun-shy, too."

Heart twinging, Annie felt his pain. Oh, the anger, the rage was there, no doubt. He wasn't going to be civil about this. At least, not up here in the cockpit.

"There's a saying back where I come from," she said quietly. "It's better that a rattlesnake rattle its tail in warning than let you step on it and get bitten."

Stymied, Jason took a deep breath. He was sweating big-time now, the armpits of his flight suit soaked. The air-conditioning cooled the cabin, but he was perspiring for other reasons. "And I suppose I'm a snake?" he rasped. He didn't like mind games.

"You're missing the point, Mr. Trayhern. I'd rather deal with someone up front, with or without diplomacy, than have them sneak around behind my back to bite me."

Sitting there, Jason found his mind reeling. "You think I'm going to bite you?"

"Would you?"

"The last two pilots sneaked behind my back and bitched to the C.O. about me. They never faced me and told me they had a problem with me."

"Well," Annie said, "that won't happen here."

"You're a damn IP, aren't you?"

The words were thrown like a gauntlet. Annie lifted her head. From her position in the upper cockpit, she could see Jason Trayhern's helmet and shoulders below her. She could see he was gripping the cyclic and collective hard, obviously upset.

"Yes, I am."

His stomach clenched. His heart sank. This was a test — the whole damn flight. What had happened to that pleasant-looking

78

woman he'd met in the hangar? Jason had found himself drawn to her, rightly or wrongly. Her golden eyes, slightly tilted, were so huge and beautiful that he'd imagined he could see sunlight dappling them, like light dancing across the rippled surface of a lake.

"And you're out to flunk me, aren't you? Orders from above? From Colonel Dugan? He doesn't want Bad Luck Trayhern in his squadron, so he's sent you to do his dirty work. Flunk me out on this flight, and that's all the reason he needs to give me a BCD outta this man's Army."

Stunned by his accusations, Annie said nothing for a long moment. "Mr. Trayhern, you are paranoid. No one has it in for you here, except maybe yourself."

"You know I got kicked out of Annapolis."

"Yes, I do."

"You've already formed an opinion of me."

"No, I haven't, but you're trying hard to make me do so now, and I don't like it."

Setting the cyclic and collective on autopilot, Jason shoved up the dark shield and shakily wiped the sweat off his brow again. Jerking the visor back down, he rested his left arm against the console and gripped the controls again. He flicked off the autopilot and took over flying once more.

"Are you saying you haven't already formed an opinion of me, Ms. Dazen?" Jason found that very hard to believe. Trying to control his breathing, he waited for her answer.

"I have another saying, Mr. Trayhern. We don't judge a person unless we've walked a mile in his or her moccasins. Now, I don't know what went on at Annapolis. Frankly, I haven't heard much about it. I do know you were caught in a drug ring, but that you were never formerly accused of doing drugs or selling them. I hope you aren't doing drugs, because if you are, I'll find out and you're outta here, anyway."

"I didn't do drugs," Jason snarled. "Now or then. So relax on that one, will you?"

"As I understand it, you can be asked for a urine sample at any time, Mr. Trayhern."

"That's right. I signed on in the Army with that agreement. They can test me until they're blue in the face, and they won't find me dirty. I've passed twenty tests in the last two years. But you probably know that already."

Annie said, "I let a person walk their talk, Mr. Trayhern. That means that your daily interface with me and my crew is what counts. We're rated top pilot and top crew here in the squadron. I want that to continue."

"And you think by being saddled with me, you won't be?"

"Dude, you are defensive! Did I say that? Did I say anything *like* that?" Annie chuckled. "I told you before, you will prove

80

who and what you are on a daily basis around here. Your past doesn't count with me, Trayhern. But your present sure as hell does. Do you understand?"

Jason closed his eyes for a moment. He heard her husky words flow over him like a calming blanket. "Yeah, I hear you." But could he trust her to do that? Or was Annie Dazen like the other pilots who had screwed him? Just waiting to catch him making a mistake so they could run screaming to the C.O. and nail him? Only time would tell.

Chapter 4

"We need to talk — privately." Annie kept her voice low and firm, brooking no argument from Trayhern, who only furrowed his broad brow, his eyebrows drawn down in a V.

Gripping his helmet, Jason nodded curtly, walking beside her toward their office in the hangar. Humiliated because he had felt the eyes of her crew on him as they got the bird's blades tied down and chocks around the three wheels, he ground his teeth. For two hours she'd grilled him in the air, making him feel like a child. Jason wanted to dislike Annie. But he couldn't and he didn't know why. Had it been her whiskey-smooth voice in the earphones of his helmet? Her pointed questions about his ability to trust? The answer escaped him and he kept his silence, studying her profile. Her hair was in disarray now that she'd taken off her helmet, and flyaway black strands glinted with reddish highlights in the sun.

Once inside the air-conditioned office, Jason dropped his helmet into one of the two chairs that sat in front of the green metal desk. When he heard the door click shut, he rounded on her, his rage barely held in check. Her golden eyes were narrowed and assessing, and he was surprised at the strength that suddenly emanated from her as she stood toe-to-toe with him, her helmet still beneath her left arm.

"Okay, Cowboy, let's have both barrels. You're spoiling for a fight and this is the place to have it." She jabbed a finger at the door. "This is where you and I tango. Never while in flight and never in front of our crew."

Jason was taken aback momentarily at her use of the word *our*. When had any other pilot ever done that? Blinking a couple of times, he felt his mind spin. Yeah, he was angry, but suddenly he felt as if that wasn't appropriate. Annie had said "our crew." *Our.* She trusted him. She must. Why?

"Maybe," he growled, "I'm just uptight because of the unexpected test you pulled on me."

Giving him a taut smile, Annie turned and placed her helmet on a hook. She moved around the desk, smoothed her hair with her hands and sat down. The chair creaked.

"You have a right to feel stressed. I would, too."

Dammit, she wasn't like male pilots. When Jason challenged them the way he'd challenged her, he blasted them. Yet he didn't feel an urge to fight back. Instead, he sat down and ran his fingers through his damp hair. "Why'd you do it?"

"Why wouldn't I?" Annie opened her hands. She saw the confusion in Jason's eyes. Because she was highly intuitive, she could feel the range of emotions he was experiencing right now. Something told her that he wasn't as much angry as he was worried that she wouldn't accept him as a full partner in the cockpit and on the ground. "From where I sit, I'm pleased with how you handled the bird." She pointed to her clipboard, which held the test scores he'd earned. "I'll give you a copy of the results and we'll talk about them. We'll make strengths of any weaknesses I saw before we leave for Afghanistan. You don't have the flight hours I feel you need, so we're going to be doing a lot of flying between now and then to sharpen your reflexes and get more of your skills up to par."

Jason digested her huskily spoken words. So much of him was drawn to her. What *was* it about her? He'd never been as fascinated by a woman as he was by Annie Dazen. Maybe it was her slightly tilted eyes that shone like warm, golden sunlight tinged with cinnamon? Or the way her full mouth turned soft with compassion. Or her openness toward him.

"I thought you wanted to get rid of me. That's what the other pilots did," he growled. "I thought you were pulling this test to find a reason to write me up and get me out of the squadron."

Her heart gave a tug. Whether Jason knew it or not, in that moment, he looked like an abandoned little boy, not a twenty-four-year-old man. She had a gift of perception that she'd inherited from her mother. At times she could see beyond the normal range of human comprehension. As she looked across the desk at Jason, any defensiveness she may have felt toward him melted away. It was the look in his eyes; for a second, he seemed like a hunted, haunted animal on the run from . . . what? Who?

"I hope you don't paint me with the same brush, Mr. Trayhern. I have no desire to set you up to fail. I want to get to Afghanistan and do a little damage to El Quaida. And whether I like it or not, you're my new copilot."

"Who would want me for a copilot with my track record? You probably see me as an instant liability to your hopes for promotion." He knew a bad junior pilot could drag the best pilot's career through the mud, and hurt his or her chances for advancement.

Shrugging, Annie sat up, placed her elbows on the desk and looked him squarely in the eyes. "Look, Mr. Trayhern, I have no ax to grind with you. If you do what you say you'll do, I'll have no problem with you."

Blinking, Jason sat there and looked at her

sincere, open features. Her hands were clasped in front of her, her voice low and warm. That warmth cascaded through him like heat against a glacier, melting a frozen part of him inside.

"Then . . . you're giving me a chance?" *A real one?* Oh, God, how he wanted that! Wanted to halt the downward spiral of his career. Wanted to try and hold on to something, to pull himself up by his own bootstraps. Studying Annie's features with something akin to amazement, Jason realized that she was his last hope. If he couldn't turn his life around with her help, he really was done. And he couldn't stand the shame that would place on his family, or himself. He'd finally hit bottom.

"You'll be giving yourself that chance, if you want it," Annie told him. "I'm going to work your butt off for the next thirty days."

"That doesn't bother me."

"Then what does?"

"That you'll sandbag me, Ms. Dazen. That you're waiting in the weeds like those other two pilots I flew with, looking for a chance to nail me."

"I'm not like that." She sat up, then leaned back in the chair. "But you'll find that out sooner or later. Right now, you need a shower and a change of clothes. When you're done, come back to the office and we'll discuss your test results."

Jason stood up. "Okay, fair enough."

"The showers are just off the locker room. There're always towels, washcloths and soap available." She looked at her watch. "Be back here in thirty minutes?"

Moving toward the door, he muttered, "Yeah, I'll be back."

Annie watched him pick up his helmet in his long fingers. He had the hands of a pilot, there was no doubt, even though his flight suit was stained with sweat.

When the door closed and she heard him walk away from her office, Annie blew out a long, unsteady breath. Relief washed through her. She didn't like confrontations like that.

"Some days are more trying than others," she muttered. "Why am I getting this guy, Shaida?" Shaida was the name of her spirit guide. Every Indian Annie knew of, especially one who came from a medicine family as she did, had a guide. Although Annie couldn't see hers, she knew she was there. She'd grown up with her. As a child, she had often seen the lithe, two-hundred-fifty-pound black jaguar, who used to sit and watch her with large, golden eyes. Annie had always felt safe as a child when Shaida was with her. And the Great Spirit knew, she'd always been in some kind of trouble, needing protection. Shaida was her guardian angel, there was no doubt.

Annie rubbed her brow now and stood

up. She nervously wiped her sweaty palms on the sides of her flight suit and went out into the hangar to talk with her crew. They'd brought the bird inside the hangar already and were working on maintenance. Pride in her crew swelled within her as she walked across the clean and shiny concrete floor. Well, it would be a pleasant half hour before she had to bang heads with Trayhern again.

"So that's the bottom line on your test results, Mr. Trayhern." Annie tossed the clipboard back on her desk after giving him a copy of the test and the percentages he'd earned on each of the flight functions she'd assessed. "Overall, not bad. I don't think you got the air time you needed with the other pilots. I think these grades reflect your lack of flying time. That's something we can quickly remedy around here."

Jason took the papers and glanced at them. He felt a lot more comfortable sitting in front of her desk in a clean, dry flight suit. A shower had been just what he'd needed, for many reasons. Water was always soothing to him, a calming balm to any fractious state. It allowed him to relax and let go.

Looking at the test scores and then up at Annie, he said, "No, I didn't get a lot of flight time." Mainly because he'd been squabbling so much with his copilots that they wanted to avoid him, so his flight hours dipped accordingly.

"Because?" Annie was bound and determined to find out what was eating Trayhern. He'd not only showered, but he'd shaved as well, which pleased her. He didn't have to. It was near 1700, quitting time. He had taken extra pains, she hoped, to show her that he cared enough to try.

"Because," Jason growled, "I wasn't exactly pleasant with my command pilot."

"Why?"

He eyed her. "You don't mind asking hard questions, do you?"

Her mouth quirked. "Not when my life depends on it."

Managing a sour grin, Jason said, "I was in his face because I was constantly questioning why he was doing something."

"That implies a lack of trust in the command pilot."

"Yes . . . I guess it does." He dropped his head and stared at the test scores. Annie Dazen had given him relatively high marks on most of the flight maneuvers, which surprised him. His other command pilots had consistently rated him at the bottom, just above the seventy-five percentile passing mark. She, on the other hand, had given him scores in the eighties and nineties, which buoyed his sense of confidence in himself — and in her. It looked as if she really wasn't out to get him.

"Why didn't you trust your command pilot?"

The words were spoken so softly and gently that Jason felt the doors of his heart fly open. It shocked him. He sat there, staring down at the papers in his hand, as he mulled over his emotional response to her. Finally he forced himself to look up. When he did, he was once again surprised. Annie's usual poker face was soft and readable. He saw a burning look in her golden eyes, as if she genuinely wanted to know the truth.

Sighing, he whispered, "Look, I've never talked about this to anyone before. . . ."

"You have to give me some sign of trust, Jason." Annie deliberately used his first name, and saw the impact that instantly had on him. There was such struggle evident in his eyes — between shame, anger, hope and something else she couldn't decipher.

"Yeah . . . I hear you. . . ." The papers fluttered nervously in his hand. "I expected you to fail me like the others did."

"You aren't a failure. You're just rusty, is all. There's a huge difference." Annie's heart bled for him. For an instant, she thought she'd seen tears in his eyes, but just as quickly, they were gone. His mouth was twisted in a tortured line. Her gut instinct was to get up, walk around the desk and slide her arms around his shoulders as he sat there. Clearly, he was suffering from some terrible past event that haunted his present. She didn't dare reach out to him that way. But the very idea of doing so was startling to her.

"I can see that. . . ."

"Then help me to help you," she beseeched softly, leaning forward, her hands opening. "Tell me what's behind your lack of trust. I need to know."

Though he wanted to look down at his polished black leather flight boots, Jason forced himself to meet Annie's gaze. Her expression was so open, so tender. Her lips were slightly parted. Beckoning . . . Damn, but he wanted to find out if her lips were as soft as he thought they might be.

Giving himself an internal shake, Jason realized that his life as an aviator hung in the balance, depending on whether or not he came clean with Annie. Somehow, in his deeply wounded heart, he knew she would be fair with him — but only if he was honest with her. He saw that in her eyes, in the way they glinted. She had such gentle, yet strong, power. Jason would trust her with his life in that cockpit because she radiated a kind of quiet confidence he'd looked for all his life, and never found — until now.

Clearing his throat, he looked at his watch. "It's 1700. Quitting time."

Shrugging, Annie said, "I have all night, if

that's what it takes."

Relief flowed through him. His stomach muscles unclenched a little. "Yeah, okay . . ." Frowning, he looked around the office, trying to gather his thoughts. Finally, he looked back at her, after clearing his throat.

"When I was six years old, I was kidnapped by a drug lord. My father, Morgan Trayhern, ran a supersecret organization called Perseus." Frowning, Jason muttered, "He still does."

Annie looked at him in surprise. "You were kidnapped?"

Jason studied her face. There was such openness in her expression. It gave him the courage to go on. "Yeah. I was playing in my little sister Katy's room when the bad guys broke in. They shot my mother and father with darts that knocked them out."

"That's terrible!" Annie searched his brooding features. "What did they do to you?"

"I remember them bursting into the room. They were dressed in civilian clothes and looked like anyone you'd see on the street. I remember getting up. I had heard the scuffle out in the front room, where my parents were. I felt scared. I knew the big guy coming toward me was going to hurt me. I was too scared to scream, but that's what I wanted to do. . . ."

Swallowing hard, Annie held his gaze.

"What happened next?"

"The dude put a cloth over my face and I blacked out. I woke up, I don't know how many hours later, on the island of Maui, Hawaii. I learned later they left Katy behind. They didn't want her."

"How awful."

"Yeah, it was."

"You have full memory of this?" Annie knew that many times, in trauma, the brain conveniently tucked away details of an experience because it was too terrible for a person to bear.

"Full memory," Jason said.

"I'm so sorry." Annie realized that his trust had been broken during that trauma. And she could easily understand that if a child's trust was not healed, the adult he became would have a hard time trusting anyone. Which was why Jason hadn't trusted the two other pilots he'd flown with. *Maybe.* She had to learn more in order to put this puzzle together. "Did both your parents survive the kidnapping?"

"Yeah, eventually." Jason looked down at the floor. "My mother was drugged and raped repeatedly by a drug lord in the Caribbean. My father was taken to South America and tortured for months. In the end, other members of Perseus, my father's agency, mounted a rescue effort and several elite mercenary teams found them and brought them home, back to the States."

"And what about you?"

"They sent a team to find me. And they did."

"How long were you a captive?"

Shrugging, Jason said, "A month or so . . ."

She saw the pain in his eyes. "Can you tell me what you remember of your captivity?"

Shifting uncomfortably in the chair, Jason said, "Yeah, I guess . . ."

Annie waited. She could feel the tension radiating from Jason, saw the way his shoulders hunched, as if to deflect a coming blow. Her questions must be like blows to him. She had so many questions she wanted to ask, but she had to be patient.

"The dude that took me was an old man. He hated my father for disrupting the world-wide drug trade. Every chance he got, he'd make sure I heard how bad my father was."

"And did you talk back to him? Fight or resist?"

Mouth thinning, Jason said, "Yeah . . . at first. I used to yell at him that my father was a good man. Every time I did, he'd slap me."

Wincing inwardly, Annie said, "I'm so sorry. . . ."

Again, her soft words haunted him, touched his aching heart and soothed him in a way no one ever had. Jason stared at her wordless for several seconds before he continued. "I learned real fast not to stand up for my father. And when the old bastard kept brainwashing me on how bad my dad was, I would cry instead. I cried out of anger, because what I wanted to do was punch out the old man's lights, but I knew he'd kill me if I tried. He always had two goons with guns hanging around the room when I was there. I knew they'd kill me."

"So you cried? Out of fear and frustration?"

"Yes."

"What else happened?" Annie dreaded asking this, but she had to in order to understand the man Jason was today.

"I got regular beatings from him when I cried. So I eventually learned to say and do nothing."

"To swallow all your feelings. To say nothing and stay silent."

"Exactly." He gave her a level look. "You understand."

"Yes . . . I do. Prisoners of war often experience the same thing you did."

"I was a prisoner of a war. I learned to trust no one there. I was watched twenty-four–seven, and I got at least one beating a day from the old dude, or from one of my guards. They said it was for being Morgan Trayhern's son. When they finally rescued me, I was black-and-blue, I had a broken nose —" he touched it with his finger "—

and several cracked ribs."

Closing her eyes, Annie placed her hand across them. Her heart swelled with anguish for Jason. No wonder he didn't trust! Allowing her hand to fall away, she opened her eyes and stared at him. He sat there tensely, as if expecting a blow. "That's really terrible. You were badly abused by them."

He chuckled darkly. "You've said a mouthful, Ms. Dazen."

"Did your parents get you therapy?"

"Oh, yeah . . . all kinds. The shrinks said I had PTSD, post-traumatic stress disorder." He flexed his fingers and chuckled again. "No surprise there."

"And how did you do with the therapists?"

"Not well, I guess. I didn't trust them."

"Of course not. They were adults."

"That's right," he said grimly.

"You probably felt abandoned by adults in your time of need. And the adult who held you prisoner hurt you badly."

"Yep, that about sums it up."

"And have you had problems trusting adult males since that time?"

"A little," Jason muttered, looking away. "I'm not on good terms with my father, either."

She hurt for him, because she saw undisguised pain over that admission not only in his narrowed blue eyes, but in the thinning of his full mouth. "I'm sure your father tried to regain your trust?"

"Oh, yeah. He did. . . ."

"But?"

"It didn't take. I was — I *am* — angry at him for what happened. He should have protected us, his family. Instead, he was arrogant and felt we were safe enough in Washington."

Annie sighed. "What about your mom? How did she get through this mess?"

"She had a lot of years after the kidnapping when she wasn't really available to us kids. I mean —" he opened his hands "— she was raped. I'm still angry over that. I see what it did to her . . . and how it's affected all of us. . . ."

"And now?"

"She's pretty much worked through the worst of it, although I still see it in her from time to time. I've learned what rape does. It's a terrible thing. It murders part of a person and you never get back that piece again."

"It sounds like the drug lords got the revenge they wanted."

"And then some."

"Your father must have been affected by this, too? You said he was tortured?"

Jason nodded. "Yeah, nonstop. You can see the scars on his arms and legs when he's in a bathing suit or a short-sleeved shirt."

"And how has he recovered from the kidnapping?"

"Better than any of us, but then, he'd been

97

wounded in the head during the Vietnam War, and had amnesia for years after that. The U.S. government screwed him, too. He didn't know who he was, and eventually joined the French Foreign Legion. Several years after that, he suddenly got his memory back and went home to the U.S.

"From there, he met my mother, Laura, and they were finally able to find the men responsible for branding him as a traitor, and to get his name cleared. My dad is a hero to a lot of people." Jason looked away. "So, my two cents' worth is that because of his past experience, he was able to roll with the kidnapping better than my mother or myself. He seems the least affected by what happened."

Annie nodded. "Thank you for telling me this. I promise it will go nowhere, but it helps me to understand you."

She saw him lift his head and study her, and instantly, her heart flew open. The look in his eyes was one of relief and hope. There was no more anger or distrust there. How badly she wanted to get up and throw her arms around Jason. Annie sensed that being held was exactly what he needed — and that, since the kidnapping, he'd never let anyone beyond those armored walls he'd built up.

Somehow, Annie knew he'd let her in. And that realization was as startling as a lightning bolt.

Chapter 5

"Have you found out anything, Morgan?" Laura asked as she laid out china plates of a colorful floral pattern on the kitchen table. It had been two weeks since she'd talked to Jason, and she hadn't heard a word from him since. She didn't know who worried more about their son, her or Morgan.

Wiping her hands on her peach-colored apron, she moved back to the counter. Today, Kamaria was being watched by their baby-sitter, Crystal Harding, a local woman from Phillipsburg who dearly loved the little tyke. Crystal and Kamaria were in the toddler's bedroom at the other end of the large, two-story home, having Kamaria's favorite lunch of peanut butter and jelly sandwiches while watching reruns of *Mister Rogers* on television.

Scowling, Morgan went to the drain board and picked up the bowls of salad Laura had made for them. "I just got off the phone with Red Dugan," he said as he placed the wooden bowls on the table.

"And?" Laura shot him a questioning look as she placed pink linen napkins and silverware next to the teak bowls. Morgan pulled out her chair and she sat down. One of the many things she loved about her husband was his gallantry. She knew it came from the fact that he'd been a Marine Corps officer, a throwback to another time, but she loved his sensitivity toward her in this way. Smiling to herself, she realized she was most likely a throwback, herself.

Watching as Morgan sat down at her left elbow, she waited impatiently to hear what he had to say about Jason. Because of her husband's broad intelligence network, which spanned the world, and his contacts with the higher-ups in every military branch, it was easy for him to pick up a phone to check in on Jason or Katy without their knowledge.

Picking up a bottle of light Italian dressing, Laura unscrewed the cap. With the advent of menopause, she found she gained weight quickly, so was dieting to help keep herself in shape. As she squirted some dressing on the colorful salad, she felt a tad guilty about Morgan initiating this behind-the-scenes checking on their children. But in Jason's case, Laura was glad he had the contacts. Jason usually called weekly, but that was it. He rarely wrote a letter. Then again, she didn't know many military men who wrote letters to their parents. Phone calls usually had to do. Jason didn't e-mail her, either. . . .

Katy wrote e-mails all the time from her secret operating base down in Colombia, and Laura was always eager to hear from her. Laura worried about her daughter, who lived in constant peril while flying the Seahawk helicopter and delivering Marine Recon teams to key locations to help Colombian government soldiers fight the rebels. And soon Jason was going to be in Afghanistan. The idea made her stomach knot. She grimaced and passed the bottle to her husband.

"Thanks . . ." Morgan took the dressing and spread some over the crisp romaine, endive and butter lettuce. Setting it down, he gave her a slight smile. "Relax, honey. You're worried about Jason, I can tell."

"So, it's good news?" *For once.*

"Seems to be. Red said that he'd just had a private conference with Jason's command pilot, Annie Dazen, a CWO2. I guess she's been flying his butt off the last two weeks, at least three hours a day in the cockpit."

Laura chewed a bite of salad and swallowed. "Why so much air time?"

"Because, from what I can understand, Jason wasn't getting the hours he needed with the other pilots."

"The personality conflicts with them, that's why. They kept him out of the cockpit."

"Well," Morgan grunted, "you become a pain in the ass and that can happen."

"So," Laura murmured, picking up half a

mushroom, "does this mean he *likes* Annie Dazen? If she's flying with him, it would seem they're getting along?" She popped the mushroom into her mouth.

"Apparently so. Red said that she's a qualified IP and used to teach green students how to fly the Apache before she was assigned to his squadron. Looking at Jason's flight numbers, Red says he's improved dramatically in two weeks."

Laura heard the lightness in Morgan's deep voice, saw relief on her husband's scarred face. Her heart lifted because she knew just how much Morgan worried over Jason. Placing her hand over his forearm, she whispered, "This is wonderful."

"Yes," he said, turning his hand over and squeezing her slender fingers, "it's the best news we've had in a long time when it comes to Jason."

"I wish he'd call."

Chuckling, Morgan speared a slice of tomato with his fork. He liked the fact that there was tasty feta cheese sprinkled over the salad. Laura made meals like this zesty. "Well, according to Red, Chief Dazen has him going nonstop. She's always pushing him, making him accountable on the ground and in the air."

"And he's actually doing it? Working? Not digging in his heels and being stubborn like he was before?" Laura wanted to believe it, but she knew that her son was stiff-necked, just like his father. They were made from the same cloth, as far as she was concerned. Jason was a younger version of Morgan, whether either of them liked to admit it or not.

"Red said Jason was busting his tail." Giving her a slight smile, Morgan pulled over a file folder he'd brought in with him. "I had my assistant, Jenny Wright, do a little snooping on Annie Dazen. Here's her personnel record. Take a look at it later."

Shaking her head, Laura murmured, "Oh, Morgan, you know this isn't right." Her husband could get the scoop on anyone, at any time, since Perseus was a deep undercover operation involved with the CIA. She eyed the file with a little more eagerness and curiosity than she cared to admit.

Shrugging, Morgan attacked his lunch with renewed interest. The news on Jason lifted his spirits as nothing else could. For once his son seemed to have gotten lucky. "We'll keep it between ourselves," he told her. "I want to know who's making our son come to heel."

Laura couldn't stand it. "Is there a photo of her in there?"

"Yeah, go ahead, peek. It won't hurt." He grinned widely as Laura gave him a censoring look, then reached over and flipped open the file.

"She's beautiful, Morgan!"

Chuckling, he said, "No kidding. Tall, dark and dangerous is the category I'd put her in. She's a full-blood Apache from a reservation in Arizona. She's known hardship and was raised in the mountains there." Motioning to the woman's official military photo, where Annie Dazen stood decked out in her class A green uniform, her hair in a black knot at the back of her head, he knew why his son was being good. "I'm sure Jason likes her."

Laura picked up the large, glossy photo. "What's not to like?"

It felt good to laugh instead of cry over Jason. Morgan buttered his whole wheat bread with long, smooth strokes. "No kidding."

"Oh, she is so pretty, Morgan. Look at her gold eyes. Cat eyes. They're so wide. That's a sign of high intelligence."

"I think Annie Dazen has the goods on Jason. She sees through him and knows how to reach into his heart instead of running up against his bullheaded mind."

Laura looked up and quirked her lips. "Gee, that bullheadedness sounds like someone else I know. . . ."

They laughed quietly.

Laura studied the photo of Annie in her uniform. "An Apache Indian piloting an Apache gunship. Isn't that interesting?"

"Annie has been a poster child of sorts for Boeing, which makes the bird, and for the

Army, which wants to entice more women to volunteer for the service." He motioned toward the thick file. "I managed to get all the ads on her standing with her helo. You'll find it all interesting." Knowing his wife would make it her business to know all the details, Morgan glowed inwardly as her face grew pink.

"We should feel really bad about having Annie's file," Laura chided him, putting the photo down and firmly closing the file flap.

"But you don't."

"No, I don't. I'm just . . ." she looked at him ". . . relieved."

Gripping her fingers momentarily, Morgan murmured, "So am I, honey. So am I."

"And in two weeks, they go to Afghanistan. . . ." Laura whispered.

His fingers tightened over hers. "I know." He saw the worry eating at her, making her soft mouth thin and her eyes darken with fear. This was war, and they could lose their son. Neither of them wanted to talk about that.

"It looks like Annie knows her stuff," he told her, trying to sound upbeat. "She's the best and the brightest the Army has, man or woman. Her scores are higher than everyone's. So I think Jason got put with the best."

Nodding, Laura released his hand and reached for a slice of bread. "I don't know how to react to the fact that she's Apache. I know so little about Native Americans, their belief system, the way they see the world . . . and I'd hate to label her with stereotypes."

"Like the belief that Apaches were the fiercest fighters in the West? That Geronimo fought against the Army and brought it to a standstill with a handful of warriors?"

"Things like that." She slowly buttered her own bread, deep in thought. "Personnel records only show you so much."

Morgan smiled wryly. "I had Jenny compile information on her mother and father. You'll find it in the back of her file. Her mother was an Army nurse. Her father was in the Army, too."

"Morgan!"

"Well, I had to do it, Laura. I want to know about this woman who seems to be turning our son around."

"You really ought to feel bad about this," Laura said, eyeing the file with renewed interest.

"But I don't. It's not hurting anyone, Laura. We need to know, for a lot of reasons. I think once you read up on her and her family, you'll feel very good that Jason is under her wing. She comes from warrior blood. In fact —" he smiled again "— Jenny found out by snooping through the archives that her family has direct lineage to one of the woman warriors who rode with

106

Geronimo. That's good news. Warrior blood runs in Annie's veins."

"Still," Laura murmured, setting her knife on the plate in front of her, "this isn't right. I just hope we're forgiven for all our snooping without their permission. . . ."

Jason Trayhern sat on the concrete floor of the hangar, going over software manuals that showed new and updated information on HUDs, the two TV-like screens in each Apache cockpit. Using heads-up displays, pilots could see the enemy in real time, infrared or radar mode. The HUDs allowed pilots to look through the blackest night to ferret out the enemy.

Sweat worked its way down his spine. The hangar doors were open at both ends to catch any sluggish breeze that might pass through. Muted voices echoed through the hangar as crews worked on the various Apaches. Kat Lakey had just handed him the updated software manual, and he'd plunked himself down next to their bird to look at the upgrades. He and Annie had to get the modifications fixed in their minds fast and then practice them like hell.

He heard footsteps coming in his direction and looked up from where he sat cross-legged. By now, Jason knew Annie's step. How beautiful she was! Poised and confident, too. Even though she wore desert-fatigue pants and a loose green T-shirt, her outfit couldn't hide her decidedly feminine assets. She was eye candy.

Giving her a slight smile, he held up the new handbook. "More work."

"When isn't there?" Annie halted in front of Jason and took the manual with a nod of thanks. When their fingertips met, a pleasant warmth moved up her arm. In the last three weeks, Jason had made incredible strides. She knew it was due to their personal chemistry, and that was okay by her. She'd use whatever it took to get inside his armored walls.

"Thanks." She looked at the thin manual in her hands. "Upgrades."

"Yes, and you sound about as happy about it as I am."

A half smile twisted her mouth as she quickly perused the pages. "I heard Boeing was trying to get us the latest dope on the HUDs before we left for Afghanistan. This is good."

Jason tore his gaze from Annie's face. In the last three weeks, he'd come to trust her like no one else in his life. Every time he'd challenged her, she'd met him halfway, and then some. She was so solid emotionally and mentally . . .

Frowning, he moved his gaze back to his own manual, which he placed on his left knee. Though he had learned through crew chief Lakey that Annie didn't have a boyfriend, Jason couldn't contemplate a relationship with her. Annie was a CWO2 and he was a CWO3, making him a junior officer. And the Army frowned upon personal relationships between a senior and a junior officer. He could get booted out of the service for having an affair with her, and that was something he wasn't going to risk. For once, things were going right in his career, and he wasn't about to screw it up this time.

"Geez, they really did make some changes," Annie muttered, studying the manual intently.

"Good ones, though," Jason said.

"Looks like it. Hey, I just got a call a minute ago in the office. You're to go over and see Colonel Dugan."

His heart thudding in fear, Jason got to his feet. "Colonel Dugan?"

"The one and only."

"What's up?"

"I dunno, Jason."

He liked it when she called him by his first name. Usually, she said, "Mr. Trayhern." Sometimes, though, Annie would use his first name, and he'd come to realize she'd do it when he was worried or anxious about something. Sort of like soothing a horse by patting it, he supposed. Peering into her gold eyes, so deep and unreadable, he asked, "Have I done something wrong?"

Her lips pulled up in a smile. "Not from

where I stand. Maybe it's *good* news for once. Did you ever think of that, Mr. Bad Boy?"

Chuckling, Jason closed the handbook. She would teasingly call him that when he got into a snit and reverted back to his old ways and habits. "Good news? That isn't part of my life." Dusting off the seat of his cammos, he tried to sound nonchalant.

Annie watched his blue eyes turn stormy and knew he was feeling anxiety. He stood there, his large, square hands on his narrow hips, looking out the hangar door, lost in thought. Or, more than likely, in silent panic — but panic just the same. Jason was very good at keeping in his feelings. But then, Annie ruminated, what man wasn't? They all stuffed their feelings in some dark, deep hole inside — to their own detriment. She was glad to be a woman and able to get her emotions out when she needed to. Better out than in, as far as she was concerned.

"Well, hotfoot it over there, soldier. Colonel Dugan doesn't like squad members showing up tardy when he's asked for them."

Giving her a mock salute, Jason said, "Yes, ma'am!"

Jason stood at stiff attention in front of Red Dugan's desk. The commander had a personnel file in front of him, and Jason guessed it was his.

"At ease, Mr. Trayhern."

110

"Yes, sir." Jason assumed the position, feet slightly apart, hands behind his back, looking straight ahead. His heart was pounding. What had he done wrong now? Since coming here, he'd tried to keep off the radar screen of the commander and H.Q. Was he going to get kicked out? Court-martialed? His mind whirled over what he might have done to deserve this. Annie had shown him his marks after every flight, and they'd been climbing steadily. She'd talked their C.O. into giving them more hours in the air. Aviation fuel wasn't cheap, and the squadron had a certain supply budgeted monthly for each pilot. Somehow, Annie had gotten Dugan to give them a lot more gas to fly the Apache. Was it about that?

"Well, son, it looks like you've turned a corner." Dugan gazed up and smiled briefly. Opening the personnel file, he said, "Congratulations. You've just been promoted to CWO2."

Stunned, Jason looked down at him. "Sir?" His voice cracked. Jason knew he'd been denied this opportunity in the past because of his problems in the other squadron. In fact, he was long past due for the promotion.

Tapping the file, Dugan said, "Mr. Trayhern, since coming here, you have shown dogged determination to make things right after your experiences in your other squadron. It was brought to my attention

111

that you were overdue for a promotion, so as of today, you are CWO2. The ceremony will take place in my office, at 0900 tomorrow morning. Ask Chief Dazen to be there. I think she's had a great deal to do with your turnaround, don't you?"

Drilled by the colonel's narrowed eyes, Jason tried to keep the joy out of his tone. "By all means, sir. Yes, sir, Chief Dazen *should* be there!"

Smiling again, Dugan said, "Good." Rising, he thrust his hand across the desk. "You're making us proud, Mr. Trayhern. Keep it that way."

Gripping the C.O.'s hand, Jason murmured, "Yes, sir, that's exactly what I intend to do."

"Hey, you got a minute?" Jason called to Annie. She was in the hanger, with Spec 2 Bobby Warner. The blond mechanic and she were appraising the chain gun below the carriage of the Apache.

"Sure." Annie saw an undefinable joy lurking in Jason's eyes now. The darkness was gone. He stood in front of the helo, shifting from one foot to another like a little boy with a huge secret he could barely keep to himself. Grinning widely, Annie knew that whatever Dugan had called him in for had been good news. Finally! No one deserved it more than Jason at this point. Getting up, she dusted off her hands and walked with him out of the hangar. They stayed a few feet apart, stopping in the shade of the building.

When Jason turned and looked down at her, a smile lurked at the corners of his mouth — a mouth that more than once Annie had dreamed of kissing. Oh, she knew that was wrong. There was no fraternizing allowed between pilots, especially when they were a rank apart.

"Spill it before you explode."

"I want to ask you out tonight. To dinner at La Fontaine."

Stunned, Annie gazed at him and saw merriment dancing in Jason's blue eyes. "What? Well . . . er, we can't, Jason."

"Can't or won't? Why wouldn't you go out with me?" He felt like a salivating wolf watching his prey. He'd wanted to take Annie out to dinner from the day he'd met her. Regs wouldn't allow it, of course, but now the tables were turned.

Heart racing, Annie stood there, for once without a glib retort. "Well, uh, can't, I guess."

"But if I were a CWO2, you'd think about it?" Never had Jason wanted anyone to say yes more than her. He stared into her uplifted gaze, drowning in the darkening gold of her eyes. Her mouth parted and he groaned inwardly. Oh, how he wanted to kiss those soft-looking lips.

"Well . . . geez, Jason, this is kind of sudden and unexpected."

"If I were a CWO2, would you go out with me?"

Shrugging, Annie turned and looked back toward her hardworking crew, buying time to think. Jason was keeping his voice low, but this conversation wasn't one she wanted anyone to overhear. Looking up at him, she said, "Yeah, I'd go."

"Good." He rubbed his hands together. "Because Colonel Dugan just called me in to give me a promotion up to CWO2. You and I are on an equal footing now, and I can ask you out."

The pleasure radiating from him made her dizzy. Annie took a step back and absorbed the information, then laughed shortly. "You got a promotion?"

"Yeah. *Me!* How about that?"

In the next second, Annie squealed, threw her arms out and wrapped them around Jason's broad, strong shoulders. She didn't care who was watching. She felt him recoil slightly, his hands closing automatically around her waist, in shock from her unexpected move.

"Oh! That's great, Jason! Just great!" She released him and stepped back. Where his hands had rested on her hips, her flesh tingled. Quickly smoothing her hair, she laughed nervously. What had gotten into her? Oh, it was that spontaneous Apache blood of hers, she supposed.

He stood there, stunned by her quick, puppylike embrace. Where her cheek had touched his, he'd felt her soft, velvety warmth, and his hands ached to reclaim her waist. The deviltry dancing in her eyes lifted his pounding heart as nothing else ever could.

"Then . . . you'll really go out to dinner with me? You're sure?"

Laughing, Annie looked around. She saw her entire crew watching them. "Yeah, very sure, Cowboy. Now I gotta go repair the damage my wild spontaneity just caused."

Grinning, Jason felt euphoric. "I kinda liked it."

"You would."

"How about I pick you up at 1800 at your apartment?"

"You know where it is?"

"Of course I do."

She gave him a wry, chastising look. "I shoulda known."

Feeling cocky, Jason said, "Why wouldn't I know where you live?"

"I won't answer that on grounds that it could incriminate me. I'll tell the crew about your promotion. They'll understand why I hugged you."

Standing there, Jason put his hands on his hips and laughed. It was the first time in a long time that he'd honestly laughed. It felt good having that sound rumble up from his chest. As he watched Annie head back into the hangar, his heart opened wider. He was even more pleased about her going to dinner with him tonight than he was about getting that promotion.

Everything had happened so quickly. He scratched his head and ambled back toward the bird, watching as the crew encircled Annie and she told them the good news. As he headed toward them, Jason pondered her unexpected embrace. Her tall, firm body had felt so damn good against his. How long had it been since he'd actually lusted after a woman? A long time. And Annie flipped every switch he had, whether she knew it or not.

As he approached the crew, everyone turned toward him with sincere smiles of congratulations. Crew chief Lakey was the first to stretch out her hand to him. "Way cool, sir. Congrats on the CWO2 promo."

"Thanks, Lakey," he murmured, pumping her hand. He saw Annie step back so the others could surround him. For the first time, Jason actually felt like part of a team. As he shook each crew member's hand, and heard the sincerity in their voices, he understood how important it was to belong. Really belong. It was a new feeling for him. As he held Annie's glowing golden gaze, Jason began to truly realize how important it was to be a part of something larger than himself. No longer was he a loner, a troublemaker. He was a respected member of a team.

"Sir, can we be at your promotion ceremony?" Lakey asked.

Stunned that she would ask, Jason looked over at Annie for help.

"Sure, you can all come," Annie told them with a grin.

Lakey smiled. "That's wonderful."

Jason thought so, too. Though he'd walked into their lives just three weeks ago, the crew had adopted him like part of their family — no small thanks to Annie Dazen. But then, she inspired people, like the good leader she was, to work together for a common cause.

"Hey, it's 1700," Annie said. "Let's close up shop for the day."

More than ready, Jason seconded her order. In an hour, he'd be alone with Annie, on an equal footing, man to woman, and frankly, he couldn't have been given a finer gift than that.

Chapter 6

Jason thanked his Naval Academy training for making him an officer and a gentleman. At the French restaurant he'd chosen, he was on his best, most suave behavior. The maître 'd took them to a private table with black leather seating in a horseshoe shape. The table was set with white linen, polished silverware and elegant white china trimmed with a thin gold stripe. Jason offered his hand to Annie as she gathered her gossamer lavender, ballet-length skirt to sit down. The maître 'd, dressed impeccably in a black suit and white silk shirt with a conservative, pale blue tie, smiled and nodded approvingly.

Jason found it a thrill to see Annie out of uniform for the first time, and wearing feminine attire. A lavender top with cap sleeves showed off her upper body. What drew his attention was the two-strand necklace that fell between her breasts. It was an interesting piece of jewelry and obviously one of a kind. In the low lighting, her straight black hair gleamed with reddish-gold tones as it moved like a shining cape about her shoulders.

"Thank you, sir," she said, releasing Jason's hand and grinning.

He smiled back. He'd taken great pains to look good. Though he'd been living out of suitcases at the B.O.Q., he was glad he'd brought along his navy-blue blazer, white silk shirt, red silk tie and tan chinos to wear tonight. "You're welcome, ma'am."

The maître 'd handed them white leatherbound menus embossed with fleurs-de-lis.

After the California chardonnay they'd ordered was poured, Annie looked around the small, intimate restaurant. "This is a nice place."

"Only the best for you and me," Jason murmured, meaning it. He'd gladly blow his whole month's pay to give Annie what she deserved.

"Cowboy, you got more lines than a herd of horses."

Chuckling, Jason held up both hands. "Guilty as charged."

Laughing softly, Annie absorbed his playful smile. He was terribly good-looking. How he'd been able to get back to the B.O.Q., shower, shave and make it back to her house in an hour, she couldn't guess. It must have been a feat. She lived on the outskirts of the base.

"You know," Annie murmured, picking up her glass of pale golden wine, "this is our first and last date."

Raising his eyebrows, Jason lifted his glass and clinked hers gently. "That's a helluva way to start off a date — giving it the ax."

Sipping the slightly fruity wine, Annie smiled and set the crystal goblet down on the pristine tablecloth. "All next week, I'll be at my apartment, packing and putting everything I own in storage. We're going to be gone for a year over to Afghanistan. So I'm gonna be a little busy packing up my apartment, as well as loading up our helo and the C-141 Starlifter with supplies."

Nodding, Jason said, "I know. I don't like it, but you're going to be busy. Then once we're over in Afghanistan, it's going to be all business."

"That's right," Annie said. She didn't like to say it, but where they were going, there would be no time for personal relationships. The country was at war and they could be killed anytime, day or night, at their base or flying missions for the Rangers or Special Forces.

"Let's get back to the good things of life for a little while, then," he said. He motioned to her necklace. "That's a beautiful piece of jewelry. Can you tell me about it?" She wore a set of matching gold earrings set with three round pink gemstones. The jewelry seemed to frame Annie's natural beauty. Jason wanted to take a photo of her before they left the restaurant. He had his digital camera with him, in his pocket, and he was going to ask her to pose later if she agreed.

Touching the necklace with her fingertips, Annie smiled softly. "This is where you start getting educated about Indians. It's called a rainbow medicine necklace and it has been passed down through the line of women on my mother's side for over a hundred years. The necklace is given to the firstborn daughter of every new generation when she matures. My mother gave me this in a ceremony when I turned eighteen. It goes everywhere with me, though I rarely wear it in plain sight." She smiled, running her fingers gently across the rounded beads of green and pink tourmaline.

"Why? It's a knockout." And it was. Jason couldn't keep his eyes off it. Or her.

"Because people are drawn to its power, its healing energy, and they automatically want to reach out and touch it, even if they don't know why they want to do so."

He sipped the wine. "What is a medicine necklace? You said it heals?"

"Native Americans use natural things to help heal themselves," she explained. "They know that each rock, tree, flower or bush possesses a living spirit that is part of the Great Spirit. We are all related." She brushed the stones with great reverence. "Each time the medicine necklace is passed on, the story — part of our verbal tradition — goes with it."

"Can you share it with me?" The velvety look in her golden eyes enthralled him. The huskiness in her voice was charged with emotion. He liked seeing this side of Annie.

"Sure. One of my relatives, an Apache woman warrior, rode with Geronimo. We've always had women warriors within our nation, and do to this day." Annie smiled slightly. "My relative, Isdan Shash, Grizzly Bear Woman, went on a vision quest when she was younger. In her vision, she was told to leave Arizona and go to the land bordering the great ocean of the west, which we know today as California. Isdan Shash was led by the vision, and a spirit that went with her, a black jaguar. In those days, jaguars, both the spotted type and the black ones, lived in our land. Her spirit guide took the long journey to the west coast with her. On a hill near San Diego he told her to start looking around. She did and she found these beautiful green, pink and blue stones just lying on the ground. The guide told her to gather up a handful of them and put them into a leather pouch. Today, we know them to be the gemstone tourmaline. The Pala Indian Reservation, near San Diego, has a tourmaline mine with the same name nowadays.

"Then the jaguar guide took her south, into what we know as Mexico today, to the Huichol people, the people of the Copper Canyon area. There, she was given this."

Annie held up an oblong-shaped, dark blue gemstone. "This is druzy quartz. And this is a dark blue color. After that, the jaguar guide told her to turn around and go north once more.

"She traveled many, many months and it got colder and colder. Nearly freezing to death in the winter of that year, she was rescued by an old Eskimo in Alaska, a medicine woman. They couldn't understand each other's language, so they communicated in their heads." Annie tapped her temple. "Mental telepathy bridges all languages. And the Eskimo woman gave her this." Annie held up a yellow-white oval stone wrapped in gold wire, so that Jason could look more closely at it.

"It's a woman's face," he murmured. "Enclosed by wings? What kind of wings? Eagle?"

Annie smiled and allowed the pendant to once again drop between her breasts. "Isdan Shash found out that this old woman, when she went on her own vision quest in Alaska, was shown an ancient animal that had died. It had huge tusks sticking out of the ice and snow. The medicine woman was directed to take a piece of the tusk and carve this woman's face with snowy owl wings surrounding her head."

"That's an incredible tale," he murmured, enthralled. Annie was a great storyteller, and

Jason found himself mesmerized by her graceful gestures, her low, melodic voice that held his rapt attention.

"Yes, it is." Annie got choked up and felt embarrassed for a moment. She patted the beaded strands gently. "Every time I speak of this necklace's journey, it touches me so deeply I usually end up crying, so don't get alarmed if you see tears coming, okay?"

Jason reached across the table and clasped her hand briefly. "Okay." He didn't want to let go, but knew he must.

It took Annie a moment to recover from that tender contact. She was warmed by the velvety look in Jason's eyes. There was no question that he liked her. Swallowing hard, her hand tingling from his masculine touch, she tried to think coherently. "I learned about the woman enclosed by the owl wings on the woolly mammoth tusk through my great-grandmother, who researched the places mentioned in Isdan Shash's story and found all those mines do exist."

"Amazing," Jason murmured, studying the engraved face on the tusk. "And I may be crazy, but you know what? That looks like *your* face, Annie. Have you noticed that?"

Nodding, Annie said, "Yes. Isdan Shash was told that the carving would magically change to look like every woman in her family who wore it."

Shaking his head, Jason murmured,

"Nothing in my life has trained me for what you're telling me."

"As I said, our world is very different from yours." Annie grinned and took a sip of wine. "And far more interesting, as far as I'm concerned. But on with the story.

"Isdan Shash survived the winter with this old Eskimo medicine woman. She was then sent by her black jaguar guide back down the coast to the desert hill where all the tourmaline lay scattered about. This time, she was met by a Coast Indian medicine woman, Badger Woman, who gifted her with this." Annie pointed to a rectangular pink-and-green gemstone that hung above the blue druzy quartz. "Badger Woman had been told where to find this clear tourmaline stone, and she spent years honing it, rubbing it and polishing it to what you see today."

Jason studied the large emerald-cut stone, wrapped in gold wire on the shorter strand of the necklace. "That's phenomenal. To get that kind of polish by hand . . . I know a little about gemstones and you need polishing agents and a wheel to get that kind of luster."

"Right on," Annie murmured. "It was Badger Woman's life work to do this. And then she gave it away to Isdan Shash. The medicine woman also showed her how to hand grind and shape the stones she'd gathered for the rest of the necklace.

"Finally, after another year staying with the medicine woman and polishing the stones by hand, Isdan Shash was sent home, to the east, by her jaguar guide. She continued to hand polish each of these beads as she walked. Over the years, she fashioned and shaped every one of these stones you see here." Annie's fingers brushed the roughly rounded stones. "She got thin, fine gold wire from a miner who traded it for a horse. Over time, Isdan Shash wrapped the wire very carefully around each of the gemstones so they could never fall off or be lost by accident.

"When the U.S. Army came and started hunting our people, she wore this necklace at all times. And when one of the warriors would get injured by a bullet, she would lay the necklace across the wound and he or she would be miraculously healed. That's why it's called a medicine necklace — it possesses special energies and healing qualities."

Jason raised a brow. "That's magic, then." He itched to reach out and touch the necklace, but decided against it.

"Yes," Annie murmured, "it is."

"So, what does it mean that you have it? Do you heal people with it?"

Shrugging, Annie sipped her wine. "As the eldest daughter, I was supposed to go into training to learn how to become a medicine woman. But I didn't. I chose to go into the Army instead. My father was a helo pilot in the service and I fell in love with flying because of him. I wanted to follow in his footsteps, not my mother's. She, by the way, is in the medical field. She was also in the Army as a registered nurse when she met my dad. And today she's a medicine woman on the reservation, helping our people."

"Then you've broken the family tradition?" Jason found that ironic. So had he.

"Yes, I have. In our nation, I have done nothing wrong, though. My decision is honored. There's no right or wrong to it." She touched the necklace reverently. "It's mine until my daughter turns eighteen. Until that time comes, I keep it with me at all times."

"I've never seen you wear it at the base."

Smiling, Annie said, "I always keep it in my trouser pocket, where it can't be seen or crushed."

"I see. . . ." He held her luminous gold gaze. Right now, Jason wanted to kiss that lush, ripe mouth of hers. He was interrupted by the waiter approaching. Disgruntled, but not showing it, he leaned back as they placed their order. Alone with her once more, he settled his elbows on the table and leaned forward. "Does it have magic? Have you seen it work?"

Laughing, Annie said, "I saw my mother place it on many a child or baby, and watched them get better immediately. I grew up with her wearing it. And when she'd take it from her neck, she'd place it gently on the person, wherever they hurt, and they'd always get relief or a cure."

Shaking his head, Jason said, "That's a lot to swallow."

"I know it is. But I saw it with my own two eyes."

"What does it do for you? Is it working?"

"It always feels warm and comforting to me. Right now, it's very warm — much warmer than my skin or body temperature. And I find it very calming when I get into sticky, emotional or stressful situations. It soothes me immediately. I really wouldn't know what to do without it now. I rely on it. It keeps me clear and in better emotional balance."

"Have you used it on others?"

Annie chuckled, shaking her head. "Me? Gosh, no! I'm not a trained medicine woman. I wouldn't have the first clue about how to use it."

"I thought you just laid it on the person?"

"Well, there's more to it than that, Jason. My mother trained for years to remember certain chants, songs or prayers specific for each type of illness. You don't just slap this necklace on someone and say 'heal!' "

Jason nodded, his blue eyes full of mirth. "I thought it was too good to be true."

"Hey, it still is alive, and I love its energy. It helps me a lot."

The waiter came then with their shrimp cocktail appetizer. Annie loved the classical music that was playing quietly in the background. It was still early, and she knew most patrons wouldn't start coming until 8:00 p.m. or later.

"Well," Jason murmured, picking up his fork and dipping a shrimp into the sauce, "I do share one thing in common with you and that magic necklace."

"What?" Annie picked up her own fork.

"Neither you nor I took the path our parents wanted us to. My father wanted me, the firstborn son, to go to a military academy, and then on to some superstar career, just as the eldest son of each generation for the last couple of hundred years had done." Jason glanced over at Annie, who was looking very serious now. "I blew the Academy by getting caught up in a drug scandal and being kicked out. So I've blown the eldest-son expectation big-time. I'm a disgrace to my father now, and to the family heritage. As a matter of fact, my sister Katy went though Annapolis and did great. She's carrying on in my father's footsteps instead."

Annie heard the pain in his voice, the confusion, and saw a spark of anger in his eyes. She knew she had to tread carefully. After nibbling on her shrimp, she murmured,

"There's nothing wrong with a woman carrying on a tradition for a family. In our eyes, that's just as expected as a male doing so. To us, there is no difference."

"Well," Jason muttered, "that's not how it is in this family of mine. It's the eldest son or nothing."

Smiling briefly, Annie finished the last shrimp and then wiped her fingers on her napkin. "I doubt your father sees you as a disgrace, Jason. Maybe you feel badly that you disappointed him? From what I've heard of your dad, he sounds like an honorable man. And you said you were innocent in that scandal —"

"I was."

His voice was hard. Defensive. Annie sat back a little, digesting the sudden tightness in his tone. Treading softly, she added, "Then all the more reason that your father wouldn't consider you a disgrace. Mistakes happen, but if a family is strong, spiritually speaking, then they get over it, move on and love their children, regardless. Life happens, you know?"

"Is that what they did with you when you turned down medicine training in front of a pair of gold wings? You weren't in disgrace because you didn't uphold your family traditions?"

"My family honors whatever decisions I make. We don't see a person's choices as right or wrong. Our heritage is resilient enough to encompass all our choices." Annie smiled gently. The pain in his eyes made her ache. Jason was like a little boy in that moment, so filled with hurt, and no one was there to hold him, rock him or make him feel safe. Impulsively, she reached across the table and placed her fingers on Jason's arm. She felt the nubby texture of the sport coat he wore, but beneath it, the strength of him as a man.

"My heart and gut tell me your parents love you deeply, Jason. No matter what happened, or the choices you made." She liked the power in his arm. Liked it a little too much. Jason was in superb physical condition, his body hardened by long hours of exercise in a gym, no doubt. Annie saw his blue eyes darken instantly as she touched him. She'd never seen that look before and it sent a spiral of awareness through her. And then, just as quickly, she saw him suppress the feelings he had when she'd grazed his arm. Why? Was he afraid of human contact? Contact with her, perhaps? She forced herself to remove her hand.

"My mother forgave me. She loves me no matter what I do or don't do," he mumbled.

"And your father?"

"He's distant, so cold he couldn't hug a tree, much less one of his kids. Well, I shouldn't say that." Jason wiped his mouth with his napkin. "He never hugged me or Katy. Years later, when the twins came along, he changed."

"How?" Annie ached for Jason. She could see that his father had never held him, or told him that he loved him. And more than anything, that was what Jason needed.

"I guess the kidnapping snapped him out of his cold-fish routine," Jason said. "With the twins, Pete and Kelly, he was warm and hugged them a lot."

"You're angry. Maybe jealous of them?"

Shrugging, Jason sighed. "Yeah, I'm sure I am. Not that I don't love my little brother and sister. I do. And I'm glad they have a different father than we had."

"But if he changed, can't he hug you now, too? Tell you that he loves you?"

Shaking his head, Jason said, "Listen, it's a Mexican standoff between him and me. Every time we get together, it's a battle. He tries to tell me what to do and I fight him every inch of the way. He thinks he knows what's best for me. He doesn't trust me to know what's right for me. It's always a one-way street with him — his way or no way, and I'm not going to be a part of that."

"And your mother? You love her a lot? Get along well with her?" Annie instantly saw the tension in Jason's face dissolve and his eyes lighten with happiness as he pulled out his wallet. Opening it, he showed her a picture of a blond-haired woman.

"This is my mother, Laura Trayhern. She's a military writer. She's got two books published, plus over a hundred articles on different military subjects."

Annie took the wallet, their fingertips meeting. His were cool against her warmer ones. "She's beautiful." Smiling up at him, Annie said, "You have her eyes."

"Yeah, the rest of me, unfortunately, looks *exactly* like my father."

"Do you have a photo of him in here?" Annie began to flip through them.

"No. But here's Pete. And that's Kelly. They're fraternal twins and are still at home. Both are juniors in high school. And here's Katy. She's 22 and second oldest."

Annie memorized each of the children's faces, although she knew they were nearly adults now. Turning another leaf, she saw Laura with a baby. "Oh, a new baby? There are *five* of you in the family?"

Smiling, Jason said proudly, "That's Kamaria. My parents adopted her. My folks were caught in that Southern California earthquake less than a year ago. Kamaria lost her mother, and while my mom was in the hospital with a broken ankle, she helped the nurses in the baby section because they were so shorthanded. This little tyke —" he pointed to the baby's photo "— was my mom's charge. She fed her three times a day, changed her, took care of her."

"And your parents fell in love with Kamaria?" Annie studied the infant's round, pink face and dark, curly hair. She was so cute.

"My mom did. She persuaded my father to adopt her. They call her Kamaria, which is African for 'beautiful like the moon.'"

Annie saw him beaming like a proud older brother, and her own lips lifted. "She's a beautiful baby. And how old is she now?"

"About two . . . I don't remember exactly."

"And you've seen her in person?"

"No, just pictures."

Annie gently closed his wallet and handed it back to him. "So you don't go home much?"

Sliding the wallet back into his pocket, he shook his head. "No."

The waiter came with their next course and took away the appetizer dishes.

Annie sighed and picked up her soupspoon. It was a lentil soup, one of her favorites. "Don't you miss going home, Jason? To see your brother and sisters? Your mom? Isn't that a heavy price to pay to avoid seeing your father?"

She was right, he realized, distractedly stirring his soup. "When you put it that way, yeah, it sounds kinda dumb, doesn't it?"

"We get thirty days leave every year," Annie said between spoonfuls. "And I can't *wait* to get home to see everyone. I love going home to the mountains, the tall pines and that dry, hot air."

"We have another thing in common," Jason said, finally taking a taste. "Our families both live in mountain country. My parents have a two-story cedar home on the outskirts of Phillipsburg, Montana. The Rocky Mountains are their home. I love the tall pines, too. I love to fish in the cold streams and catch trout. Do you have trout where you live?"

She grinned. "You bet we do. The best in Arizona. My reservation runs a brisk tourist trade, with fishermen who pay for licenses to use our streams and lakes."

"Funny, I always thought of Arizona as desert."

She noted the warmth in his gaze. When Jason spoke of his mother, his voice softened and he opened up, becoming less armored. Maybe that was a key to him; women had not abandoned or hurt him, and he was more likely to trust them, as much as he could trust anyone, as a result. His trust issues made handling him even more of a delicate dance, from a psychological point of view. But Annie's heart had a mind of its own and she liked him, regardless of his wounds and defenses.

She smiled. "Arizona is what I call the land of extremes. In the south, we have the Sonoran Desert and saguaro cactus. In the middle of the state, we have bluffs, piñon, cypress and juniper trees. In the north, we have the Grand Canyon, tall mountains, pine trees and plenty of lakes and rivers. It is a beautiful state and offers something to everyone."

As she sat there sipping the chardonnay, Annie wondered what she was getting herself into with him. Jason was not a man she could keep at arm's length. His boyish smile, his raw honesty and his wounds all appealed to her. And they would be going to war together shortly. A part of her was glad, because she could trust him; he was a fine aviator. But her heart cringed at the possibility of losing him, too. War took lives. For the first time in her life, Annie felt torn. She was falling for this cowboy, warts and all. He wasn't a bad person, just a hurt one. And Jason was genuinely trying to be a team player, sensitive to the needs of others now, not always focusing on himself.

"Well," he said, his voice turning husky, "if you are a prime example of that state, then it must be beautiful."

Chapter 7

Jason stood on the porch of Annie's apartment, a redbrick structure, two stories high. The night air was heavy with humidity, and the fragrant scent of the gardenias that grew on either side of her home intoxicated him. Once Annie had unlocked the door and turned to him, he wanted to kiss her. Beneath the porch light, her eyes were dark and unreadable. Did she want him to? He wasn't sure.

"Thanks for a great dinner, Jason." Her heart thundered in her breast. The look on his shadowed face, the narrowing of his eyes, scared her and thrilled her.

"It was great," he murmured. He shoved his hands in his pockets. Mouth dry, he said, "I'm feeling a little nervous right now."

Laughing breathily, Annie said, "Me, too."

"What do you want me to do? Kiss you? Shake your hand? Hug you?"

"You're a man with options. I like that." Her mouth tingled. Oh, Jason had a very male mouth, no question. Strong, uncompromising and filled with power and promise.

"I thought I'd better give you the list and

let you decide. You're pilot in command here."

Reaching out, she slid her fingers along his upper arm. At the flex of his biceps, she felt her heart lurch. "This is a shared activity," she said, dropping her hand.

"You're scared."

It was a statement, not an indictment. "Yes, Jas . . . I am. For a lot of reasons I haven't shared with you — yet."

Nodding, he rocked back on his heels. The sweet, heavy fragrance of the gardenias surrounded him like a lover's perfume. Annie looked lovely, her hair slightly curled from the humidity. He found himself wanting to smooth back the strands. "I understand."

"And we're going to war. . . ." Leaning against the door, Annie sighed.

"War makes it hard to forge a relationship," he agreed quietly. There was real sadness in her eyes. Jason found himself wanting to ease that emotion. The urge to step forward and embrace her was nearly his undoing. She held her small white purse in her hands, her head bowed.

"I want to kiss you, Jason." There. It was out. When she lifted her head and connected with his feral gaze, she felt her body blossoming beneath his heated look.

"I hear hesitation." Even as his heart lifted with joy, he remembered his past, how easy it was to crash and burn in a relationship. The confusion in Annie's large, tilted eyes tore at him.

"Yes, there is. I've gotta have time, Cowboy. Plenty of it. I learned the hard way about rushing in where fools fear to tread."

"Oh, that one. Well, join the crowd," he said, giving her a slow, sensual smile meant solely for her.

Absorbing the heat of his longing, his need to kiss her but at the same time not overstep the boundaries she'd put in place, Annie thirstily drank in that very male smile. Did Jason know how damn sexy he was to her? Maybe, she thought, seeing the glimmer in his eyes. Her lips curved.

"At least we have common ground to work from."

"Seems to me we do have a lot in common."

"You white man, me Indian . . ."

"Okay, Tonto, we'll just be the good team we're working at being for now. Okay?" Jason lifted his hand toward her. She looked at it and then at him, her smile making her face glow in the low lighting.

"Okay, Lone Ranger, you got a deal." And she slid her hand into his. At the feel of his warm flesh, she felt an ache building deep within her, hot and hungry. Reluctantly, Annie removed her hand.

"Listen," Jason said, "until we leave, we're

going to be moving at mach three with our collective hair on fire. You have an apartment's worth of stuff to get into storage. Do you want some help?"

"Well," Annie said, "I was going to have a moving party on Tuesday. I'd invited the crew over to help me for the day. We were going to round robin it. Kat Lakey lives in Army housing with her husband and two kids, so she doesn't have to pack. But Bobby and Lance both live off base, in an apartment together. We were going to take Wednesday night and pack their place. Want to help?"

"Sure. Thanks for letting me be part of the team."

"Good. That's what we do, Jason. We look out for each other's backsides."

Smiling, he reached out and tamed some of those shiny strands back into place. "See you tomorrow, early, at the base. Good night, sweet pea."

Her scalp tingled wildly where he'd grazed her hair. How she wanted to step forward into his arms! But Annie stopped herself. She saw that lazy smile linger on his mouth. "Sweet pea? That's not my call sign, Cowboy."

"Yeah?" he taunted. Her call sign was Jaguar. Every pilot had a handle, and that was hers. She had changed his to Cowboy, and he didn't mind the new nickname.

"Sweet pea doesn't exactly sound like a warrior."

Stepping off the porch, he chuckled. "No, it doesn't, but you remind me of them. My mom loves them. She always plants them along the white picket fence around our place every spring. As a kid I used to go out there and bury my nose in them. I liked them because they were the colors of the rainbow and they smelled so great. I used to pick them and put them in my pockets."

Warming to his admission, she said, "Okay, you're forgiven. Just don't call me that in front of my crew."

"Not to worry, Jaguar. Your alias is safe with me. . . ."

The evening was turning out nearly perfect. Annie opened the door and stepped inside. "See you, Jas. Thanks for a wonderful dinner."

Nodding, Jason stepped back. Annie had flushed as soon as he had called her "sweet pea." Secretly, he felt she liked the endearment, and that made him feel good. "My pleasure. I'll see you tomorrow. Good night . . ."

Annie went inside and turned on the lights in the foyer. Heart pounding, she placed her hand against her breast as she walked to the right, into the small living room, and turned on a table lamp. Had she done the right thing by not kissing Jason? Great Spirit knew,

141

she wanted to! Groaning to herself, she dropped her purse on the coffee table, along with her car keys. It was 2200, or 10:00 p.m. She remembered she wanted to call her parents and say goodbye. Annie knew they were worried about her year-long duty coming up in Afghanistan.

Going to the kitchen, she flipped on the light switch. The phone was on the wall, next to the table. Punching in the numbers of her family's home on the White River Reservation, Annie pulled out a chair and sat down.

"*Nohwich'i adach'idiigo.* We greet you."

Just hearing the Apache language once more sent a wave of peace through Annie. Smiling, she answered in the Apache tongue, and then switched to English. "Hey, Mom, am I calling you too late?"

"Why, no, child," Lane Dazen, her mother, replied in a husky voice everyone said sounded just like Annie's. "You never call too late. Hold on a moment. . . ."

Annie could hear her put her hand over the phone as she called her husband, Canyon Dazen, to the kitchen. Smiling softly, Annie sighed and closed her eyes. She deeply missed her family, her roots. Being in the Army was an incredible warrior adventure, but it did not fulfill her spirit entirely. Her homeland, her people, poured such love back into her thirsty soul.

"Hey," Lane said excitedly, "your dad is

coming. He was watching a baseball game on television."

"That's okay, I'll wait till he gets on the other phone and then we can have a three-way conversation."

"Yes. You sound good. Things are going well?"

"Very well, Mom."

"Pumpkin?"

It was her father's jovial voice, deep and filled with happiness. Annie felt her heart swell with emotion. How she missed her parents and her siblings!

"Hi, Dad. Sorry to pull you away from your favorite sport, but tonight is the only time I can talk to both of you before we leave for Afghanistan. Next week is going to be crazy and I won't have time to talk like I can now."

"Oh, don't worry about a silly game, Pumpkin. We're so glad to hear from you."

Pumpkin was the pet name that her father had given her when she was a tyke. Annie had been told often that as a two-year-old, she had liked to sit out in the squash garden her mother had sown, next to a big orange pumpkin that had grown there. It had become her friend, and she'd talked to its spirit all the time. Her parents had encouraged her to water it, take care of it and converse with it.

"When are they shipping you out, Annie?" her mother asked.

"Seven days from now. We'll be going over in the Air Force Starlifter. We're being sent to Kandahar, where we'll replace the Apache squadron that's been there since October of last year."

"And how are you sitting with this?" Canyon asked.

"Okay, Dad. I'm afraid. Excited. Worried. I worry about my crew, and how to keep them safe. I want everyone to come home in one piece."

"Spoken like the true leader you are, Pumpkin."

"What about your new copilot? Jason Trayhern?" Lane interjected. "The last time we spoke, which was three weeks ago, you sounded unsure of him."

Laughing, Annie said, "Oh, him. Well, he's doing fine now. Really fine . . ."

"Hmm," Lane murmured, "somethin's goin' on there. Your voice changed just now after I mentioned his name."

Shrugging, Annie said wistfully, "He's a nice person underneath all that armor he keeps in place. The more I've gotten to know him, the more I like him. Not just professionally, but personally, and therein lies the rub."

Lane chuckled. "Well, your father and I can't sit here and tell you that wartime relationships don't happen, because they do."

Annie knew the story of how her parents

had met. Her mother had been an Army nurse, her father a U.S. Army helicopter pilot working behind the lines in South America in the 1970s. Her mom had been part of a secret medical team flown in to Colombia, where his unit was located. "Well, I'm not saying it's that kind of thing," Annie protested.

"Of course not," Lane said dryly. "But you're happy with him? He's a good flyer? Good hands?"

"Yes, he's come along really well. Jason's a hard worker, and he's learning how to become a team member, which is really important."

"Most important," Canyon agreed grimly. "That guy has to watch your back, Pumpkin. We'll both rest easier knowing he can do that."

"I'm sure he will."

"When you get to Kandahar, will you be able to e-mail us? Call us?" Lane asked worriedly.

"Mostly e-mail, although I understand communication is set up once a week for calls home, so I'll definitely be in touch with you and my brothers and sisters."

"Good," Canyon murmured. "Just stay very alert, and don't let your guard down. It's when things become routine that stuff happens."

Annie absorbed her father's warning. He

should know — he'd been a combat helicopter pilot who had been shot out of the sky by a local drug lord. For weeks he'd subsisted in the jungle, evading their forces. "I will, Dad. I promise," she said fervently.

"You have the medicine necklace?"

"You bet I do, Mom."

"And you wear it daily?"

"I'm never without it." Annie touched the beads where they lay against her chest.

"Good," Lane said, relief in her voice. "Always keep it with you, Annie. Listen to it. Listen to the jaguar guide that comes with it. Together, they'll help keep you safe."

"I know that, Mom. I talk to my spirit guide all the time. I've been lucky not to have my crew ask me what I was muttering about," she laughed.

"They saved my life more than once," Lane said, her voice strained. "It seems like the path of this rainbow necklace is to go from one war to another. Our ancestor, Isdan Shash, wore it for the first time when the U.S. Army went after Geronimo. And our grandmothers wore it during World War I, and II. And Korea. Then me, while part of the secret ops with the Army in Colombia." She sighed. "The women in our family have never been without it during wartimes. Now you're going to war, halfway around the world, to Afghanistan."

Smiling softly, Annie murmured, "That's

146

so, Mom, but look. Look what it has done. It saved every woman who wore it going into war. It's like a spiritual shield that protects us."

"Yes, that's true. That's why I don't want you to be over there and *not* wear it!"

"Don't worry," Annie laughed, "this necklace is a *part* of me."

"Well," Canyon said good-naturedly, "at least until you settle down with some guy and have your first baby girl. Then, when she's eighteen, we'll have a ceremony here for her, and it will be passed on."

Warmth moved through Annie's heart. As her father spoke those words, she pictured Jason in her mind. What would it be like to love him? To carry one of his babies? The thought was as unexpected as it was intense. Her abdomen felt heated and heavy all at once.

"Now, Dad," Annie teased huskily, "I'm not ready to settle down yet. I'm only twenty-four. I like late marriages. From what I see out there today, early marriages are like dimes and nickels — they're thrown away. I want something that lasts, like your relationship, and our grandparents'. I want to grow old with the guy, like you two are doing."

Hearing her parents' mutual laughter made her feel safe and good.

"Pumpkin, when the right guy comes along, you'll know it. Instantly. That's how it was with your mother and me. The moment I laid eyes on her, that was it. I knew she was the gal for me."

"Well," Lane chuckled, "I wasn't so sure!"

"Yeah," Canyon said, "I had to drag you kicking and screaming all the way to the altar. You were one wild filly."

"I'm an Apache warrior," Lane reminded him archly. "You think we know the word *surrender?*"

Annie loved their kibitzing back and forth. *Surrender* was not a word the Apache people used often. In their belief system, the only one they surrendered to was the Great Spirit, a higher spiritual power — never a human one. Geronimo had never surrendered, either. He had stopped running to save what was left of his people. The Army had not trapped him and forced him to quit; he'd stopped because of his love of his people and their unmitigated suffering at the hands of the relentless Army that hunted them.

"Okay, you two," Annie said, "I gotta go. I promise to e-mail you as soon as I can, so you know I'm safe in Kandahar."

"I'll do a safety ceremony for you," Lane said.

"I'm so glad you're a medicine woman, Mom. Thanks. I can use all the help I can get."

"What about saying a little prayer for that

young man of hers? Jason?" Canyon asked his wife.

"I suppose I can. Do you think he'd mind, Annie?"

"No, that would be great. He's a white man, but he's really interested in how we see the world. He's not like all the other Anglos I've known, thank goodness."

"Good," Lane said. "We love you, child. May the wings of White Owl Woman enclose you, hold you close to her and keep you safe. . . ."

Annie wanted to stay on the phone forever with them. Just hearing their voices, even the little bit of Apache language they shared, made her homesick. She spent thirty days every year, in the fall, when it was cooler, at their homestead on the reservation. Always, it renewed her spirit and filled her heart.

As she placed the phone back on the wall cradle, Annie stood up. Smoothing her skirt, she walked slowly through the kitchen, the bright yellow walls reminding her of Father Sun. The cheery white-and-yellow-flowered curtains on either side of the window in front of the counter always lifted her spirits. Her mother had made those curtains for her from cloth bought at the local trading post. The flowers, evening primroses, reminded her poignantly of home. Those blooms would open just once, in the evening. Annie loved to ride her horse along the red clay road and watch them opening up at dusk.

A certain large moth, almost the size of a hummingbird, would hover around the flowers and pollinate them. The fragrance of the primrose was sweet, the dusk air perfumed as she rode back home, situated on a hill crowned with pine.

Moving to the bedroom now, Annie flicked on the light and began to undress. After laying her skirt and top on the bed, she finally took off the rainbow necklace. A deerskin pouch sat on her dresser and she placed the beads gently within it. Removing her earrings, Annie set them in a nearby box. She always kept them separate, the necklace in the pocket of her flight uniform, the earrings safely stored away except on special occasions like tonight.

Feeling warm and open, she went to take a shower in the bathroom that adjoined the bedroom. Stepping under the hot, invigorating spray, she relished the feel of the water pummeling her face and soaking into her long, thick hair. Closing her eyes, she found the image of Jason floating gently in her mind's eye. How she ached for him. Their lives seemed opposite when it came to their families. She had a close, positive relationship with hers. He seemed to almost hate his father, avoiding contact and communication.

Annie scrubbed her flesh with hand-milled soap made by her mother from the sacred sage that grew in great profusion on the hills of the res.

She lathered her face, still thinking of Jason. He loved his mother, no question. He seemed to love his siblings, too. After all, he had photos of them in his wallet, and it was obvious as he'd shown her the pictures that he was proud of all of them. His father had been the only family member missing. Annie wondered what Morgan Trayhern looked like.

From her perspective, it seemed as if the man was a very wounded warrior, just like his son. He'd probably had a hell of a time trying to adjust to becoming a parent. Jason was the firstborn, the "trial" child — the one parents made the most mistakes with and, hopefully, learned from, so that the rest of the children didn't suffer as much as he had.

Scrubbing her hair with the soap, Annie turned and allowed the warm, pummeling water to strike her neck and back. So Jason had a dysfunctional father probably suffering from PTSD. And he'd likely been so absorbed in getting adjusted to a normal family situation that he'd had neither the time or energy to devote to his firstborn son, even though he may have wanted to. Annie had seen many such cases in her psychology classes. It was hell on a family, and she intuitively knew that Jason had suffered from his father's wounds. And now her copilot carried those wounds in him. The emotional distance

Morgan had resorted to after his injuries was perceived by Jason as a lack of love. An abandonment that was only highlighted when Jason was kidnapped.

After rinsing her hair with a concoction of sacred sage and soapweed yucca, Annie threw her head back and stepped out of the shower. Leaning over the sink, she squeezed the last of the moisture from her long, dark locks. Grabbing a soft green towel, she wrapped it around her hair and then took a second towel to dry her body.

The wounds of the father were the wounds the son carried. Annie frowned as she considered that probability. Based on what she'd learned in her psychology classes, she felt her assessment was correct, but there were a lot of things she still didn't know. Jason's trust in women seemed to be intact, and that was what was making their relationship work.

Hanging the bath towel back on its hook, she unwrapped the one around her head. And to make this dilemma even more personal, Annie realized she *liked* the man, wounds and all. She'd seen him throw his shoulder into the harness and work hard for the good of their crew.

Dropping the towel on the commode seat, Annie reached for her comb and began to gently run it through her damp hair, untangling the strands. This was a ritual she loved. Given the hot, humid climate, she looked forward to washing her hair nightly.

Annie's thoughts turned to Kandahar, and she wondered if she would be able to wash her hair very often. Was there water available? She knew they'd be behind the airport defenses, living in makeshift housing — tents with wooden platforms for a floor, and cots for beds.

Fear threaded through her as she finished combing her wet locks. Fear of the unknown. Fear of dying. Yeah, that was it. But worse, fear of being wounded and crippled for life. Annie scowled and picked up her hair dryer. She also feared that Jason might get hurt, too. Right now, her heart was wide open to him, making her feel more vulnerable.

What would Afghanistan bring?

Chapter 8

"Happy Winter Solstice," Jason told Annie as he slipped inside a supply tent with a small gift he'd wrapped in bright red-and-green paper. It was dusk, the gray light softening the harsh winter landscape. The Afghan hills were barren and the blue mountains that ringed the plain were swathed with snow.

Annie smiled. "A gift? Hey, I didn't get you one, Cowboy." Eagerly, she took the small parcel. It was December 21, a day that her people celebrated. She relished the fact that he had come to meet her with the present. The tent was their "away place" from the stress of the war. Supply had hundreds of canvas tents set up on the base, but this one was their hideaway from the world. The small tent at the north end had proved to be the quietest, and because of its distance from the others, it was unlikely that a supply person would come barging in to grab boxes of MREs to feed the troops at this time of day. When Jason and Annie weren't flying missions, they usually met here. Annie had come to love this private place, where they could be with one an-

154

other on a personal basis.

"What is it?" she asked excitedly, turning the package around and then holding it next to her ear and shaking it.

Grinning, Jason sat down on a box across the aisle from her. Leaning over, arms coming to rest on his long thighs, he folded his hands and watched the delight in her face as she turned the box between her slender fingers. She had beautiful flight hands and Jason yearned to know the feel of them grazing his body. His need for Annie was so powerful that at times he felt overwhelmed by it. He'd never felt like this about any woman before. Yet the war gave them no time for such intimacy. Trying to push his yearning for her aside, he gave her a slow smile. "What is it? Now, sweet pea, if I told you what it was, it wouldn't be a surprise, would it?" His heart swelled with joy. Annie was in her flight suit and flak jacket, as was he. Their helmets sat on the wooden floor of the tent, always nearby. In less than an hour they had a mission with a platoon of Rangers going into a known Taliban village fifty miles north of Kandahar. The Apache helicopter would be their air defense in case a firefight broke out.

"No, but I had to try," Annie said, laughing. "Jas, this is great!"

"You've taught me a lot about your traditions over the last few months," he said, a note of pride in his voice, "and I remembered that you celebrated the equinoxes and solstices as Mother Earth's birthday."

Marveling, she murmured, "I only told you that one time in passing," as her fingers flew ripping the paper aside.

His smile grew wider. "I listen well, sweet pea." He saw the tenderness shining in her eyes as she stopped and studied him across the aisle.

"I should have gotten you something, Jas. . . . You celebrate Christmas Day."

"You have." When he saw her confused look, he added, "You're my gift."

Her fingers hesitated midair. The husky inference made her heart pound with happiness. Lifting her chin, Annie willingly drowned in his blue eyes, which had a feral look in them. "You really know how to get to me. That's a beautiful answer, and I know you mean it."

"No, it's not a line. Thank you." His lips lifted in another grin. Motioning to the package in her hands, he said, "Go ahead, open it. . . ." Would Annie like his gift? He wondered. Would it be in keeping with her Apache traditions? Jason wasn't sure. She had taught him a lot about her culture and the way she saw the world. And in the end, Jason found that his belief system and how he saw the earth was closer to hers than to the Anglo way of seeing things. That was a good discovery for him. Annie often teased him that his family tree must have a Native American somewhere in it that no one knew about. She said that something about him gave her the sense that he had an Indian ancestor. Jason recalled how he'd refused to learn about the long line of Trayherns from his father because he didn't want to be around him. Now he was sorry he hadn't taken advantage of the opportunity to learn about his ancestors. He made a mental note to e-mail his mother and ask if there was, indeed, a Native American in their family history. Deep down inside, he hoped so. He liked the idea of having that kind of connection to Annie.

Jason enjoyed watching Annie as she bent her head and tore the package open. She was like an excited child, her enthusiasm infectious and uplifting. She made life here at Kandahar bearable for him. And how beautiful she was! His mouth ached to touch her lips and yet, in all this time, Annie had not made a move to kiss him. And that's what Jason wanted — her to come to him of her own free will. She was Apache and she'd told him a long time ago an Apache woman chose her man, not vice versa. So Jason waited and hoped. What he'd found out about Annie only deepened his feelings for her.

"Oh!" Annie cried. "Oh, wow! Dude, this is great!" She pulled a brown leather pouch from the box. Eyes widening, she searched Jason's features. "What kind of skin? Goat?" Her old deerskin pouch that held the rainbow medicine necklace was thin and hard with age.

Annie remembered pulling the pouch out one afternoon here in the tent to show him the necklace after she'd explained its full history. When she had, part of the pouch had crumbled and broken off because it was so old. She had carefully picked up each shred of deer hide and gently placed it in the bottom of the pouch. Realizing Jason must have remembered this and had gone out of his way to do something about it made her go warm inside with gratefulness.

"Naw, not goat. It's deer hide. I got an old man from a nearby village who hunts deer for his family to make it for you." Jason swallowed hard. "Do you like it? Will it replace the old one or not?" He knew now that every animal hide held a spirit, which had great meaning to Annie. Not just any hide would do, Jason had realized after discussing it with her one time. And God knew, he'd scouted relentlessly for months to find someone who hunted deer in the nearby mountains. Not that the animals were plentiful with the war going on. The conflict compounded the problems of finding the right hide and then finding someone who could tan it and make it into a pouch for her necklace.

The long search had been worth it, judging from the look in Annie's eyes. Even in the dimming light, he thought he saw tears in them as she reverently turned the handmade pouch over and over in her long fingers.

"Jas . . . this is so . . ." Annie choked up. She studied him in the shadows, his face strong and vulnerable. As the months had flown by, Annie had been allowed to meet the real Jason Trayhern, part wounded child, part adult learning to be a man. She saw him struggle to put his traumatic past into perspective so that it wouldn't haunt him for the rest of his life.

Getting to her feet, she took that one step across the aisle and settled her arms around his shoulders. Jason opened his legs so that she could crouch down between them. Annie lifted her face upward and tightened her arms around him.

Surprised by her actions, Jason looked down into her dazzling golden eyes and saw they were filled with tears. Her expression tore at him. Without thinking, he placed his hands on her shoulders and moved them in a soothing motion.

"Hey . . . I didn't mean to make you cry. . . ."

Sniffing, Annie shook her head. "You don't understand, Jason. I never told you. . . . The deerskin pouch wears out from time to time, and it is the man whom we've chosen to share our life with who makes us a new one for the necklace. Somehow . . . you knew. You knew. . . ." Then she strained upward and placed her lips against his.

First contact for Jason was shocking. Heated. It made him hungry. As her lips moved gently, almost in adoration across his, he pulled her powerfully against him, pressing her breasts to his chest. He heard Annie moan softly. Feeling her mouth curve against his, her arms tighten around his neck, he was certain she wanted this. Wanted him. Wanted to share this first, dizzying kiss with him. Jason had not gotten the pouch just to get her to come to him. He knew better than that. Apache women were defiantly independent and called their own shots. They were not moved by manipulation or games.

"Ohh," Annie sighed, "you are a *great* kisser! I knew you would be." And she moved her mouth more strongly against his smiling one. Hearing Jason chuckle, the rumble vibrating through his chest into hers, she arched willingly against him, showed him how much she cared for him. Oh, Annie knew she loved him, no question. She had for some time now. As Jason's breath grew ragged, his mouth wet as it slid hungrily against hers, she knew that he loved her, too.

Her heart had opened slowly, like the shy, yellow evening primrose that grew along the road where she used to ride her horse each evening on the res. There had been no rush, no hurry. Each small touch, given at rare times, had been like gifts shared between them. In their world of war, there was precious free time to spend with one another.

As Annie moaned, she felt Jason's hands move reverently across the back of her flight suit and linger hesitatingly against the sides of her breasts, as if he wasn't sure she wanted to be touched there. Oh, she did! Her flesh heated up wherever he grazed her. Her nipples hardened and she ached to have him touch her even more intimately.

Breathing hard, Jason slowly eased back from her soft, searching mouth, which tasted like life itself, precious and sweet. As Annie dazedly looked up at him, their noses nearly touching, he heard her breathing chaotically. Her hands ranged restlessly across his upper arms. "We'd better stop," he said. "I don't want to, but I'll be damned if I'm going to love you for the first time on the floor of a supply tent."

Laughing breathlessly, Annie nodded. "The first time is special. I agree."

"I want you, Annie. *All* of you . . ." Jason lifted his hand and gently smoothed the errant strands of dark hair across her crown. Then he gave her an awkward smile. "I have for a long time . . . since I met you."

"I know."

"You did?"

"You were kinda obvious, Cowboy. . . ." She laughed softly and got to her feet. If she didn't move, she was going to take Jason all the way on the wood floor of the tent. Annie had no problem with that. There were other issues, however — someone discovering them by accident foremost among them. So Annie put her hunger and need of him on the shelf for now. Maybe another time, in the future, the sweet possibility would present itself. Besides, in less than thirty minutes they had a mission to fly. Loving Jason, enjoying his body, his mind, and melding as one with him was something she did not want to rush.

Jason felt himself hardening, heat pooling into his lower body. Annie stood before him and dug her hand into her pocket, withdrawing the pouch that held the special necklace. She sat down on her supply carton. The light had faded, and he could barely see her at this point. She opened the new pouch and carefully placed the old one inside it.

"There," she said, satisfaction thrumming through her. "The necklace has a new home."

Jason smiled and rested his elbows on his thighs again. "You really like it? It's appropriate?"

"It's perfect, Jason. Perfect." Annie stretched out her leg so that she could slide the pouch back into the thigh pocket before she sealed it with Velcro. Pulling her leg back, she reached across the aisle with her hand and grasped his folded ones between his legs. "Thank you . . . with all my heart. That was such an incredibly thoughtful gift. . . ."

"You are looking like you never thought I would do something like that," he said with a chuckle. Her fingers were strong and warm against his, and felt good. It was cold here in December. Very cold. A dry cold with a lot of nasty wind that made the windchill often dip to well below freezing.

"Guilty as charged," Annie murmured. She withdrew her hand. Lips tingling, she wanted to kiss Jason again — and again. And never stop. Jason's mouth was perfect for hers; it was a mutual fit in every way.

"Not all Anglos are blind."

Laughing quietly, Annie held up her hands. "You're right and you're on a roll with me, Cowboy. You know how to impress an Apache maid, believe me."

His smile dissolved and Jason became very serious, holding her joyful golden gaze. "I listened to you, Annie. I wanted to learn about your ways, and how you see the world around us. These months have been the best I've ever spent because you've taught me how to appreciate you."

His words blanketed her with a warmth that made tears sting her eyes. Bowing her head, Annie sniffed and wiped her nose. "You know what?"

"What?" How Jason wanted to go over there and sit beside Annie. Time was short. It was never on their side, he realized as he glanced at his watch.

"I was wrong about you. When I first met you, you were wearing armor a mile thick." She studied his features in the dim light, her voice low with feeling. "I didn't think you'd let me in."

"Why wouldn't I? You were never out to hurt me like other pilots were, Annie."

"I know, but . . . your awful past . . . I mean —" she opened her hands helplessly "— I understand why you were the way you were. If all that had happened to me, I don't know if I could have overcome it as you have." She gave him a soft look. "Yet you've opened up and let me in. I like the man who lives inside." She pointed a finger toward his heart. "I like him a *lot.*"

"Enough to think of keeping our relationship moving forward over time?" Jason's heart was suspended with dread and fear of what her answer might be. He loved her. Fiercely. Completely. And he knew it wasn't the right time to tell her that. Their relationship was organic, deepening over time, and he found himself enjoying the slow, unfolding process. Annie was no flash in the pan, no overnight lover or bed hopper. No, she was honest and she played for keeps.

Wiping her eyes, Annie nodded, her throat choked with emotion. Searching his serious features, his blue eyes narrowed on her, she managed to whisper, "Yes, I like what we have, Jason. Not even war can stand between us. I know it's frustrating. We can't get the time off to be together like this, only once or twice a week. . . . But I'm willing to wait. I saw my mother and father work at their relationship. They've told me many times that their love for one another was strong when they met, but they took the time to evaluate it, test it and discover one another. The pace we're moving at feels right to me."

Reaching over, Jason took her right hand and held it between his. It was freezing in the tent, the flaps shaking in each brisk gust of wind. "It feels right for me, too, Annie." Her fingers were cool and he rubbed them gently between his own. "I'm trying to court you the Apache way, not the Anglo way." And his mouth lifted in a smile.

"You're a warrior at heart," Annie whispered, closing her hand over his. "You're courting me in a way that fits in with our customs." How warm and strong Jason was. And tender. He wasn't like a lot of other Anglo men Annie had had the misfortune to run into. All they wanted was the instant gratification of a one-night stand they could walk away from the next morning. Sex was a game for them. And it wasn't to her.

Drowning in Jason's sincere gaze, she added, "We need to go. We have to get out to the bird. Our crew will be wondering where we are. . . ."

Nodding, Jason released her. "You're right." He sighed. Stepping to the rear flap of the tent, he poked his head outside. It was almost dark. He saw no guards, but knew they were around. "It's all clear, sweet pea. . . ."

Stepping out of the tent, Annie adjusted her flak jacket and put on her helmet. It was cold and she wrapped her arms around herself. As always, one of them left before the other. Jason would wait five minutes, then head in the opposite direction so that no one would spot them walking together.

Jason watched Annie hurry between the other tents and disappear. Glancing at his watch, he timed her. She would go to the hangar, get her gear and then go out to the bird. The crew would be there, waiting for her. Then he would arrive, roughly five minutes later.

As Jason waited, he looked up. The sky was clear, the stars so near and bright. The Afghan sky was like a field strewn with diamonds. It was a hard, wild, beautiful country, and as harsh as the landscape was, the beauty of the night sky more than made up for it. His mind turned back to Annie. She was a diamond of another type. More precious to him than anything else. With his heart swelling with joy, his lower body still aching with need of her, Jason knew he had to divert his attention. The flight would take one hour, providing nothing happened, and he hoped it didn't. When he got back, he would go to the small office that he shared with Annie in the hangar, and write a letter home. It would be his overdue Christmas present to his parents.

"Morgan, there's a letter from Jason!" Laura quickly pushed open the front door, stomping the snow from her boots on the woven rug before she entered. Breathless, she swiftly shed her dark green wool coat and hung it up in the foyer. Her boots came off next. She set them aside on another rug beneath the coat rack to let the snow melt off them. Today was Monday, and Morgan had agreed to baby-sit Kamaria while she went into town, did some quick grocery shopping and picked up the mail at the post office.

She heard Kamaria giggling in the living room, and headed in that direction. Morgan was sitting on the bearskin rug in front of the fireplace, playing with the child. Their daughter looked cute in her tan corduroy romper and red, long-sleeved cotton turtleneck. Her dark hair spilled in soft ringlets about her tiny shoulders, her blue eyes shining as she reached out for her father.

Morgan's hand was so large and scarred compared to the child's tiny pink one. Laura loved these moments her husband spent with the baby of their household.

"A letter from Jas?" Morgan asked, grinning playfully at Kamaria, who threw herself at him. He gave an "oomph" as she crashed into his chest. Wrapping his arms around his daughter, he laughed with her. This was a game she loved to play. She would run into his open arms where he sat on the rug and he would grab her and make growling sounds, all the while kissing her neck where she was ticklish.

"Yes, a letter!" Laura held it up triumphantly. "At last! I thought he'd broken both hands." She laughed breathily. Going over to Kamaria, who was standing now, her arms held upward, Laura gave her daughter a quick hug and a kiss on the noggin. Satisfied, Kamaria turned back to Morgan and threw herself on him once more. Laughing, Laura sat down on the couch nearest the bear rug.

"She's full of it today."

Kamaria was shrieking and wriggling like a puppy as Morgan kissed her repeatedly on the neck. "No kidding," he murmured, releasing her, then grinning as she assaulted him once more. Glancing over at Laura, who looked comfortable and pretty in black wool slacks and a soft yellow angora sweater, he smiled. "Hurry up. Rip it open. Let's hear what Jason has to say." Releasing Kamaria again and cushioning her as she fell onto the thick bearskin, Morgan watched his blue-eyed daughter gurgle and kick her arms and legs as he made feinting attempts to tickle her ribs.

"I'm hurrying, I'm hurrying. . . ." Laura slit the thick envelope with her finger. "It's a *big* letter, Morgan."

"Maybe the writing bug hit him," Morgan said, watching as Kamaria quieted down. It was near her nap time and she sighed and rolled onto her side, gazing at the crackling fire in the black, wrought-iron fireplace insert. Morgan gently began to rub her back with his hand. Kamaria loved to be touched, and he marveled over that as he massaged her tiny back until she finally closed her eyes. Deep in his heart, he held grief over not doing this for Jason or Katy. He'd never played with them. Not like this. And he should have. Because the loving bond he'd established with Kamaria was so rich and beautiful, Morgan realized now how much he had neglected his first two children. He hurt for them. He hurt for himself.

"Okay," Laura whispered excitedly, gathering the pages in her hands and resting her elbows on her knees, "here's what he has to say. . . ."

"Dear Mom, Brother, Sisters and Father,

this is a late Christmas gift to you. I'm sorry I couldn't write sooner, but the missions have been many and often. You know how that goes. Anyway, I just got off a flight, and it's midnight. I'm too wired to sleep, so I thought I'd write and try to catch you up on life around the base here.

"I'm fine. It's colder than hell here, just like the Rockies, except the snow falls in the mountains, not on the plain. We get a few flurries here, but mostly it's the wind that bites us and rain that soaks us. With the windchill often making it feel like zero, we try to stay inside as much as we can. The wind is always blowing here. The dust, as you know, is terrible. It gets in your eyes, nose, mouth and places I won't mention. And let me tell you, a tepid shower once a day is something we really look forward to.

"I wanted to thank you for your Christmas box. I gotta tell you, all the goodies you packed into it were so welcome! I shared them with our crew. Except for the homemade chocolate chip cookies, which I only shared with Annie. She loved them. She said she'd like your recipe, Mom, because they tasted so good. Maybe, if you have time when we get back next June, you could give it to her? She loves to cook, too, like you.

"As a matter of fact, Annie got the cooks over at mess to let her make her favorite winter stew with mutton. She made a huge batch for the whole base and had a lot of fun doing it. The Afghan people eat a lot of lamb, and Annie was raised on it, too. I got to peel a ton of potatoes and chop up a lot of onions for her stew. She made fifty gallons of it to serve the base at lunchtime. That shows you how many people we have here.

"Annie's mutton stew went over great with the soldiers here. They now call her the 'diva of gourmet cooking.' The mess cooks are begging her to come back and make some more Apache food. Everyone wants her to, but we're so busy that she hasn't had the time. That stew sticks to your ribs, I'll say that. She went out with some local folks and gathered herbs to put in it. The local Afghans love her. They are very close to the earth, very much a part of it, and so is she.

"When we get time off, which isn't often, we'll hop a ride with a ranger detachment in a Hummer and go to a local village for the day. Many Afghan women are incredible weavers, and Annie has a teacher, an old woman called Fatima, who has been teaching her how to weave on her loom. When we go to her house, which is made out of mud bricks, we always bring goodies — like canned fruit, cereal and stuff. We get the leftovers from the supply sergeant, who doesn't mind if we feed the village. He says it's good PR, and we agree with him.

"Life around here is bearable because of Annie. She's a fantastic pilot, Mom. Good flight hands. And she makes me laugh. A lot. No other woman in my life has made me feel so good about myself as she does. I know there's a war going on around us, but with her here, I can put up with it. I look forward to each day now. Life is good even if we are over here. So don't worry about me, okay? I know you do.

"I hope you don't mind, but I read Annie your letters. She and I have a secret meeting place in the back of a supply tent. When I get a letter from you, we choose a time, grab some cans of fruit and make a celebration out of reading it. She's learned a lot about our family through what you've written. And when her parents write to her, she reads their letters to me. It's a great way to get to know one another. So your letters are more important than you think!

"When we get rotated back to Fort Campbell in June, we'll have thirty days leave coming. I'd like to come home and introduce you to Annie. Would that be okay?

"Well, I'm getting sleepy now. I'm gonna hit the sack. Give everyone a hug for me, will you? And thanks for sending the updated pictures of Kamaria. She sure is growing up in a hurry. Annie thinks she's beautiful. So do I. Merry Christmas. Jason."

Laura smiled softly and touched the crinkled notebook pages covered in handwritting. "Oh, this is the best letter he's ever written to us, Morgan. It's so personal."

Morgan gently touched his daughter's shoulder as she slept on the bearskin. Nodding, he gazed over at Laura, who had such joy shining in her eyes. "This letter from him *is* different." For her sake, Morgan was relieved. Jason's letters were usually curt and short, certainly lacking the downhome flavor that this most recent letter had.

"I know why," Laura said primly, folding the letter carefully and putting it back in the envelope.

"Why?"

"Well, didn't you hear it in Jason's letter?"

"What?" Morgan shook his head and saw the utter frustration on Laura's face. "Hey, you women always see things before we do." He chuckled indulgently.

"Annie! Annie Dazen is making the difference with him, Morgan. Jason is finally opening up. You can see the progression in the letters — what few he's sent. In each one, he's more accessible."

"It sounds as though Annie makes him happy," Morgan murmured.

"He loves her."

Morgan frowned. "How do you know?"

"I just *know*, Morgan." Laura touched her heart and smiled. "It's a gut intuition."

Groaning, he said, "Okay, I know better than to go there."

"And I'm always right about it, too. You know that."

"No question," Morgan agreed with a chuckle. He saw the light dancing in Laura's wide eyes. "So he wants to bring Annie home and introduce her to us?"

"Yes. He's never done that before, darling. Annie means a lot to him, I'd guess."

"I agree." He unwound himself and moved to the couch. Placing his arm around Laura, he said, "Maybe after all the crap he's gone through, she's straightening him out. It sounds like it."

"Well, I'm sure Annie is, darling, but she's not forcing him to do it. He loves her. That's why he's opening up and becoming more available." She patted the envelope in her lap. "Oh, this is *such* good news! I'll write him back today. And I'll ask him to ask Annie for her mutton stew recipe. This is a woman I want to know. She's done more good for Jason in five months than we have in a lifetime."

A wave of pain moved through Morgan's chest. He carried such a heavy load of guilt about Jason. He tightened his arm around Laura's shoulders, giving her a gentle squeeze. "Yes, she has, and no one deserves this break more than our son. I'm just hoping that if Jason loves her, she loves him as much."

"It sounds like it," Laura murmured, resting her head against her husband's shoulder. "Oh, I hope so, Morgan. I want to see Jason happy. . . ."

Chapter 9

Jason couldn't get warm inside the tent. It was late February and there had been a rare snowstorm shortly after they'd hand landed, two hours ago. They had just gotten off a mission protecting a Special Forces team east of Kandahar. The Taliban had struck, and Jason and Annie had used their rockets to successfully defend the soldiers. He'd had weapons duty tonight instead of flying the helo. Every other night, he would switch off as PIC — pilot in charge — with Annie, and work the weapons console, choosing the firing options.

What had jangled his nerves the most was that they'd had a Stinger missile fired at them. If not for Annie's quick reflexes they would have been shot down. As it was, the Stinger missed them by a few feet, flying beneath the undercarriage of the Apache. Jason had never felt so scared. Maybe that was why he couldn't sleep now; adrenaline was still flooding his bloodstream from the close call. When it happened, Annie had given an Apache war cry that had just about split his eardrums. Her shout was so unexpected that

Jason didn't have time to react. He'd jerked, froze and then gasped when he saw the missile coming directly at them.

Annie had brought the Apache around in a tight, driving turn, and he'd shaken off his reaction and quickly put the chain gun into action. They'd destroyed whoever had fired the missile at them.

He moved restlessly on his cot and it squeaked every time he did so. Jason turned toward Annie, who lay asleep across the aisle from him. He couldn't see her in the darkness, but he could hear her soft, shallow breathing. He thought about how amazing she had been that day. They'd come within seconds of being shot out of the sky and killed, and when they'd landed, he'd seen her eyes blazing like those of a warrior in the midst of battle. The smile on her face had been tight and grim. There was no fear in Annie, he realized. But he'd been shaking like a proverbial leaf and had problems walking a straight line, the adrenaline letdown had been so strong. Annie had seemed unfazed by it, acting higher than a kite. Jason acknowledged that some people took to combat better than others, and Annie had a glow around her that made her seem invincible. He felt far from that.

The wind gusted and the tent groaned. Although tied shut, the flaps protested. Sighing, Jason tried to get his mind off their close call. Maybe if he thought about the nice, gentle things in life, his adrenaline would calm down. . . .

Like Annie . . . He loved her, there was no question about it. Frowning, Jason repositioned his hand beneath his lumpy pillow. Frustrated because he couldn't make love to her here, and saw no way to do so before they got back to Fort Campbell in June, he grimaced. War was hell on relationships. For the first time in his life he had fallen in love, in a situation where his hands were tied.

The wind howled, then eased off before slapping viciously at the tent again. Jason felt the dregs of exhaustion creeping up on him. He felt sorry for the Ranger teams that had to protect the base perimeter by Humvee. Everyone hated nights like this, he knew. With dust mingling with the snow in the air, visibility was poor, making it easier for the Taliban to slip close. All the enemy had to do was fire off an RPG — rocket-propelled grenade launcher — then scurry for the scrub-covered hills nearby.

Jason turned over again, his back to Annie. She was able to sleep through the worst wind, storms and rocket attacks. Marveling at her ability, he recalled her telling him one time that it was the rainbow medicine necklace that helped her sleep. Maybe if he pictured that beautiful piece of jewelry in his mind, which was what she had urged him to do, it might help him fall asleep. Right now, Jason was willing to believe in magic just to get a decent night's sleep. So often they were running on nerves, increasingly sleep deprived due to escalating missions against the Taliban.

The last thing Jason remembered as he began to drift off was seeing the beautiful pink, green and blue tourmaline stones. The face of the woman who so closely resembled Annie, slowly appeared before him. The wings of the great snowy owl were pure white surrounding the golden glow of the face carved into the mammoth tusk. He saw the wings begin to open and widen. To his surprise, he felt them enfold him almost protectively. The sensation was warm and comforting, and Jason felt an unbelievable peace begin to flow through him, loosening his tight muscles, allowing him to breathe deeply and fully. As he spiraled into a deep, dreamless sleep, he absorbed the chiseled features of White Owl Woman. It was Annie's face — a visage he loved with all his heart and soul. She was his peace. His sustenance.

The first *carrummp!* jerked Annie out of her sleep. Her eyes snapped open. Groggily, she started to push the thick woolen blanket off her shoulders and sit up. RPGs! Grenade launchers. Attack! The wind buffeted the tent. She heard the two pilots at her feet stir in their cots, too. Jason was snoring. Like everyone else, she wore her clothes to bed except for the cumbersome flak jacket and her boots.

As she saw the flash of red-and-yellow light as the grenade hit, she gasped. It was only two hundred feet from them! Terror surged through her. In that split second, as Annie turned over on her side to push back the blanket, a second grenade landed — in their tent.

One moment she was starting to sit up, the next she felt everything blank out. And then she felt the shocking wave of an explosion against her chest. The air was knocked out of her lungs. She tasted fire, the heat tunneling up her nose and into her open mouth. She tried to cry out as everything erupted in a fireball around her. Heat, burning and savage, attacked her. Flying . . . she was flying! Bright red-and-orange light blinded her and she was sailing through the night air. With an "oomph" Annie landed hard, the air torn out of her lungs.

Gasping, she lay there, numb. Though her mind gyrated, she couldn't think. Screams drifted into her semiconscious awareness. Gunfire. A helicopter taking off in pursuit of the attackers. The fire! Face pressed into the snow and mud, she forced her eyes open. She lay on her side, unable to move. Terror was the first feeling that bolted through her.

Jason! Where was he? Jason? Struggling to sit up, gasping and clawing for air, Annie shut her eyes, sobbing.

Trying to move, she saw dark shapes racing through the deep shadows nearby: men running to get fire extinguishers. Five tents were on fire, and the explosions were still coming. *Oh, no! Jason! Where was Jason?*

Grunting, Annie forced herself to move. Dragging her legs beneath her, she saw the light from a sixth explosion expose three prone bodies where her tent had once been. None were moving. One of them was Jason. She recognized his form even in the darkness rimmed with firelight. Tears flooded her eyes.

"Help . . . !" Her voice was strained and weak. Had anyone heard her? More and more people were running toward them. So many tents were on fire!

Jason? Annie was numb all over. What was wrong with her? Why couldn't she get up? Mouth open, she struggled to stand. *Get up!* Annie couldn't feel her own body. Jason lay unmoving a hundred feet away. She had to get to him! He was hurt! Tears stung her eyes. Gasping, Annie managed to get to her knees.

But when she tried to lean on her left hand and push herself to her feet, she collapsed back in a heap, falling face first into the mud. Through her flared nostrils she breathed in the hideous odor of burning flesh. Instantly, her mind rejected the smell, the taste. Panic set in. Why wouldn't her left arm hold her? What was wrong with it? Annie rolled over on her back and began to probe her arm with her other hand. Her fingers encountered a sticky, wet substance at her elbow, but she felt no pain. Her mind gyrated back to Jason, his still form. Once again tears jammed into her eyes.

"Help!" Her voice was scratchy. It sounded a million miles away, as if she were standing at the end of a very long tunnel. Shadows, long and dark, ran around her. The screams and shouts of the wounded rang in her ears. She felt warm blood gushing out of her nose, and then pain began to slowly drift into her left arm and up to her shoulder.

"Jason!" Annie focused every molecule of strength she had to cry out his name. Out of the dark came her black jaguar. It was her spirit guardian. Shaida's mouth was open, her tail twitching. Annie called to her, asked her to go to Jason and help him. She watched as the jaguar turned and trotted toward Jason. She heard footsteps. Heard someone slide to a stop near her head.

"Here's another one!"

Annie didn't recognize the voice. It was a man. A man with fear in his tone. Gripping her left arm, her fingers now wet with blood, Annie closed her eyes to fight the nauseous waves assaulting her. Gritting her teeth as the man leaned over her, she whispered, "Jason Trayhern . . . get to Jason. He's not moving. . . ."

The phone was ringing. And ringing. Morgan groaned and rolled over onto his side. He frowned when he realized it was the secure phone, the one connected to his office at Perseus, that was ringing. Rubbing his eyes, he sat up and fumbled for it as Laura gently stirred beside him. The secure phone didn't ring often, but when it did, it usually meant one of his teams out in the field was in dire trouble.

Sitting up, he shoved the bedcovers aside and dropped his legs over the edge of the mattress. The cedar floor was cool under the soles of his feet. "Trayhern here . . ."

"Morgan?"

Frowning, Morgan opened his eyes a little more, trying to erase the deep sleep he'd been in. He had been expecting it to be Mike Houston, who was pulling duty last night, but it wasn't. Morgan couldn't place the voice, but it sounded familiar.

"Who am I speaking to?" he demanded, rubbing his face.

"Morgan, it's Red Dugan."

An ominous feeling filled him, as if someone had just gut punched him. The shock of finding Jason's C.O. on the other end of the phone jolted him wide awake. He sat up straighter, gripping the phone. "Red? What's wrong?" His stomach shriveled in terror. It was about Jason. *No . . . oh, God, no!*

Trying to steel himself against whatever Red might say, Morgan automatically pressed his free hand to his stomach.

"I'm sorry to call you, Morgan, but I thought you'd want to know first rather than get a letter or call tomorrow. Jason was in his tent sleeping last night when the base got hit with multiple RPG attacks by the Taliban. They took out five tents where my people were sleeping. Jason is in critical condition. We've already got him on a flight to a hospital in Germany. I'm sorry to have to tell you this, but I knew you'd want to know right away."

Cold, biting sweat popped out on Morgan's wrinkled brow. *No! No!* He wanted to scream. Instead, he clenched his hand into a fist against his aching gut. "How bad? Where was he wounded?" His voice was unsteady and harsh. He felt Laura sit up beside him.

"Head injury, Morgan. I don't know how bad. A grenade landed at the foot of his tent. The other two warrants are dead. Annie, his pilot partner, was also wounded, but not critically. She's on the same flight to Germany. We got real lucky in one respect. There was a C-9A Nightingale jet already here from Ramstein, Germany. The jet had been scheduled to pick up a bunch of Afghan kids to-morrow and take them to Landstuhl Regional Medical Center for routine medical checkups. Instead, the medical jet, which is fully equipped to save lives, was used to transport the wounded from this attack back to Landstuhl. If that jet hadn't been here we'd have never been able to give Jason the type of emergency attention he needed so quickly. The last I heard from the head nurse on board was that he was critical but stable."

Placing his hand across his eyes, Morgan whispered, "That is good news, Red." The Boeing Nightingale was a huge modern jet. It was the only aircraft dedicated solely to aeromedical evacuations. The Ramstein Air Base in Germany was the only one in Europe that had them. And the Landstuhl Medical Center stood only a few miles outside the giant air base. What a stroke of luck! Morgan tried to gather his spinning thoughts. "We'll grab the first flight we can over to Germany. Thanks for letting me know, Red. I'm sorry . . . for all the families. . . ."

"I'm sorry, too, Morgan. We're all praying that those who survived so far pull through. I'll try to track you down if I hear anything more before you arrive in Germany to see your son."

"Yeah. Thanks, Red . . ." He quietly hung up the phone, dreading telling Laura the news. This would gut her. She'd suffered enough over the years, and Morgan felt helpless to protect her from this news, even though that's exactly what he wanted to do.

"Morgan?"

He cringed inwardly, and turned on the bed to face her. Laura sat up, looking so beautiful in her pink silk gown, her blond hair tousled and her eyes sleepy. "Darling," he said, his voice cracking as he reached for her hand, "I've got bad news. That was Red Dugan from Afghanistan." He saw her eyes widen. He heard her gasp.

"Oh, no! Morgan!" Laura grabbed at his hand. "Jason? Is it Jason?"

Wincing, he saw her eyes go wide with shock. With denial. And then he saw her pain. Forcing out the words, he rasped, "He's been wounded, Laura. Critical condition but stable. A head injury." He would not spare her the details. Morgan knew from long experience it was better to get the whole truth out and not leave family members in the dark. "There was a grenade launcher attack. Five tents were blown up. Jason's was one of them."

Leaning over, he switched on the lamp sitting on the bed stand, blinking as light flooded the room. Laura had grabbed his hand, her nails biting into his palm as she struggled to get hold of herself. At that moment, he saw his wife's true courage. Yes, there were tears in her eyes, but the set of

186

her soft mouth told him that she was going to remain strong through this.

"We need to get to Ramstein, Germany. Now," she whispered, releasing his hand. Scooting off the bed, she grabbed her pink chenille robe and threw it on.

"Yes," Morgan muttered, "as fast as we can." His heart was reeling with grief. With fear. "I'll call Mike. He's duty officer over at Perseus tonight. He'll use our connections to get us a ride on an Air Force transport going to Europe. One way or another, we'll get there as fast as humanly possible."

"I'll call Crystal Harding. I'll ask her to come over now to take care of Kamaria while we're gone." Laura wiped the tears from her eyes. Jason was hurt. How much had he suffered? Was he in pain? Would he make the flight out of Afghanistan alive? A head wound. Oh, God, that was the worst kind of injury! Would he survive? All the questions terrified Laura and she struggled valiantly to put a cap on her mounting fears.

"Yes," Morgan muttered, "do that."

"And then I'll start packing."

Laura was calm now. And thinking. He wasn't. It felt like a mass of writhing snakes had been released inside his gut, nipping at him and making him feel so much pain that he thought he might be having a heart attack. Getting up, Morgan rubbed his hairy chest with his hand in an effort to try and make the oppressive ache go away. He wanted to cry. He wanted to scream. This couldn't be happening. Everything had been going so well. Jason was fitting in. He was happy over there. He loved a woman named Annie.

Frowning, Morgan picked up the secure phone to call Mike Houston. Mike would get the ball rolling on the fastest way to get from Montana to Germany.

Laura emerged from the bathroom.

"What about Annie, Morgan?" she asked, walking quickly to the master closet and hauling down two pieces of luggage. As she threw them on the bed, she saw him put the phone down and turn toward her. Seeing the grief ravaging his narrowed gray eyes, she went over to him.

Morgan opened his arms, needing Laura's warmth and womanly strength right now. As her arms closed around him, he rested his head against her soft, silky hair.

"Annie was wounded, too. Not as bad, Red said. She's not critical, but she's on the same flight to Germany with Jason."

Giving him a hug, Laura said, "You know, we have Annie's parents' phone number. Jason put it in his last letter to us." Looking up at him, she said, "Call them, Morgan. I know you can move heaven and earth to help them get over there, too. Will you, darling?"

Having something to do made him feel less

188

out of control. "Yeah, that's a great idea."

"Good." Laura reached up and pressed a kiss to his hardened mouth. "I have to call Crystal. You call Annie's parents. They need to know her condition."

The constant reverberation of the C-141 Starlifter's multiple engines tremored through Morgan. He and Laura, dressed in jeans, warm shirts and leather coats, sat in the belly of the monster Air Force craft. It was now 1:00 p.m. The nylon seat wasn't uncomfortable, and Morgan could easily get up and thread his way through the pallets of supplies to the cockpit, where they had coffee brewing. Laura was stretched out on four of the empty seats, asleep. He was glad she could sleep. The day was fully upon them now and they'd been in the air for six hours and had just started to span the upper Atlantic. Below them stretched the snow-covered, icy tip of Greenland.

The loadmaster, a forty-something Air Force sergeant by the name of Jerry Forester, nodded a greeting when Morgan ambled into the tight quarters where coffee and food were stored for the trip. The man was short and boxy, with a set of shoulders like a bulldog. His close-cropped, dark brown hair had a little gray at the temples.

"Sergeant, you got any fresh brew?" Morgan asked him.

"Yes, sir, I do. Just made some," he answered with a smile, picking up the pot and pouring him some. "You musta smelled it drifting back through our girl, here."

It was such an effort to talk, to be polite, when all Morgan wanted to do was scream out his anguish and frustration. "Yeah," he muttered, lifting the black, steaming coffee to his lips, "that was it."

"We'll be landing in Germany in five more hours, sir. About 1800 hours. The pilots requested special flight clearance to move this girl at top speed so we'll get there sooner."

"I appreciate it," Morgan said, meaning it.

"Would your wife care for a cup of java, sir?"

Shaking his head, he said, "No, she's asleep."

"That's good, sir."

"Yeah, it is. . . ."

"Excuse me, sir, but the pilots were wanting fresh coffee up in the cockpit."

Morgan eased out of the tiny space and ambled back along the metal decking. There wasn't much room between the massive pallets stacked with food supplies and the fuselage of the plane, lined with nylon net seats. The deck vibrated under his feet, soothing his apprehension somewhat. Flying always lulled and calmed him. Morgan couldn't explain it, since he was a Marine groundpounder at heart.

As he eased around the last pallet, which was strapped tightly to the deck so it couldn't move, he saw Laura sitting up. Her face was pale, her eyes huge with grief and worry. He went over to her and gently smoothed some of the softly mussed strands of her hair away from her face, tucking them into place.

"I thought you were sleeping."

She caught his hand and pressed a kiss into the palm of it. "I was, but I heard Jason screaming. I woke up." Lifting her face, Laura saw that Morgan's gray eyes were dark, with shadows beneath them. The stress made his face look rock hard and emotionless, but she knew better. She knew Morgan was twisting and dying inside just like she was. They both remained silent in that moment, listening to the sound of the jet engines around them.

"I couldn't sleep. I was afraid if I did, I'd have nightmares about him, too," Morgan replied, seeing his wife's eyes fill with tears. Laura hadn't cried yet. He wondered if she would let those tears fall now. He wanted to cry, too, but he didn't know how. And then he saw her straighten her back, set her lips and force the tears away.

"I had bad dreams for you," she offered, managing a twisted smile. "Any word? Have they called the pilots?" Morgan had set up a direct line of communication with the

Landstuhl Medical Center to patch in a call aboard the jet once Jason was out of surgery. When she and Morgan had left Montana, Jason had just arrived at the hospital and was being taken into the operating theater.

"No, nothing . . ."

Sighing, Laura stood up, smoothing her hands over her jeans. Adjusting her dark brown leather coat around her and retying the pink silk scarf she wore around her neck, she said, "I don't know whether that's good or bad, Morgan. Do you?"

Shaking his head, he murmured, "No, honey, I don't. Come on, the loadmaster just made a fresh pot of coffee." He held his mug up. "It's pretty good for the Air Force," he joked, trying to lift his lips into a smile to buck up her spirits, though he could barely manage it.

Laura rubbed her face. She'd lost track of how long they'd been in the air. Managing to grab a commercial flight out of Anaconda for Spokane, Washington, they'd gone over to Fairchild Air Force Base and caught the C-141 heading for Germany at 0700. It had been sheer luck that this flight had been scheduled. They were the only two civilian passengers on it, and they would never have been allowed aboard, except that Perseus was part of the CIA, which gave Morgan carte blanche to use military transport anytime he wanted. She was glad.

"Come on, I'll walk you up front," Morgan murmured, putting his hand on the small of his wife's back. She was so petite, yet so damn strong. Morgan knew Laura's strength. He'd seen it today just as he'd seen it years earlier, after she had suffered the ordeal of the kidnapping. But nothing — nothing on the face of this earth — prepared parents for a child who might be dying.

What would they find at the hospital? Morgan had arranged with the base commander that their jet be met on the tarmac and they be whisked by an official DV — distinguished visitors — car to the hospital. He was grateful for all his military connections, because right now they needed every last one of them.

"I don't know how most parents of children in the military handle this," Laura murmured as she poured herself a cup of coffee. Pulling down the sugar dispenser, she added several teaspoonfuls to the coffee. "Most of the time, all they can do is sit home and wait. Wait and worry for hours, days . . . God, that must be torture. Pure, hellish torture. . . ."

"Well," Morgan said, watching her fix her coffee, "we've at least got the Dazens on another flight. They're headed to Germany, too, just like us."

Giving him a warm look, Laura stirred her coffee. Her stomach was in knots. She

193

wanted to cry. She wanted to wail out her heartache, her terror that her son might be dying. Never had Laura felt so helpless. Not since she'd been drugged and kidnapped. This was the same horrible feeling. She had to pull on the strength she'd discovered from that experience to keep her emotions at bay now. No, she couldn't afford to lose control. Not now. Not yet . . .

"That was so good of you, Morgan. You mentioned they're getting a flight out of Luke Air Force Base in Phoenix. There was a C-141 leaving from there at noon for Germany, right?"

Looking at his watch, he said, "Yeah, they should arrive about six hours after us. I'll have a staff car there to pick them up, too, and take them to Landstuhl Hospital."

Laura moved out of the small room and leaned against the aluminum siding. Her cup between her hands, she said, "I'm so glad that over the past months Jason told us about Lane and Canyon. I feel as if I already know them through his letters."

Morgan joined her, leaning back against the metal wall. "I was surprised when he sent us a photo of them, since Annie had two. . . . Because they're both ex-military, they know the ropes. They'll handle this flight fine."

Closing her eyes, Laura bowed her head. "Oh, God, Morgan . . . this is so awful. I know Jason is in love with Annie. He was so looking forward to coming home in June and bringing her to meet us. . . ." Tears closed off her throat.

"Drink a sip of your coffee, sweetheart. . . ."

She did as he instructed. The knot in her stomach dissolved a little, though tears burned her eyes. "I feel like we're in a bad dream, Morgan. Nothing feels real right now. It seems as if I'm out of my body, somewhere else . . . but I don't know where. As if I'm flying apart and can't put myself back together again. . . ."

Hearing her anguish, Morgan placed his coffee on the nearby counter and faced her. Hands on her small shoulders, he forced a smile he didn't feel. "It's going to be okay, Laura. I know it."

Sniffing, she gripped her coffee in her hands. "Oh?" Her voice was wobbly. "And who told you?"

Pressing a soft kiss to her brow, he whispered, "Lane Dazen. She said Annie had a rainbow medicine necklace. She said it would help both of them."

A ragged sound escaped Laura's lips. "I want to believe her, Morgan. I really do. . . . I believe in the spiritual world. In unseen help."

"I don't, but right now, I want to. It's all I have to cling to. . . ."

Chapter 10

Laura Trayhern tried to keep her gnawing fear at bay as the C-141 landed at Ramstein Air Base in Germany at 1750. It was snowing lightly. The sky was a thin, milky gray and the dusk light feeble through the thick snowflakes. As she and Morgan left the huge cargo plane after thanking the crew for their kindness, they were met by a staff car and Air Force Lieutenant Liz McConnell, a woman with short red hair who held a cell phone to her left ear as she greeted them.

Their driver, Staff Sergeant David Haley, opened the door of the black Mercedes Benz. Laura thanked him and quickly ducked inside and slid across the leather upholstered seat, Morgan following behind her. As they got on their way, Lieutenant McConnell twisted around from where she sat in the front seat.

"Sir, I'm patching you through to the surgery floor. There's a nurse there on duty, Lieutenant Evans. She'll give you an update on your son."

Relief flooded through Laura. She barely saw the hangars they passed as the car snaked along the wet, slushy streets. As Morgan took the cell phone from Lieutenant McConnell, Laura clenched her hands in her lap. Was Jason still alive? *Oh, God, please let him be okay. . . .*

"Lieutenant Evans? This is Morgan Trayhern. Can you please give me an update on my son, Jason?"

Laura stared hard at Morgan's profile, hoping to hear something . . . anything. She saw her husband's tense face fall a little.

"He's still in surgery? Ten hours? Stable? That's good. When do they think he'll be out? Two more hours. I see. You're sure he's stable?"

The terrible fear that was gnawing at Laura dissolved just a little. Feeling her nails biting into her palms, she flexed her hands then tugged at Morgan's elbow.

"Ask about Annie Dazen."

"Oh, yes, Lieutenant — his copilot, Chief Annie Dazen was brought to your medical center, too. Can you give me a status report on her? Yes? Good. Okay, we'll be there shortly. Thank you for all your help. Goodbye." When Morgan got off the phone, he thanked Lieutenant McConnell and handed the phone back to her. Turning, he studied Laura's tired eyes.

"Jason is stable. He's had ten hours of surgery, with two more to go at the most. They've got the top neurology team in Europe in there for him. They were having a conference on neurology at Landstuhl Regional Medical Center, and the very best neurosurgeons in the Air Force and Army were here."

"Oh, thank God. . . ."

"Yeah," Morgan whispered, "it looks like Annie's medicine necklace has been with Jason from the get-go."

"What else? What else did she say?"

"That his head wound is serious. He's stable, and that's the best news. They said he was young and strong, and that's in his favor. In two hours or less they'll transfer him to ICU, where we can see him. The chief surgeon, Dr. Pointer, will meet us as soon as he's done, and give us an update on Jason's condition."

Closing her eyes, Laura reached out and gripped her husband's hand. It was comforting to feel Morgan's strong fingers fold around hers. "Thank God . . ." She opened her eyes. "And Annie? What about her? Is she there?"

"Yeah," Morgan said, rubbing his watering, smarting eyes. "She's out of surgery. Her left shoulder's involved. Right now, they have her in a private room at Landstuhl. She's awake and going to be okay. They say she's in fair condition."

"Is there any way we can patch this info through to the Dazens? Maybe if we got

198

through to the flight commander, he or she could convey the news to them?" Laura looked to the young, red-haired lieutenant in the front seat.

"Oh, of course, ma'am, can do. Once we get to the medical center and I direct you to the proper people, I'll be happy to contact them."

"Thank you," Laura murmured gratefully. "You've all been so kind."

"Ma'am, we understand. The Landstuhl Regional Medical Center has been used in just about every war theater we've ever had in Europe or the Mediterranean." She smiled a little. "That's why the C-9 Nightingales are based here. We can use them to transport, like we just did out of Afghanistan."

Morgan shook his head. "It was damn lucky that C-9 was on the ground at Kandahar."

"Yes, sir, they had flown in to take twenty-five Afghan children who needed pediatric care to us." Shrugging, she added, "But none of them have life-threatening problems. Most need prostheses for lost limbs due to stepping on land mines. We'll send the C-9 back tomorrow to pick them up."

Nodding, Morgan looked out the window of the Mercedes Benz. They had just left the large base that was home to a C-131 Hercules squadron, the lifesaving C-9s and other Air Force units.

"Sir, I don't know how familiar you are with Landstuhl, but you're probably going to be talking to both Army and Air Force personnel. It's a mix-and-match military medical center, roughly seventy-five percent Army and twenty-five percent Air Force. With all the Army bases surrounding Ramstein, it's a real hodgepodge."

"Thanks for the info, Lieutenant. It's been awhile since I was here at Ramstein."

"Of course, sir, and just to let you know, the base general, Paul Lanyard, has authorized DV quarters for you. When you're done at the medical center, the staff car will take you to a house on base and you can get some rest."

Morgan was familiar with distinguished visitors quarters — posh houses on base kept ready for important people who visited. "Thank you, Lieutenant. I intend to talk to General Lanyard in person in a little while. What about quarters for Chief Dazen's parents? Where are you putting them?"

"Oh, sir, we've already got a suite for them at the Fisher House, just a quarter of a mile from the medical center. It's a huge brick home that has ten suites in it. Each suite is fully equipped with a kitchen and all the amenities they might need."

"Excellent," Morgan murmured. "And you'll be meeting them on their flight coming in? With a staff car?"

"Of course, sir. General Lanyard made it clear that you and the Dazens are both DVs." She smiled proudly. "We'll make sure that all of you have no stress or problems while you're with us. We'll take care of everything. If you need something, just say so and we'll get it done."

Relief wound through Laura and she leaned back and stared out the window, her head spinning with exhaustion. The snow made the German homes and surrounding landscape look like a picture postcard, the redbrick stark against the fresh white blanket. The streets were slushy but passable. At this time of night, there was little traffic out and about.

Her mind gyrated back to Jason. A head wound. Had the injury destroyed part of his brain? Would he be on life support? Would he be able to breathe on his own after surgery? The questions continued to eat at her. Very soon, two hours or less, they'd know Jason's condition for sure . . . one way or another. . . .

"Your son is stable," Dr. Harold Pointer told them in his office on the surgery floor. He was still in his light blue surgery gown, though he had removed the sweat-stained blue cap from his head and dropped it on the maple desk in front of him. "The reason it took so long was that when that grenade

201

exploded, it must have landed to the left of your son. We had to pick out close to a hundred fragments of sand and other debris from the opening in his skull. The wound is located on the left temporal area of his head, just above his ear."

Laura sat close to Morgan in front of the gray-haired surgeon's massive maple desk. Her hand clenched Morgan's as she sat there, tight-lipped. A hundred questions wanted to rush out, but she knew she must let the colonel give them a full report first.

Pointer sat down and took a sip of his coffee. "Your son is in critical condition and will remain in ICU. But he's like a workhorse. He's got a good strong heart and he's fighting back, so that's a good sign."

"What about brain damage?" Morgan asked.

Shaking his head, Pointer murmured, "I'm sure there is some, but how much? We don't know. For the next seventy-two hours, we're purposely keeping him in a comalike condition so that we can pack his head with dry ice, to continue to reduce the swelling of the brain due to this trauma. Further, we have him in a special suit that covers his legs and chest. Water is pumped through it, keeping his body temperature down to thirty-two degrees Celsius. It's like putting the brain on ice to give it time to heal itself. Plus, it decreases some of the abnormal chemical reactions that take place after a brain injury. If we don't keep him sedated, then we can't control the fluid level in his brain. If the pressure builds up too much, it will destroy more of the brain and impair your son. Keeping that pressure low is our only goal right now. When you see him shortly, don't be upset because he's in this body suit. He's unconscious due to the drugs we're giving him. We *must* keep the brain from swelling, although there is still a hole in his skull."

"A hole?" Laura whispered, her heart thudding hard in her chest, underscoring her fright. Her hand tightened around Morgan's.

"Yes. The blast of the grenade destroyed part of his bony plate," Pointer said. "Don't worry. Later, when he's recovered sufficiently, we intend to go back in for another operation and put in new bone, to grow over that area and enclose it."

"Oh, God . . ."

"It's okay," Morgan whispered, giving her a comforting look to ease her shock. Laura's face was waxen, her fingers pressed against her lips. Turning to the doctor, he said, "Isn't that dangerous? Leaving an opening in his skull?"

The neurosurgeon sipped more of his coffee. "No, not really. Please, Mrs. Trayhern, this is not as terrible as it sounds. I'm sorry for being so blunt. I can see I've upset you, and that was not what I meant to do." He managed a slight smile. "The hole is covered and no infection can get in there."

Trembling inside, Laura nodded and allowed her fingers to drop away from her lips. "Thank you, Doctor. I'm just . . . well, a little shaken up. I — it sounds so horrible. . . ."

"Understandable." Pointer picked up his cup. "I think seeing your son is what you need. Come on, I'll escort you to ICU."

Laura tried to gird herself as they got off the elevator. The ICU nursing station was on the left, and several women in white uniforms and caps were manning it. The place smelled of antiseptic. All the ICU rooms were on the right, with walls of glass so that the nurses could see in and make sure the patients were all right. Gripping Morgan's hand, Laura forced herself to walk slowly, though she was in a hurry. She had to see her son.

Pointer stopped in front of one of the rooms and pushed open the glass door. "In here. You can stay up to ten minutes. With any kind of brain injury, holding his hand and talking to him is very beneficial."

"Thank you," Morgan said, his voice tight.

"I'll arrange it so that you can come up here anytime you want, sit with your son, talk to him, read to him. . . ."

Laura reached out and squeezed the doctor's long, spare hand. Hands that had helped save Jason's life. "Thank you . . . so much. . . ." She forced back the tears as the surgeon nodded curtly.

"I'll leave you with your son," he murmured.

Laura turned and walked into the room. There were beeps and sighs coming from the monitors. Morgan moved to one side of the bed, and she approached the other. Tears filled her eyes as she took her son's limp, cool hand in hers. His head was swathed in white bandages and gauze. He was on a respirator that would breathe for him. Everywhere she looked, he was hooked up to machines. There was an IV in each of his arms, and a tube down his throat to help him breathe. Laura shut her eyes.

"Oh, God . . ." she whispered. Then she sniffed and got hold of herself. Jason's eyes were taped shut and she thought of him as a child, remembering his thick, long lashes, and how deep his blue eyes had been. If only she could see Jason open them one more time. Just once . . . Compressing her lips, she studied the left side of his face, where the wound extended from his temple to his square jaw. The stitches were nearly invisible beneath the surgical tape that held the thin red line together.

"He's got a wound on the same side of the face as I do," Morgan said in a choked tone.

Touching his own scar, which traveled the same length as his son's, he looked over at Laura in amazement. He saw her nod, her eyes luminous with tears. Laying his hand on the blue bedcovers, Morgan opened his fingers and slid them toward his son's hand. He knew Jason hated him, but Morgan loved him, and right now, more than ever, needed to touch him. As his fingertips met his son's, he wondered how long it had been since he'd been able to reach out and hold him in any way. Unbearable pain stabbed at Morgan as he slowly enclosed his son's hand in both of his, trying to warm him up. Jason's skin felt so cool and lifeless.

Jason's flesh reminded him of cold marble. There was no color in his cheeks, which were usually ruddy looking. The slackness of his son's strong mouth and the way his eyelids were taped shut nearly undid Morgan. Tears burned in his eyes, and he wiped them away with his fingers.

"We need to talk to him," Laura said unsteadily, looking over at her husband. Morgan hadn't shaved for hours, the dark stubble making his face appear grim. "Positive things . . ." And she leaned over and placed a soft kiss on Jason's uninjured cheek. Just holding her son's hand helped stabilize Laura. She saw the terror in Morgan's watery eyes, the terrible vulnerability revealed in his parted mouth. He was holding Jason's hand so gently, his large hands covering his son's so protectively. Laura knew he was grieving for what had never been shared between them, father and son. Reaching across the bed, she ran her palm down Morgan's sleeve.

"Listen to me, darling. Don't remember the past. This is the present. Use this situation to start a new chapter in your life with Jason."

Morgan lifted his hand, gently touching Jason's clean-shaven jaw. It was such a stubborn jaw. Of all the children he and Laura had been gifted with, Jason was nearly a spitting image of him, even down to that square jawline. And now a scar would be with him for the rest of his life, to remind Jason of his war duty. Just as Morgan was reminded by his own scar of that fateful day when his company in Vietnam was overrun by the North Vietnamese Army, NVA, and only he and another man survived the murderous attack. Every morning when he shaved, that scar reminded him of that event. Over the years, he'd been forced to make peace with what had happened in Vietnam. The loss of his men, and the suffering of their families was forever etched in his mind, just as the names of those who had died were etched on the black wall that stood as a monument in Washington, D.C. Morgan had his own personal black wall. There wasn't a day that went by when he didn't remember something about one of the men he'd lost. He allowed the memories to come as a way to atone for the guilt he'd felt over the loss. Though he'd been vindicated from the claims that he'd left his company open to attack, in his heart, Morgan felt responsible. Until the last breath he took, he would remember each of the Marines in his company. It was the only way he could honor the sacrifice they'd made to their country and to him.

Now, as he looked at his wife, heard her plea that he forget his bad past with Jason and focus on the future, he felt fresh grief. "Yes," Morgan whispered unsteadily, "I'll try to do that, Laura. I really will try. . . ."

Just then, the nurse came to the door and gently opened it. Laura looked at her watch. Where had the ten minutes gone? It was as if they'd just gotten here.

"Mr. and Mrs. Trayhern? I'm sorry, but time's up for this hour. Dr. Pointer has left some information for you at the desk. Come and get it when you feel like it."

Laura turned and looked at the dark-haired nurse. "Yes. Thank you . . . We'll be there shortly."

The door shushed closed. Laura leaned over, kissed Jason on the cheek and then caressed his shoulder, which was covered in a blue hospital gown. "We'll be back, honey. Don't worry, your mom and dad are here. We'll be with you all the way. Keep fighting,

Jason. Come back to us. There are so many who love you. . . ." She sobbed once, then straightened her back, forcing herself not to cry. Slowly, reluctantly, she slid her fingers away from Jason's. Looking at Morgan, she saw his eyes burning with unshed tears. More than anything, he needed to cry.

"I — I can't remember the last time I told him I loved him . . ."

Laura stood very still. His face was tortured. Tears were streaming down his cheeks. Morgan leaned over and pressed a light kiss on the gauze that covered his son's brow.

"I love you, son. I know . . . I know there's lots of bad blood between us, but we're going to work through it. I promise." Morgan squeezed Jason's hand firmly. "We're going to get through this together, son. As a family. We're going to surround you with our love. . . ."

Tears leaked out of Laura's eyes as Morgan slowly unwound his hand from his son's cool fingers. His eyes were red-rimmed from exhaustion, with terrible emotions burdening him from the past. Laura knew she couldn't take that burden from him, no matter how much she wanted to. Moving to the end of the bed, she reached out and gripped Morgan's elbow. Pulling a tissue from her pocket, she pressed it into his hand.

"Here, darling." She pulled one out for herself and blotted her eyes. Giving him a wobbly smile, she said, "Let's go see Annie. And then we'll go home to the DV quarters and get some sleep."

Annie heard the door to her private room open. Still doped up on drugs after having come out of surgery half a day earlier, she slowly turned her head toward the sound. It was probably the nurse, Lieutenant Betty Harper, checking in on her. When she saw two people coming toward her, she frowned. They looked familiar, but who were they? Her mind was sluggish, the drugs making her feel woozy.

"Annie?" Laura said, coming to the side of the bed. "I'm Jason's mother, Laura Trayhern. And this —" she gestured to the man at her side "— is Morgan, his dad." She gently touched Annie's hand, which was marked with abrasions from the grenade blast. "We've come to see you and Jason. How are you doing?"

The information overwhelmed Annie for long moments. Trayhern. Jason's parents. Her left shoulder and arm were heavily bandaged and she could barely move. The warmth of Laura's hand on hers was startling and felt good to her.

"Jason?" she whispered hoarsely. "You . . . Jason . . . how is he? Is he alive?" Her heart beat hard in her chest beneath the blue gown she wore. She felt Laura's fingers tighten momentarily on her own.

"Yes, he's alive." Laura slowly went over all the information with her. Now that she saw Annie in person, she understood why her son had fallen in love with her. She was beautiful, with strong features and high cheekbones. Her black hair, recently washed, lay around her like a black halo, shining dimly in the fluorescent lighting.

Though Laura had to repeat the update on Jason several times for her to understand it, the information sank slowly into Annie's drugged brain. Jason was alive! Closing her eyes, Annie felt tears seeping from beneath her lashes and slipping down her cheeks. She felt Laura gently dab them away with a tissue. A sob worked its way out of her. When her body jerked, she felt pain briefly floating up her injured arm.

"It's okay," Laura said softly, slowly stroking Annie's thick black hair. "He's alive."

"I — I love him so much. . . ." The words were torn out of her.

Morgan looked at Laura as Annie began to cry, shaking her injured shoulder in the process. Pulling her hand out of Laura's, she held the heavily bandaged area to try and ease the building pain.

Almost helplessly, Laura leaned over and placed her hand lightly on Annie's right shoulder. "It's all right," she whispered unsteadily. "He's alive, Annie. And God willing, he'll come out of this so all of us can love him. . . ." She bowed her head and pressed her lips gently against Annie's brow.

Morgan stood back, unable to say anything. Annie's sobs were animal sounds wrenching from deep within her. Laura had been right; Jason and Annie were in love. And Annie was so beautiful. More important, she loved Jason. Rubbing his face with exhaustion, Morgan found the sound of weeping too upsetting in light of the emotional hell he was suffering over Jason. Yet Laura had an incredible ability to reach out and care for others when he knew she was ready to keel over from the long flight and the shock of seeing Jason for the first time. Morgan felt as if he should do something, but he didn't know what. Annie's parents would be coming around midnight. At least he could give her that good news, because he knew she wouldn't expect them to be able to fly here and see her so quickly, if at all. Most families wouldn't be able to afford it.

Stepping forward, he gently rubbed Laura's back. As Annie's weeping abated, Morgan leaned down and whispered to his wife, "Why don't you tell Annie her parents are going to be here in a couple of hours? I think that will help her a lot."

Gazing up into Morgan's sad features,

Laura saw tears still swimming in his dark blue eyes. Giving him a slight smile, she nodded. Tears were running freely down her own face and she didn't even try to blot them away. "Yes . . . yes of course . . ."

Chapter 11

With her father's help, Annie sat down very carefully in the wheelchair provided. Her mother stood behind her, gripping the chair so it wouldn't move. They had just had lunch together and for the first time since she'd been injured, Annie had an appetite. Her dad had brought in her favorite food: pizza. He'd found a little German pizza shop not far from where they were staying, and she'd wolfed down half of the pie while her parents split the rest. It was wonderful having them here to share her lonely days.

"Thanks," Annie whispered, vague pain drifting through her left shoulder. She'd suffered a broken upper arm — a compound fracture — a separated shoulder and some nerve damage, all of which made her arm fifty percent weaker. The sling she wore helped to support it. She smoothed her uninjured hand over her blue gown and bathrobe, then smiled up at her father, who had a concerned look on his face.

"I'm okay, Dad. Really." She twisted to look at her mother. "Let's go. . . . I'm really anxious to visit the ICU and see Jason."

Today was the day. They'd taken Jason out of the cooling body suit twenty-four hours earlier, and Dr. Pointer was finally allowing him to become conscious. The good news was that his brain had not swollen to the extent where more damage could have been done. He was past that particular crisis, and the doctors had taken him off the drugs that had kept him in a coma.

Because of her own injuries, Annie hadn't been able to leave her bed until today. How badly she wanted to see Jason! Having to lie in a room knowing that the man she loved was two floors above her had nearly driven her insane. The yearning to see Jason, to touch him, had eaten at her daily.

If not for her parents' arrival, Annie wasn't sure she'd have stayed in her bed. Jason needed her. He needed the medicine necklace. Lane had taken it to him at her urging, and placed it beneath Jason's pillow, with the approval of his parents. Whether they believed in the magic of the necklace or not, the Trayherns seemed eager to do anything possible to help Jason survive.

Annie gripped her hands excitedly in her lap as Lane wheeled her toward the door. Canyon moved ahead and opened it.

"Do you think he'll be awake, Mom?" Being a nurse, her mother understood Jason's condition more extensively, because of her medical training.

"I don't know, Pumpkin," she murmured, hesitantly. "He's been heavily sedated for seven days. *If* he comes out of it, then it usually takes twenty-four to forty-eight hours to become conscious. Every patient is different when it comes to brain injury, Annie, so it's a tough call to make. Jason is strong and young, so he might bounce out of this coma today. Let's hope so."

As her parents wheeled her slowly down the immaculate, blue-tiled hall, where nurses and visitors streamed past, Annie wanted to hurry. It was frustrating being in the wheelchair, but she wasn't at all steady on her feet yet. When she tried to walk, the pain was excruciating, and she'd quickly decided a set of wheels was a good idea, at least temporarily.

Oh, how she missed Jason! How desperately she wanted to be at his side to comfort him. Morgan and Laura had told the nursing staff that she and Jason were engaged to be married. A blatant lie, but it meant that Annie was "family" and therefore allowed to visit Jason in ICU; otherwise, she would not have been able to.

"You said some people with brain injuries never regain consciousness." Her heart beat with dread at that thought. Jason *had* to wake up!

"A low percentage don't become conscious. I hope for your sake and for his family's sake, he does. He has the medicine necklace beneath his pillow. I know it will help him."

Nodding, Annie moistened her lips. She had told her parents of her black jaguar guide going to Jason's side during the attack. Her mother said the guide probably helped to save Jason's life. Annie knew it was true but she never shared that with the Trayherns, unsure of how they would receive such information. "I'm so glad Morgan and Laura let you put it there. I was worried they'd say no."

Lane smiled briefly. "I feel Laura very much believes in our world as we know it. Morgan doesn't, from what Laura said, but he's desperate, so he allowed me to put it beneath Jason's pillow." She patted Annie's good shoulder. "Jason's life is in the hands of the Great Spirit now. All we can do is pray for him, and hope."

Annie knew she'd say that. It was true, but she wanted to do as much as possible to help him. "The doctor said Jason sustained that wound on the left side of his head, Mom. What does that mean?"

"Jason took a hit to the temporal lobe or the temple area. My area of expertise is emergency room care, so I'm a little rusty on traumatic brain injuries. Basically, that lobe of the brain deals with our ability to hear, our memory, visual perceptions and categorization of objects."

Annie frowned as they halted in front of

the elevator. "Mom, what does all that gob-bledygook mean? You're speaking medicalese again."

Gently laughing, Lane gazed down at her daughter, who had a stressed look on her face. "I'm sorry, Pumpkin."

Canyon pushed the button for the elevator. "Your mom is fluent in Apache, English and medicalese. That's pretty impressive, speaking three languages."

Managing a thin smile, Annie nodded. "Yeah, and now I need a translator."

Canyon grinned and held up his hands. "Don't look at me, Pumpkin. When she comes home from the Fort Apache Medical Clinic, I just let all those fancy words drift right over my head. Not that I'd understand them anyway."

Once again Annie twisted to look up at her mother, who stood behind her. Lane's black hair was arranged in two thick, long braids. Her black wool pantsuit was set off with a red blouse that made her look elegant and yet completely Indian. Annie was proud of her mother and of her heritage. "Okay, the English translation, Mom? Please?"

Lane grinned at her husband, who looked every inch an Indian himself in a Western shirt and jeans, and then gazed down at Annie. "Two against one. That's no fair. Okay," she said, watching the elevator doors open, "here's what it can mean. The patient may have difficulty recognizing faces, even of those he loves. Trouble understanding words is very common, so when Jason wakes up, be sure to speak very slowly and clearly to him. Enunciate each word." She pushed the wheelchair into the empty elevator. Canyon hit the button for the ICU floor. As the doors closed, Lane turned the wheelchair around.

"Jason might have selective attention regarding what he sees or hears. Something might catch his notice and he could become riveted on it to the exclusion of all other things that are going on around him."

"Sort of like obsessiveness?" Canyon wondered aloud, shoving his hands into the pockets of his jeans.

"Exactly. See, Annie? Your dad knows more than he lets on."

"You two are good for me." Annie smiled brokenly, reaching back and gripping her mother's warm, strong hand. "I'm so glad you're here. . . ."

"Thank Morgan and Laura," Canyon murmured. "We owe them a lot. If not for them, we'd still be back in Arizona, wondering how you were and waiting to hear from you."

"I know," Annie whispered, releasing her mother's hand. "The Trayherns are such wonderful people. They feel like old friends to me because of the letters Jason shared with me from Laura. She's a great writer, and I got to sit and listen to him read her weekly letters, plus a bunch of e-mails. Laura is really good about e-mailing, but Jason was pretty slow in answering them."

"The Trayherns are good people," Lane said quietly. "I pray Jason pulls out of this, for them and for you."

The doors whooshed open and Lane steered the wheelchair out of the elevator. On the walk down the hall toward ICU, she continued explaining the symptoms Jason might suffer as a result of his injury. "In medicalese, we call what Jason sustained a TBI — traumatic brain injury. So if you hear the doctor throwing that term around today, you'll understand it. TBI of his type can mean Jason might have difficulty identifying objects or verbalizing about them. He might recognize something, but be unable to tell you what it is. Or he might suffer from short- or long-term memory loss. There's also potential for increased or decreased sexual behavior, or aggressive behavior for no apparent reason. And lastly, categorization of objects. For example, Jason might see a can of soup on the shelf, but not know what it's for."

Frowning, Annie rubbed her head. "None of that sounds very good, Mom."

"No, it doesn't. We'll just have to wait and see. No one can accurately predict what a TBI will do to a person. We have to wait until he becomes conscious before we know."

"If he has any of these symptoms, will he ever get over them?"

Lane slowed the wheelchair. Up ahead, Laura and Morgan Trayhern stood waiting for them at the ICU nursing station. Laura was wearing a cinnamon-colored wool pantsuit with a pale pink silk blouse. Morgan had on a pair of dark blue chinos, a red polo shirt and a blue wool blazer. They broke into welcoming smiles. What courageous people they were.

"The answer is yes and no," Lane murmured quickly. "Sometimes a symptom is there at the beginning, but slowly goes away over time. Or the person can have spontaneous or miraculous changes from bad to good. Or he might not change at all."

Annie nodded. "I like the idea of miraculous, sudden changes, Mom."

"Well," she cautioned, "there is plenty of proof that it does happen, but it's rare, so don't go getting your hopes up too high."

"Thanks for letting me know, Mom. I'd rather know than not know. At least I can be prepared. . . ." That was a lie. Deep down inside herself, Annie was afraid. What if Jason didn't recognize her? What if he didn't remember their love? Shutting her eyes for a moment, she wrestled with the panic and grief those questions brought to her.

Lane nodded. "TBI is going to stress his family in the worst sort of way, Pumpkin. In

221

the next two to three days, the Trayherns will know, most likely, what they're up against — that is, if Jason comes out of the coma. We're going to try and be there for them, no matter what the outcome. They're going to need support if this goes badly. . . ."

"He *has* to be all right!" The words exploded from Annie's lips in an intense whisper. "Jason *has* to come out of this okay!" Biting her lower lip, she felt her mother's comforting touch on her shoulder. Right now, she needed her stabilizing touch to combat the ugly fear roiling within her. Annie wondered if the Trayherns knew about the possible symptoms Jason might suffer. If they did, they sure didn't look like it. Annie studied their faces. Both of them looked so hopeful, their eyes shining with subdued excitement. Dr. Pointer had said Jason would likely awaken either this morning or later in the afternoon. And why shouldn't Laura and Morgan be excited? Jason was their son. Annie knew now just how much they loved him, even though Jason had minimized it to her.

Laura Trayhern came forward with a warm smile. She embraced Annie's parents, then turned to Annie.

"You're looking good today, Annie. More color in your cheeks and your eyes look clearer. How are you feeling?"

"Better, because the docs are finally allowing me outta that bed so I can see Jason." Laura looked thin in the pantsuit, the pink silk blouse matching the color in her cheeks. Her blond hair always look slightly mussed around her oval face. Annie thought she was beautiful, and she could see Jason got his good looks from both his parents.

Morgan came up and shook Canyon's hand, hugged Lane and then looked down at Annie.

"Big day today for all of us, Annie. Dr. Pointer said Jason could become conscious anytime in the next twenty-four hours. We're pretty excited about that. And I'm sure you're more than ready to see Jason yourself, right?"

"Am I ever! Can we go in?"

Morgan smiled. "May I wheel her in, Lane?"

"Sure. An ICU cubical isn't built for five people. Go ahead, Canyon and I will wait out here," Lane agreed with a smile.

"Thanks for understanding," he murmured, then wheeled Annie into the cubical. He positioned her wheelchair on one side of Jason's bed. "I'll let you stay with him for ten minutes. That's all the time they'll give us each hour, Annie." He saw the riveted expression on her face as she looked at Jason, who lay white and still. Putting his hand on her good shoulder, Morgan said gently, "You okay? Do you want me to stay? Or have one of your parents in here, instead?"

Choking back tears of shock, Annie shook her head. She felt the stabilizing warmth of Morgan's strong but gentle hand on her shoulder. Tearing her gaze from Jason, she looked up at him. "No . . . I'll be fine, sir. But I'd like to be alone with Jas, if it's okay with you?"

"Of course," Morgan murmured, and he left.

The quiet settled around Annie. Looking over her shoulder, she saw Laura ushering her parents toward the ICU nurses' station.

She sighed. She was finally alone with Jason. Reaching out with her right hand, she slid it beneath his. Oh, how pale he looked! It frightened her. His head was swathed in bandages, especially the left side. He was breathing on his own, and her mother had told her that was a good sign. Annie curled her fingers around his limp, cool ones.

"Jas? It's Annie. I'm here . . ." Her voice cracked. Hot tears stung her eyes. "I love you. I never got to tell you that, Cowboy. I sure hope you can hear me. Mom said you can hear us and that I should talk to you as if you were awake, so that's what I'm going to do. I'm okay. I got a broken arm and separated shoulder, so I walked away lucky. There was a Taliban attack inside Kandahar. They targeted us with RPGs, Jas. There were five of them with grenade launchers, and five

224

tents took direct hits. One of them was our tent, Jas." She bowed her head and tears streamed down her cheeks. Gulping rapidly, she rasped, "Our two tentmates, Chuck and Jim . . . they're dead."

Sniffing, she gripped his hand a little more firmly. "In all, we had twenty people hurt. And eight are dead. It was awful." Her voice broke again and she gave a sob. Struggling with her emotions, Annie hung her head and pulled her hand from Jason's. She took an edge of the thin blue bedspread and wiped her eyes. Sniffing again, she dropped the bed-spread and wrapped her hand around his once more.

"Your parents are here, Jas. Morgan has been in touch with our squadron. He says they caught the bastards who did this, so that's good news. They're on their way to Guantanamo Bay, where they'll be put in prison. It's the least they can do to them after what they've done to all of us. . . ."

Annie absorbed his silent features. Jason was clean-shaven. His lips were parted and his chest rose and fell with shallow breaths. The beeps and sighs of the monitors around him comforted Annie. "Your parents love you so much, Jas. That's so wonderful. Every hour, they spend ten minutes with you. My mom and dad are here, too, thanks to Morgan. It's so good to have them with me. I'm lonely without you, but having my parents here helps me a lot. . . ."

Annie pulled her hand from his and wiped her eyes and face once more with the edge of the bedding. Sliding her hand back into his, she whispered, "Listen, you're going to be okay. You hear me? I'll be with you all the way, Cowboy. I love you and I'm in for the long haul. I know you love me, too, Jason. It showed in your eyes, in your face. You showed me in a hundred small ways. . . ." She gulped and bowed her head. "Just wake up, okay? Come back to us. You are so loved. . . ."

Jason heard voices, but they were far away, as if he were standing at the other end of a long tunnel. He heard women's voices. Men's voices. Who were they? He didn't know, but something pushed him to try and get in contact with them. Struggling, he saw light at the end of that tunnel. It was very dark where he was standing. He heard a deep, contented purring. Looking down at his side was a black jaguar. The cat rubbed against him and looked up, his yellow eyes large with huge black pupils. The feeling came over Jason to follow him. Moving away, the black jaguar swayed languidly. He had to follow! Somehow, Jason knew he had to follow this powerful, wild animal or die. He didn't want to die!

He felt as if he were wearing huge, oversize

weights on each foot as he willed himself to move toward the light. In fact, he felt so heavy that every step was a gargantuan labor for him to perform. One step at a time. Jason had no sense of time in the dark space he was in, only that it was getting brighter and lighter as he struggled. He felt as though he were imprisoned in deep water, with sunlight dancing off the surface far above him.

The voices became clearer. He could hear low tones of a man and the softer tones of two women. Finally, the light showered around him. He'd made it! He was bathed in it. Feeling lighter, although utterly exhausted, he struggled to open his eyelids. The voices, excited and hushed now, continued around him. He had to pry his eyes open. He had to!

With every effort and what little energy was left within him, he felt them begin to part. As they did, the bright light instantly stunned him. He wanted to shade his eyes but he was too weak to lift his hand. Tears jammed into his eyes in response to the blinding light and he could feel them trickle down the sides of his face. Pain . . . he was aware of a terrible headache throbbing and pulsating like the waves of an ocean beating against a concrete wall within his brain.

Slowly, Jason's eyes adjusted to the light. Now he could see blurred shapes. One was on his right, two on his left. He felt someone's hand enclose his right one. It hurt to move his head, but he did so anyway.

The person on his right was short. As his eyes adjusted, he saw her hair — a shining cape of black around her blurred face. She was holding his hand.

Mouth gummy, Jason thirsted for some water. He opened his lips, but only a rasp came out.

"He's thirsty," Annie whispered, gazing across at his parents. She looked back at Dr. Pointer, who stood to one side of her. "Can we give Jas some water, Doctor?"

"Yes, you may. Mr. Trayhern? You're nearest. Pour your son a glass of water. Very gently slide your arm beneath his head and raise it ever so slightly. Let him suck on the straw."

Morgan did as the doctor instructed. A thrill arced through him as he slid his arm beneath his son's damp neck, below where the bandages encased the rest of his head. Holding him as if he were a little boy once more, a boy he'd never cradled like this, Morgan held the straw to his son's chapped lips. Jason sucked awkwardly several times, until Laura leaned over and held the straw steady. Instantly, Jason began to drink, and soon the water was gone. Joy flooded through Morgan and he gave his wife a tender look of thanks, then glanced back at the doctor. "Can he have more?"

Pointer smiled. "All he wants. This is a very promising sign. His motor reflexes are looking good."

"Thank God," Laura whispered, clasping her hands before her. Already, she could see the color returning to Jason's face. Her heart swelled with emotion as Morgan handled his son with loving gentleness, giving him a second glass of water.

Jason felt the man's arm slip from beneath his neck, and he missed the contact instantly. But the water tasted so good. . . . Moving his lips, he whispered, "Thanks. . . ." It took him a good minute to get the word out. What was wrong with him? He knew what he wanted to say, but the words seemed stuck in his brain.

Over the next hour, his vision began to improve markedly. No longer were the faces surrounding him blurry. As he lay there, most of his attention was fixed on the black-haired woman. She looked anxious, and nervously held his hand. Worry was clearly written across her beautiful copper features. What he liked most were her luminous gold-brown eyes. They were so large, and burning with such tenderness, that Jason found himself mesmerized by them. A part of him simply wanted to drown within them and let the rest of the world go away.

Then another man moved closer to the bed. "Jason, I'm Dr. Pointer," he said very slowly, enunciating his words clearly. "I'm your doctor. I'm going to shine a light into your eyes and check your pupils, son. . . ."

Annie watched the doctor. Her heart was pounding with dread, with joy. Jason was alert! He'd drunk water. He'd spoken a word. Outside the ICU, her parents stood and watched, their hands pressed to the glass, their faces anxious and filled with hope.

Pointer quickly flashed a small penlight across each eye. Straightening, he murmured, "Good. Your pupils are reacting normally. That's a *very* good sign." Tucking the light into a pocket of the white coat he wore, he held up his hand.

"How many fingers do you see?"

Jason stared up at the doctor's lean, long fingers. Struggling for long moments before the word would come out, he rasped, "One."

"Excellent!" Pointer picked up Jason's left hand. "Now I want you to squeeze my hand as hard as you can."

Jason fixed all his attention on the hand holding his. It took a huge effort to make his fingers work, but they did.

"Good," Pointer murmured. "Not bad for a first try, son."

Pointer looked around at the others. "He's responding very well, considering everything. He's got reflexes and his pupils react. We're making progress. Let me check his right hand."

Annie used her feet to push the wheelchair back so the doctor could get near the bed and test Jason's reflexes. Holding her breath, she saw that, again, Jason could slightly squeeze the doctor's fingers. Hope arced brightly in her. She wanted to cry. She wanted to give an Apache victory whoop, but it wasn't the right place or circumstances to cut loose with that kind of joyful ululation. Instead, she grinned widely and thrust her thumb upward to denote victory to her parents, who looked on from outside the cubicle. They smiled back.

Pointer smiled paternally and patted his patient's shoulder. He took time to explain to Jason where he was, what had happened and how long he'd been here. Then he asked Jason if he understood.

"Y-yes . . ."

"Good, son. Listen, you have some people here who love you very much. I'm going to give them ten minutes with you, and then let you rest. You've done a lot in a little time. I know you're tired."

Pointer moved to the door. "Don't overstay, folks. He's about ready to go to sleep on you. Right now, he needs a lot of rest."

"Of course," Laura whispered, unable to keep the joy out of her voice. Heart pounding, she moved to Jason's bedside. Morgan's hand came to rest on her shoulder as she leaned over and picked up Jason's fingers.

"It's so good to have you back, honey," she whispered, looking into Jason's dulled blue eyes. "We love you so much. . . . And it's so good to have you back with us!"

Confusion filled his mind. He stared at the blond-haired woman, who had tears in her eyes. Searching her face, he frowned slightly. "W-who are you?"

Annie's eyes widened. Gasping, she pressed her hand against her lips. Laura recoiled, shock in her face. Morgan scowled. They both looked at Annie, then at one another. Annie saw the dismay in their eyes, in the grim line of their lips. Jason didn't recognize his mom.

Maybe it was a mistake. Annie stared disbelievingly at Jason, who appeared genuinely confused. Her heart broke with compassion for him. It had to be the TBI. Her mother had said he might not remember. . . . A cold fear washed through Annie. Choking down a sob, she saw Laura wrestling with the realization. What would it be like to have your child suddenly not recognize you? Annie's heart bled for her.

Gulping hard, Laura took a deep breath. She tried to calm herself. This couldn't be happening. No, Jason *must* recognize her! Dr. Pointer had warned that he could have amnesia, but Laura didn't want to even consider that possibility. She'd seen what it had done to Morgan and his life. For nearly a decade after his own trauma, he'd had amnesia, not remembering who he was, and worse, that he had a family who deeply loved him and had no idea where he was. They'd hung in limbo for a whole decade while Morgan was "missing" — in reality enlisted in the French Foreign Legion under another identity.

Grappling with her panic, Laura moved closer and looked down into Jason's half-closed eyes. "Jason, I'm your mother. Laura Trayhern. You're our firstborn son. We love you so much. . . ." She tried to sound up-beat, but she felt fear strike at her as she noted his confused expression before his eye-lids closed. His mouth worked, but no whispered words came forth. Clenching his hand, Laura felt an ache build deep within her heart and soul. No, this couldn't be happening! Jason *had* to remember her. Remember his family. *Oh, God, please don't do this to us again!* Gripping his hand, she kissed the back of it. "Darling, I'm your mother. Please try to remember me?"

Blinking, Jason opened his eyes again and studied the blond woman. Fatigue lapped at him. He heard the raw desperation in her voice, and felt bad for her, but he truly didn't recognize her. "I don't know you. . . ." he said huskily. "And I don't know who *I* am. . . ."

Annie moved forward, fear eating at her. She watched as Laura straightened and

233

looked toward Morgan, her face filled with anguish. Picking up Jason's other hand, Annie got his limited attention.

"You're Jason Trayhern," she told him quietly. "You're Morgan and Laura Trayhern's firstborn son."

Closing his eyes once more, Jason felt the weight of tiredness sweeping through him. He'd seen fear in the faces of everyone surrounding his bed. "I — don't know any of you. . . ."

Annie squelched a cry as she saw him close his eyes. His fingers grew limp within hers. There was no connection. None.

Shock warred with grief within her chest. Jason didn't know her. Oh, Great Spirit, how could this be happening? How? They all watched as he fell into a deep sleep, his lips parting and his breathing growing shallow once more. But despite his peaceful state, it felt as if a bomb had struck the ICU cubicle.

Morgan gently squeezed Laura's tense shoulders as she clung to Jason's hand and stared down disbelievingly at her sleeping son.

"Dr. Pointer said many things could happen, darling. Jason doesn't know us now . . . but he may later." Morgan looked across the bed at Annie. He could see she was heartbroken, just as they were, her gaze riveted on Jason, her hands clenched in her lap.

"Listen, we need to get up to speed about TBI." Morgan heard his voice shaking. He swallowed hard and looked down at his feet while he struggled with the mass of emotions writhing within him. Looking up, he pinned Laura and Annie with a firm gaze. "Dr. Pointer said it would be a rough road for us, and we didn't understand until now what he meant. We need counseling, and fast, so we can help Jason get his memory back. I'll make an appointment with the TBI counseling unit here at Landstuhl. We aren't going home empty-handed. We're going to know what we're up against and how best to help Jason recover."

Annie pressed her hand against her eyes, afraid she was going to cry. "He doesn't remember what we had . . . how much we loved one another. . . ."

"I know," Morgan whispered, his heart shattering for Annie. "Listen to me, young lady, this isn't over by a long shot. Trayherns aren't known to be quitters. The old saying that when the going gets tough, the tough get going fits our family. We'll do whatever we have to do to get Jason brought home to us — to all of us."

Looking up, Annie whispered, "What do you mean, sir?"

Laura smiled gently and stroked her sleeping son's cheek. "Annie, it's obvious to us that you and Jason loved one another very much," she said unsteadily. "Morgan's working with the Army right now to see about getting both of you flown to Anaconda, Montana. There's a Veterans Administration hospital there. You'll be near where we live. We can take care of both of you, if you want. . . ."

Two shocks in one day were nearly too much for Annie to cope with. She used to be able to handle the world with no problem, but since her injury, she felt terribly unstable and vulnerable emotionally. The nurses had told her it was because of the trauma she'd survived. Little things often made her cry, and ordinarily, she would never be so prone to tears. Staring at them, seeing the suffering in their faces, she quavered, "You'd do that? You'd let me stay with Jason?"

"Of course," Morgan answered promptly. "If Jason doesn't get his memory back on his own, then the people who love him may be able to pull it out of him. You're the person he was closest to, Annie, besides my wife. We want you there, if you want to be there with him."

"Well, sure . . ." Annie's head spun with questions. She saw her parents watching raptly through the glass panel. She wondered how they would feel if she went home with Jason instead of them.

Morgan held up his hand. "One step at a time, Annie. Your parents are in favor of it, too, in case you want to know. We talked to them about the possibility yesterday, after the briefing Dr. Pointer gave us on the possible ramifications of TBI and what might be necessary for Jason's recovery."

Hope flared Annie's heart, though she felt raw and unprepared in a world suddenly gone mad. Only her love for Jason kept her from feeling as if she was spinning completely out of control. Suddenly, her stable world had been upended in a way she'd never fathomed, and she was being hurled into chaos, with no control over her actions or decisions. Staring into Morgan's dark blue eyes, which reminded her so much of Jason's, she whispered, "Yes, sir, I'd like that, like anything you can do. . . . I just want to be with him. With Jason."

Chapter 12

It was snowing again and Jason felt incredibly depressed. As he stared out the window at the snowy landscape of Anaconda, his head ached. When didn't it? Only morphine-derivative drugs could partially dull that bursting sensation in the left side of his head. Mouth twisting, he watched the thick white snowflakes twirl downward from the gunmetal-gray sky.

Bracing a hand against the wall to steady himself, he stood before the window. Though he was dressed in his blue pajamas, a thick, fleecy robe and warm sheepskin slippers, he still felt a bit of a chill. And why wouldn't he? He'd lost twenty pounds in the last four weeks, the doctors had said. For the first two weeks since he'd become conscious, Jason had been bed-bound in Germany. Being transferred to the George C. Marshal Veterans Hospital in Montana had been a godsend to him. His neurologist, Dr. Susan Dorf, told him that getting out of bed would be good for him. She said it would help lift the dark mood he was always in. To a degree, it had.

Jason scowled at the wheelchair beside him. He hated having to rely on it. He wanted to walk on his own and not depend on some contraption to get him around. But every time he stood, dizziness assailed him. Still, something drove Jason to stand every chance he had instead of getting right in the damn wheelchair. Oh, he was careful not to fall. He was sure that if one of the medical orderlies caught him standing like this, all hell would break loose. They rarely came to his private room unless it was time for him to take his meds, which wouldn't be for another half hour, when lunch arrived.

Though he felt a little better because he was able to stand, his mood wasn't any lighter.

The door quietly opened and closed.

Jason knew better than to try and turn around in a hurry; the vertigo would nail him and he'd pitch forward on his face. He slowly turned, his hand on the wall to steady himself. It was Annie Dazen. She stood there bundled up in her Pendleton coat of blue-and-green plaid, her left arm in a movable cast.

"You know, if the orderlies catch you standing . . ."

"Yeah, I know. What are they going to do? Beat me in the head? Make a second hole?" He lifted his hand, pointing at his heavily bandaged skull. The hole was still there, but a clean bandage was placed over it daily. Sometime in the future, Dr. Dorf said, when he was much improved, they'd perform a bone graft to patch it closed.

Laughing, she said, "No, I don't think so, Jason." She wriggled out of her wool coat. It was awkward with her left arm still in the cast, and she was glad it was due to come off shortly.

Giving her a sour smile, Jason watched her remove the coat and place it and her red neck scarf on a hook. "I'm jealous, you know."

Running her fingers through her long black hair to tame it into place, she grinned wickedly and picked up the sack she'd brought. Every time she saw Jason, her heart opened with such a fierce love for him that Annie had to watch carefully what she said. "Of what?" How tough it was to be "just friends" with Jason. Every day, she hoped that he'd remember his love of her and her love for him. As of now, all Jason knew was that they'd flown together in Afghanistan, and he was her copilot, nothing more. "What are you jealous of?" she asked.

"You. For getting out of this place. I miss you coming in at all hours to see me."

Annie halted by his bed, the covers of which were strewn about haphazardly. "Hey, I got my freedom yesterday, Cowboy." Damn! She'd slipped. Frowning, she opened the sack, studying the contents with more interest than she felt. Would Jason wonder at her nickname for him? She hoped not. She didn't want to confuse him.

"Cowboy?"

"Er . . . yes . . ."

"Am I a cowboy, too?" he wondered. Turning, he flattened his back against the wall so he wouldn't fall. Annie's cheeks were flushed, her hair deliciously mussed. For some reason, he felt a powerful familiarity with her. He didn't understand why, yet his heart always lifted when she came for a visit. And it always sank when she left. Yesterday she had been released from the hospital. Now she had a small apartment two blocks away, and a car that Morgan had leased for her.

"Well . . ." Annie hesitated, pulling out a small carton from the brown paper sack. "It's a euphemism, a slang word. Army aviators all have handles, or nicknames. I always called you Cowboy." It wasn't the whole truth, Annie knew. The word to her was an endearment — much more than just a military nickname, that's for sure. But Jason couldn't know that. She hoped he would accept the explanation. Day by day, his wit, his ability to speak, to use words, was improving remarkably. And that was good. Annie wanted the old Jason back, but the truth was, he was different. Not bad different, just not himself. He seemed more open. More vulnerable.

Without his defenses in place.

Lifting her head, she said, "Come over here, I got you lunch. A McDonald's burger, fries and a chocolate milkshake." She smiled at him. "They were your favorites before you got hit in the head, Jason."

"They were?" He looked at her wide golden eyes, and realized how happy he was to see her today. Since they'd arrived at the VA hospital, Annie had visited him often every day. When she was released yesterday, the frequent visits had ceased, much to his frustration. Having Annie nearby lifted his spirits. He always felt better when she was around.

"Yeah. You used to bitch to me about how you wished you had some of this greasy, fattening food over in Kandahar. That's what you missed most — junk food." She chuckled. Secretly, Annie hoped the food would pry loose an old memory in Jason. Dr. Dorf had told them to ply him with what he was used to before the TBI in hopes it would jog his memories to life once more.

Jason snorted softly. "I have exactly four weeks of memory, you know, and the nurse that comes around to give me food never put this stuff on my menu."

"Well, tell you what, Cowboy, if you don't like this, I'll eat it myself, okay?" Annie's grin grew wider as she approached Jason. "Come on, I'll help you get back into your wheels. . . ." And she maneuvered the chair around so he could sit down.

"I hate this thing."

"I know."

Carefully turning, Jason gripped first one chair arm and then the other. He knew better than to sink down with a plop. His head would explode with such pain that he would want to curl into a fetal position and moan. "I keep pestering Dr. Dorf about getting out of here. I feel like a trapped animal."

Although her arm was healing, Annie had to be careful how she used it. The doctors said she had two more weeks before the bones would be knit completely. And then she could get rid of the cast once and for all. Still, she could use her good arm and her body weight to wrestle the wheelchair around with Jason in it. Pushing him to the side of the bed where he could reach the food cartons she'd laid out, she said, "I think that might happen soon. Go ahead, eat. . . ." She set the brake on the wheel for him.

"What about you?" he asked, unwrapping the paper from around the burger. It smelled incredibly good.

"I already ate. A salad, by the way. Not this junk food stuff." She chuckled, sitting on the bed. With interest, she watched Jason's physical efforts. Every day his dexterity improved a little. That was good. At first, he could barely hold a cup or wrap his fingers around a fork or spoon.

She pushed her hair away from her face, feeling glad to be dressed in regular clothes once more. The wool sweater and jeans she wore today made her feel human again. Grinning, she watched as Jason wolfed the food down.

"My, my, feed you junk food, Jason, and you'll gain back all that muscle mass you lost. You never dive into food the hospital orderlies give you. . . ." Annie smiled hugely, watching as Jason stuffed more of the salty fries into his mouth. Her heart went out to him. He looked like a vulnerable little boy in that moment, with a few strands of dark hair falling over his broad brow, and his blue eyes gleaming with humor.

"This *is* good," he murmured around a bite of food.

"Jason, slow down. You're not supposed to talk when your mouth's full."

He cocked his head. "Why not?"

"It's bad manners," she told him. Annie had been surprised that Jason seemed to have forgotten many of the normal social graces. She and his family had been retraining him in this area. She picked up a paper napkin. "Here. Before you eat, you're supposed to put this in your lap."

"Why?" He jammed six more fries in his mouth. The salt tasted incredibly good to him.

"Because in case food falls out of your mouth, it lands on the napkin and not your clothes." She suppressed a smile at the sight of the fries sticking out of his mouth. "And," she said lightly, "you put food *in* your mouth. You don't leave half of it hanging out like you're doing. Okay?"

Shrugging, Jason poked the errant fries into his mouth.

The room was warm. Annie saw that the television was off. "You were standing at the window, Jason. What were you doing?"

He bit into the second burger, ketchup oozing out one corner of his mouth. "I told you, I feel like a trapped animal. I want to go outside. I really need to feel the weather. I like the snow. . . ."

Leaning over, she picked up his napkin and wiped the ketchup from his mouth. A mouth she had kissed only once before. A mouth that had ravished hers in return, sent her soaring into a rainbow-filled world of joy, heat and love. Her hand hesitated fractionally near his lips, then she gave them a second gentle swipe.

"If food comes out on your mouth or chin, you have to wipe it away, Jason. You never leave it there."

"Okay . . . ." Her touch was gentle, and heat purled in his lower body. Stymied by that sensation, he frowned as Annie put the napkin back on his lap. What *was* it abou her? She made him feel good. So good. And happy. Only Annie was able to lift the awful gray cloud that enveloped him twenty-four hours a day. She was his sunshine.

Annie straightened. "So, you like the snow. Do you have a memory of that?"

"No . . . it's just . . . I want to feel what it's like to be outside. I *need* it, Annie. I feel like I'm dying in this hot, stuffy room."

"I see. . . ."

"I wish I could remember." Jason stared up at her. "I wish . . . God, I wish so much I could remember. . . ."

"This is progress," Annie murmured sympathetically, gesturing to the window. "You like the great outdoors. You like fresh air. See? You didn't know that before, Jason."

"It's not coming fast enough," he growled, finishing off the last of the fries.

Annie sat there, hands in her lap. "Well, there are some nice surprises heading your way. I met Dr. Dorf in the elevator when I was coming up here. She says it's time for you to start physical therapy. They've got you slated to do some stretching exercises down in their gym this afternoon."

His brows rose. "Yeah?"

For a moment, when she saw the look that came to his blue eyes, she recognized the old Jason. Annie's mouth lifted. "Yeah." Usually, the expression in his eyes wasn't quite right. Sometimes Annie saw Jason "home" in his body, but a moment later he was gone again. His eyes no longer held that devilish spark of biting humor he'd had before, that playful, teasing glint. How badly Annie wanted him to come back, to return to his body, to stay here and be truly home once more.

"What are you wearing under your sweater?" he asked, gesturing to the bulky outline he could see around her neck.

Annie smiled. "My necklace," she murmured, her hand coming to rest against her sweater.

"Can I see it?" he asked, picking up his napkin and dutifully wiping his mouth.

"Sure. Hold on. . . ." Annie tugged open the front of her sweater and gently withdrew the necklace, allowing it to come to rest again between her breasts. She slid off the bed and came up to Jason, leaning down so he could see it. She noticed his eyes suddenly focus on the carved figure of the woman's head enclosed by the snowy owl's wings. Would he remember that? She prayed so. Her hands on her thighs, Annie leaned patiently forward while he studied it.

Sometimes Jason would suddenly, obsessively, hone in on an object and stare at it for minutes at a time. Annie knew that that was a TBI symptom. Now Jason seemed transfixed by the carving. He lifted his hand, touching it very carefully with his index finger.

Annie held her breath. They were so close! She shut her eyes, absorbing his nearness. It was all she had — unexpected moments like this, which were gifts to her. She felt him touch the necklace lightly, as if it were a fragile egg that might break if too much pressure were brought to bear upon it. Opening her eyes, Annie watched as he used his thumb and index finger to feel its smooth quality. Mammoth tusk, Annie had discovered, had a warm, buttery smoothness, unlike any other animal tusk she'd ever held.

"What is it, Jason?" she asked, not daring to hope that he might remember their many conversations, the story of the necklace.

"I — don't . . . Wait, I *know* this necklace, Annie! I know I do!" Jason closed his eyes and saw the necklace. Annie was wearing it. "I see you. . . ." He compressed his lips, his brows dipping as he fought to hold on to the fleeting image. Oh! It was gone! Frustrated, he opened his eyes. "I saw you wearing it."

A thread of joy flowed through her. Tears came to her eyes as she heard his voice go suddenly raspy. "Tell me what you saw?" She held her breath.

"You were wearing a lavender top." He smiled briefly. "You looked beautiful. . . ."

Gasping, Annie whispered, "Yes! Yes, I did! Do you remember where, Jason?"

"N-no . . . it happened so fast. I had this feeling of knowing the necklace, and then I

248

felt this . . . thing come into my head. I felt pressure, as if I was being pulled from a very deep, dark place . . . and then I saw this flash of you sitting somewhere. Your hair was down like it is now, and the necklace was around your neck." He frowned and tried to remember more. "You were wearing something else. Earrings . . . but I can't remember them exactly. . . ."

"Yes, yes, you know this, Jason." With a small cry, Annie spontaneously threw her good arm around him and gave him a careful hug. Not wanting to release him, but knowing she must, she leaned back and smiled at him. He seemed pleased with the contact, but his gaze was still fixed on the piece of jewelry she wore. "We were at a restaurant. I wore it that night I went to dinner with you. Do you remember what we ate?"

"No . . . just you sitting there," he murmured, gazing at the piece.

"Still, this is wonderful, Jason! Your first memory. Oh! Your family is going to be so excited to hear it!"

He continued to touch the necklace. The pendant was warm and smooth between his fingers. Annie was so close that he could smell the scent of sweet sage in her hair. Inhaling her feminine fragrance, he saw tears glimmer in her eyes.

"Why are you crying?"

The old Jason would never have asked such

a question, Annie realized. The new Jason, the man who had no defenses, would. She met Jason's darkening eyes and drowned in them. So close. Oh, he was just inches from her mouth. How badly Annie yearned to press her lips to his, to feel his mouth cling hotly to hers, the heat they generated boiling and scalding between them. . . .

"Because you remembered something, Jason," she said throatily. "You remember us. That night we shared a dinner together at Fort Campbell, Kentucky. We'd gone there to celebrate you making warrant officer two."

Studying the pendant he held, Jason said, "But this necklace is familiar in another way to me, Annie, and I can't place it. . . . I'm trying, but my mind feels like it's stuck in concrete. It means something else to me. . . ."

"It's from our past," she agreed softly, stopping herself from reaching out and gently grazing his cheek. "Just holding it is sparking another old memory of yours." Joy bubbled through Annie. Pushing back the tears, she gulped and remained very still.

Jason released the mammoth carving and slowly moved his fingers upward to trace the large double strand of tourmaline beads she wore. Her skin beneath her sweater reacted wildly to his brief touch as his fingertips lightly traced the stones. He was exploring, trying to remember. She saw it in his furrowed brow. Was the necklace healing him? Annie knew it could. His touch wasn't intimate, man to woman; he was like a child exploring his new world, and the necklace was the center of it right now.

"How about if I take it off and you hold it? Maybe by touching it more, you might have another memory come back."

There was something so right about touching Annie, even accidentally, Jason realized, gently tracing each translucent tourmaline gemstone. The colors — pink, green and blue — enthralled him. Reluctantly, he pulled his hand away and said, "I like touching you, Annie. You feel good to me."

Her heart clenched. As Annie slowly straightened, her feelings soared. She ached for Jason. Fumbling for the clasp, she whispered, "I hope someday you remember what we shared, Jason. . . ."

Studying her face beneath the fluorescent lights, he saw the anguish banked in her half-closed eyes. He saw the corners of that delicious mouth drawing in with what could only be described as pain. Jason felt guilty, because he didn't want to hurt Annie. He didn't want to hurt the people who said they were his family, but how could he not? There wasn't an hour that went by when he didn't wish he could remember them, to ease the suffering he always saw in their eyes no matter how hard they tried to hide it from him.

Annie took the necklace off and carefully placed it in his hands. "You said we were friends?" Jason saw the struggle in Annie's broad face as she sat back on the bed, her legs dangling over the side.

"Yes. Good friends. We liked one another." *A lot*. But she didn't stay that.

"I see," Jason murmured, reflecting upon the double-strand necklace now draped across his palm. "I like this necklace, Annie. It feels good to me."

"It is very special," she murmured.

"Yes . . ." Jason gently rubbed the beads. "It feels . . . warm. Maybe because it was against your skin."

"Maybe," Annie murmured, watching Jason become lost within the beauty of the necklace. She prayed to the Great Spirit to let the healing powers of the stones reach him. Annie had no way of knowing *what* the necklace would or would not do. There were stories from the past that her mother had verbally passed on to her. But Annie wasn't a trained medicine woman, so maybe the necklace wouldn't work with her. She simply didn't know. But as she watched Jason slowly turn it around and around, then hold it up to the light to look through the glimmering gemstones like a child mesmerized by its beauty, her heart lifted unaccountably.

"It's so pretty," Jason murmured. He curled the necklace into one of his palms and placed his other one over it, then closed his eyes.

Annie could barely breathe. Jason ordinarily had very wan looking flesh. Now she could see a glimmer of his former ruddiness returning. Sitting up, her hands clasped against her heart, she began to feel hope. And Annie prayed.

For ten minutes, Jason sat with his eyes closed, simply holding the necklace between his large, square hands. As he did so, Annie saw his face gradually lose its tension. His well-shaped mouth softened. She knew he often had blinding headaches. He had a low-grade one all the time, so the corners of his mouth were continually pinched inward. Now they relaxed.

Annie barely breathed, not wanting to break the tender silence that swirled between them. She hoped no orderly would burst in and break the spell.

With a long, ragged sigh, Jason finally opened his eyes. He saw Annie watching him intently, and he smiled. "I'm really tired. I need to sleep. . . ."

Sliding off the bed, Annie murmured, "That's fine, Jason. You just ate lunch." She quickly pulled the covers back and smoothed the white sheet for him. Turning, she saw him slowly reach out with his left hand, grip the bed and try to stand. Moving quickly, Annie grasped his elbow to help steady him.

"Take it easy, Jason. . . ."

"I know, I know. . . ." He took mincing steps to his bed, then lay down and stretched out on his back, the necklace in his hand, draped across his stomach.

Annie adjusted the covers. She wasn't going to try and get him out of his robe or slippers. When she turned around, his eyes were already shut, his mouth slackening in sleep. Surprised, she stood there, uncertain. His hand had slipped off his belly, the necklace still wrapped in his fingers.

Tears flooded her eyes. Annie sniffed and quietly backed away after making sure the wheelchair was nearby in case he needed it when he woke. What had just transpired? Though she was uncertain, Annie did know that was not common behavior on Jason's part. Usually he had trouble sleeping and was unable to get the deep, healing rest he really needed. In the last two weeks here at the hospital, he never slept at noontime.

As she tiptoed toward the hook that held her coat and muffler, Annie wondered if the necklace had given him peace. Peace to sleep. Moving to the door, she quietly opened it so it wouldn't waken Jason. His sleep was so light that he often came to with a start, sometimes even shouting. Dr. Dorf said he had classic post-traumatic stress disorder symptoms, and restless sleep was one of them.

Compressing her lips, Annie headed out the door. Let Jason hold on to the necklace. It would never hurt him; it could only help. Once out in the shiny green-and-white-tiled hall, she looked toward the nursing station at the other end. She headed in that direction, wanting to tell the nurses not to disturb Jason, that he was sleeping. She'd tell them about the necklace, too, in case they didn't realize it was hers and that she'd given it to him.

As Annie finished speaking with the head nurse, she heard Laura's voice drifting from the elevators. Turning, she saw Jason's mother, her arms loaded with photograph albums. With her were Pete and Kelly, her twins. They were all joking and smiling as they walked toward Annie.

Hope burned in her breast. Dr. Dorf had been a guardian angel to them. A Navy commander on the neurology staff at the hospital, she'd had a family meeting with all of them a week ago, and had urged the Trayherns to bring in photo albums to show to Jason. By telling him stories of his past, Dr. Dorf hoped, they might jog his injured brain and release all those buried memories.

Annie found her heart expanding with happiness now as she saw the Trayherns. The twins were juniors in high school. Kelly had dyed her spiky hair bright red, and her gra eyes shone as she walked confidently in h long wool coat beside her mother. Pete, dark-haired and also gray-eyed, wore grunge look, his jeans hanging midhip, with the ends flopping over his running shoes. He wore a baseball cap backward, the bill brushing the nape of his neck.

Laura's face lit up with pleasure when she spotted Annie. More than anything, Annie wanted to share the good news with them — Jason's first memory! They could leave the photo albums here, and the nurses would put them in his room after he woke. Yes, she had some good news for them — finally.

Chapter 13

Morgan nervously wiped his hand down his pinstripe suit as he walked out of the elevator at the veterans' hospital. Under his arm he carried a very special photo album — one devoted entirely to Jason's growing up years. Heart beating with dread and anxiety, Morgan tried to quell his terror. Ahead, he could see the busy nurses' station. There seemed to be a lot of activity for 11:00 a.m., but then, it was nearly lunchtime.

Running his finger beneath the collar of his white silk shirt to loosen his tie, he felt a trickle of sweat on his right temple. Grimacing, he quickly wiped it away. He didn't want his son to see him sweating bullets. Morgan moved forward at a slow pace, not his normal brisk one. Jason's private room was near the nurses' station, and Morgan was in no hurry to get there.

For nearly two decades he and his firstborn son had been detached, disconnected from one another. Rubbing his chest over his heart, Morgan took a deep breath, then opened the button on his gray pinstripe jacket. He'd dreaded this moment ever si he'd heard the doctor tell them, as a family, that the best way to jog Jason's memory was to show him pictures and tell him the stories behind each one.

For the last two weeks Jason had slowly but continually improved, and now Dr. Dorf had given the go-ahead to start teasing old memories out of him. Before, Jason had needed lots of rest to help him heal from the trauma. Now, he was bored and wanting something to do as his health continued to return. It was a perfect time to snag his attention with photo albums.

Mouth tightening, Morgan tried to get hold of himself. Laura and the twins had been doing all the work, showing Jason the photo albums these past two weeks, and now it was his turn. This was the toughest thing he'd ever done: face a son who no longer responded to or remembered him as a father. To Jason, he was merely a friend, that was all. Though he didn't treat Morgan like his father he also didn't seem to remember the unpleasant past that had haunted both of them.

Maybe that was good, Morgan thought. Maybe this TBI was a chance for him to start all over with Jason, as Laura had said. A new day. A new relationship. Since Jason didn't remember the past that had flowed like toxic waste between them, it was Morgan's opportunity to begin afresh. Laura had urged him to respond to his son as he had with his later three children.

Shaking his head in frustration, Morgan decided that learning how to be a good parent was the hardest damn challenge he'd ever faced. And the price for his inability to be one had been paid by his first two children, unfortunately.

Gripping the album a little tighter in his left hand, Morgan knocked lightly at the green door and then entered.

Jason stood by the window, dressed in a pair of tan chinos, a rainbow-colored wool sweater and his sheepskin slippers. He turned his head and then smiled. "Hello, Morgan."

It felt odd that Jason would call him by his first name, and not "Father," but Morgan had been warned by the doctor this would occur with memory loss.

"Hello, son." Morgan was not going to treat Jason like a friend. He refused to. Jason was his child, memory or not. The doctor had said that was fine, as long as Jason didn't respond negatively to the label, and so far he hadn't. Morgan always thought he saw faint amusement in Jason's blue eyes when he used the term "son," but that was okay. Morgan could live with that far better than if Jason rebelled at him using the term at all.

"Yesterday, it was Laura, Pete and Kelly visiting me. Today I get you. I guess Dr. Dorf told you I was getting bored." Jason allowed his hand to drop away from the venetian blinds he'd been looking through. Sunlight peeked through the broken gray clouds outside, making him feel a tad better.

"Yep, we're on a mission with you, Jason." Morgan laid the hefty leather album down on the unmade bed. He moved over to his son, who was easing himself back into the wheelchair. "How's the dizziness today?"

"Better, actually," Jason said. Morgan leaned over and unlocked the brake, swinging the wheelchair around to move Jason closer to the bed.

"And your headaches?"

"They're better, too. Not so painful. Like someone has turned down the volume." Once the brake was set, Jason got up under his own steam and maneuvered himself onto the bed next to the dark brown leather album.

"That's great," Morgan said. Shedding his coat, he hung it on the hook by the door. Unbuttoning his cuffs, he rolled his sleeves up to his elbows and looked into Jason's face. His son was an alarming thirty pounds underweight. Muscle atrophy had been terrible. Jason had lost twenty in Germany and another ten here. Dr. Dorf said this was normal, but Morgan remained concerned about it. He knew Jason had always been in such good athletic condition from the photos he'd sent home to them. Now he resembled a stick figure. It broke Morgan's heart.

"Yesterday, Annie left her necklace with me." Jason pointed to it lying on the bed stand next to the water pitcher. "I slept with it. This morning when I woke up I felt a lot better."

Nodding, Morgan hitched himself up on the bed. "That's great news." He picked up the album and laid it across Jason's lap. "I think Annie's good for you."

Fingering the first page of the album, Jason nodded. "She always makes me feel better just by being around."

Morgan heard the hesitant tone in his son's softly spoken words, and saw him knit his brow. He knew now that that look of concentration meant Jason was struggling to remember something. Understanding that, Morgan reached out and placed his hand over his son's for a moment. He'd never touched him like that before, and he should have. Children needed to be touched and comforted often by their parents, but he'd found that out too late. They needed to know that they were loved and protected. Now he was being given a second chance, and he wasn't going to blow it. Patting Jason's hand gently, he murmured, "Listen, son, I had a TBI just like you. And I had amnesia for many, many years afterward."

Turning, Jason studied him. "You did?" Astounded by the information, he said, "Cou you tell me about it? You got your mem

261

back, right?" Hope suddenly flared in him.

"I did. It came back spontaneously, off and on over several weeks' time." Morgan pointed to the scar that ran from his temple to his chin. "If you ever doubted you were my son, the fact that we've shared such a trauma and have a scar on the same side our face ought to tell you we at least share a similar history."

"I saw your scar after I woke up. Annie pointed that out to me." Jason tentatively touched the scar on his own cheek. It was healed now, but still a bright pink and hell to shave around. "Like a mark, huh?"

Managing a twisted smile, Morgan said, "Yeah, it's a mark all right. I'm not sure if it's good or bad, son."

Shrugging, Jason felt the man's warmth and interest in him. He wanted to call him Dad, but the word just wouldn't come out of his mouth. The concern radiating from the older man's eyes made Jason feel oddly cared for. Morgan was tall, strong, confident and someone Jason automatically looked up to with great respect. When Morgan had touched his hand, Jason had felt cherished.

"Tell me about your experience, okay?" Jason asked.

"Of course." And Morgan launched into he story, leaving nothing out. It took half an ur to tell all of it. Jason sat there atten-ly, his hands clasped on the photo album.

"The sins of the father visit the son?"

"Maybe," Morgan said, unhappy with the analogy. Jason had been reading voraciously since coming home, and there were many library books in his room, mostly classics. He said reading helped his eyes focus and took his mind off the continual headaches.

"Or a blessing in disguise?" Jason felt bad when he saw how his words impacted on Morgan in a negative way. Pain registered in the man's narrowed eyes.

"I don't know, son. I really don't. The Trayherns are usually a tight-knit family. We fight together, love together and defend our country together."

Opening his hands, Jason studied the album that lay across his lap. Pointing to the first picture, that of a baby wrapped in a blue blanket, he said, "Is that me?"

Relieved to focus on the album, Morgan smiled briefly. "Yeah, that's you. A strapping eight pounds nine ounces. Your mother said she felt as if she were carrying an elephant."

Chuckling, Jason looked at the next photos which showed Morgan standing beside Laura as she held the baby. The pride in Morgan's face was unmistakable. Laura looked tired but happy. Jason supposed the infant in her arms was him. "I obviously can't remember this time."

"No," Morgan said, "of course not. But let's look at when you were six years old. Dr

Dorf said most of us have memories beginning then." He flipped past several pages to find pictures of Jason at that age. "I'll leave this album with you afterward, so you can look at the pictures whenever you want. . . ."

"You're leaving already? Are you short on time?"

"No," Morgan said, lying. He had intended to leave because he had several appointments scheduled back at his office. Before, he'd used Perseus, his supersecret company that supplied mercenaries for global missions, as his excuse to avoid the intimacies of family. He realized he was doing it again, and that was a mistake, judging from the stricken look on Jason's face. Business could wait. Morgan would learn that lesson, or else. He felt heartened that Jason wanted him to stay. His son enjoyed his presence. That alone brought a wave of relief cascading through him.

"Okay, here . . ." Morgan pointed to a color photo of Jason standing by a wide river, fishing rod in hand. "This is you. We lived near Washington, D.C., at that time. I taught you how to fish in the Potomac River."

Studying the photo, Jason saw a young, dark-haired boy grinning proudly, standing on a grassy bank. In the distance was a bridge. Running his fingers across the photo, he murmured, "I like to fish?"

"Yes. Just like me."

"Yeah?"

"I like fly-fishing. My dad, Chase Trayhern, taught me when I was your age, so I wanted to pass that skill on to you when you turned six. Living here in Montana, I find one of my favorite things is to get away from the office and take my rod and tackle out to a little stream north of Phillipsburg. I often bring home fresh trout for dinner. Your mother has become an expert at cooking trout in butter, you know."

"Sounds good," Jason said, almost tasting it. And then he straightened, his voice raising in excitement. "Hey! I remember what trout tastes like!" He sat there, savoring the memory. It had come out of nowhere, but it was real. Jason's lips parted in awe.

Heart beating with joy, Morgan gripped Jason's hand. "Wow, son. That's great!" And it was. He saw the light in Jason's face, the relief in his expression as he digested the tiny, seemingly insignificant memory.

"Trout . . ." Jason closed his eyes, feeling the warmth and strength of Morgan's hand on his. "It tastes sweet . . . and it's flaky and moist. I like it with butter and lemon juice and a little basil on it. . . ." The memory was incredibly joyous to Jason. He felt Morgan's hand tighten around his.

"Yes, you love basil. You throw it on everything. Most kids poured ketchup on their food, but you used basil." Morgan didn't try to disguise the quaver or emotion in his voice.

Jason opened his eyes and turned, a huge smile pulling at his mouth. For the first time, Morgan saw hope in his son's expression. The light of discovery. Of happiness. Without thinking, he released his hand and slid his arm across Jason's shoulders. How thin and fragile he felt as Morgan embraced him gently and quickly.

"This is great," Jason said, finding himself wanting to return Morgan's hug. But he didn't, because he felt a little awkward about suddenly getting personal with him. Still, Jason absorbed the unexpected embrace like sunlight pouring into his cold, dark soul.

As they moved apart, Morgan felt hot tears come to his eyes. He looked away so Jason wouldn't see them. And then he realized he was reverting back to a time when that's what he'd done: hid his feelings from his children.

Lifting his head, Morgan allowed his son to see the tears dribbling down his cheeks. And to his everlasting surprise, he saw tears on Jason's cheeks, as well.

Giving an embarrassed laugh, his son said, "Look at us. Two crybabies. Over what? A fish story?"

Morgan managed a soft smile. "Men do cry sometimes, Jason. We can share our feelings with one another, son."

"I still have no feelings toward you," Jason claimed, wiping his tears away. "I mean, I like you. But . . . well, father to son? It's just not there. . . . I keep hoping it will come back. And I can see you care for me. . . ."

Jason's admission sent another wave of relief through Morgan. He whispered, "I love you very much. But listen, don't worry about not feeling that connection with me. With time, I know in my heart all your memories will return. The one thing I found when I had amnesia was that I couldn't force myself to remember. Just ease off trying so hard. When I had amnesia I learned to live one day at a time. Stay in the present, and trust me, the past will eventually catch up with you. Okay?"

Nodding, Jason said, "That's what I'm trying to do." Sighing, he looked around the room and then back down at the album. "When I see the pain I'm causing you and Laura, as well as my brother and sister, I feel so bad. I wish I could remember. . . ."

"They know and understand that, son. Don't be so hard on yourself. Let's enjoy the little victories like this one. Consider it the first brick of your foundation. There will be more to follow."

Jason trusted Morgan on that because the man had had a similar trauma. Hitching his shoulders, he muttered, "I'd give *anything* to get out of this room. I want to be outdoors, Morgan. I want to walk in the snow. To feel the wind on my face, to breathe the cold air. . . ."

"I have some good news for you, son." Morgan saw Jason twist his head in his direction. "A week from now we're driving you home to Phillipsburg. We own a small cabin twenty miles from our house. It's a summer place for Laura, the kids and me. There's a trout stream nearby, and a hot spring right outside the cabin. It's our getaway place when we've had a tough week. Usually we drive up there on weekends. Right now, Laura is hiring a housekeeper to get it cleaned up and ready for you."

Lifting his eyebrows, Jason said, "Really?"

Hearing the hope, the eagerness in his voice, Morgan grinned. "Really."

Closing his eyes, Jason whispered emotionally, "I so much want to get out of this hospital. . . ."

"I understand that," Morgan chuckled, remembering when he'd been hospitalized in Japan with his own amnesia. He had hated being bedridden.

Opening his eyes, Jason scowled. "What about Annie? She's coming, too, isn't she?"

Morgan heard the little-boy plea in his voice. Dr. Dorf had warned them that a person with TBI could sometimes revert to the immaturity of a child. It was just something that happened, and they'd have to deal with it. "Well . . ."

"She's my best friend, Morgan. You are letting her come along, aren't you?"

He hadn't thought of that angle, and was caught off guard by Jason's emotional overture. "Well, er, sure. But first we'd have to ask Annie about it. . . ."

"I'll ask her," Jason said, feeling triumphant and happy. "I *know* she'll say yes."

Morgan sat there thinking out loud. "The cabin has three bedrooms, so that's not a problem. And it has a full kitchen. There's a fireplace, too. A nice one that will heat the entire home."

"Annie likes the outdoors just as I do," Jason said stubbornly. "She'll want to come. I know she will."

Smiling a little, Morgan said, "I'll find out."

"No, I'll do it."

"Okay . . . sure. No problem." He looked at his watch. It really was time to go. Just then, the door opened and an orderly brought in Jason's lunch. The middle-aged, blond man said hello and placed a tray on the bed stand.

After the orderly left, Morgan asked, "Is Annie coming for a visit today?" He got off the bed, unrolling his sleeves and rebuttoning the cuffs.

Jason looked up at the clock on the wall. "Yes. She said she'd be here this afternoon sometime."

"Good. So talk to her, okay? Your mother will be here at ten tomorrow morning to continue looking at your album with you." Morgan opened the closet and removed his coat, then shrugged it back on. Jason looked relieved — greatly so. Even if his son didn't remember he loved Annie, a part of him still had feelings for her. That must be why he was so vehement and emotional about her coming along to the cabin with him.

Would she? Morgan wasn't sure. And he'd have to let his son find out for himself, although Morgan wanted to go to her now and find out. If Annie said no, it would devastate Jason. And that was the last thing Morgan wanted. He felt highly protective of his son, but knew better than to run interference on this issue with him.

"You haven't used the phone yet," Morgan told him, pointing to the device on the bed stand. "After you talk to Annie, how about you call and let us know her decision?"

Jason looked over at the black phone. Beside it was a list of numbers that Laura had written out for him. Taking the tray of food and setting it on his lap, he said, "Sure, I can do that."

"Good." Morgan went over and placed his hand on his son's shoulder. "I'll see you in a couple of days, Jason. I think we made great progress today."

Grinning, Jason studied the older man's

face, his shoulder tingling where Morgan had squeezed it. Absorbing the man's obvious love for him, he said, "I'll look forward to it. Who knows? Maybe I'll remember something else when you're here."

Morgan murmured, "I sure hope so. I know Dr. Dorf will be thrilled to hear that you remembered your trout and basil."

Laughing shortly, Jason lifted his hand. "Goodbye, Morgan. And thank you — for everything. . . ."

Everything . . . Morgan left the room and walked down the hall, deep in thought. He'd hugged his son today just as he had wanted to so many times in the past. He felt euphoric, as if he were literally walking on air. And he felt a thread of deep satisfaction that he'd never experienced before. Even more importantly, they'd cried together over the memory Jason had had. Such a small thing, and yet so healing and filled with hope.

Morgan remembered that day fishing with Jason. It had been one of the few times he had set aside to spend with his son as he was growing up. Oh, they hadn't caught any fish, but Morgan remembered how much fun they'd had sharing the afternoon together. But after that he hadn't had time for Jason. Why hadn't he made time for his son? Realizing he'd started the disconnection right there by not doing more things with him,

Morgan tasted the bitterness of his bad judgments.

As the elevator doors whooshed open and several medical personnel exited, Morgan waited, remembering the tears he had shed. Tears of joy. Oh, why hadn't he let his children see him cry? Why did he always have to be such an unfeeling bulwark of strength for them? Entering the elevator, Morgan punched the button for the first floor as the doors closed behind him.

Once in the busy lobby, he shrugged on his black wool coat. Sunlight was filtering through the clouds outside and his heart was buoyed with such joy he thought he might die from it. But what a way to go!

Nodding deferentially to those who passed him, he walked with a new confidence out the sliding glass doors. The wind was cold, the sun bright in his eyes. Burying his hands in the pockets of his coat, he headed for the visitors' parking lot beside the massive hospital. The sidewalk was wet with melting snow, the temperature just above freezing. Along the walk he saw the first green shoots of spring: the tips of daffodils. Breathing the cold, crisp air deeply into his lungs, Morgan spotted his black Mercedes-Benz. His son wanted to experience the out-of-doors, and very shortly, he'd have that opportunity.

It felt so good to give Jason something that would make him happy. Because of the past,

272

Morgan felt he had to make up for the pain he'd caused Jason. Before, they'd shared a sullen, bitter relationship, one filled with angst and unhappiness.

As he opened the car door and slid in, Morgan worried, though. What would happen when Jason's memory came back? Would he hold the past against Morgan? Would Jason's old anger sabotage the new relationship Morgan was so desperately trying to build with his son? Would he have the chance to right the wrongs he'd done to Jason by being a negligent parent?

As he turned the key in the ignition, the motor purred to life. Morgan sat there for a moment, his hands resting on the wheel. Dr. Dorf knew that their relationship had been fraught with anger and distrust. She knew of Morgan's abandonment of his son. And what she'd said to him haunted Morgan daily, at work and at home.

"You have a second chance here, Mr. Trayhern. Your son doesn't remember your checkered past together. Sometimes amnesia is like a gift of sorts. It wipes the slate clean. If you can forge a new and more positive relationship with him now, there's every hope that when his old memories do return, he will remember *both*. And if you're able to create a happier relationship with him now, then he has a choice to make. What that choice will be, I don't know. But at least you have a chance to rescue your son, and let him know you love him and that you aren't abandoning him now, in his hour of need."

With a grimace, Morgan thought of Annie, hoping she, too, wouldn't abandon Jason in his hour of need. He knew she had already spent so much time away from her own family. He only hoped that she would stay with Jason a little longer. . . .

Chapter 14

"Annie!" Jason couldn't contain his eagerness as she entered his hospital room. Today her hair was arranged in braids woven with red ribbons. The white mock-turtleneck sweater she wore showed off her copper skin and emphasized her huge, slightly tilted golden eyes, which shone with joy when he called her name.

"Hey, Jas! Sorry I'm late." She laughed and pointed to the left side of her face. "I had to visit the dentist. One of my fillings came off last night when I was eating a piece of pizza." Shedding her plaid Pendleton coat, she tossed it on the end of the bed and rubbed her hands against her dark blue Levi's. "So I had to find a dentist in a hurry. Luckily, I found one who would see me late this morning, and my tooth is fixed now."

"I've been waiting for you."

Smiling tenderly, Annie couldn't stop the huge avalanche of feelings that always came with seeing Jason. She fell more and more in love with him every day. What was she to do? Though she felt like a puppet in Jason's hands, she bore him no ill will. Dr. Dorf

275

didn't think it was a good idea for him to know that they had loved one another, and Annie agreed. The doctor felt he was strained to his fragile emotional limits.

She came around the bed and gave his shoulder a playful tap. "So what have you been up to?" She had had her cast removed this week and was feeling up to speed again.

Laughing, Jason patted the spot next to him on the bed. "Sit here? With me?"

Raising her eyebrows, Annie stood in front of him, her arms crossed. "I dunno, Jas. You've got a glint in your eye, as if you're up to something. . . ." She could sense his ebullience from the light in his eyes and the way the corners of his mouth were lifting. Jason rarely smiled. He seldom laughed, but right now he seemed like a wriggly child with some huge secret he could barely contain. What had happened?

"Did you get some memories back?" Annie asked, letting her arms fall at her sides. Oh, she hoped so! How handsome Jason looked today. The pink scar on the side of his face was slowly losing its color. It would never fully go away, but would remain a constant reminder of that terrible moment in his life. Jason was filling out, however, and every day looked more like the man she'd loved before he'd been wounded.

"Yes . . . I did! Morgan came and he showed me this." Jason pointed to the photo album on the bed stand. Words tumbled out of his mouth as he breathlessly related how he had remembered what trout tasted like and the fact that he loved basil on his food. When Annie's eyes lit up, he smiled. "You look so pretty when you smile," he told her.

Annie stopped herself from reaching out to touch him, though she ached to do just that. Her lips twisted and she drowned in his alert gaze. Today, Jason seemed the best he'd been since becoming conscious. "Thank you, kind sir. You don't look half-bad yourself. I think this is the first time I've seen you smile since Afghanistan."

Pushing the strands of hair that dipped over his brow back into place, Jason shrugged. "I wish I knew what I was like then, Annie."

"Every day we're showing you a little more of your past," she said gently, sitting down next to him. Annie was careful to keep a comfortable distance between them. She wanted to snuggle in Jason's arms, feel his breath against her face as he held her and kissed her brows, her hair, her cheek. . . . Annie forced herself to stop remembering how well Jason kissed, his mouth so strong and confident sliding across hers that one time.

"I know. You help me so **much**."

Grinning, Annie patted his **hand**, which lay on his thigh. "Your dad **made the** breakthrough with you, Jason, not me."

"Yes . . . that's true. But you make me feel hope, Annie. No one else does that but you. . . ." Jason held her startled gaze. He turned completely toward her, his knee against her long, curved thigh. Grasping her hand, he pressed it between his, though it took all his courage to do so. Something unknown was driving him to touch her. Jason didn't understand it, but he was feeling so driven by this desire that he acquiesced to the feeling.

"Annie, I have news so important to me that if I don't tell you, I'm going to burst." He smiled nervously and skimmed his fingers back and forth across the top of her hand. Her skin was dark compared to his. He loved the color, that copper-red tone, because it reminded him of the fertile red earth. Annie was of the earth, Jason sensed, although he didn't remember anything specific about her background. He simply knew, without understanding how he did so.

"What is it, Jason? What do you want to share with me?" Annie held her breath for a moment as he cradled her hand between his own. Nervously, he licked his lower lip, his gaze skittering from one side of her face to the other, not quite meeting her eyes. Jason hadn't touched her since the incident. How should she interpret this gesture? Was it one of intimacy? Friend to friend?

Unsure, Annie found her heart aching because she wanted to slide her arms around Jason and hold him. Just hold him and allow her love to saturate him in silence as they clung to one another. That was a dream she had several times a week. Annie would wake up crying, and then she'd curl up into a fetal position and hold herself as she felt the loss of Jason's love.

"I'm afraid, Annie." Jason feared his heart would burst. What if she said no? He couldn't imagine his life without her in it.

Reaching out, Annie gently curved her hand against his scarred cheek. "Whatever it is, we'll handle it together, Jason." She saw the terror in his eyes. His brow was beading with droplets of moisture. Never had Annie seen him so agitated as now. Dr. Dorf had warned them that Jason could become very dramatic and overemotional about certain events. Tensely, she said, "Tell me, Jason. Just tell me. . . ."

He hung his head. Annie's hand was warm between his. Just touching her gave him a sense of renewed stability. Frightened, he forced himself to look at her. "I need you to come with me, Annie."

"Where are we going?" Her tone was teasing, though she saw the frantic, panicked look in Jason's blue eyes as he wrestled with his words. Whenever he got excited, he had to struggle to talk coherently. "Just take your time, Jas. Breathe deep. . . . Take some deep breaths. . . . There you go. Now a few more . . ."

Fear ate at him as he drew a final deep breath. Clinging to her hand, he whispered, "Come home with me, Annie. Please? I know I don't always do things right, and my words come out wrong . . . but I *need* you. I don't want to go home without you. Please say you'll come with me?" He gave her a beseeching look, his voice breaking with emotion.

Frowning, Annie stared at him. Jason's hand was strong and firm around hers. She placed her other one on top of his. "Go home with you? What home are you talking about, Jason?"

"Morgan told me today that I was going home soon. He said there's a cabin twenty miles away from their home. Laura is getting it fixed up for me." Absorbing the shock in her widening eyes, more fear stabbed at Jason. "It's a large cabin, Annie. Big enough for both of us. I told Morgan I wanted you to come there to be with me. To help me . . ."

Clearing her throat, Annie looked away for a moment to gather her thoughts. Jason's urgency was real. She felt his sincere plea vibrating through every cell of her being. Turning, she held his pleading gaze.

"What do Morgan and Laura say about

this? Do they want me there with you?"

Shrugging, he said, "Morgan doesn't care. I told him I'd ask you when you got here today. I told him you'd come. Will you?"

"Oh, Jason . . ." Annie choked back so many unexpected feelings. "My mom and dad want me home now that I've been released from the hospital."

Frowning, Jason kept moving his thumb against her soft, warm flesh. "You would leave me?"

Torn, Annie bit her lower lip. "I don't want to, Jason . . . but you don't remember. . . ." She stopped abruptly. If she didn't, she'd blurt out the truth — that they'd been in love with one another. The last thing Jason needed right now was one more emotional commitment he had to try and live up to. Annie had seen him work so hard to pretend to be the son Morgan and Laura wanted him to be, memory or not. And every time they left, he was limp with fatigue from the huge emotional expenditure. Annie wasn't about to saddle him with their former relationship, too.

"I know I don't remember, Annie, but I *like* you. You're good for me. When you're around, I feel *hope*. You make me feel like I'm not drowning, when I know I am. I try so hard to remember for Morgan and Laura, but nothing comes. I see their pain. I want to cry for them. . . ."

Heart breaking, Annie turned and gently touched his cheek. "You try too hard, Jason . . . and they understand. You need time."

Hitching one shoulder, he stole a look at her frowning features. "Will you leave me, Annie?"

The words, like those of a hurt child who had lost everything in his world, stabbed deeply into Annie's heart. The last thing she wanted to do was make Jason feel even worse. She had seen his daily struggle with depression, and she'd cried internally for the suffering he was experiencing.

"Jason, this decision involves more than just me."

"Your mom and dad?" He knew how close she was to them. Watching her mouth thin, he saw anguish register in Annie's glorious gold eyes.

"Yes, them . . . and my brothers and sisters, Jason. They're all expecting me home soon. . . ."

"They miss you, I bet."

His words sounded so desolate and lifeless. Annie saw Jason hang his head and close his eyes. His lips parted and she felt his suffering as if it were her own.

"Listen," she pleaded softly, "let me make a phone call to them, okay? I need to see how they would feel about this."

"I know you miss them," Jason told her

quietly. He lifted his head and slowly straightened up. "Sometimes I see you standing over there, looking out the window. You're far away from me, Annie. I know you're dreaming of your home, the mountains and your family."

How much more could she take? Annie sat very still as he spoke about how he had watched her, how he had felt her distance from him. Jason's newfound simplicity was heart-rending and eloquent. What he didn't know was at those moments she was reliving what they'd once had, remembering that kiss, a conversation, a laugh shared between them. Taking a halting breath, Annie whispered, "Some days I do get lonely, Jason." That was the truth, but not the whole truth. Annie was lonely for Jason's touch, his ebullient personality and teasing humor. The man who sat at her side on the bed was different — gentler, accessible and gut-wrenchingly honest. Those weren't bad qualities, Annie realized, just different from the old Jason she'd known before.

"I don't want you to be unhappy, Annie." He caught her gaze and tried to smile, but failed. "I don't want to see you cry. I don't want to make you cry."

His words shattered her as nothing else could. Rubbing her wrinkled brow, Annie whispered haltingly, "Let me make a phone call, Jason. If my family doesn't mind, I'll go home with you and stay for a while, okay?"

Brightening, he nodded. "I'd like that, Annie."

Annie sat on the couch in her third-floor apartment, the phone in her hand. It was early evening and she had just gotten home from the hospital. Jason had wanted to play a game of checkers. Dr. Dorf had heartily endorsed the idea as the game helped him think. Annie had entertained Jason for several hours, purposely losing to him in order to build his confidence in his own thinking processes, which were still childlike at this stage of his recovery. As they played the game, she'd seen the fear eating at him over the possibility she wouldn't be going home with him. There was little Annie could do to relieve him of his anxiety, even though she tried.

"Hello? Lane Dazen speaking. . . ."

"Hi, Mom, it's me, Annie."

"Pumpkin, what a nice surprise. It's only Tuesday."

Annie sat up, leaning forward, her elbows on her thighs. "I know, Mom." Usually, she called every Sunday.

"What's wrong, Annie? I feel it around you."

Her mother's psychic ability never failed to impress her. Giving a slight, strained laugh, Annie said, "Well, it's not really anything

284

bad, Mom. Just . . . gosh, different. I'm beginning to hate that word — *different.*"

"Your arm okay?"

"Oh, yeah, I've got the cast off and my arm is fine now. I still have nerve damage in my two little fingers. They don't seem to be improving, but the doctor said it could take a while. At least I'm not in pain, so that's good. Don't worry, I'm almost a hundred percent now, Mom."

"Good! And Jason?"

"That's why I'm calling, Mom. I need your advice real bad. I don't know what to do, I'm so torn up over this. . . ." Annie pressed her fingertips to her closed eyes. "Jason is going to be released shortly. His father said he was preparing a cabin near where they live for him. Jason asked me this afternoon if I'd come and stay with him, Mom." Anguish filled her. Tears stung her eyes. "I don't know what to say. I want to come home and heal. . . ."

"I understand, Pumpkin. This is very hard for you, I know."

A quivering sigh broke from Annie compressed lips. "It's torture, Mom. There're days when I'd rather be dead than be around Jason and remember what we had together. It's so gutting to me. . . ."

"My poor little dove," Lane murmured. "My heart hurts for you."

"Every night I dream of Jason. I dream of

what we shared — the conversations, the kiss. . . . We never made love, Mom. We were waiting until we got home. Now I often lay here wondering why I didn't love him in Afghanistan. Every day I see him, my body aches for him. It's awful. I don't know what to do with myself, Mom. I want to be intimate with him like I was before this happened, but he doesn't remember. . . ."

"Do you want to go with him to the cabin, Annie?"

Her mother's voice, low and coaxing, broke through her roiling emotions. "A part of me does. Another part, the me that's feeling like a whipped animal, doesn't. I don't know if I can emotionally handle having Jason in the same house with me. I'm afraid, Mom."

"Of what?"

Annie leaned back on the couch. "Of the feelings I have for him. Do you know how tough it is not to call him by the endearments we once used? Not to touch him? Kiss him? Be playful with him? Be teasing . . ."

"But you love him, Pumpkin."

"Don't remind me! No . . . I didn't mean that. I really didn't. I'm just so frustrated. . . ."

"You were never very good at being patient."

Annie's laugh was low and broken. "Yeah, I know, Mom. Do you think this is the Great Spirit getting even with me now? Making me learn patience this way?"

"I don't know, Pumpkin. I know the Great Spirit loves all of us, cares for us and tries to help us."

"I'm so lost, Mom. It's hell being here with Jason every day, and yet I wouldn't give it up for the world. I feel torn apart. My heart is bleeding. . . ."

"I know, I know. . . ."

"What should I do, Mom? Should I come home? Should I stay with Jason?"

"I can't tell you what to do, Annie. This is one of those life decisions you must make on your own. I can tell you that we'd love to have you come back to the res. We have already repainted your bedroom for you."

Closing her eyes, Annie whispered, "I miss you so very, very much. I feel so alone out here, not being with my own kind. . . ."

"You have the necklace, Annie. Remember your ancestors that had it before you. Each of us went through some terrible test where we were pulled apart just like this. Maybe the circumstances weren't the same, but the tests that the Great Spirit gives the women who carry the rainbow necklace are huge and sometimes overwhelming."

"What did you do, Mom? You were shot down in Colombia, in the jungle. You were the only survivor and were being chased by bad guys. That was your trial."

She laughed shortly. "Oh, yes, it was a terrible test! I wasn't sure from one hour to the next if I was going to survive, Annie. Life was so tenuous."

"That's how I feel right now, Mom. Tenuous. Like no matter which way I step, I'm going to get hurt again and again. . . ."

"I understand."

"What helped you, Mom? I need to try and get myself off this tightrope I'm on."

"Well, you know that after two days, Canyon flew over in his helicopter, trying to find the downed crew. He didn't know I was the only survivor. And when his chopper was shot down and only he survived, we were on the run together."

"At least you had company."

"You do, too, Annie. You have Jason at your side."

"Not like I want."

"I didn't get along with Canyon very well, either. He was more a pain in the butt than a help at that time."

Annie chuckled. "Yeah, a little like Jason on some days . . ."

"See? There *are* similarities. The medicine necklace tests each woman who wears it. You must prove yourself strong, Annie, where you are presently weak. You must walk through that gauntlet of hell and fire and come out the other end of it alive."

"That's where I feel I'm at right now — walking through a gauntlet of fire. I feel

…d. I feel trapped. There are
want to scream, Mom. I want to
a wolf and let go of my pain, my fi
and fears about Jason's recovery."

"When we're tested, daughter, our fa
muscles and our tendons are stripped a
leaving our inner core. That's where we f.
the strength to survive the harsh trials w
must make it through. It really is a test of
life and death. That is how true spiritual
strength is created: by the tests such as this.
You are the daughter of a medicine woman
and you walk this path even though you've
never taken the training. It's about becoming
strong inwardly in order to do the work and
help others."

"There are days when it seems like I'm
dying, Mom."

"Yes, I know the feeling. But you know
what? You have the strength of your grandmothers behind you. I know some days seem
so dark that you'll never see the light
again . . . but the light will come, Annie."

"Is that a promise?"

"Yes, it is."

Chapter 15

"Here you go, Cowboy," Annie said, the endearment slipping out naturally as she walked out on the rustic pine porch of the cabin, two cups of green tea with honey in her hands. The mid-May sun's rays had just topped the mighty Douglas firs that surrounded them. Jason sat bundled up in his dark blue nylon coat, hiking boots on, a loose knit cap of red on his head to protect his ears from the biting air, which hovered just above freezing. Annie was discovering it was very cold in the mornings at this time of year in the Rockies. Usually, the temperature rose to the sixties in the afternoon.

There were days when she regretted her decision to stay here at the cabin instead of going home, but they were less and less frequent as Jason began to grow out of his childlike demeanor and take on more adult ways. Still, as Annie stood there gazing down at him, she couldn't protect herself from the love that grew every day despite his lack of memory about their relationship. Nor could she keep her raw heart from yearning for him. But she was beginning to see some of the old Jason emerging here and there, and it gave her hope . . . enough hope to hang on.

Jason pulled his gaze from the top of a fir tree, where a raven was balanced. The pleasant thunk of her boots across the pine slats of the porch eased the anxiety he was feeling in his chest. Giving Annie a smile, he reached for the large white steaming mug of tea that she offered him.

"How did you know I was out here?" Usually, Annie was in the shower this time of the morning and he was in the gym that was set up between the bedrooms, working out to increase the muscle mass he'd lost.

"Just a feeling," she said, sipping the tea and standing near the old pine rocking chair. Looking across the yard, which was surrounded with a white picket fence, Annie absorbed the warmth of the burgeoning sunlight as it danced across the tops of the mighty conifers surrounding the cabin. Earlier that morning, in a small meadow not far away, she'd said her morning prayer to Father Sun, the rainbow medicine necklace in her hands.

The tea was hot and sweet. Jason sipped it gingerly, the mug warming his hands. Just having Annie this close to him made him feel better. Steam rose from the mug as he drew it away from his mouth and set it carefully on his lap.

"You look tense," Annie noted. Her heart

ballooned with such a fierce love of him. He looked so much better now. In two months' time Jason had regained twenty pounds, his face filling out so he looked much like the old Jason she remembered. Cooking three square meals a day for Jason had turned into a pleasure for Annie. He seemed to devour her home-cooked dishes compared to how he had nibbled at the hospital fare. And yes, she used lots of basil, because he loved that seasoning. It was the only memory from the past he had conjured up so far, except for that of her wearing the necklace.

He shrugged, sipping the tea eagerly. "You know the PTSD symptoms Dr. Dorf said I had?"

"Which ones?" Annie set her hand gently on Jason's broad shoulder. Instantly, she saw some of the tension melt from his face. Her touch was magical to him and she knew why. But he didn't. It hurt that he saw her only as a "friend" and nothing more. Though Jason was seeing life in its more complex facets, a love life wasn't in the picture. At least, not yet. And maybe never. That was what scared Annie the most. Caressing his nylon coat with her fingers, she said, "Feeling uptight? Tense?"

"I was working out in the gym with the weights and all of a sudden I panicked. I wanted to run, Annie." Jason twisted to look up at her. "So I ran out here to greet the sun and say hello."

When his mouth stretched into that able smile, Annie's heart squeezed yearning. Oh! How she wanted to lean de and caress that mouth, taste Jason and him know the love she held for him. Instead her fingers tightened momentarily on his shoulder. "That was a good plan, Cowboy, coming out here."

"Every morning at sunrise you get up and come out here. Why?"

"It's the way of my people, the Apache." Annie lifted her hand and pointed toward the sun. "Each morning, I rise and come out here and greet Father Sun. I greet the day. I say a prayer."

"What kind of prayer?" He absorbed her huskily spoken words. Annie's profile was strong and beautiful. Jason never tired of looking at her. The inflection of her voice was so calming, her touch even more so. This morning, her long hair fell like a black waterfall across her proud shoulders, set off by the plaid wool coat she wore. Of late, he had been wanting to touch her hair. To feel it.

"A prayer for thanksgiving, mostly." Annie sat down beside the rocker, her feet on the damp ground. It had rained two days ago, even though snow could still fall at this time of year.

"Share it with me?"

." She lifted her right hand toward n. "Father Sun, it is I, Annie Dazen, greets you. I thank you for allowing me be alive this day. Guide me, help me, let e always stay in touch with my heart and with Mother Earth and all her relations. Aho." She turned and looked at him. His face was pensive and serious. "That's it. Short and sweet."

"And you do this every day?"

"Ever since I can remember."

"That's nice. I like it. Can I do it, too? Or do you have to be Apache?"

Giving him a soft smile, Annie whispered, "The Great Spirit sees us all as one, Jason. We are all related. So, yes, you can say it whenever you want."

He reached out and slid his fingers through her thick, silky black locks. "Your hair reminds me of a living waterfall, Annie."

Shocked by Jason's unexpected touch, by the tremble in his low voice, she froze momentarily. Annie tried to process her feelings, which were in chaos. Was Jason touching her as a lover? Or merely out of curiosity? By now, she understood that adult awareness was not really a part of his world. Every day she taught him a little more about what was appropriate and what was not. But touching her? This was only the second time he'd done it. Heart aching, she felt his fingers tremble slightly as he drew them through her hair. Closing her eyes, her hands tight around her mug of tea, Annie tried to draw in a deep, steadying breath.

"Your hair is like a living river," Jason murmured, mesmerized by the reddish color within the ebony strands as he lifted them in his hands, holding them up in the sunlight. "I like to watch you walk when your hair is down. It's so long and beautiful. It's alive. Like you."

Getting a grip on her pounding heart and trying to ignore the tingling of her scalp, and the rampant, yearning feelings that clamored to be acknowledged, Annie took a slow, deep breath. She looked up and saw that same fixed look on Jason's face. Every so often he would stare as if obsessed by something for minutes at a time, and then, just as suddenly, look away. One of the TBI symptoms, she realized. Heart breaking, Annie decided Jason's response was not an emotional one but rather like that of a small boy fixated on something bright and shiny that drew his attention.

She allowed him to explore her hair, but she didn't fool herself. She knew Jason wasn't doing this out of love for her, but merely out of curiosity.

As Annie sat there, enjoying the warmth of the sun, she watched frost on the dead, bedraggled plants inside the picket fence slowly melting. Any touch was better than none, even if Jason didn't realize how much this meant to her. And like a famished wolf, she absorbed each gentle stroke of his hand on her hair, allowing it to feed her starving heart.

"You said you had to go somewhere today?" Jason asked as he eased his fingers from her hair.

"Yes, I have to go to the Veterans Hospital to find out about some tests." Annie didn't add that she was going to find out if she would be allowed to stay on in the Army as a combat helicopter pilot or not. The injuries to her shoulder had created nerve damage in her left arm, especially her last two fingers. Dr. Dorf had put her through a battery of exhausting tests last week, and now Annie would find out if she had a career or not.

Fear filled her as she sat beside Jason, sipping tea in silence. What would she do if the Army released her? She had no vision of her future, no money other than a small nest egg she'd saved. She'd have to get a job. But doing what? Worst of all, she'd have to leave here. Leave Jason. There were no jobs in Phillipsburg; she'd checked out the situation — just in case.

Closing her eyes, Annie felt her gut knot in turmoil. The rest of her life was going to be decided this afternoon. . . .

Jason jerked awake. He lay in the large

queen-size bed, the duvet, a rainbow-colored patchwork quilt stuffed with goose feathers, keeping him warm. A sound. He had heard a noise. Or had he? So often he'd snap awake in the middle of the night hearing awful sounds. Screaming. Shrieks of pain. They haunted the halls of his mind on some nights, and he knew it had to do with the attack on Kandahar he'd nearly died in. Not that he remembered it, but some portion of his brain obviously did.

Throwing off the covers, he got up slowly so that dizziness wouldn't assail him. The wooziness was mostly gone, except when he rose too quickly. There was a light on near his opened door. There. He heard it again. Soft weeping.

Frowning, Jason scrubbed his eyes and forced himself to wake up. This wasn't a dream. No, it was real. Reaching for his burgundy robe at the bottom of the bed, he slipped his feet into his wool slippers. Standing, he shrugged into the robe and tied the sash around his waist. There it was again. Muffled sounds. He was *sure* this was weeping.

Moving slowly toward the door, Jason got his balance. Hand resting against the doorjamb, he peered down the hall. There were night-lights stationed in every hall in the house so that if he got up in the dark, he wouldn't accidentally run into something and hurt himself. His bedroom was at one end of the cabin. The gym was on his right. To his left was the bathroom. At the far end of the hall was Annie's bedroom, and the door was wide open. Frowning, Jason recalled that she always closed it at night. Something was wrong. His heart started pounding slowly with dread.

He stepped out into the hall, then stopped, uncertain. There! Frowning, he started along the passageway once more. Halfway down, he turned left, past the bathroom, and moved into the living room. The fireplace was bright with warm yellow-and-orange flames. Looking at his watch, he saw it was 3:00 a.m. The crying was muffled. Surely it was Annie, but why would she be crying? Scowling, Jason made his way to the kitchen.

Moonlight cascaded through the large window over the sink, filtering through the white, frilly curtains that hung there. Jason walked to the back door, and when he reached it his heart stopped. Steadying himself on the door frame to keep his balance, he saw Annie sitting on the porch, bent over, her head buried in her arms. She was in her yellow fleecy robe, her moccasins on, her hair like a black coverlet across her shaking shoulders.

His heart squeezed with pain. Her pain. Jason twisted the doorknob and quietly opened it. He stepped out into the freezing, wintry air. The sky was clear, the moon hanging like a luminescent, glowing globe.

The old pine boards creaked as he walked across them, and Annie looked up. Her vision was blurred with hot tears, her nose running. Jason stood there uncertainly, his shadowed face torn with anguish.

"Oh, no . . . ! I'm so sorry I woke you up, Jason." Annie quickly tried to wipe her face dry, but it was impossible. The look in his eyes tore at her vulnerable, raw heart. Sniffing and choking, she felt awful that she'd disturbed his sleep. Jason slept lightly anyway, and she'd tried so hard to be quiet. She'd come out here to allow Mother Earth to absorb her tears.

"It's okay. . . ." Jason whispered unsteadily, as he sat down next to her. Putting his arm around her shoulders, he drew her against him. Somehow, he knew this was what she needed. Hadn't Annie held him on bad days when he would cry for no reason? Dr. Dorf had said he would go through storms of emotion, suddenly and without warning. Jason knew Annie had lived through that attack at Kandahar, too. Just as she had comforted him, he would comfort her now.

"Let me help?" he whispered, touched to the point of tears himself. When she lifted her tearstained face, her eyes seemed to be wounded holes of grief. Whispering her name, he drew her gently into his arms. She came without resistance, and his heart soared with relief.

"Just let me hold you, Annie. That will make you feel better. . . ." He smiled and closed his eyes as she sank against him, her face pressed to the column of his neck. He could feel the wetness of her tears and the warmth of her skin. It was a beautiful, delicious sensation — a new one that he savored, like the sun touching the tips of the firs. Her hair slid like soft silk over his arms. Annie smelled of fresh sage, and he inhaled her unique fragrance.

Patting her awkwardly as she sniffed, Jason whispered against her hair, near her ear, "Whatever it is, it's going to be okay, Annie. I promise. Just let me hold you. When you hold me, I always feel better."

Jason's words tore her wounded heart open even wider. Without thinking, Annie slid her arms around his waist. More sobs erupted. She couldn't stop them! For so long she'd been able to control her feelings around Jason, but not tonight. Yesterday had been hell. Her whole world was hurtling out of control and she had no way to stop it. Only Jason's warm, supportive arms around her made her feel any sense of stability. How badly Annie wanted to think that he'd come out here to hold her because he loved her, but she knew that wasn't possible. Those memories were gone. All he was doing was emulating what she, Laura and Morgan had done for him so often, which was to hold him when he was hurting.

And yet as Annie buried her face against his neck, and felt Jason's hands moving gently across her back, she lost herself in memories of their old life together. And as she sobbed her heart out against the man who held her, but who had forgotten their fierce love, Annie felt her whole life crumbling into dust and moving back into the hands of Mother Earth.

As he rocked her gently, Jason found incredible solace, having Annie in his arms. He couldn't think of anything that had ever felt so good, warm and comforting to him. Jason continued to stroke her head with his hand, rocking her in a slow, gentle motion. Gradually, her weeping abated, replaced by her soft breathing. Feeling the moist warmth of her breath against his chest, he smiled.

"You feel so good in my arms. Why haven't I held you like this before?"

Annie tried to wipe her runny nose. It was no use. She had to ease out of Jason's arms and dig into the pocket of her robe to find a tissue. As he released her, she felt as if she were being thrown out into the cold once again. Bereft, she blew her nose and then wiped it.

"I — I'm sorry, Jason. I thought by coming out here I wouldn't wake you. . . ."

Annie's profile was filled with suffering as she looked down at the crumpled tissue between her hands. Something made Jason lift his arm and place it around her shoulders once again. Pulling her close, he said, "You do this for me, Annie, when I cry. Why can't I do it for you?"

Lifting her head, Annie drowned in his dark, shadowed gaze. His mouth was parted, his eyes questioning and filled with concern for her. Or was it love? She wanted to believe it was, but she simply wasn't sure. She tried to smile and failed. Wiping her eyes with the tissue, she whispered unsteadily, "I got really bad news yesterday, Jason. That's why I was out here crying. I couldn't sleep. My mind was going a million miles an hour."

Frowning, he moved his fingers along her shoulder. "What bad news?"

"Remember I went to the VA hospital yesterday afternoon for that appointment with Dr. Dorf?"

He lifted his head and frowned. "Yes . . . you did. What happened? Is something wrong?"

Annie's lower lip trembled and she systematically tore the tissue into little pieces. "Yeah . . . a lot is wrong, Jason."

"Well, why didn't you say something? I could tell at dinner you were sad, but you never shared it with me. Why?"

"Because you don't need to be upset by

my problems, that's why. Dr. Dorf thinks you need a pleasant, calm place to recover. My news isn't good." Annie shook her head. "That's why I didn't share it. . . ."

"What's the bad news, Annie?" He held her a little more closely as he felt her tense.

"Well, uh, my left arm . . . You know it's weak? Remember I told you before that I'd suffered some nerve damage in it?" Annie held up her hand for him to see.

"Yes?"

"Dr. Dorf says the damage is permanent. What that means is that the Army is no longer interested in keeping me on as a combat helicopter pilot. I no longer have the reflexes I need. It means I'll be receiving a medical discharge and I'm out of a job. I have to give up flying, Jason. And there's nothing I want to do more."

Jason sat there thinking through what she'd said. He cursed his lack of memory. "Jobs are important."

"Yes." Annie sniffed, leaning her head against his shoulder. "Without one, you can't put food on the table, Jason. You can't pay your bills. It's a terrible state to be in."

"And the Army is no longer paying you?"

"That's right," she sighed. "You got it."

Sitting there, absorbing the feel of her body against his, Jason stared out across the dark yard. For long minutes he tried to grasp the implications of what she had told him.

"You're crying because you lost a job that paid you money so that you could pay your bills?"

"That's right, Cowboy. You've hit the nail on the head."

"Can't you fly ever again?" Jason knew how important it was to Annie to fly. He didn't remember his own fondness for it, but when Annie spoke of flying her eyes glowed with such joy, and her voice grew excited, and he shared that with her.

"Well," she mumbled, wiping her eyes with her fist, "I can. But not in the military. Reflexes, instant ones, are necessary in combat. I don't have those reflexes anymore because of the nerve damage. Dr. Dorf said I could fly commercial helicopters without a problem. I'd be able to pass the FAA, Federal Aviation Agency, medical exam and be able to get a job doing commercial flying."

"Okay, that sounds good." He looked down at her face, at her half-closed eyes, her mouth pulled in with suffering. It made his heart ache. His Annie — his best friend, who had helped him so much over the past months — was hurting so badly. Jason had never seen her like this before, and he felt helpless. Frustrated, he didn't know *what* to do. So he decided to follow his heart. Dr. Dorf had told him to follow what felt right, and now he was going to do that.

"Come here, Annie. . . ." he entreated, his

voice husky and unsure. He opened his arms and drew her tightly against him. Placing small kisses on her hair, he quavered, "It's going to be all right. I don't know how I know this, but I do." The strands of her hair were smooth and sleek beneath his lips. With each small, careful kiss, he felt Annie melt a little more against him, her arms twining around him.

Heart soaring with joy, Jason sensed this was the right thing to do. Overriding everything was his need to assuage her pain, to somehow take it away from her. "You're such a good person, Annie," he whispered near her ear, giving it a kiss. "You help me all the time. Now, finally, maybe I can help you. Your crying hurts me. It claws at my heart. I don't know what to do. I just want to help you. . . ."

"Oh, Jason . . ." Annie closed her eyes and sank fully against him. He was kissing her! She felt his strong mouth against her scalp, against her ear. His breath was warm and soothing to her. Hearing the beating of his strong heart in his chest, Annie tightened her arms around him.

This was new. This wasn't simply Jason emulating her. The discovery was heated. Frightening. Beautiful. Annie was feeling such loss within herself that she heedlessly absorbed each hesitant kiss Jason gave her. How she wanted to lift her head and kiss him in return. But what would that do? No, her heart told her to remain on the receiving end of his feelings.

They were in new territory now. This wasn't friendship. It was something else, and Annie was too afraid to name it.

Chapter 16

"What can I do for you, son?" Morgan sat down at the small pine table in the cabin. Morning sunshine lanced through the kitchen window. He'd received a phone call at 8:00 a.m. from Jason, one of the few his son had made since leaving the hospital, and Morgan had driven up immediately to find out what was going on.

"Thanks for coming," Jason said. He'd made coffee and poured two cups minutes earlier in anticipation of Morgan arriving. "I know you like your coffee black. You probably need some?" he said, motioning to the cup at Morgan's elbow.

Morgan was dressed in a charcoal-gray suit, a starched white shirt pressed to flawless perfection, and a light blue tie. He always looked strong and powerful to Jason.

"I can always use a cup." Morgan nodded his thanks as he placed his hands around the white mug. Studying Jason across the table, he could see his son was visibly upset. Jason's blue eyes were stormy looking, his mouth set. Dressed in a red flannel shirt, jeans and hiking boots, he looked almost

307

normal to Morgan. The bandages were gone, since the bone graft operation had taken place successfully nearly two months ago. His hair was growing back, to the point where no one could tell he'd been injured, except for the scar on the left side of his face. Morgan knew that scar would be there like a brand to remind Jason — and him — of a tragic time in their lives.

"Well, uh . . ." Jason cleared his throat. "I don't know where to start . . . Dad." He gave Morgan a searching look. "I hope you don't mind me calling you that? I've been thinking a lot about this. I feel like your son even if I don't remember anything."

Warmth flooded through Morgan. Thunderstruck, he stared at Jason. He saw desperation in his son's eyes, the fear that he might be rebuffed by Morgan. "Why, no, son. I like it — a lot. I'd love for you to call me Dad if you want to."

"I don't know what I called you before, but . . ." Jason looked down at his cup of steaming coffee and then back at Morgan. "I just feel the need somewhere in me . . . to do this. To say it. . . ."

Pleased beyond belief, Morgan smiled gently. He reached out and placed his hand on Jason's. "This is a gift to me, son. I've always dreamed of you calling me Dad someday. Thank you. . . ."

The contact was comforting and soothed

308

some of Jason's anxiety. When Morgan lifted his hand away, he asked in a low tone, "What did I call you before?"

Grimacing, Morgan murmured, "Father. Like I said before, son, you and I had a very cool, distant relationship before your TBI." He searched Jason's earnest face. He'd just shaved, and he'd nicked himself on his jaw, near the scar. Morgan remembered it had been hell shaving around his own scar, and he felt for Jason.

"You're not cool or distant," his son muttered. "You've been here for me — and Annie — every step of the way. Why would I be distant with you?"

"It's a long story, and I don't think you called me up here for past family history this morning. You sounded upset. We can talk more about the past relationship between us later if you want. I'll be happy to go over it with you." That was a lie. Morgan dreaded talking about it, but he knew he had to be brutally honest with his son, because if Jason's memory came back and he realized Morgan had lied to him, it would only cause more problems long term. Morgan cleared his throat. "I like you calling me Dad. I've wanted you to call me that for a decade, and it means more than you'll ever know. But now I want to know what was on your mind when you called."

His mouth curving slightly, Jason said,

"You're pretty smart, Dad. How did you know I called you up here for another reason?"

"You hardly ever phone me, son, that's why. And I could tell in your voice that you're upset about something."

"Oh . . ." He gave a sour smile.

"What's bothering you, Jason? How can I help?" Morgan saw his son's brow wrinkle. There was confusion in his narrowed blue eyes as he turned the mug restlessly around in his large, square hands. Flight hands. And he'd never fly again.

Pain grated Morgan's heart over that realization. Maybe it was just as well that Jason didn't remember how he loved to fly. If he ever got his memory back, it would be such a crushing blow.

"It's . . . about Annie," Jason choked out in a strangled whisper.

"Oh? Is she all right?" Morgan frowned. Jason's face was tense with anxiety. Earlier today, Annie had driven down to their home and picked up Laura for a day's shopping in Anaconda. Morgan hadn't seen Annie, had only heard her voice. He'd been in his study when she had come by to get Laura.

"Well, no . . . I don't think she is." Jason looked around, trying to keep his feelings controlled, but finding it impossible to do. His emotions were always on tap and he never tried to hide them. "I found Annie out

310

on the porch at 3:00 a.m. sobbing her heart out."

Morgan scowled. "Crying? Why?"

"The Army gave her a medical discharge, Dad." Jason held up his left hand. "She has too much weakness in her fingers to fly for them anymore."

"Damn . . ." Morgan muttered. "I didn't know. She found this out yesterday?"

"Yes . . . She didn't tell me, either. When she came home in the late afternoon, she looked sad and I wondered why. But she never said anything."

"How bad is the nerve injury?"

"Dr. Dorf said she could fly commercial helicopters but not combat ones."

Relieved, Morgan sat back. "That's good news. She's just lacking the fast reflexes needed for combat."

Mouth quirking, Jason leaned forward over the table, his coffee mug gripped between his hands. "Dad, she's scared. And so am I."

"Why?"

"She says she has to leave!" The words came out in a cry. Jason gulped. "I don't want her to go. She said she has to get a job and make money now that the Army fired her." He searched Morgan's dark, scowling face. "Please . . . can't you do something? I — I don't know what I'd do without her here, Dad. . . ."

Morgan saw tears drifting down Jason's

311

face. How vulnerable and open he was compared to his previous personality. Touched, Morgan rasped, "She's not going anywhere, son. Don't worry, I'll think of something."

Breathing hard, Jason added, "When I woke up and heard her crying . . . it hurt me, Dad." He rubbed his chest, confusion in his tone. "I don't know what's going on. I feel so many different feelings here for Annie."

Swallowing hard, Morgan nodded.

"What *was* our relationship like before my TBI, Dad? Annie's and mine?"

"Son, you'll have to ask her about that. It's not for me to tell you. Have you asked her?"

"N-no . . . I didn't think to, really. Not until . . . well, last night . . . I just feel as if there're snakes running around in my chest. When she cried, I hurt. I cried with her and held her. There was so much pain. . . . I don't like to see her hurting like that, Dad."

Jason's pleas tore at Morgan. "I understand, Jason." *Love does that,* was what he wanted to say. *When you love someone, you hurt for them.* But he kept quiet. Jason had such a bewildered look on his face as he slowly rubbed his chest. Even though he didn't remember their love from the past, he was obviously falling in love with Annie all over again. And Morgan knew that the feeling was shared.

He saw how Annie constantly stopped herself from becoming too intimate with Jason. She understood, as Morgan and Laura did, that if he was to love her, he had to come to her first. And now Morgan knew without a doubt that Jason was falling in love with her.

"You and Annie share something special," he rasped quietly, wanting to wipe his son's tears away, but knowing he couldn't. Jason took a swipe at them with his trembling fingers. "I'll help her, son. I'll put a plan together so she can stay here with you and have a job, okay?"

"You can fix this?"

Smiling a little, Morgan said, "I think so. I'll make a cell phone call to her and ask her to drop by the office this evening when she and your mother get back from Anaconda. But remember, it's Annie's decision in the long run. I can offer her a job, but I can't guarantee she'll take it. Okay?"

Clenching his fists beside his coffee cup, Jason whispered, "She *has* to, Dad! I — I don't want to be here without her. I don't want Annie to leave. . . ."

Annie wondered why Morgan wanted to see her at the Perseus office. She'd just returned from Anaconda with Laura. Shopping had helped relieve some of her deep sadness over her plight and being able to talk to Laura about it relieved Annie of a lot of stress. Laura's sympathy and understanding helped a great deal. Annie had to call her parents, and she knew they'd be just as devastated by the news as she was.

Golden evening light hung above the Douglas firs as she walked from the small parking lot to the three-story Victorian. The house was a cover for the offices of supersecret Perseus, which were located below ground, in the basement. Morgan had gone into hiding to protect his family from ever being kidnapped again.

As Annie took the elevator down to the offices, she ran her fingers through her hair. The welcome warmth of mid-May allowed her to dress in something other than winter clothes. Today she'd worn a burgundy skirt and a very feminine cotton top. It was still chilly, so she had a soft pink pashmina thrown around her shoulders.

The doors opened and she saw Jenny Wright, Morgan's assistant, sitting behind her desk. The blond woman looked up and smiled.

"Hi, Annie! Morgan is expecting you," she said, getting up to open the dark maple door that led to his office. "May I get you something to drink? Coffee? Tea?"

"No thanks, Jenny. I just came from Anaconda with Laura. We had a great lunch and I'm still stuffed like a buzzard."

Laughing, Jenny opened the door. "I understand."

Morgan looked up from his large desk. Papers were piled around him in neat stacks, begging for attention and signatures. "Hi, Annie, come on in." He rose from his chair as Jenny closed the door. Gesturing to the leather couch nearby, he said, "Let's sit over there, shall we?"

"Of course, sir." Annie could never quite lose the "sir" with Morgan. He was a tall man who walked proudly, his shoulders squared like the Marine Corps captain he'd once been. Dressed in his dark suit, he reminded her of a sleek, powerful corporate executive. What did he want with her? Annie wasn't sure.

Sitting down on one end of the couch, she arranged her skirt, which hung to her ankles. Pushing back the pashmina, Annie allowed the ends to drape over her arms.

"Did you and Laura have a good day up at Anaconda?"

"Yes, sir, we did."

"Shop till you drop?" he asked, grinning. Annie was trying to be chipper, but he saw the sadness in her gold eyes. Her hands were clasped in her lap, fingers fidgeting and giving her away. She was beautiful inside and out, Morgan thought, and he understood why his son loved her. She was a good person.

"Well . . ." Annie laughed, but the sound was strained. "Laura did."

"Not you?" Morgan studied her half-closed eyes. She would barely make eye contact with him. He saw the corners of her mouth pull inward.

"No, sir . . . not me. . . ."

"Why not?"

Sighing, Annie said in a low tone, "Because I don't have the money, if you want an honest answer."

Nodding, Morgan sat back on the other end of the couch. "How would you like to earn seventy-five thousand dollars a year, Annie?"

Shocked, she lifted her chin and stared openmouthed at him. "Sir?"

Uncrossing his legs, Morgan leaned his elbows on his thighs. "Jason told me what happened. That the Army released you from obligation." He nodded toward her. "Your left hand sustained some nerve damage. You don't have the reflexes required for combat anymore."

Pain gutted her. "He told you. . . ." she whispered, hanging her head and staring at her clenched hands.

"He called me after you left to go shopping with Laura."

"I'm sorry. You folks have enough to handle with Jason, let alone my problems."

"You weren't going to tell us?"

"No, sir, I wasn't."

"Because?"

Sighing, Annie whispered, "Because you're a wonderful family and you've done so much for me already. Your focus should be on Jason, not me. I know how much this has stressed all of you, getting used to the 'new' Jason, to his lack of memory, social skills and such."

Giving her a gentle smile, Morgan said, "Annie, you're important to our family, too. Jason loves you."

"Well," she muttered, closing her eyes, "he *did*." Heart aching, she wanted to cry all over again.

"I know he still does. . . ."

Opening her eyes, she stared at Morgan. "He said something to you today about that?"

"Not in so many words, Annie, but his heart is there with you. I had a talk with him this morning. I know he's not able to express himself quite yet, but he kept rubbing his chest and saying he had all these feelings for you. He's confused because he doesn't know what love feels like, so he can't quantify it — yet." Searching her taut features, Morgan held her golden gaze. "I asked him if he'd told you how he felt, and he said no. I urged him to talk to you directly. He also asked me about the relationship between the two of you before his TBI."

Annie bit her lip. "What did you tell him?" Fear threaded through her.

"Nothing. I told him he had to ask you directly."

"Oh . . . good. Because right now we have a friendship and nothing more."

Shrugging, Morgan smiled a little. "Well, I think it's more than that, from his view of things, Annie. I think what happened last night changed that perception for him. Maybe you need to sit down and divulge a little more about your past relationship? He's maturing rapidly now and I think he's ready for some of the truth about you two."

Pressing her face into her hands, Annie whispered, "Things are such a mess. . . ."

"Let me help you straighten some of them out, Annie." Morgan reached forward and placed his hand momentarily on her shoulder. Right now, Annie didn't look like a combat pilot. She looked like a woman carrying more loads than she could handle. Patting her shoulder gently, he said, "I'm serious about you earning seventy-five thousand a year. Do you want to hear my offer?"

Annie pushed her hair away from her face and straightened up. Just Morgan's paternal touch steadied her chaotic feelings within herself. "Y-yes. I'm sorry. I'm listening."

He smiled a little. "Don't apologize, Annie. You're going through the shock of losing your world. I know you loved being a combat pilot. You were very good at what you did.

But at least you can still fly, so that's good news."

"Commercial," she muttered in a strangled tone. "But that means going to a big city, and I hate cities, sir. I'm a country girl. And the only way I can see to fly in a rural area is to become a crop-dusting pilot." Grimacing, she muttered, "I don't believe in poisoning Mother Earth with all those chemicals. I just couldn't do it." Opening her hands, she said, "So I don't see myself being able to fly anymore, and I'm trying to come to grips with that. I can't lie to myself and trot off to a big city to become a pilot for some private concern. Cities will kill my spirit. I can't stand the pollution, the people running like rats everywhere, every day, so out of touch with Mother Earth. . . ."

"Slow down, Annie." Morgan gave her a slight smile. "I think I have a solution for all your concerns."

"How?" she murmured, her voice strained.

"Well . . ." Morgan got up and went to his desk, where he picked up a folder ". . . here's the plan." He handed Annie the file. "Open it up and take a look. It's a proposal I've been sitting on for some time, and it looks like now is a good time to act on it."

Frowning, Annie opened the folder and read the proposal. It was for the acquisition of a commercial helicopter for Perseus, to be housed at the small Phillipsburg airport, and to be used to fly Morgan or his mercs to various places in the region. She looked at the money available to buy a helicopter, and farther down, at the salary for the pilot who would fly it. Frowning, she looked up at Morgan, who stood leaning against his desk, a slight smile on his face.

"You're wanting a helo and pilot for your firm?"

"That's right. And whoever I decide to hire will be responsible for putting in a bid to several helicopter manufacturers to get us a bird. Driving to Anaconda, which is Perseus's main jump-off point insofar as getting commercial air flights for my teams, slows things down. With a helicopter available, we'll be able to fly teams in and out of the city whenever needed, in less than thirty minutes' time. I also need a bird to fly to Helena, and other cities within the fuel range. I simply can't be wasting ground time driving anymore."

Her heart thumped once. Hard. Her fingers trembled as she looked down at the proposal. She couldn't believe her eyes. It was all here. The money. The proposal.

"A-are you asking me what I think you are, sir? To be a pilot for Perseus? To fly this bird for you? For your teams?"

Morgan grinned. "That's *exactly* what I'm asking, Annie. Are you interested? You'd be here in the Rocky Mountains, close to nature. Phillipsburg is a small town, not a city. I think you'd be happy here."

So many emotions suffused Annie. She slowly closed the file, her hands resting lightly on it.

"But . . . what about Jason? I mean, how do you see it all happening? Do you want me to move out? I don't understand. . . ." She searched Morgan's pensive face, those gray eyes broadcasting such warmth. Annie had come to know why his teams loved him so fiercely. Morgan Trayhern emanated a warmth and caring that made the person he focused on feel damn special.

Easing away from the desk, Morgan came and sat down on the couch. "Annie, I'm not going to interfere with whatever is between you and Jason. I'm offering you a job. If you want to move out of the cabin and get an apartment at one of the condos we own here, you can do that. I don't want to tell you how to live your life. That's up to you." He pointed to the file in her lap. "But I do need a pilot. And I need a bird. If you want the job, it's yours."

Gulping, Annie took in a huge, ragged breath, her heart filled with joy. "Oh, yes, sir! I'd love the job!"

"Good! Then see Jenny about getting signed up for Perseus as an employee. She'll help you through the considerable paper-work."

Sitting very still, Annie compressed her lips. "You said I could move to a condo if I wanted?"

"Yes. We had thirty of them built several years ago to house merc teams that were either coming back from a mission or prepping to go out on one. Most of the employees who work here have bought condos at a very reasonable price from Perseus. It won't break your piggy bank, I promise." Morgan grinned a little at the relief he saw shining in her eyes.

"Well, sir . . . if it's okay with you, I want to talk to Jason about all this. See how he feels. . . ."

"How do *you* feel?" Morgan hoped — no, prayed — that Annie would remain with Jason. But he also understood the pressures on her. Even though a physical therapist came in every other day to work with Jason, and a special-ed teacher helped him with communications skills, Annie was his full-time caretaker. Morgan wasn't sure she wanted to continue in that vein or not, and would certainly understand if she didn't.

With a breathy laugh, she said, "There's no contest there, sir. I *want* to stay with Jason. We have a great friendship. I love him . . . even if it's at a distance and he doesn't know it. No, I'd rather be with him than separated. But let me talk to him. He needs to be a partner in this process, too." She searched

Morgan's face, noting his pleased expression. Morgan's ability to work with people was legendary, and now Annie knew why. When the man focused on you, you felt like the center of the universe. But she'd already experienced that with Jason.

"Fair enough." Morgan got up and buttoned his suit coat. "I think it's quitting time, Annie. Why don't you go home and study that proposal? Once you get done signing up with Perseus, your next order of business will be to find us a helicopter."

Slowly rising to her feet, Annie rearranged the pashmina across her shoulders and looped the ends in front. "I will, sir. . . ."

"Good. Now, go home to Jason. I know he's eager to see you. . . ."

Chapter 17

"We need to talk," Annie told Jason after she took off her coat and hung it up. It was nearly 6:00 p.m. and she found Jason standing at the kitchen counter, carefully cutting up vegetables for their nightly salad. When he raised his head and looked at her, her heart squeezed with such a fierce love for him she didn't know what to do except stand by the door. Jason looked scared. He probably thought she was going to leave.

"Yes . . ." he said, carefully placing the knife and the carrot aside on the wooden cutting board. Lifting a towel from a hook at the end of the cupboard, Jason wiped his wet hands.

Annie pulled out a chair for him at the kitchen table, then sat down in another. Jason gave her a soft, uncertain smile. It was that little-boy smile that went straight to her heart, that got her every time. As he sat down at her elbow, their knees brushed. Without preamble, Annie launched into the day's amazing events. At the end of the explanation, Jason looked relieved. She saw hope burning fiercely in his blue eyes. How she wished he could remember their love! It was a bittersweet moment.

"You will stay with me?" Jason gestured around the cozy kitchen. "Here?"

"If you want me to, Jason. Yes. But you may want to live alone. So it's up to you." Annie hated saying that, but she had to for Jason's sake. Daily, he was maturing, and Annie didn't want to keep making decisions for him. It would do no good to push herself into his new life if his need for her had changed.

Jason felt roiling sensations in his chest and he frowned and rubbed the region. "No . . . I like having you here, Annie. I would miss you. You don't want to leave, do you?" He anxiously searched her darkened eyes. Her lips were set, her hands folded on the table in front of her.

"I'd like to stay, Jason. Only if it works for you, okay?" Annie swallowed hard. She wanted to say *Living with you is the rightest thing in the world for me, Jason. At least I can love you at a distance, which is better than nothing. . . .*

"Good!" He reached out and gripped her hands. "Then let's celebrate, okay? I was making us a salad."

His simplicity was endearing. Annie squeezed his long, lean fingers momentarily. "Yeah, let's celebrate, Cowboy. . . ." As she released his hand and slowly stood up, Annie decided to call her mother tonight, after Jason was in bed and asleep. She had some serious stuff to speak to her about. Besides, her parents would be thrilled to hear of her new job. She'd dragged her feet about calling them to tell them that the Army had summarily discharged her. Now that she had a new future ahead of her, she looked forward to talking to them about it.

"Mom, I need your help." Annie sat curled up on the leather couch near the fireplace. It was midnight and she'd awakened her mother. She had had no choice, because Jason hadn't gone to bed until an hour ago. Annie had made sure that he was sleeping deeply before making the call.

"Sure, honey, no problem. Just let me rub the sleep out of my eyes. . . ."

Annie heard her get up and set the phone down on the bed stand. She heard her father mutter something, and her mother shushing him back to sleep.

"Okay," Lane said then. "I'm out in the kitchen. Hold on, I want to put the phone back in the cradle in the bedroom — be right back."

Annie waited patiently. When her mother returned on the line, she said, "I'm sorry to call you so late, Mom. I have some great news for you, and I also need your counsel on something else."

"Sure. What's going on?"

Annie filled her in on the Army discharge and getting the job with Perseus as a helicopter pilot.

Lane sighed. "Wow, what a day!"

"Tell me about it," Annie griped. "My head's still spinning from it all."

"And Jason wants you to stay?"

"Yes."

"And you're coping?"

Annie grimaced. "Barely, at times . . . But then there's good days, too, so I'm not complaining."

"He's maturing before your eyes, Annie. He was very childlike at first and now he seems to be in his late teens, from what you've shared with me. That's a good sign that his brain is healing."

"I'm glad to hear it," Annie said quietly. She lifted her head and looked to the living room entrance to make sure Jason was still asleep. She heard him snoring off and on. "Mom, I remember stories told by Grandma long ago, when I would sit at her feet on a winter's night in front of our fireplace. She'd spin stories about being a shaman."

"I remember those times very well. You'd sit there in rapt attention, and even when she got tired, you'd beg her for one more story." Lane laughed softly.

"I never forgot any of them, Mom. Grandma

was a shaman, and she trained you to be one."

"That's right. And you could, too, if you want. I would love to train you to do the work."

Compressing her lips, Annie said in a sad tone, "I wish I had become a medicine woman, Mom. I could sure use that knowledge right now to help Jason. Remember when Grandma would talk about people losing pieces of their spirit? That these pieces of energy were stuck in the time when they'd experienced some sort of awful trauma?"

"Of course. That's what happens, dear."

"And you're familiar with this?"

"Yes. It's part of the knowledge my mother shared with me."

"What do you call it? I know there's a name for it, but I can't remember the words she used. . . ."

"Soul recovery."

"Yes! That's it!" Annie curled up on the couch and tried to keep her voice low even though she was excited. "Mom, I'm positive that Jason has lost a piece of his spirit due to that RPG exploding in our tent. He's not really here. I remember Grandma saying that people who had lost a piece of themselves had a faraway or vacant look in their eyes. Ever since the explosion, Jason's eyes have been dull looking, when they used to sparkle. I loved gazing at them because they shone with such energy, warmth and humor.

Now . . ." Annie's voice dropped. "It's as if he's half-alive, Mom. He's not whole. . . . Something's missing. I can *feel* it. And I'm frustrated. I don't know what to do about it . . . how to help him . . . or if he *can* be helped to get back his missing piece."

"You're right," Lane said gently. "He lost part of himself due to that trauma. That much I can tell you. In training with my mother I learned that people can lose a piece of their spirit in many ways. For instance, in a car accident. Or from any kind of shock that could affect a person on a mental, emotional, physical or spiritual level."

"So Jason lost a part of his spirit in the attack?"

"Correct. But a person could do so by tripping and falling, or maybe receiving bad news, like being fired from a job, or being told your spouse wants a divorce, or suffering through the death of a child or another loved one. All these situations can affect a person's spirit. There's no way to tell who may or may not be affected, Annie, but there are definite signs of what we call soul loss. And when we see them, we perform a ceremonial shamanic journey on that person's behalf to retrieve the missing piece, and bring it back."

"That's what I thought!" Hope stirred in Annie. "Mom, I know I'm not trained — and I'm gonna rectify that shortly — but is there *anything* I can do right now to help Jason retrieve that lost piece of his spirit and bring it back to him? Anything?" Her voice cracked. Annie closed her eyes, praying that her mother would say yes. She had no training, no knowledge of this secret and sacred information. It was passed on verbally from mother to daughter, one generation to the next. Native Americans never wrote anything down, but passed on their wisdom one-on-one.

Sighing, Lane said, "Let me think a moment, love. . . ."

Fear ate at Annie as she sat there tensely, gripping the phone at her ear. She prayed to the Great Spirit that there was something that could be done. Usually, a person went to a medicine woman or man, but Jason wasn't up to traveling yet. Annie wasn't sure that he would agree to such a healing, either — but then again, he might. She simply didn't know.

"Okay, here's what you can try, Annie. But I'm not guaranteeing it will work. You understand me?"

"Sure, Mom. Tell me?"

"Build a sweat lodge. Have Jason help you. Teach him what a sweat is all about. You can't help someone retrieve the lost piece of themselves without their knowledge and approval. As you build the sweat, talk to him. Tell him about soul loss and recovery."

"Okay . . . I build a sweat. What then?"

Her heart leaped with such hope that her voice wobbled with excitement.

"The necklace, Annie. Have him hold the rainbow medicine necklace in the sweat. You've done many sweats yourself and know how to conduct the ceremony. He's to go into the sweat with you. And Jason has to pray to the Great Spirit to bring that lost piece back."

"I understand."

"Annie, there's no guarantee it will work."

"But there's a chance, Mom. A chance!"

"Yes, but Pumpkin, you won't know for sure for some weeks. You will know if his eyes change — if he regains that sparkle in them. If the piece is brought back through his desire, through his heart, with the help of the Great Spirit and the energy of that necklace, you will probably know within thirty days. It takes a full moon cycle for the piece or pieces to reintegrate and become a part of his spirit again. Sometimes, depending upon the loss and how large it is, it can take up to ninety days. You won't know right after the sweat ceremony, so don't set yourself up to expect that, okay?"

Annie laughed softly, joy filling her. "I know, Mom. You've said it thousands of times to me over the years — expect nothing, receive everything."

Lane laughed with her. "That's right. And listen, you first need to check with his doctor to make sure he can be in a sweat. Let the doc decide if he can handle that range of temperature and humidity. It will raise his blood pressure, and the last thing you want is to have the fluid levels in his brain increase and put pressure on that newly healed area. Okay?"

"Yes, Mom, I promise to talk to Dr. Dorf about this first . . . and I'll also talk to Morgan and Laura, even before I ever talk to Jason about it."

"Good," Lane stated. "So, now that I'm awake, what *else* is going on? I've been picking up on you all day. Tell me more about your new job. I know Canyon will fire off a hundred questions at me tomorrow morning across the breakfast table, so tell all. I want to be prepared to answer them."

Annie laughed quietly. "A lot has happened. Let me fill you in. . . ."

"Annie, you're saying that this Apache healing ceremony might help our son? And that Dr. Dorf has approved of it?" Morgan demanded.

Annie sat in a leather chair opposite them in their large cedar living room. Morgan and Laura sat on the couch together, their faces showing concern and hope. "Yes, sir, she has. I've told you everything about it. Native Americans have used the sweat lodge as a healing tool for thousands of years. Leading a sweat is a serious task, and I was trained to do so by my mother for many years. I've seen miracles happen in it. Miracles." Annie held their doubting gazes. "I know this isn't a medical technique that you're familiar with . . . and I'm sure it's not a part of your belief system." Annie knew they went to the Presbyterian church every Sunday, and they gave a great deal of money to the church to help the poor through the worldwide charities.

Laura smiled a little. "Annie, I've seen healing take place in many places, not just in a church. I'm very open to alternative medicine. A few of our mercenaries are trained homeopaths and I've seen it help people." She looked at her husband, who was frowning. "I've read enough books on complementary medicine to know that Native American ways of healing are respected. Furthermore, they are being looked into by medical researchers because they *are* effective." She took her husband's hand. "Morgan?"

Shrugging, he muttered, "So long as Dr. Dorf has okayed it, I'm all right with it." He studied Annie. "But I don't know how a necklace could help Jason. I just don't understand it."

Opening her hands, Annie said, "I know the world is a mysterious place and cannot be explained, sir. Our medicine tradition is to tend first to a person's spirit. We know the spirit can be wounded or split off during a crisis, and believe all healing must begin there. I can't convince you, and I'm not trying to. I just want your blessing to try it. Jason isn't all here. Even you can see that. You see it in his eyes. . . ."

Laura sighed. "She's right, darling. Jason's eyes are so much dimmer now. There's no spark, no life in them."

"Look at it this way," Annie urged. "Undergoing a sweat lodge ceremony to call back his spirit isn't going to hurt Jason." She tried to smile to ease the worry she saw on Morgan's face. "If nothing else, he'll have a good sweat and wash out the toxins from his body."

"True," Morgan murmured. He looked over at Laura, squeezing her hand. "What do you say?"

"I have a good feeling about this, Morgan. I think it will help Jason in some way. Call it a gut hunch."

Annie watched the couple with trepidation. She badly wanted to give Jason the chance to get his spirit back, but his parents had to approve. Laura's face shone with eagerness. Morgan remained reticent and unconvinced.

Annie pulled a small book from her bag. The cover was blue, with a yellow circle on the front. Flying across the circle was the silhouette of a great blue heron. "Sir? I managed to find this at the Phillipsburg library yesterday." She walked over to Morgan and handed it to him. "I did a lot of research trying to find if any Native American had written about soul loss." She smiled briefly. "Ours is a verbal tradition, and we usually hand info down that way." She pointed to the small volume in Morgan's hands. "This book is called *Soul Recovery and Extraction* by Running Elk, a shaman from the Cheyenne nation. She doesn't give away the actual techniques that a shaman uses to bring back soul pieces, but she does explain about the process in easy-to-understand terms. More importantly, she has cases in there about people who have suffered soul loss and how they have returned to health once a sweat was done for them."

"This is wonderful!" Laura whispered, eager to look at the book Morgan held.

"Yes," Annie murmured, shoving her hands in her jeans pockets as she stood near the couch. "The author names all the symptoms of soul loss, too, so people can identify it. There are quite a few, and I think you'll note a number of them in Jason. Anyway . . ." Annie backed away from the couch. "I don't want to overstay my welcome here. It's almost dinnertime, and I have to drive back to the cabin to help Jas fix a meal."

Morgan thumbed through the small book. "I'm glad to have this, Annie. It should help me understand it all."

"I know, sir. We're of two different cultures, I realize. But if something might help, why not try it? There's no guarantee, of course, so I don't want you getting your hopes up too much, either."

Nodding, Morgan gave the book to Laura, who eagerly took it. "Give us a few days, Annie? We'll let you know after we've read about it and discussed it."

"Of course, sir." She lifted her hand. "No rush." *Liar,* she thought, turning to get her jacket. Annie wanted them to be as eager as she was. She'd watched her mother perform soul retrieval ceremonies and she'd seen people come out of them feeling much better. They usually healed completely within several months.

Trying to tame her impatience, Annie grabbed her light yellow jacket and, saying her goodbyes, let herself out of the house.

It was warm on this late May evening. Spring was in the air. Shrugging into her coat, Annie headed for the gravel drive where she'd left the car. Her feet were light. She felt hope. Would Morgan and Laura allow Jason to try an unconventional means of healing? Traditional medicine had done everything it could for Jason. Now it was time to try an alternative, to help him in the next steps of his recovery. As Annie opened the door to her car, pulled the seat belt across her lap and started the engine, she felt a strong surge of hope in her chest.

"What can a sweat lodge ceremony hurt?" Laura said as she sat with Morgan in the breakfast nook three days later. The soul recovery book was on the table between them, along with cups of coffee and plates of eggs and bacon. She lifted her cup to her lips and sipped it as she eyed her husband. Sunlight shifted through the three-sided alcove, illuminating the Pothos plants that hung in each window.

Stabbing at his home fries, Morgan said, "I don't think it will hurt anything." He looked up, fork halted in midair. "Frankly, when I read the signs of soul loss, I saw a lot of them in Jason. I was amazed, Laura." He popped the food into his mouth.

"I know." She picked up the book and turned a few pages. "Here are the signs he has — depression. Asking 'why am I here?' A feeling of detachment. He's always saying he wished he could connect emotionally with us, Morgan. I see him struggle with that all the time."

"I don't know who hurts worse from it. . . ."

"Blocks of memory loss. That is a *big* one in his case." Laura read down the list. "A vague feeling of impending doom." She lifted her head. "He has PTSD, and that's a definite sign of it."

Morgan slathered strawberry jam over his English muffin. "I saw that one symptom and thought the same thing."

"I was very taken by the things people say when they've experienced soul loss," Laura murmured. "This author listed twenty different cases, and I wrote down those I've heard Jason say, such as 'I don't feel whole,' 'I can't sleep well at night,' 'I feel as if there's a gaping hole here.' You know, he's said that and pointed to his head injury time and again."

Morgan nodded, moving the scrambled eggs around on the plate with his fork. "What got me from the book was the person who said, 'My senses feel dead, I don't feel any joy or sadness.'" Sighing, he added, "Based upon that book, there's no question Jason has soul loss. But I find it so weird, Laura. That's a world I've never been in. It rings of voodoo to me."

Laura buttered her muffin. "You know who you might talk to about this?"

Disgruntled, Morgan looked up. "Who?"

"Your second in command, Mike Houston. He's known as the Jaguar God down in Peru. He's part Peruvian Indian, and his mother was a Quechua medicine woman. I've had more than one lunch with Anne, his wife, and she's told me some *very* interesting things about Mike's spiritual background. According to her, he's a shaman himself, Morgan."

"Huh?" He looked up, frowning. "Mike? A shaman? Like the type Annie is talking about?"

"Yes, love." Laura reached over and patted Morgan's hand. "Men never talk about personal stuff, you poor dears. Women, on the other hand, explore our personal lives endlessly with one another. That's how we find out such things. Mike is highly spiritual, and is a trained shaman through his mother's heritage. That's why, when Annie started telling us about this, I was a bit familiar with it."

"Humph."

Smiling patiently, Laura said, "Talk to Mike today, okay? Take the book with you and ask him what he thinks about this soul loss ceremony. Talk over Annie's plan with him. I'll bet he'll give you some feedback. And I think you need to educate yourself about other people's cultural belief systems so you don't feel so uncomfortable with them."

As always, Laura saw right through him. Morgan finished his breakfast and wiped his mouth with the pink linen napkin. Setting it aside, he stood and buttoned his dark brown suit coat. "Okay, I'll do just that." He saw Laura smiling like the cat who got the cream. Leaning over, he kissed her beautiful mouth. "I'll see you and our tyke at lunchtime. . . ."

Mike Houston was in his office, dressed in a red polo shirt, chino pants and tennis shoes when Morgan arrived.

"Got a minute?" Morgan asked.

"Sure, come on in." Mike got up and went to the coffee dispenser behind his desk. For him, Peruvian coffee was a must. He had the beans flown in by a friend from Cuzco once a month. "Want some?"

"No, thanks," Morgan said, sitting down in front of his desk. "I just had breakfast."

"So, to what do I owe the pleasure of this unexpected visit?" Mike asked, perching a hip on the corner of his desk, near where Morgan sat.

"Something's up that I need your help on." Morgan handed him the book on soul recovery and told him the story. He watched Mike's face closely as the ex-Army Special Forces officer thumbed through the book. He stopped drinking his coffee and listened to Morgan's story of what Annie had suggested for his son.

Once he was done explaining, Morgan looked hard at Mike, whose face was pensive and unreadable. "Well? Is this legit? Or is this soul recovery fiction? You're Peruvian Indian, and Laura said you would know."

Giving Morgan a slight smile, Mike sipped his coffee and set the book on his messy

340

desk. "Yeah, it's real, Morgan. And soul recovery works."

Scowling, Morgan said, "You've seen it work?"

"Yes, many times. Shamanism is one of the main healing methods in South America."

"And it's successful?"

"Often, yes. But there are a lot of different factors involved. Some of it depends upon the person's soul path for this lifetime. . . ." Mike's words trailed off. "Look, Morgan, we're talking pure metaphysics here. We're talking about unseen, invisible worlds and realms. You've never been steeped in these traditions, so you're looking at them like a fish out of water. My advice is do it. There's nothing to lose and everything to gain from it. It won't hurt Jason. It can only help."

"But will it work?"

"If you're asking for a hundred percent guarantee, I can't give it to you. No medicine person will do so. All we can do is try. The ceremony Annie knows, I'm sure, was taught to her by her mother. It won't harm Jason. I think you should give it a shot."

Sitting there ruminating, Morgan stared at the desk for several moments. "You're right," he sighed, frowning. "What I'm battling right now is my own beliefs versus Annie's view of the world. I don't grasp her reality as she sees it, but to be fair, I wasn't raised Indian. I was raised in a traditional church setting."

"Right," Houston said with a tight smile. "And I was raised like Annie. I grew up knowing about the invisible worlds, the spirits there. But that isn't the point here. The point is this ceremony *might* help Jason, and I think you'll give her permission based on that."

"Right as always," Morgan growled good-naturedly as he pushed himself out of the chair. "Thanks, Mike, you've helped me make up my mind on this."

"I know it sounds weird to you, Morgan, but not to me . . . not to the people around the world who deal with the spirit and use shamanism as a tool against suffering. Out there in the jungles, there ain't no doctors, and certainly no modern medicine to fix people up. Shamanism is as old as human beings here on this earth. It's not something new. It's well-established and it works."

Standing at the door, Morgan perused Mike as he slid off the desk. "Why haven't you ever told me this before?"

Grinning, Houston said, "Because you never asked. In our tradition, if you don't ask, you don't get."

Chapter 18

Jason crawled on his hands and knees through the small entrance to the sweat lodge that he and Annie had constructed earlier in the afternoon. They had built it near the natural hot springs that sat behind the cabin. The crater was volcanically heated and he'd used it often to soak in. Annie felt building the lodge nearby would be powerful. Sitting cross-legged on the earth in his blue swim trunks, a thick, large towel across his shoulders, he waited. Anxiety rippled through him as he sat opposite the doorway, which faced the east. The sun had gone down an hour ago, and the gray light of dusk was rapidly being eaten up by the approaching night.

He had another towel draped across his bare legs. Annie had told him that the towels would be necessary protection against the heat, which could become intense. He wouldn't burn, she'd said, but it might feel that way. He was glad for the towels. Between his crossed legs, he held the deerskin pouch that contained the rainbow medicine necklace. Would it work? Was there such a thing as soul loss? Had he really lost part of

343

himself during that attack?

Jason wasn't sure, but since he wanted more than anything to remember again, he was willing to try anything. Just the idea of getting better made him eager to undergo this healing method. That was the one thing in Annie's long, careful explanation that had snagged his interest. Jason didn't like living a life built upon knowledge of only the past few months. He wanted his memories back. He wanted the picture albums that he looked at daily to finally mean something personally to him.

Hearing Annie outside, Jason knew she was taking a pitchfork and scraping away coals of the very hot fire they'd built ten feet away from the sweat lodge. There were four parts to a sweat — four rounds of prayer and rituals — and seven rocks were added during each round. She was finding the first heated stone, dropping it several times on the earth to shake the ashes off it so they wouldn't fly up in the sweat lodge and cause breathing problems for him inside. Hearing her soft footsteps, he saw her legs at the door.

"Coming in with the first rock, Jason." She leaned down and expertly guided the pitchfork which carried a glowing red rock the size of a cantaloupe, into the fire pit in front of him. Earlier today, he'd dug that fire pit. It was roughly two feet deep so that it could hold twenty-eight stones.

The rock fell into the pit, and he stared at it. It was lava, the only stone to use, Annie had told him. If a sedimentary rock were used, it could explode, literally, when a ladleful of water was thrown on it. The only stones that could withstand extreme heat and then cold water splashed upon them were igneous or "fire rocks." Luckily, as they'd hunted for the right type today, they had found a plentiful supply all around the cabin.

As she added six more stones, Jason felt the heat beginning to radiate in waves throughout the small lodge. The structure was barely ten feet in diameter, created out of saplings that were skinned of their bark. His mother had come up earlier in the day and brought six old, worn blankets that they'd spread across the skeleton of bowed saplings to seal the heat inside. When water was thrown on the hot stones, steam rose inside the dark lodge. Annie had told Jason that the lodge symbolized Mother Earth's womb, being hot, moist, fertile and dark. The spirit of Mother Earth came into the lodge to help heal those who took part in a sweat.

After the first seven stones were in the pit, he watched as Annie crawled in. She wore a loose T-shirt and a pair of navy-blue shorts. Her hair was in two braids, with red yarn wound among the black strands. Small fluffy feathers from an eagle's breast were tied to the end of each braid. Sitting to the left of the door, Annie reached over and pulled down the thick flap. Instantly, the lodge was sealed and plunged into darkness, except for the reddish glow of the rocks in front of him. Already, Jason felt rivulets of sweat beginning to course down his rib cage. Wiping his brow, he said, "You were right. This is hot. . . ."

Annie laughed. She knelt over the rocks and sprinkled a tiny pinch of cedar, sacred sage and tobacco on each one, mentally welcoming it to the sweat. The odor that wafted upward was sweet and wonderful to her.

"Breathe this in, Jason. It's sacred herbs. It will help clear you and prepare your spirit for healing. . . ."

"Okay . . ." He did as she instructed. Then Annie sat down, placing a large bucket of cool water between herself and the fire pit. A wooden ladle rested on the rim of the bucket, along with sprigs of fresh sage to bless the water and make it sacred. Annie set a small drum and drumstick nearby.

Mesmerized by the ancient ceremony, Jason watched her in the dim light, finding himself riveted by each of her graceful movements. Annie picked up the wooden ladle.

"I'm going to throw water on the rocks now, Jason. It's going to get steamy in here in a hurry. After I've done so, I'll pick up the drum, beat it with a slow rhythm and start singing in Apache. This is the welcoming round. I'll welcome the four directions, Father Sky and Mother Earth to come into our lodge with us. All you need to do is sit there, eyes closed, and let the energy carry you."

"Okay. . . ."

"Scared?"

"Yeah. . . ."

"That's okay. Most people are anxious in their first sweat. Remember, if it gets too hot for you, lie down and place your face against the earth. Heat rises. It's always cooler on the floor."

"Okay. . . ." He saw her throw the first ladle of water on the glowing stones. He heard the spit and hiss of the rocks. Oddly, he thought he saw faces in the wavering heat and white steam now rising quickly toward the top of the lodge. Faces he knew . . . but who? Transfixed by them, he watched them shimmer and dissolve as the cooling water took the red glow out of the stones. The lodge turned inky black. He could see nothing.

The drum began beating. Jason closed his eyes and held the pouch containing the rainbow medicine necklace a little tighter. Annie's low, husky voice, soft and healing, began to flow around the tiny lodge. Heat prickled his ears. Jason spread the towel over his head and shoulders as Annie had taught him to do. Earlier, she'd given him a handful of fresh sage. His nose began to feel hot, as if it were being burned. He pressed the sage against his face and opened his mouth to breathe.

The moment he inhaled the sweet, medicinal fragrance of the herb he felt light-headed. A spinning sensation began deep within him, and he reached out to feel the earth, cool and stabilizing, beneath him. Annie had told him to keep his eyes closed, to go within himself once the drum started playing. Was this whirling sensation that was pulling him downward into the darkness part of the healing? Jason wasn't sure. He was afraid, and resisted it. Yet the slow, pounding beat of the drum reverberated around him, soothing him. Annie's voice seemed to be right beside him, calming his anxiety. Everything became distorted, and he could no longer separate out realities. Fear stabbed at him once more. Digging his fingers into the soft, damp earth, Jason panicked for a moment. He wanted out of here. Now.

And then he remembered that Annie had told him everyone experienced this momentary fear during the first sweat. *That is the sickness,* she warned him. *The part that makes a person want to run away.* The healthy part of his spirit would want him to stay. Taking several gulping breaths, Jason concentrated on the sweet smell of the sage entering his lungs, instead of on his fear.

Losing track of space and time, Jason

stopped fighting the spinning sensation that had captured him. The heat was getting to him, so he eased down upon his side, facing the fire pit. It *was* much cooler! Breathing a sigh of relief, Jason gripped the pouch to his chest and held it close. It felt comforting.

Eyes closed, he began to pray, as Annie had asked him to, for what he had lost to come back to him. Over and over he prayed for the piece of his spirit to return to him, to integrate with him now.

The spinning continued, and Jason surrendered to it. Sweat ran freely down his body. His skin was smarting from the heat. The darkness was all consuming. The throbbing of the drum seemed to echo the heartbeat of the earth, and it helped to stabilize him. Each time Annie stopped drumming to throw more water on the hissing stones, he missed the comforting sound. As soon as she started again, Jason felt calmer.

The second round was the prayer round. Jason remained on the floor as Annie brought in seven more red, glowing stones to add to the ones already in the fire pit. When she closed the door once more and added the water, he sat up. She drummed and sang in Apache for a short period and then stopped. Jason knew he was to pray out loud, and he did, once again asking for his spirit to return to him.

He listened to Annie's soft, husky prayers

for her family, for his family and for him. It brought unexpected tears to his eyes. The heat was stifling now, the red glow of the stones quickly snuffed out as she splashed on the water. Steam shot up and hissed throughout the darkness, and the temperature soared. Jason lay down on the ground again, holding the pouch close to his heart. This time, as the drumming began, he found himself moving in a tight, downward spiral. Eyes closed, he followed the sinking, spinning sensation, no longer afraid as before.

In his mind's eye, Jason suddenly saw the darkness begin to change. At first it was a lurid gray, and then more and more light appeared until it was as if he were standing outside on a bright sunny day. What he saw mystified him — a golden eagle sitting on the ground, looking at him.

"I am called Wambli Gleska, Spotted Eagle. Are you ready, my brother?" the bird asked.

Jason stood there, mesmerized by the beautiful, magnificent creature, its bronze plumage blazing in the sunlight. Its hooked beak was yellow, its eyes a glowing gold. The power of the eagle was unmistakable.

Jason walked nearer. "Who are you?"

"I'm your spirit guide, brother. Are you ready?"

"Ready for what?" Jason saw only the eagle. Around them was bright light, but it didn't hurt his eyes. The drumming seemed very faraway now.

"To retrieve the part of your soul that was lost. I can take you to it."

"How?"

"Climb upon my back. I will fly you to the dark world to find it."

How ridiculous! Jason stood there in front of the eagle, shaking his head. "But you're too small. You can't carry me."

"Yes, I can. Watch. . . ."

To his amazement, Jason saw the eagle grow to a huge size.

"Now, climb on my back, hold on to my feathers, and I will take you where you must go."

Astonished, he did as he was told. The instant he got into position on the eagle's back, Wambli Gleska flapped his mighty wings and they were off and flying! Jason held on to the feathers with a death grip. Suddenly, the earth was far below them, covered with fir trees. He saw the sweat lodge, the cabin . . . and then his parents' home. The eagle flew strongly and swiftly, so fast the green mountains became a blur beneath them. Jason laughed. He was flying! He could feel it. He had clamped his legs to the sides of the eagle and he felt the movement of the bird's muscles. The wind whistled past his face, making his eyes water. The beating wings created gusts of wind against his body. He was really here. He was really flying!

"Hold on, brother," the eagle warned him. "We are going to dive downward. See that hole in the ground? It is a gopher hole. We are going to dive into it and find our way down to the dark world deep within our mother."

Jason saw the hole just as Wambli Gleska stooped and went into a steep dive. Gasping, Jason held on for dear life. How could an eagle fit into a gopher hole, much less a grown man? *Impossible!* They plunged downward at a hurtling pace, so rapidly the resulting wind nearly unseated Jason from the eagle's back. He wanted to cry out to the bird to stop, but he couldn't. As he clung to his feathered steed, they zoomed down toward the impossibly tiny gopher hole visible on the flat prairie.

In a blink of an eye, they entered the hole, and it was suddenly dark. Jason gasped. He could feel the earth around them. The eagle flapped steadily, moving ever downward through the tunnel. The earth felt warm and alive around them. Jason's mind said this was impossible, yet here he was, feeling every sensation. Up ahead he saw a tiny speck of light. The eagle let out a piercing shriek and flew strongly toward it, the light growing brighter and brighter. To Jason's surprise, they burst out of the hole. What he saw made him gasp.

Below him was a swamp — a dark gray marshy area with huge cypress trees draped with long, hanging strands of moss. Wambli Gleska flew over the swamp, which seemed to stretch in every direction for as far as Jason could see. The water was muddy and smelled like rotten eggs. It made him nauseous.

The eagle flew to a barren, sandy bank and landed there. When Jason slid off its back, the earth felt solid beneath his feet.

The eagle ruffled its feathers, shook them and then folded its wings. "Brother, this is the swamp of despair. This is where many lost spirits come when they are depressed, sad or grieving. You need to stand at the water's edge. You need to call back the lost piece of your spirit. It is here."

Nodding, Jason went to the bank. Everything he saw was in black-and-white. The swamp reminded him of looking through a film negative, with shades of gray, black and a few white tones to offset the cheerless landscape. He saw cattails at the edge, the surface of the water like a mirror except where emergent plants poked their heads up here and there. Above him, the sky was a pale gray. It felt heavy to Jason, almost as if a weight were bearing down on him. It was a very gloomy place. He felt terrible here, felt a bone-gnawing melancholy that seemed to eat at him like burning acid.

Jason began to call out, "Jason Trayhern, I need you to come back to me!" Annie had told him what to say. He stood there, the rainbow necklace pressed to his heart as he looked anxiously across the swamp. Nothing moved. There were no birds, no bees. No sounds. This was truly a dead place.

"Keep calling, brother. Your spirit needs to be convinced you really want it to return to you."

This time, Jason put all his heart into his request. He kept it up, calling again and again. Finally, he thought he saw movement in the darker reaches of the swamp. Narrowing his eyes, he blinked. In the distance he detected the shadowy outline of a man, very similar in physical structure to himself. He moved slowly forward, the water knee-deep around him.

Jason heard the figure sloshing toward him with each step, and his heart raced. The light was dim and he couldn't make out the features of the person who was slowly approaching. Was it him? The piece he'd lost? Jason wasn't sure of the process.

As the spirit drew closer, he gasped. The man looked like him, only he was in a uniform, the one Jason had worn in Afghanistan. He recognized it because Annie had shown him photos she'd taken over there.

"Lie down, brother. Lie on the bank of the swamp. On your back," the eagle advised.

"Close your eyes and lie down. Ask your spirit to enter your heart and become part of you once again."

Jason couldn't tear his gaze from the soldier's face. He saw the wound on the left side of his head, the blood pumping from his cheek wound. He saw terror and bleakness in his eyes.

"Quickly!" the eagle commanded.

The spirit figure moved steadily toward him, and frightened, Jason lay down on the bank, his arms at his sides. He felt his chest rising and falling with each fearful breath, and he clenched the rainbow necklace in his left hand. Would his spirit come? What would it feel like to have it enter his heart? Would he die?

Trying to steady himself, Jason heard the figure step out of the water. Droplets struck his bare arm. This was real! This wasn't his imagination! Now he was truly frightened. Breathing chaotically, Jason squeezed his eyes shut, though he kept asking his spirit to come back to him.

Suddenly he felt a warmth radiating from his heart. It startled Jason, but he didn't open his eyes. He felt the warmth spread and then move downward, through his hips, his thighs, calves and finally into his feet. It felt good. Relaxing a little, Jason wondered if the spirit had entered him and caused this sensation. He didn't know. Now he felt that warmth spread through his upper chest, flow into each of his arms and fingers. The warmth then moved up into his neck and filled his head. The sensation of fullness pressing his brain against his skull was genuine. For a second, Jason wondered if his head was going to split open, the pressure was so intense.

Then, abruptly, he heard the loud, almost jarring beat of the drum once again. Blinking, he opened his eyes. He was lying on the cool soil of the lodge once more, and Annie was singing.

Slowly, Jason sat up, reaching out to steady himself when dizziness assailed him. What had happened? When this ceremony was over, he was anxious to talk to Annie about what had occurred. Had his spirit come back? A deep hope, clean and sharp, moved through his heart.

"And that's what happened to me in there, Annie," Jason said. He sat on the couch, wearing clean, dry clothes. After taking a shower, he'd met with her in the living room. She, too, had showered, and looked beautiful in a pink tank top and a pair of blue jeans. Her wet hair hung in long, dark strands as she combed it out.

"I'll have to call my mom, Jason, to tell her of your experience. I'm not a trained shaman, so I don't have a clue as to what happened to you in the sweat."

He probed her gold gaze. "But does it sound like my spirit came back? Something happened, Annie. I *felt* it. It was so *real*."

She smiled at him. "I'll call her and ask, okay?" She set the comb aside, went to the couch where Jason sat and picked up the phone.

Jason waited impatiently. Although he didn't feel any different, and had no new memories, something had changed in him, though he couldn't put words to it. As Annie sat beside him, he absorbed her nearness, his heart expanding with fierce new emotions toward her. Only Annie made him feel like this, and Jason savored the sensations. Just listening to her husky voice as she spoke to her mother made him feel calmer. She was always able to soothe him.

Anxiety gripped him as Annie put down the phone and twisted toward him.

"Mom says you called your spirit back. Isn't that wonderful?" Annie reached out and gave him a quick hug. That was all the intimacy she would allow herself. She wanted to kiss Jason, hug him and love him, but that wasn't possible.

"Really?" he murmured, lifting his arms. Annie withdrew before he could embrace her in return. Seeing the dancing joy in her golden eyes, he laughed a little.

"Yeah, really."

"So . . . what now?" he asked, opening his hands.

"We wait. Mom said when a piece of a person's spirit returns it can take thirty to ninety days for it to integrate. Once it has, you should get your memories back."

Her smile made him warm inside. "Is there anything I have to do?"

"Mom said to picture what you saw, each night for the next moon cycle. That's twenty-eight days, Jason. She said before you go to sleep at night, to imagine your spirit and tell it how much you love it, how much you want it to stay with you. And tonight, you're supposed to ask, just one time, 'What gift did you bring me?' Mom said you'll get your answer on that question within ninety days, too." Annie smiled at Jason. Seeing the hope burning in his blue eyes, she settled her hand on his broad shoulder. "Now we wait. . . ."

Her hand was comforting, and yet it also stirred a lost memory within him. There wasn't a day that went by when Jason didn't want Annie near him. Lifting his head, he smiled at her. "This was a crazy thing, Annie. I thought I was imagining it all. But it felt real. Very real. I felt my spirit's footsteps on the earth, the vibration as he approached me. I couldn't see him at that time, but I felt water dropping off him onto me."

Nodding, Annie said, "There is so much more to this world than what we see. My

358

mom has always said we are blind, deaf and dumb. She says that we see only half our world." Annie pointed to her eyes. "The other half is seen with our third eye, here." And she pointed to the center of her fore-head. "She calls it our movie screen. Every-one has one, and as a person opens up psy-chically, it automatically starts to function."

Shaking his head, Jason sat back on the couch. "Well, what I saw astounded me. The eagle grew huge. And then, to fit into that gopher hole, we must have grown so small. . . . I don't know how to explain it. Or how the eagle could do it!"

Laughing, Annie stood up. "Don't even try! In the unseen world, the rules and laws are vastly different from third-dimensional reality. It's a very different place, but it exists right here in this world we think is the only one." She chuckled. "Come on, I made us some fresh lemonade before the sweat. We're dehy-drated and we need to drink a lot of fluids between now and bedtime."

"I want to call my parents."

Annie hesitated. "Okay . . . I'll get us some lemonade, you call them."

"It's a deal." Jason picked up the phone.

Out in the kitchen, Annie smiled to herself. She loved doing a sweat; it always made her feel so alive, refreshed and cleaned out. There was nothing like it to clear out a per-son's toxic stuff, both physically and on every other level. Opening the fridge, she drew out the pitcher of lemonade and poured two large glasses. Looking out at the dark, starry night, she saw a meteor flash by.

That was a good sign. To her, a meteor meant a spirit was returning home. Jason's piece had come home to him. Loving how nature talked to her in its own unique language, Annie put the pitcher back in the refrigerator. Keying her ear to Jason's voice as he spoke on the phone, she heard the enthusiasm in his tone. More than anything, Annie wanted Jason to be whole. His spirit had come back. Would it integrate and stay with him? Annie knew that sometimes people rejected the piece that had returned because it came back in the same condition it had left in.

Her mother had warned her that Jason might have several days or even weeks of being emotionally upset, supersensitive, perhaps very tearful, because the piece that had returned was the one that had been lost during the explosion when he'd been badly injured. No doubt he would have recurring headaches, pain in his face where he'd been cut, and nightmares. Annie had to prepare them both for such possibilities. When these effects occurred, it was sometimes too much for the person to cope with and they unconsciously released the piece once again. If that happened, Jason would stay the same. Lane had told Annie that about five percent of the clients she'd journeyed for had such a thing happen. That meant there was a ninety-five percent chance that Jason's piece would remain with him, even though the first couple of weeks might be rough and unsettling for him.

Picking up the glasses, Annie heard Jason laugh. Halting, she realized it was his *old* laugh. Not the soft, hesitant chuckle, but full, deep laughter. Heart pounding suddenly, Annie closed her eyes. The frosty, beaded moisture of the glasses dampened her fingers. *Oh, please, Great Spirit, let Jason come home. Home to all of us . . .*

Chapter 19

The dry heat of the July day made Jason sweat freely as he dragged the green watering hose along the white picket fence that surrounded the cabin. Without fences, deer would come eat the wildflowers that Annie had planted in early June. Looking up, he saw high, thin cirrus clouds, like strands of a horse's mane, against the blue sky. The shape of the clouds reminded him of Annie's long hair. Moving along the fence, he aimed the hose at the ground, where the flowers were vigorously growing and climbing.

His mind and his heart were on Annie. How he missed her! She had left a week ago to go to the Bell/Agusta Aerospace Company in Georgia to train on the AB139 helicopter. When she became qualified to fly it she could bring it home to Phillipsburg. This had been the loneliest week Jason could recall. Every night Annie phoned him and they talked for at least an hour. How he looked forward to that! Daily, he'd mark off the hours until her call. The next two nights, however, they would not be talking. Annie was flying at night to learn the instrumentation on the AB139. Sighing, he frowned.

The warm breeze embraced him and the intoxicating fragrance of the Douglas firs filled his nostrils. Brightly colored Gaillardia, red with yellow on their happy little faces, danced beneath the spray of water. Annie loved her flowers. He recalled helping her plant them along the fence. He'd been sick with the flu on the second day of planting, so he'd stayed in bed. She had said she was planting the seeds all along the fence because he'd done so as a child with his mother. Flowers reminded Annie of the rainbow, and Jason knew the rainbow was an important symbol to the Apache people.

Well, at least he would have some company this evening. His dad was driving up from work to have dinner with him at the cabin. Tomorrow night his mother would be bringing Pete and Kelly up. Jason would not be alone, and that satisfied him to a degree. He was discovering that he didn't like living alone. He was better off with people around. It made him feel good. Annie made him happy. She always had.

Annie . . . He rubbed his heart with his hand. Jason centered on the feelings he was having presently. He'd wanted to talk to Annie about how he felt toward her, but he was afraid. Afraid that she might not feel the same way about him. That was a fear that ate constantly at Jason, nibbling daily at his consciousness. And with her gone, it only increased his fear. What would it be like if Annie decided to leave him and move down to a condo in Phillipsburg? Shaking his head, he dragged the hose farther along the fence.

As he moved to a new area, he noticed that a group of vinelike plants that had climbed a good three feet up onto the fence were finally blooming. He didn't know what they were called, but Jason was strongly drawn to them. Setting the hose down, he knelt before the plants. Annie usually put the seed packet somewhere to identify the flower species. The bright red, yellow and white blooms had an intoxicating spicy fragrance. As he gently tunneled his fingers among the rounded green leaves, trying to locate the seed packet, he smiled. There! She had stapled it to the fence so it wouldn't get wet from the hose. Leaning over, Jason gently pulled the plants aside and squinted. The sun was bright and strong overhead and he'd worn a baseball cap to shade his light-sensitive eyes.

His heart thudded. The seed packet said sweet peas.

Suddenly, Jason felt his entire world stop. He had the oddest sensation, as if there were two of him, and that one part moved like a template over the other and snapped into place, making him whole once more. Unable to describe that split-second feeling, he stared

364

at the sweet pea package. And then he gasped. Thousands of images started coming back to him, pummeling his brain. Words. Pictures. Faces. Events . . . my God! He got up, stumbling backward, his eyes widening with shock.

What was going on? What was happening? Staggering, Jason moved to the porch and sat down on the wooden steps. He held his head, for it felt as if a wild wind was whirling around in his brain. He planted his elbows on his thighs and closed his eyes tightly as hundreds and hundreds of bits of information came tumbling into him, like a swift computer downloading facts into his mind. How long he sat there seeing myriad faces from his past that he recognized instantly, remembering events, too many to count, he didn't know. Gasping repeatedly, his fingers holding his skull, Jason felt an incredible avalanche of feelings along with these old, familiar images from his past.

The sun had changed position when he finally straightened. Gradually, Jason began to hear the birds chirping and singing around the cabin once more. He heard the gurgle of the hose where it lay among the sweet peas, watering them. As he slowly opened his eyes, tears spilled out of them. He barely saw the puddle of water that had flooded a good part of the lawn.

He was remembering! He had his memory

back! All of it! *My God!* Sitting there, Jason buried his wet face in his hands. A sob tore from him. Overwhelmed with emotions, he could only sit there, blown away by it all.

The sun shifted again. It was now behind the cabin, in the west. Jason forced himself to get up and go turn off the faucet, before the lawn become completely flooded. His steps unsteady, he tried to focus on the here and now. The present. Locating the faucet on the north side of the cabin, he leaned down and turned it off. Straightening, he walked back to the corner. *Sweet peas.* The flowers came in violet, purple and pink shades as well, planted all along one stretch of the fence near the gate. Annie had planted them because she knew his favorite flower was the sweet pea. And he bet she'd planted them in hopes they might jog his memory.

They sure as hell had. As Jason stood there mixing his past memories of her with the ones he'd had since the TBI, he wanted to cry all over again. My God, how she loved him. She'd stayed with him. Taken care of him. Healed him. . . .

Jason staggered back into the cabin. In the kitchen there was a box of tissues. He took several and sat down at the table. Blowing his nose, he sat there, hands on the table. The music playing on the CD player in the background, always classical and soft, soothed his torn-up inner world.

He loved Annie. And Jason wouldn't be able to see her until she got home, three days from now. She would be flying the helicopter back across the U.S. to Phillipsburg. Rubbing his face, Jason looked toward the back door. The clock on the wall read 5:00 p.m. In less than an hour, Morgan would be here — his father — the man he now called "Dad."

Grimacing, Jason buried his face in his hands. His breath was ragged with pain. Oh, God, the war between his old memories of his father and now . . . Red-hot pain serrated his heart and he felt like claws were tearing it out. What to do? How to feel? How to treat him? Jason wasn't sure.

Messed up — that was how he felt. As if someone had just pulverized him with another story of his life — very different from the one he'd had since the brain trauma. He remained in a state of chaos and confusion.

Jason sat there and remembered how Morgan had been so attentive lately, his hugs, his talks with him . . . the tenderness he had shown him. Shaking his head, Jason leaned back in the chair, his gaze moving to the ceiling and studying the pine rafters for some simple, sane answer. Nothing came.

"Crap." Jason set the front legs of the chair on the pine floor again with a thunk. More and more memories were spewing back — from his childhood and from the kidnapping.

It all hurt. Terribly. Jason sat there thinking that not knowing was better than knowing, in the case of his father. Still, he couldn't shake the knowledge that Morgan had been a wonderful parent to him since his injury.

Oh, God, what *was* he going to do? Jason had such violent, mixed emotions about his dad. And he had less than an hour to figure them out. How was he going to act with Morgan? Cold and aloof, as he'd been in his old life? Warm and eager, as he'd been recently? Jason seesawed back and forth, fearing the moment when Morgan would step through that door.

"Jason? Son? I'm here!" Morgan shouted as he opened the back door of the cabin. He balanced a bunch of take-out boxes. Not much of a chef himself, and wanting to spare Jason cooking duties, Morgan had stopped at Molly's Restaurant on the way up here, and ordered two roast beef dinners with mashed potatoes, gravy and the works. He'd found great comfort in the fact that his son loved the same food as he had before the explosion. In fact, Jason's tastes in food matched Morgan's, which made him happy in some small but important way.

Setting the sacks on the kitchen counter, Morgan turned as he heard footsteps coming down the hall. When his son appeared at the door, terror struck Morgan. Jason's eyes were red rimmed. His face was wan, almost as pale as when Morgan had seen him at the hospital in Germany shortly after surgery. Frightened, he moved over to his son, whose shoulders were slumped, his face raw with sorrow.

"Son? What's wrong?" Morgan reached for him, curving his fingers around Jason's upper arm. "Are you okay?"

Swallowing hard, Jason stared up into his father's anxious face. This was a man he was supposed to hate. A man who had abandoned him in his deepest hour of need, when he was a helpless six-year-old. Yet as Jason searched his father's gray, narrowing eyes and felt the warm, supportive strength of his hand, he couldn't find his voice. Instead, tears trailed out of his eyes.

"Come on," Morgan murmured, seeing the tears. "Come and sit down, son. Come on. . . ." And he guided Jason to a chair. His son eased into it without a word, a stunned look on his face. Moving around to the chair next to him, Morgan sat down, anxiety riffling through him. "Are you in pain, son? What's wrong?" He gripped Jason's hands, which were clenched on the table. "Did you hear from Annie? Is there something wrong with her?"

Gulping, Jason hung his head and shut his eyes. He couldn't stop crying, no matter how much he tried. Finally, he sniffed and looked up at his father. Somehow, Morgan's grip on his hands helped him find his voice. "I . . . uh, I was watering the flowers out there, along the fence. I was really drawn to some of them, and I bent down to find the seed packet that Annie stapled nearby. I pushed the plants aside and saw what was written on it — sweet peas."

"Yes?" Morgan's heart thudded with dread. What was wrong? He wanted to help Jason, but didn't understand why he was so upset. "Sweet peas? They were always your favorite flower. Your mother and you used to plant them every spring along the fence. Do you remember that?"

Jason took an unsteady breath. He held his father's concerned stare. "Yes . . . I saw that packet . . . and all of a sudden I felt this pressure in my head. All of a sudden I was blown away by thousands and thousands of memories — from my past. They're coming back — all of them. . . ." He stared at Morgan and saw his eyes flare first with surprise, then joy and then raw terror. Jason understood his father's fear. He was afraid Jason might treat him as before. He felt his father's fingers tighten momentarily around his hands, but he didn't pull away. No, Morgan did not abandon him this time, when Jason so desperately needed him.

"You . . . your memories. You got them back?" Morgan's voice was off-key. Dread tunneled through him. Yet, through it all, he saw great sadness in Jason's damp blue eyes. Without thinking, he patted his son's hands. "That's *great*, Jason! Wonderful!" And he meant it. Morgan wondered how Jason would treat him now that the ugly, distrustful past was once again a living memory. Inwardly, he shrank in terror. Was his boy going to cast him out of his life again for the awful mistakes he'd made in the past? Searching Jason's confused gaze, a large wave of love for his son flooded through him. Morgan murmured, "Son, I love you. No matter what happens, or what you remember about us from the past . . . I love you. I always will. . . ." His voice cracked.

Jason pulled one hand from beneath Morgan's scarred one. "I — I realize that. . . ." He swiped at his eyes self-consciously. Giving his dad an uncertain, trembling smile, he said, "And I don't remember ever crying like this. God, I've turned into a crybaby. . . ."

Morgan managed a thin smile. Would Jason reject him? It was the last thing he wanted. Yet it could happen. "You've got a lot of tears buried deep in you, son," he said in a raw, painful whisper. "From the past . . . because of me. Because of my arrogance about my family's safety and my emotional aloofness. I'm so sorry, Jason! I'm sorry I put you in harm's way. What it's done to our relationship . . . well, I can't tell you how much it hurt me to see the pain you carried because of it. I . . ." Morgan felt tears flood his eyes, and he cleared his throat ". . . I hope that you'll remember how I've treated you this second time around. . . . I saw it as a chance to try and make things right between us. I didn't abandon you this time, son. I learned from my mistakes with you and Katy. I've been able, I think, to be a much better parent with Kelly, Pete and Kamaria." He grimaced. "But you, especially, paid the price for my sins. I hope . . . God, I pray, Jason, that you'll forgive me! I want to continue the relationship we've had since your injury. I love you. I want to be a part of your life, son, if you'll allow me?" Morgan searched his pale face.

Heart cracking with anguish, Jason closed his eyes, placing his hand over his father's. "Dad . . . yeah. I've sat here for an hour replaying it all." Jason's voice grew hoarse. "I can't say I'm exactly proud of myself, either. I was acting like an immature six-year-old toward you, punishing you for the mistakes you made. . . ."

Heart soaring, Morgan absorbed the feel of Jason's hand on his own. "I left you unprotected and vulnerable, son. So I don't really blame you for how you feel toward me. I deserve your anger." Jason's gesture was so rich with promise. He wasn't pulling away, and he was trying to make amends. Hope burned in

Morgan's heart as he looked at Jason's face, at his eyes, which were so much clearer now. There was no doubt the "old" Jason was back. He had that sparkle in his eyes, and for that, Morgan thanked God a million times over.

Giving his father a beseeching look, Jason whispered unsteadily, "Listen, Dad, I've got hundreds and hundreds of memories hitting me from all sides and angles. I feel like someone has squashed a lifetime of living into me in one hour's time. I'm still having memories flooding in. Flashbacks. Some good, some really bad. The kidnapping . . ."

"I know," Morgan rasped. He gripped Jason's hand between his. "What can I do to help?"

Shrugging, Jason managed a sour smile. "Just being here helps. I need somebody to talk to. Annie's out of touch. I can't get ahold of her until I see her at the Phillipsburg Airport three days from now."

"How about you come home with me?" Morgan suggested. "Be with us. We're your family. Your mother is going to be ecstatic. Let us help you, surround you, hold you close. Let us be there to listen. Please?" Morgan held his breath. He saw Jason considering it.

"Yeah . . . okay, Dad. I'd like that." Looking around, he said, "I don't want to be alone, not right now. . . ."

Those words serrated Morgan's heart. In that instant, his memory of Jason as a six-year-old, kidnapped by strangers who hated him because of his father's activities, slammed into him. The pain was so deep that Morgan rubbed his chest. The fact that Jason had forgiven him, was now willing to move forward, choked him up. Tears dribbled down his face as he looked at his son's features, calmer now that they'd talked.

"Thanks for giving me another chance, son . . . for giving all of us a chance to show you just how much we really do love you. And always have, no matter what you did with your life or didn't do. I don't care a tinker's dam about your military career. I want you to know that. I see where I went wrong. It wasn't fair of me to press you into the service because of our family's military history. I needed to see you as an individual first, not a carbon copy of me. . . ."

Morgan's apology embraced Jason like a warm blanket, relieving him of so much baggage that he had been carrying. "I'm glad to hear that, Dad. I tried to be like you . . . but it never worked. It just backfired. . . ."

"I know, and I feel terrible about it. Being a parent — a good parent — is the hardest job in the world, Jason. And God knows, I've made a ton of mistakes with you, the first-born."

Nodding, Jason whispered, "Dad, you had

PTSD. I can see it in myself, even now. I had a brain injury, just like you. Feeling how I'm feeling now . . . God, I don't know *how* you managed to think you could have a family or be a parent. Right now, I'd be afraid to have a kid. I'd be afraid that I'm not right inside myself and couldn't give a child what he or she needed."

"Well," Morgan said, sorrow in his tone, "I didn't think that far ahead. I met your mother, fell head over heels in love with her, and we both wanted a family. I never thought . . . well, I just didn't think that where I was in my healing process would impact the family we brought into our lives. . . ." He scowled and held Jason's softened gaze. "I told your mother many years ago that if I had to do it all over again, I'd have waited to have a family. I needed to sort out a lot of wounds in myself. Instead, I buried them and focused on Perseus instead. And that led me into the kidnapping situation with the drug dealers, which branded you for life. You . . . and my wife . . . have paid for my sins, and for that I'm so sorry. I don't know how I'll ever be able to make up for what I've done to the two of you. I live with it daily."

"Dad, listen to me, will you? I've had an hour to sit here, weighing my feelings toward you. If I hadn't had the same type of injuries, the amnesia you experienced, I couldn't understand your decisions at all. But I do — at least a little, I think. And no, I can guarantee you I won't be making the mistakes you made. Maybe I have learned from you, on a deeper level. I know I'm wounded. I know, emotionally, I'm screwed up with PTSD, and until I can get myself straightened out, I'm not bringing a child into the world. I won't use a kid as a way to learn and heal."

Nodding, Morgan patted his son's shoulder. "Then you've got the greatest gift I could give you — not making the mistakes your father made. That's as good as it gets."

Jason's heart swam with a fierce love for his father. He saw the pain from the past in his darkened gray eyes, the sad set of his thinned mouth. "You didn't do it out of spite, Dad. I know that now." Jason managed a wan smile. "You loved me the best you knew how."

"But it wasn't enough, son. It wasn't enough!" Once again Morgan's voice cracked, and scalding tears spilled from his eyes.

Jason whispered, "I think it was, Dad. I can forgive you." He looked at his father as he wiped the tears from his face. "Do you know what I want now?"

"What?"

"To have the relationship we established after my TBI." He smiled into Morgan's hopeful eyes. "I like the dad I have now. I like your touch. I can't tell you how good it makes me feel when you put your arm around me, hug me. I wasn't very sure of myself after the TBI. You always made me feel more stable. Loved. So I want to continue that. Let the past stay where it is. I've learned from it, I think. And it's time I grew up and quit being a six-year-old, punishing you for your choices. Don't you agree?" The corners of his mouth lifted upward.

Morgan sat there, stunned by Jason's sudden maturity and insight. Love swelled in his heart for his son. "You're more of a man than I'll ever be, son. You've grown more through this injury than I ever did with mine. And for that, I thank God, because you deserve nothing but happiness in your future."

"I think I've got it right now, Dad. Here, with you . . . and Mom, and my brother and sisters. I see this as turning the last page on the old chapter of my life. I'm starting a new one today, here and now, with you, with them."

Joy flowed through Morgan's chest. "I never thought I'd hear you say these things. I always dreamed of it, son, but never believed it would really happen."

"As Annie said, life happens. Even bad things can be good things in disguise."

"She's right," Morgan murmured, the weight of the world dissolving off his shoulders. He couldn't remember ever feeling as light as he did in this moment. He understood now that he had needed Jason's forgiveness in order to let go of all the loads he'd carried from his past. His son had just set him free.

Jason smiled wryly. "You know what? Let's not tell Annie about this. I want to meet her at the airport, bring her home and tell her here."

Smiling, Morgan said, "That's a good plan, Jason. She loves you so much. . . ."

"I know. And now I can hand my life back to her — all of it. . . ."

Chapter 20

"Mom?" Jason stood at the door to her office. In the evenings, after dinner, she usually worked on one of her many articles, which were always in high demand by magazine editors. Her back was to him, and she was seated at her computer, dressed in a pair of white slacks, a lavender tank top and sandals. Morgan had driven him down the mountain to his parents' home. Jason couldn't wait to tell his mother that his memories were back.

Chair squeaking, Laura turned, surprised to hear her son's voice. "Jason? Hi. Why are you here? I thought you and your dad were having dinner up at your cabin. What happened? Bad cooking, so you thought you'd raid our refrigerator here instead for a good meal?" She laughed lightly.

Jason looked different. What was it? Laura studied her tall, broad-shouldered son. His cheeks were ruddy and flushed. His eyes were bright and sparkling. Lips parting, she gasped. "Jason? Don't tell me!"

"Yeah, Mom, my memories are coming back!" He stepped into the room, grabbed

379

his mother and lifted her out of the chair and into his arms for a joyful embrace.

Gasping, Laura cried, "Really, Jason?" She swept her arms around his neck and hugged him back. As he carefully set her down again, her hands trailed down his arms and she gripped his hands. "Really?"

"Yeah," Jason said with a lopsided grin, squeezing her hands gently. "Really."

"Well . . . when did it happen? How? Are you okay? Dizzy? Do you need to sit down?"

Laughing heartily, Jason shook his head. "No, Mom, I'm fine. Better than I have been since I can remember — and I can remember back to babyhood now. Come on, Dad's out in the kitchen fixing us coffee. Come sit with us and I'll tell you how it happened. It was such a crazy thing. . . ."

A short while later, Laura sat next to Morgan at the kitchen table, staring in amazement at Jason, who sat opposite them. The July night was warm and they had the door and windows open. The fragrance of pine wafted into the breakfast nook as they listened to Jason's story.

"It's not done yet, is it?" Laura stated.

"No," Jason murmured, moving the cup around in his hands restlessly. "It's hard to describe. I'll see something, like a splash across my movie screen here," he told her, pointing to the middle of his forehead. "Annie told me that's where our third eye sits, the one with which we see into the other worlds."

"That's right," Morgan said, impressed. He looked at Laura. "She did."

"Yes, dear, I remember. I think it's great!" his wife whispered, wiping tears from the corners of her eyes. "And with the movie screen pictures, you get the memory?"

"Yes, all of it." Jason shook his head ruefully. "It's still ongoing. And nothing comes back in any given order. I might see something from when I was a baby, and then when I was in high school, or flying with Annie in the Apache. It's a crazy hodgepodge of info. . . ."

Laura smiled and sniffed. She had put a box of tissues on the table and pulled another one out now, dabbing her eyes and blowing her nose. "Remember? Dr. Dorf said your memory could return in one of many ways. She said a spontaneous return of memory was not uncommon."

"I'm just glad it's happening," Jason said fervently, looking warmly at his father. Morgan's face was glowing with happiness and it felt good to absorb his dad's joy for him. It was a new and wonderful gift. Why had he held a grudge, an angry, hateful one, against his father for so long? Look what he had been missing. Jason chalked it up to his own lack of maturity. But that was the past. They had a new, bright and hopeful chapter to

381

write with one another, and he was looking forward to it.

"Oh, gosh!" Laura whispered. "What about Annie? Do you remember her?"

Jason's grin widened. "You bet I do, Mom. I love her. I fell in love with her at Fort Campbell. My love for her only deepened over in Afghanistan. I remember it all. . . ."

"Oh, Jason, that's wonderful, because she loves you so much!"

"She told you that?"

"Yes, she did, son."

Studying his parents, he said quietly, "I never got a chance to tell her I loved her before I got wounded. There was never a right time." Scowling, Jason stopped turning the cup between his hands. "I wanted to . . . but we were in a wartime situation . . ."

"Understandable, son. But Annie will be back shortly."

"Yes, she needs to know," Laura murmured. "And wouldn't you like some time alone with her to do it? We could pick her up at the airport after she's flown in on our new Perseus Bell helicopter. We could take her up to the cabin, where you two could be alone. Then you could tell her. I don't think you want to surprise her in front of the family at the airport, do you?"

Jason smiled at his mother. "You're always thinking ahead and strategizing. Yeah, it sounds like the right thing to do, Mom. I want our reunion to be private."

"Women are great tacticians," Morgan said, grinning.

Laura preened. "Women are very good at a lot of things."

Chuckling, Jason said, "That sounds like a fine plan, Mom. You bring Annie home — to me. . . ."

Annie was mystified by the happiness that seemed to be mirrored in both Morgan and Laura's faces as they drove Annie up the mountain to the cabin. She chalked it up to them being thrilled with the new Bell helicopter she'd flown to Phillipsburg. It was midafternoon, the day hot and dry in the Rocky Mountains. Annie was wearing a dark blue one-piece flight suit, her hair in a thick, long braid down her back. When the Mercedes braked at the front gate, she got out and grabbed her small traveling bag. Leaning down on the passenger side, where Laura sat, she said, "I'll see you two later. Thanks for the lift."

"Take tomorrow off, Annie," Morgan told her.

Smiling, Annie said, "Wow . . . great! Thank you, sir."

Laura patted her hand. "Jason is waiting to see you, dear. He's really missed you . . ."

"I've missed him," Annie told them. Straightening, she waved goodbye and walked around the car and through the gate. The Mercedes turned and left in a cloud of yellow dust.

Once in the yard, Annie smiled over at the sweet peas, which were now blooming heavily.

"You girls didn't wait for me, but you're beautiful!" She leaned down and cupped a number of the blooms to her nose, inhaling their spicy sweetness. Behind her, she heard the screen door open and close.

Turning, Annie looked up at Jason as he stood on the porch, a silly grin on his face, his hands resting loosely on his hips. Frowning momentarily, Annie sensed a difference in him. That stance was part of the old Jason, from his days as an Apache pilot. He'd always stood like that, weight on one leg, one foot slightly ahead of the other, his long flight hands relaxing on his narrow hips. He wore a dark blue polo shirt that made the blue of his eyes stand out, a pair of jeans and tennis shoes.

"Hey, Cowboy!" she shouted, waving her hand and grinning. "Long time no see, huh?" She quickly climbed the wooden steps, dropped the canvas bag and threw her arms around his shoulders. Annie couldn't help herself; her love for Jason overrode her caution. She knew that from time to time she could get away with this intimacy and hug him.

Only this time, as she embraced Jason, she felt his arms wrap securely around her waist, lift her up and crush her hard against him. The air flew out of her lungs. Surprised, Annie automatically pushed away enough to look up at Jason. Where their bodies touched, her skin was scorched with need of him.

"Hey . . ."

"Welcome home, sweet pea. . . ." Jason whispered raggedly, drowning in her widening golden eyes. Instantly, Annie stopped struggling. Gently, Jason eased her to the ground, but he kept his large hands on her shoulders.

Stunned, Annie blinked. Jason's eyes had changed. No longer were they dull looking. No, that mischievous gleam she loved so much was back! Lips parting, Annie gasped. "Jason! You're back! You're *back!*" And she shrieked with joy, threw her arms around him and hugged him as hard as she could, laughter spilling from her.

Absorbing Annie's cry of joy, Jason laughed with her as he held her tightly against him. "Yeah, I'm back, sweet pea. *All* of me," he whispered fiercely, pressing his face against hers. Annie smelled of sage and the sweet fragrance of earth after rain. Oh, how he'd missed this! Missed her! He whirled her around on the porch, then carefully set her down.

"Listen, come inside, Annie. I'll tell you

everything." He opened the door and led her in. Once inside the living room, Jason pulled her down beside him on the couch, her hand resting on his long thigh.

"This is so wonderful, Jason!" Annie whispered, tears stinging her eyes. She smiled at him. How strong, vibrant and wonderful he looked. "Your spirit came back. It integrated. Do you have your memories back yet?" She prayed he did. He must, or why would he have called her sweet pea, that special endearment of his? Unable to keep her hands off him, Annie reached over and trailed her fingers along his jaw. Jason's recently shaved skin felt so masculine, so good.

Catching her hand and pressing a warm kiss in the palm, Jason said, "Let me tell you how it happened. You won't believe it. . . ."

Annie sat there, stunned and humbled, when Jason finished explaining. "This — this is so wonderful! I always hoped . . . but was afraid to hope too much. . . . Who would have thought that a simple packet of sweet pea seeds would be the one thing from your past to trip open all your old memories? I'm in shock."

Jason leaned against the couch, legs sprawled in front of him, Annie's hand still resting on his thigh. Her knee pressed gently against his left one. "I can't imagine the hell you've gone through, Annie. But it had to be pretty bad — to know what we had before, and for me to not remember it. . . ." Jason searched her tear-filled eyes.

Seeing her lower lip tremble, he sat up and turned toward her. Gripping her hands, he whispered, "And the worst of it was, my sweet woman, I never told you I loved you before this happened. But I will now. I love you, Annie Dazen. With my heart and soul." Tightening his hands on hers, Jason saw her eyes widen, incredible joy sparkling like a blazing sun in their depths.

Gulping back tears, Annie closed her eyes and allowed his husky declaration to flow through her. "Your words are like a rainbow to me, Jason. They touch my heart, my spirit, and they make me sing."

"I know you love me." He grinned, touched by her shaky words. When she opened her eyes and he heard her lilting laughter, his heart flew open.

"Oh, yes, I love you. I don't know when I fell for you, Jason, but I did." Annie bracketed his smiling face with her hands. "I wanted to tell you in Afghanistan, but I was afraid to. . . ."

Her hands were warm and comforting to him. Drowning in her wide, shining eyes, he whispered, "Me, too . . . I tried to find the right time, Annie, but it never seemed to arrive. And I was just as afraid. . . ."

"War is hell. We know that now, more than ever," she said in a choked voice. Touching his dark, short hair, she whispered, "You are my sun, Jason. You make me so happy. I wake up looking forward to the day, and no matter what it brings, I'm glad I have you there beside me. You give me such joy, beloved."

Her words nearly shattered him. Groaning, he gripped Annie by the shoulders. "Right now, I want to love you. Come to bed with me? Let me show you how much you mean to me?"

"Y-yes, oh, yes, Jason . . ."

Getting up, he drew Annie to her feet. Without another word, they walked down the hall to his bedroom. It was a small room with a queen-size bed, covered with a colorful quilt his mother had made long ago. The light from the only window was hazy and made the pale pink curtains glow. Jason shut the door and came to where Annie stood.

Without a word, they began to undress one another. Jason fumbled with the buttons on her flight suit and smiled. "You'd think I'd know how to undo a flight suit by now. . . ." He gave her a sheepish grin.

Laughing, Annie said, "Well, Cowboy, our flight suits were fastened with Velcro. This one has snaps. Civilian type, you know?" She felt each of the snaps open, the material curving away from her upper body. Need thrummed through Annie.

"Listen, I just got off a ten-hour flight. Can we take a quick dip in the heated pool outside, first? I'd like to get cleaned up."

"Sure . . . I'd like to sit naked with you in that warm, volcanically heated water. . . ." The idea was provocative to Jason. As he peeled away the dark blue cloth of her suit, he saw Annie was wearing a pale pink silk chemise beneath it. She wore no bra. She hated them, he knew. Her small breasts made the material swell in all the right places. As he trailed his fingers across her elegant collarbones, he saw her nipples tighten and thrust against the fabric. His heart soared and heat curled in his loins. He liked the fact he aroused Annie so easily.

As the flight suit pooled around her ankles, Annie stepped out of it. She stood in her loose-fitting silk shorts and chemise. Jason's eyes were burning with desire — for her. Every cell in her body responded to his heated look as his gaze raked her from head to foot. Giving him a careless grin, Annie lifted her hands. "Your turn, Cowboy. Let's get you out of that polo shirt, jeans and shoes, okay?"

Her hands were scorching wherever she touched him as she helped him pull the shirt over his head. Annie casually dropped it, then tucked her fingers in the waistband of his jeans. Instantly, Jason hardened. Fire exploded within his lower body and he groaned, gripping her shoulders as she opened his fly. As she pulled the zipper down, she deliberately brushed him with her knuckles. Teeth clenched, he rasped, "You keep that up and we won't be making it outside this room. . . ."

Chuckling, Annie knelt and pulled the jeans down his strong, muscular legs. Untying his tennis shoes, she eased them off his large feet one at a time. Then she peeled the jeans off the rest of the way. Rising to her full height, Annie gave him a scalding look.

"You look good to me," she whispered, sliding her hand into his. All he wore were white-and-blue-striped cotton boxers. His chest was well sprung and dark with hair. "Come on, I need to wash. . . ."

They headed out the back door. The heated pool of water was about ten feet in diameter. White gravel was spread throughout it, the stones small and tumbled smooth so they had lost their sharp edges. It was about forty feet from the cabin, sheltered by a tall stand of fir trees on one side and a rocky prominence of white-and-black granite on the other, which shielded it from the prying eyes of anyone driving along the road. Not that many people came up this road, in any case. The sweat lodge stood nearby. Today, Annie was grateful for the privacy as she released Jason's hand and sat down on the warm, smooth stones beside the pool.

Slipping out of her chemise and shorts, she hung them on a nearby branch and turned around, completely naked. She saw the hunger in Jason's eyes, felt it and absorbed it. Never before had she felt so feminine, or so strong as a woman. He stood there, jaw clenched, his eyes narrowed on her, every inch a hunter. With a winsome smile, she said, "Your turn . . ."

Giving her a dark, humorous look, Jason got rid of his boxer shorts. Straightening after he'd pushed them aside with his toes, he held her appraising golden gaze. "Like what you see?"

Her smile widened. "A whole lot, Cowboy. Come on, let's get in the water before I jump your bones here and now. . . ."

His laughter echoed around the intimate pool. "You first . . ." And he helped Annie step into the clear blue water.

As she sank to her neck, Annie moved to the opposite side while Jason slipped in behind her. The water had a slight sulfurous smell, but it was tolerable. The pool was about five feet deep, and it was easy to lean against the side. Annie began to scrub her skin, splashing her face with handfuls of the 104-degree water. The water felt wonderful, invigorating and so healing. Jason, too, began to wash himself.

He came over to her side after she was done, sliding one hand across her shoulders and turning her gently in his direction.

"I'm not gonna last, Annie. I want you so much. Here and now . . ." Jason leaned down, cupped her chin and moved his mouth commandingly against hers. The water was warm, inviting, sliding like raw silk as their bodies met and melded hotly together.

Jason groaned as she smiled beneath his mouth. "Oh, yes . . ." Annie sighed against his wet lips. "Right now . . . here . . ."

Her hands moved boldly across his chest, fingers entangling in his hair, causing a hundred little jolts of pleasure on his taut flesh. As her fingers ranged down across his torso, to his hips and to his hardness, Jason groaned. He gripped her shoulders as her fingers grazed and teasingly stroked his throbbing organ. Clenching his teeth, he hissed out his breath.

"Damn . . . Annie . . ."

"I know what I'm doing," she laughed breathily, looking up into his slitted blue eyes. Releasing Jason, she moved against him, her breasts brushing boldly against his chest, the sensation hardening her nipples. The water only enhanced the tactile feelings spreading wildly throughout her body. "You think I'm gonna sit back and let you make love to me?" she whispered, biting his right earlobe with her teeth. "Think again, Cowboy. It's the right time of month in my cycle, so we don't need to worry about protection. You have a wild woman on your hands. . . ." And she laughed huskily as she pressed her hips demandingly against his. The hardness of his body against the softer, more yielding curves of hers made her moan.

If Jason was shocked by her sweet assault, he didn't back off. No, she knew him to be a brave man, with a strong, giving heart. As she wrapped her arms around his shoulders, her mouth coming to rest against his, she felt his hands slide down her hips and grip her buttocks. He clearly wasn't put off by her challenge.

Jason lifted Annie upward, the heat of the water flowing between them. Her legs curved behind his back and she locked her ankles together, bringing herself fully against him. The sweet firmness of her body made him tremble with hunger. As he brought her down, down upon him, their bodies sheathed together for the first time. He didn't want to hurt her, so he allowed Annie to descend by tantalizing increments. Each sleek, sliding movement was pure hell on him. He gripped her hips hard, his teeth clenched, his head thrown back. She was hot and tight as she slowly slid lower, taking him into herself bit by bit. The moments fused together in a pleasure-filled haze. Her face was pressed against his, her breathing ragged, their heart-beats pounding in unison. He felt her arms tighten around him as she flowed in a rhythmic motion. How was he going to stop from exploding in her?

Sweat beaded his brow. His breath came in ragged gasps. She melted against him, and he could feel her every breath, the rise and fall of her rib cage.

As Annie settled around him, she tightened her legs and surged against him. Her lips found his once more and she kissed him deeply, her tongue thrusting daringly into his open mouth. Nostrils flared, Jason followed her bold lead and brought his hands down beneath her buttocks, pressing her hard against him. Heat raged within Jason. He heard her moaning, felt her teeth nip at his lower lip, her eyes narrowed with raw desire.

Loving her with a fierceness that surged through him as never before, Jason gripped Annie as he felt her stiffen against him. She cried out and threw back her head, her hands splayed against his shoulders. He knew she was gifting him with her climax, and in that moment he gritted his teeth and forced himself not to release, not just yet. The water churned wildly around them, mimicking the wildness of their coupling. Just as Annie began to go limp against him, Jason released his passion into her. The explosion was so deep, so hot, that all he could do was growl and hold her against him, his face pressed against her damp hair, nostrils flared and mouth parted to suck in gulps of air.

Annie sank against Jason as he leaned against the wall of the pool. Sobbing for breath, she laid her head on his shoulder, her cheek pressed to his. Her body still trembled, and the languidness she felt made her smile softly in the aftermath. Barely able to move, and weak with pleasure, she whispered in his ear, "Dude, you are *good.* . . ."

With a half laugh, Jason opened his eyes and pulled Annie away from him just enough to drown in her drowsy gold eyes, which were shining with joy. Feeling very good about giving her pleasure, he rasped, "Sweet pea, you aren't bad in the clutch yourself."

"I'm not bad?" Annie pouted playfully for a moment and then laughed. "I'm *very good,* Cowboy." She poked at his chest. "And don't you forget it!"

Laughing with her, Jason pulled her close again. He liked feeling her still wrapped around him. He grazed her smiling lips with his. "Oh, I'll never forget this — or you."

"Better not!"

Moving his hand against her damp cheek, he kissed her brow, her nose and finally her wet lips. "I won't ever forget. Never again, Annie . . ."

Chapter 21

Annie was rocking gently in the porch swing, watching puffy, cauliflower-shaped cumulus clouds turn pink as the sun set in the west behind the cabin. She heard Jason's sure, solid footsteps coming down the hall. Turning her head, she saw him push the screen door open and pin her with a dark gaze. Smiling, she patted the green-and-white-striped cushion next to her.

"Dishes done, Cowboy? Come and join me. Let's watch the sunset together." They had a deal: after she made the meal, he cleaned up. That was fair.

"You got a deal, sweet pea." Jason thunked across the porch to sit beside her.

She saw something in his right hand. "What have you got?" Loving how his weight felt next to hers, she smiled up at Jason. The last three weeks had been pure heaven for Annie. Indeed, the old cocky, confident Jason was back. He was even better, having integrated his old personality with the new one that had emerged after the TBI. Searching his face, she saw he seemed more at peace than ever before. There was a soft smile lurking at the corners of his mouth as he turned and placed his left arm around her shoulders.

"Oh, I'm up to no good as usual," Jason teased.

"Yeah, something's up, because you've been driving back and forth from the cabin to Phillipsburg a lot lately."

Raising his brows, he said, "Well, I was on a mission, Annie."

She laughed. "Uh-oh . . . I thought you were going to start training with Mike Houston next week, learning how to run Perseus. Is that what this is about? You couldn't wait? You had to get back in the saddle on military stuff and learn your father's job sooner rather than later?" Jason was torn between working with his father and going back to college to become a forest ranger with his love of biology. Morgan had supported whatever Jason wanted to do. Annie felt he would sort out careers over time. And right now, she knew Jason wanted to work closely with Morgan because their father-son relationship was so important to both of them.

Jason caressed her hair. Annie wore it in two braids, for the weather was too hot in July to have sheets of hair hanging around her shoulders.

"Well," Jason hedged, "not exactly, although you're right, I've been down to

Perseus daily for the last three weeks." He smiled into her wide, dancing gold eyes. Annie lifted her right leg and hung it across his. His love for her welled through him and he stilled his hand on the back of her head. "I have a story to tell you . . . one I think you'll like."

She cocked one eyebrow. "If it doesn't have a happy ending, Jason, I'm not interested. I've had enough fireworks in my life since you busted into it — falling helplessly in love with you, and then losing you. . . ." Annie reached over and caressed his cheek. How handsome he looked in the tan polo shirt that outlined his wide chest. A chest she loved to run her hands across. Her body glowed from the lovemaking they'd shared late this afternoon. They couldn't get enough of one another right now, and Annie understood why. Both of them had been waiting a long time for the intimacy they now shared and the wait lent an urgency to their lovemaking, which was hungry, gratifying and often.

"Hmm," Jason murmured, looking down at the box in his hand. "Well, I don't know the outcome of the story — not yet at least, sweet pea." He lifted his head and grinned, "But let me tell it, okay? I think you'll like it."

Pouting playfully, Annie placed her hands across her stomach and leaned against the back of the swing. "Okay, Cowboy, but this had better be *good*."

Chuckling, Jason said, "Okay, here goes. My great-grandmother, Lexa Trayhern, was a nurse during World War II. She was twenty-six at the time. She was considered an old maid because most women married in their late teens and had babies by the time they reached age twenty. She was a highly intelligent woman. Her mother was once a suffragette, so she came from a family of rebellious, independent women long before it was acceptable for a woman to be that way."

With half-closed eyes, Annie grinned. She loved to watch the evening light playing upon Jason's strong face and his chiseled jaw. "So, your great-grandmother was a suffragette demanding the vote for women in this country. I like her already! Go on, this is wonderful!"

Gloating, Jason said, "See? I said you'd like this story."

"Stop being so smug, Cowboy. On with the tale. You got me hooked."

Jason sat back, content to have Annie's leg lying over his. He rested his head against the soft cushion and said, "Lexa was a real fighter for women's rights. She was an Army officer, a lieutenant and registered nurse. And because she had such fire in her heart, such moxie, she was always at the front of any battle, helping to take in casualties directly off the field of fire. She was one of the few women who were allowed that close to the fighting. The men worried that if a MASH unit was overrun, women would be taken prisoner, and that just couldn't happen. But Lexa didn't care. She wanted to be where the action was because she knew the injured would have a better chance of surviving if they got swift medical attention."

"She was Apache by proxy," Annie murmured. "With the heart of a warrior. This is good to know, Jason. I love family stories because they reflect future generations." She lifted her finger and poked at him. "And her blood, her fire, her courage flows through your veins, too."

Grinning, Jason said, "Yeah, she sounds a lot like you . . . like your mother, Lane. A lot of moxie. Bold. In your face."

"It's the way to be." Annie grinned lazily. "Your sister Katy has that same warrior blood in her veins. Look at her — on the front lines fighting the drug war down in South America. So, on with your story. I love hearing it."

Jason smiled widely. "Lexa met my great-grandfather, Captain Wesley Alexander Trayhern, in Europe, right after D-day. He was an Army Ranger leading a squad of men. They had parachuted in behind enemy lines to raise hell with the Germans and to pull their attention away from the D-day landings. Lexa was in the spearhead Army and her group got cut off by the Germans. In trying to escape, she ran right into Wes and his men."

"Saved," Annie said.

"Well, yes and no. I'm giving you the short version of this today."

"Bummer. I like long stories. They're parables we can learn from. That's why the Apache sit around telling their stories and verbally handing them down from one generation to another."

"Well, my mom will give you the long version when you want it. She's got their photo album, and you can sit with her for hours — she knows their lives by heart. Anyway —" Jason waved his hand in the air "— on to the ending."

"Happy ending, Cowboy."

"Of course. By the end of the war, Wes and Lexa decided that they'd been battling one another enough, and in 1946, he proposed to her. The Trayherns have always been financially well off. Lexa came from a poor but very highly educated family. Her eyes were emerald green." Jason sat up and turned toward Annie so she could see the box in his hand.

"My great-grandfather traveled down to Colombia, to the Munoz Emerald Mine, and got Lexa an emerald instead of a diamond engagement ring." He opened the black velvet box and showed an emerald solitaire and a simple gold wedding band to Annie.

"Oh . . . that is gorgeous!" She sat up and took the box carefully in her palm. Barely touching the large, square emerald, Annie whispered, "Oh, Jason, this was hers?"

His throat tightened. He slid his hand across her shoulders. "Well . . . they're yours — if you want them, sweet pea. I talked to my parents and they agreed that you should have them . . . if you want to marry me?"

Annie's head shot up. Eyes widening, she saw both hope and uncertainty in Jason's narrowed ones. "Really? I mean . . . marriage? You never said anything about that before. . . ."

"When did I have time? I wanted to spring the question on you in Afghanistan, but it was the wrong place, wrong time. And then when I got dinged in the head, I didn't remember anything . . . but I was still falling in love with you all over again, Annie." Jason gave her a hesitant, searching look. "Well? Would you marry me? Be my wife? My best friend? My partner for life? The mother of our children when we know we're ready for them?"

Tears flooded Annie's eyes. The two rings blurred before her. Sniffing, she looked up. "Y-yes, I'd love to marry you, Jason Trayhern. You already are my best friend. You treat me as an equal and we have a good relationship."

Hardly daring to believe his ears, he said, "You're sure? We had a rough, rocky start with one another."

Wiping her eyes, she said, "Well, as soon as you lost that damn chip on your shoulder, things went fine. I haven't seen it come back since then. . . ."

"This is great!" Jason whispered, taking the box and picking up the emerald solitaire. "Give me your left hand, Annie. . . ."

She held out her hand and watched as Jason gently slid the emerald engagement ring on her finger. To her amazement, it fit perfectly. Jason looked up and she saw the pride and joy in his eyes as he held her hand tenderly in his.

Snapping the box closed, he whispered, "Listen, I know this is kind of sudden, and I don't want you to feel pushed. I really like your mom and dad, and I think a wedding at your reservation, Apache style, is in order. I already talked to my parents and they honor your culture. I don't know what an Apache wedding is like — or what has to be done or how long we should wait — but I'll wait forever for you, Annie. You make me so damn happy that I wake up every morning wondering what I did to deserve you. . . ."

Tears crowded into Annie's eyes again. "I love you so much, Jason!" She leaned over and threw her arms around his shoulders, dragging him against her. The swing rocked gently as Jason embraced her in return. Feeling his mouth brush her hair, then her cheek, Annie turned her face and met those strong, searching lips of his. As they closed across her mouth, she moaned. Jason's hands moved to frame her face. He caressed her lips, sipping from them, tasting them and then claiming her with a power that took her breath away.

Breathing hard, Annie tore her mouth from his. As the dusk deepened around them, she smiled into his stormy blue eyes, their noses touching. "I love you so much, Jason. . . ."

"Then you'll marry me? Someday? When it feels right?"

"Yes, I will. . . ."

"Good. I knew you would." And he flashed her a gloating grin as he caressed her cheek. In the semidarkness Annie's high, broad cheekbones emphasized the tilt of her huge, intelligent eyes.

"You're such an egotist!"

"Well," Jason demurred, "I *am* a good catch, you know. I'm attractive. . . ."

"Oh, dude, you are out of the water!"

"Single. I'll have a good income, either working full-time at Perseus or getting a job with the forest service —"

"Like I'd marry you for those reasons!" Annie playfully punched his arm. "Security is within ourselves. And money? That doesn't make a marriage work or make it happy."

"But I *am* good-looking."

Rolling her eyes, Annie moaned in protest, "Pulleeze!"

Chuckling darkly, Jason said, "Come on, you have to give me that. I *know* I'm handsome. Look at my father. Even in his fifties, he's still a good-lookin' dude."

Sighing, Annie ruffled his short, dark hair. "Okay, I'll admit it. You're easy on the eyes, Cowboy, but that's not what attracted me to you."

"No?" He pulled Annie across his lap and into his arms. She laid her head in the crook of his shoulder, her arm around him, her other hand pressed against his beating heart. She was tall, strong, all warrior, and he loved her with a fierceness that nearly overwhelmed him as he rocked her gently in the swing.

"Of course not!" Annie gave him a playful look. "I liked what I saw in your heart. You were a good person despite all the stuff I'd heard about you."

"And you gave me a chance," Jason whispered, kissing her cheek. Her flesh was warm, and her hair smelled of cinnamon. Earlier in the day Annie had baked an apple pie with a number of spices. Inhaling the scent clinging to the soft, silken strands, he pressed his lips against them.

"Apaches' foremost criteria is whether a man walks his talk. And you proved that daily to me, sweetheart." Annie brushed his cheek and smiled. "Every day you showed that you cared, you were sensitive to others and you learned how to work with my crew and me. That's what I judged you on. Not your past."

Sighing, Jason said, "I like the way you see the world, Annie. And I think you gave me a chance because of your Apache ways."

"Guaranteed," she chuckled darkly, "because the Mr. White Man way had already nailed you to a cross and judged you. Right or wrong."

Frowning, Jason said, "Well, my experience at Annapolis is a part of my history. It's something I'll take to the grave with me."

Searching his dark eyes, Annie said, "And that drug scandal will never be totally erased."

"It's okay, sweet pea. What happened was that my roommate, Peter Quinn, was dealing drugs and, unknown to me, using my laptop computer and e-mail program to send out information to other cadets who wanted to buy off him. So when he got found out and busted, the investigators confiscated our computers. His e-mails on my machine implicated me."

"Damn."

"And I couldn't prove that I wasn't a part of the ring. After all, the e-mails were on my computer." Frowning, he muttered, "I couldn't clear my name, especially when my roommate said I was in on it. We never really got along. More like oil and water. A couple of times, he wanted to sell me papers and test answers, and I refused, so that pissed him off, too. He always called me a white knight and said my morals were too strong."

Snorting, Annie growled, "Oh, sure! The bastard!"

"Want to know a terrible twist in this?"

Annie eyed him. "What?" She saw Jason frown.

"Quinn got kicked out, but he went over and joined the CIA. He never got caught. They could never prove he did it. The others in the ring never ratted on one another. Annapolis kicked out the lot of us, anyway. So, the bad guys never got taken down. They walked away, free and clear. Guess where Quinn's stationed?"

Eyes widening, Annie growled, "Don't tell me. South America?"

"Yes, and he's working directly with my sister Katy."

"Oh, geez, Jason! Does she know about him? What he did to you?"

"Of course she does."

"How's she handling it?"

"Not very well. I just got a letter from her the other day and she said she's ready to kill him herself. I guess he's a screw-up in the jungle down there." Katy had been thrilled he'd recovered from the TBI.

"There're people like that in the world. Talk about karma," Annie murmured with a shake of her head. "Can't she get him transferred?"

"No, because he's the one who's been down there working in the bush with the farmers, to fight off rebels that are trying to take over. He knows more about the political ins and outs in that region than anyone."

"I see . . . He's made himself indispensable, then."

"Looks like it." Jason stared at Annie, who was obviously angry. "I still don't get it. Why would the CIA hire a known druggie?"

Snorting, Annie growled, "Hell, they do that all the time in police departments. They hire them as snitches. Because they couldn't convict Quinn, the CIA probably thought he was a good catch. Maybe that's the role Quinn's playing down there."

"What I'm worried about is that he's probably high on cocaine most of the time. He's the one giving Katy and her helo teams the info. What if he's wrong? They could be shot down by rebels and killed."

"It's not a pretty picture. All we can do is pray for her, Jas. She's strong and she's smart, like you." Annie smiled briefly, seeing the concern for his sister banked in his eyes. "Don't worry, she's got nine lives like all you Trayherns. You might go through the fires of hell, but you do survive them."

"Katy is tough," Jason acknowledged. "Still, if this thing hadn't happened at Annapolis with me . . ."

"You can't change it, sweetheart. Sometimes bad things happen to good people for a reason. And few know what the reason is. We just have to try and muddle through."

Shrugging, Jason said, "The rest is history, that's true. I went down with the drug ring because Quinn wouldn't testify that I was innocent. It was his way to get even with me. He didn't like the fact I was a Trayhern, with a two-hundred-year military dynasty behind me. I think he chose me on purpose just for that reason. He wanted to see me fall. My dad . . . well, hell, Annie, I was really hurting over that whole situation. I knew I was a huge disaster, a disappointment to him. He had so much riding on me, the first-born son, to make the Trayhern dynasty live on like it had in the past. . . ."

"Have you told him all of this?"

Nodding his head, he said, "Yes, I have. It's Mom I haven't told yet. But I will. Soon. I need to spend time right now with you, more than them. I'll know when it's right to sit down with Mom and let her know the truth. Dad understands. He was relieved to hear the rest of the story. I should have told them right when it all happened, but I was too immature, too embarrassed and angry at Quinn. I didn't do anything right. Plus, my dad was furious because he believed all the newspapers. I just clammed up. I let him think the worst. Stupid, looking back on it."

"And your mom will accept it, Jason. I know she will." Annie smoothed his wrinkled brow with her fingertips.

"I really got screwed there. It was a helluva ugly situation."

"You know what, Cowboy? People are either going to or not going to believe it. They either will judge you on your actions today with them, or they'll choose to remember that incident. You don't want to be surrounded by people who cling to your past. We all make mistakes. If they can't forgive you, even though they don't know the truth, then they aren't worth knowing or dealing with."

"I like the Apache way of seeing life — take no prisoners. . . ."

Laughing softly, Annie hugged him. "The man I know — the man I love — is a hero in my eyes! He always has been and always will be. . . ." She drew back enough to search his stormy blue eyes, which burned with such tenderness toward her. "You'll make mistakes in the future, and so will I, Jason. The deal is that we forgive one another and move on. If we learn from our mistakes, that's the best it can be. Because —" Annie pressed a soft kiss to the hard line of his mouth and felt it soften beneath her lips "— we're going to make plenty of mistakes over our life span. . . ."

Kissing her back, Jason whispered, "I'm going to like making mistakes with you. You love me. You'll understand and be forgiving."

Giggling, Annie kissed him again and then pulled back to meet his gleaming gaze. "Life is hard, Jason. We know that better than most people our age. But we have one another. Together, we can weather the storms life throws at us."

"Well," Jason murmured, sliding his hand across her abdomen, the denim material rough beneath his fingertips, "I don't know about you, but when we decide to become parents, I'm looking forward to our first baby being a little girl, and watching her grow up to be just like her mom. And then I'm looking forward to her eighteenth birthday, when you pass the rainbow medicine necklace on to her. . . ."

Sliding her hand to where his lay on her belly, Annie whispered, "Me, too. . . ."

"This is funny," Jason said, laughing softly. "Here we are — warriors from two family dynasties marrying. The women went to war on your side of the family, the men on the Trayhern side."

"Well," Annie said archly, "that's changing. Katy, your sister, has graduated from Annapolis and is now flying helicopters down in South America. She's carrying on the flag for the family military dynasty in that sense."

Nodding, Jason said, "Changing times. Instead of the first male always carrying the dynasty forward, it's the first woman."

"And about time," Annie said with a grin. "I've never met her, but I hope to soon. She sounds like a real butt kicker."

"Yeah," Jason chuckled, "my sister is a mirror image of you . . . only maybe worse than you. . . ."

Laughing, Annie hugged him. "She's got warrior blood in her veins. What do you expect? Our children will have a double dose of it, too."

Kissing her smiling mouth, Jason whispered, "Yes . . . and I'm looking forward to making every one of them. I like large families. . . ."

She felt him tenderly caress her belly. "How about two? Unless you want to stay at home and be a mom, so I can go off and fly the skies, Cowboy? Parenting will be done by both of us. That's the deal. . . ."

Laughing, Jason murmured, "No question there, sweet pea. We'll both put in time with them. I won't make the mistake my dad made with me. I *want* to be there for their first steps, their first words . . . all of it. That's what is really important in life. . . ."

Annie closed her eyes, holding Jason tightly against her. The pain he had endured over his fatherless childhood had taught him a valuable lesson that he would never repeat with his children — their children. Opening her eyes, her lashes beaded with tears, Annie looked off into the night sky, which sparkled with stars so close it seemed she could reach out and touch them.

"We'll love our babies with a fierceness that you never knew, sweetheart, but you'll be able to gift them with the childhood you didn't have. Love," Annie whispered, embracing him, "is our gift to them."

About the Author

A homeopathic educator, Lindsay McKenna teaches at the Desert Institute of Classical Homeopathy in Phoenix, Arizona. When she isn't teaching alternative medicine, she is writing books about love. She feels love is the single greatest healer in the world and hopes that her books touch her readers on those levels. Coming from an Eastern Cherokee medicine family, Lindsay was taught ceremony and healing ways from the time she was nine years old. She creates flower and gem essences in accordance with nature and remains closely in touch with her Native American roots and upbringing.